'A gripping psychological thriller'
Essentials Magazine

'This is a fantastic, all-consuming read'
Heat

'[A] gripping story'
Hello!

'The cold, snowy cover and winter setting make
this a great stocking filler for your mum or sister'
thelittlewildwoodkitchen.com

'The book is full of mystery and intrigue, successfully
keeping me guessing until the very end . . . An evocative
read, full of dramatic secrets that will make the reader gasp'
www.novelicious.com

'A poignant, sophisticated and romantic love story'
www.handwrittengirl.com

HER
FROZEN
HEART

Lulu Taylor's first novel, *Heiresses*, was nominated for the RNA Reader's Choice award, and she has gone on to write eight more well-received books. With *The Winter Children* and *The Snow Rose*, she became a *Sunday Times* top ten bestseller. After many years in London, she now lives in Dorset with her husband and two children.

www.lulutaylor.co.uk
@misslulutaylor

HER
FROZEN
HEART

LULU TAYLOR

PAN BOOKS

First published 2017 by Pan Books
an imprint of Pan Macmillan
20 New Wharf Road, London N1 9RR
Associated companies throughout the world
www.panmacmillan.com

ISBN 978-1-5098-4071-7

1 3 5 7 9 8 6 4 2

A CIP catalogue record for this book is available from the British Library.

Typeset by Ellipsis, Glasgow
Printed and bound by CPI Group (UK) Ltd, Croydon, CR0 4YY

Visit www.panmacmillan.com to read more about all our books
and to buy them. You will also find features, author interviews and
news of any author events, and you can sign up for e-newsletters
so that you're always first to hear about our new releases.

To Mickey

διδάσκαλος καί φίλος

with love and thanks

Prologue

June 1940

Tommy was coming back across the fields when she saw Bertie Potter cycling up the lane. It had been a beautiful afternoon, the colours of early summer almost too much to bear. She was dazzled by the intense cornflower blue of the sky flooded with golden light, the deep lush greens of the woods and fields, the blues, whites and vibrant magentas of the meadow flowers. The birds had been going crazy all day, thrilled by the onset of warmth and burgeoning growth; they'd zipped about the hedgerows and sung wildly from the trees. One robin had accompanied her in fluttering dashes as she'd walked the dogs up to the cottages and back. Spotty had met her there – *no, not Spotty, Mr Spottiswoode, I must remember to call him that* – and they had inspected the living conditions, to see if they were suitable for the girls coming that summer to help bring in the harvest. Greaves, the tenant farmer, had joined them, grumbling about having women working on the farm, even though he could remember the same thing happening in the last war.

'Modern girls won't be like the other ones,' Greaves had

declared. He was grizzled with age and decades of labouring outdoors. 'They don't know what hard work is. Only bothered about dancing and hairstyles and lipstick.'

'Let's give them a chance, Greaves, shall we?' Tommy had said lightly. 'They might not be as bad as you think. We're all trying to do our bit with things going so badly abroad.'

That had shut Greaves up. Everyone had been pulling together so much in recent days, since the disaster at Dunkirk – *not disaster*, she reminded herself, *miracle*. But the news was pretty awful and people were nervous about the future. If things went on this way, they didn't stand a hope.

We have to keep on. It's all we can do.

Tommy had thought of Alec, far away in France. He hadn't been evacuated with the others. He was still there, fighting, or on the move; no one knew. She imagined him for a moment in the French countryside, the enemy nearby; then swiftly banished the image. These days she tried to think of him as little as possible. It helped.

It's here and now that matters. The children. The family. The house. Looking after them is how I can help.

Spotty – *oh crumbs, Mr Spottiswoode, I mean* – had said that if the cottages were spruced up, the land girls could be paid less in consideration of their better boarding conditions, and Greaves had clearly liked the idea, but Tommy had said she didn't agree, they'd get their money and a decent lodging too, and then she left the men to it. No doubt they were cursing her name and wondering why they were having to obey her, and not her brother, but she didn't care. Let them.

Striding back across the fields, she breathed in the sweet air and the calm of the afternoon. There was barely a sound, except for the birds chirruping and tweeting away. A blur of wings darted past her, and her robin eyed her from the nearby hedge, before swooping away again. The sun shone brightly and a line of sweat prickled at her hairline. Her jersey was uncomfortably hot so she took it off and slung it over her shoulders, letting the sunshine warm her skin through the light cotton of her blouse. The long grass waved against the bare skin of her legs below her skirt line.

I feel . . . I almost feel alive again.

Of course, she never would be, not in the way she once was. And why should she, when miles away frightful battles were raging, men were dying, ordinary people's lives and homes were being destroyed? A great black cloud was rolling towards them, engulfing everything in its path, bringing death and chaos.

Coming over the brow of the hill, she saw the house, ancient and beautiful, sitting just below her. The sight comforted her. It was home, an enduring shelter, a place of safety. It would surely continue to exist as it had for centuries. In the garden there was a flash of movement and the children appeared briefly, two small dots with bright red jumpers and bare legs, before vanishing behind the house. Where were they going? To the paddock? Into the woods? How wonderful to be so carefree.

Then she saw him. Bertie Potter, his cap pushed back on his head, cycling along the lane towards the house.

Tommy stopped with a gasp and her skin turned cold. For a moment, she stood staring, watching the little figure getting closer and closer to the old manor. She started walking, quickly now, oblivious to her robin, marching out through the long grass. Her heart was pounding and her face pale, but she strode on, calling to the dogs when they lingered, watching Bertie reach the house, drop his bicycle on the lawn in front before running around the side to the kitchen door. She couldn't see him now but she could imagine him rapping on the old door, opening it to shout across the scullery to the kitchen. Out would come Ada, wiping her hands on her apron, to take his little envelope in her hand.

Tommy knew what it was, and who it was for. She'd been waiting for this moment for weeks, though she hadn't realised it.

He's dead. They're going to tell me that he's dead.

It seemed to take hours to reach the lane, but it was only about ten minutes. In that time, Bertie had gone. Ada had summoned the others. Tommy walked into the kitchen, the dogs at her heels, to see them waiting for her. Her mother was there, her expression grave, and behind her Gerry, her face white, her eyes wide and frightened, biting her lip. Ada hovered about the sink, sighing and muttering, moving things for no reason, while Thornton stood against the larder door as if hoping to disappear through it.

'It might be all right,' Tommy said in a flat voice, but she already knew what the envelope her mother held out to her would contain. As she turned it over, she saw the cross stamped on it that meant the worst news of all.

Not a prisoner. Not injured.

She stared at it for a long time, her heart racing, hundreds

4

of images of Alec tearing through her mind. The last time she had seen him: calling goodbye at the station as Alec leaned out of the train window, tiny Antonia waving a white handkerchief in farewell. Tommy had held Harry up high so he could get one last look at the baby. Alec, in his scratchy great coat and cap, kit bag still over his shoulder, had waved back, his dark eyes unreadable, a cigarette dangling from his lips, before he'd ducked back into the carriage and disappeared.

Suddenly she looked up and handed the envelope back to her mother.

'Aren't you going to open it?' Gerry asked in a small, scared voice.

'You open it. I know what it says.' She turned to the scullery doorway, a square of sunshine beyond the gloom of the kitchen. 'I'm going to find the children. I must tell them first of all.'

'Oh Tommy.' Gerry's voice broke on a sob. 'How terrible this is!'

'We're sorry, Thomasina,' her mother said in a quavering voice. 'You must be suffering very much.'

'Yes,' Tommy said, in the same blank tone. At any other time, her mother's sympathy might have touched her, but not now. 'Thank you. But I must go.'

She went out into the warm afternoon.

Alec is dead.

Her life would never be the same.

Chapter One

Present Day

'Come on, Max,' Caitlyn pleaded, almost falling under the force of her son's embrace. She dreaded this. Every time she hoped it would be different, but it never, never was. 'Let go, darling. Let's go inside.'

They were standing on the gravelled drive in front of the school's grand entrance. Caitlyn's hopes had been raised when she had managed to get Max and all his kit out of the car and right to the door, but it hadn't lasted. At the sight of the open front door, he'd lost it, dropping his hockey stick and back-pack on the ground and grabbing her. Now he was holding her tight, his arms clamped around her, his sobbing harsh and unceasing. With what breath he had left, he was stammering, 'Don't go, Mum, don't go, d-d-d-d-don't leave me!'

Other parents went past, herding their own small boys, shooting her sympathetic looks or politely ignoring the weeping Max and Caitlyn's efforts to prise him off her. None of the other boys seemed to be having anything like Max's reaction to going back to school.

Max's abject grief was almost more than she could stand. She hated leaving him here, especially when she hadn't really wanted him to come in the first place, but Patrick had convinced her that it was in Max's best interests. He'd been in love with the whole idea of prep school and what he thought it entailed: cricket, dorms, tuck, midnight feasts, high jinks, life-long friendships.

'It's what I want for Maxie,' he'd said firmly, but Caitlyn had suspected it was what he wished he'd had himself.

The only concession she'd managed to win was that Max wouldn't go till he was ten years old. Patrick wanted him to go at seven, but Caitlyn couldn't bear it while Max was still holding her hand and skipping as they walked to school, and still needed to hug his teddy and snuggle up to her while she read a bedtime story. Even then, when Max turned ten, he still seemed too young to go away from her.

'Please let go, Maxie!' Tears were pricking her own eyes as she attempted to peel back his arms. He was immoveable, his grip rock solid around her as if he really believed that by hanging on long enough, he could make her give up and take him home.

'We have to go in!' she said, almost sobbing now herself. He was practically pushing her over with the force of his embrace and she stumbled on the gravel. 'I'm sorry, Max, I hate it too, but you have to stay.'

'Here – can I help you?' It was Max's housemaster, a young man with a beard and glasses and a friendly smile. Someone had obviously sent him downstairs to them. 'Hey, Max! Great to see you, pal.'

Max ignored him, his torrent of tears unceasing.

'I'm sorry, Mr Reynolds,' Caitlyn said, raising her voice over the sound of Max's crying, anxious in case the housemaster should be offended by Max's evident disinclination to see him. 'He's still finding it hard . . . you know . . .'

'Of course I do.' Mr Reynolds smiled at her. 'He's not the first, don't worry. He'll be fine once he's upstairs. Honestly. C'mon, buddy.' He put his hand on Max's arm and patted it.

He means so well, she thought. *He's a nice man.*

Mr Reynolds was one of the reasons she could bear leaving Max behind. He was young, empathetic, and relentlessly positive. He radiated good humour and tolerance, and when Max was being at all upbeat about school, it was clear he rated Mr Reynolds very highly, from the way he was always up for an after-supper game of football, to the eagle eye he kept on them all, alert to signs of any trouble among his charges.

But none of that had made any difference to Max's despair at parting.

Mr Reynolds put his hands on Max's heaving shoulders and began to pull him away from Caitlyn. With his mother tugging at his arms and Mr Reynolds pulling from the back, Max began to release his grip. It was time to give in. He had made his protest, but he knew how it had to go.

'I'll be back soon, darling, you know I will. Daddy and I will come and see you at the first opportunity. His bags are here, Mr Reynolds.' She gestured to Max's pile of kit on the gravel: sports bag, trunk, tuck box, shoe bag, school bag, and a small pile of outdoor things plus a blazer.

'Thank you, we'll sort it out.' He grinned at her and nodded at the car. 'I think you'd better head off while you can.'

Caitlyn cast one last forlorn glance at Max, who seemed to have given up the fight and was leaning against Mr Reynolds as his sobs calmed a little. 'Goodbye, darling. I'll see you soon. I promise.'

Is it worth it? she asked herself on the way back to London. *There are almost three more years of this. Surely he can't go on being so upset whenever I go? He's got to settle sometime. Perhaps the summer term will make it easier – longer days, games in the evening.*

But she wondered for the umpteenth time if she ought to put her foot down and tell Patrick enough was enough, and they must take Max out of Spring Hall.

It wouldn't happen. When had she ever made Patrick do something he hadn't wanted to?

He was back tonight and she was looking forward to seeing him. Life lost its velocity when Patrick wasn't around. Sometimes she felt as if she was on an exciting ride, and Patrick was the pilot while she had to cling on for dear life as he took corners too fast or made madcap turns. It was mostly thrilling but it was Patrick who was in charge.

Was that how it was from the start? Or did it gradually become that way? I really can't remember. I don't suppose it matters anyway.

As she finally pulled up at the house, she wondered if she let herself be too much of a doormat. Ought she to protest more, make more of a stand about things?

But Patrick knows his own mind. I don't think I ever know what I really want.

Patrick was so good at persuading her round to his point of view. She would set out with a firm idea but within moments Patrick would make her see everything in quite another way and her own opinion would wobble, turn puny and collapse.

Caitlyn sat at the kitchen table with her cup of coffee and flicked through the Sunday papers on her tablet, Chopin nocturnes wafting down gently from the concealed sound system. There had been an email waiting from Mr Reynolds to say that Max was calm and happy, watching television with the other boys, and there was no need to worry. Comforted, Caitlyn settled into the calm and quiet. This was where she was happiest. She wished that Patrick was reading on the downstairs sofa, stretched out in that way of his, the book held up high over his face like a shield, and Max was sitting on the floor, playing with his Lego as he had been this morning, and all she had to do was have a bath and go to bed. As it was, Patrick was due home in an hour or so, and she would cook dinner: one of his homecoming favourites. The porchetta, perhaps, or the soy salmon; there were the ingredients for both in the fridge. It didn't matter to her, she wouldn't eat either of them. They would open a fresh bottle and talk about his trip, catch up on all the news. Then he would unpack his travel case, no doubt with a bottle of expensive scent for her from whatever airport duty free he'd lingered in that afternoon.

She remembered that last time he had brought her a bottle of Fracas.

'How lovely, thank you!' she'd said, and then laughed.

'What?' Patrick had said at once.

'Nothing. Only . . . it's Sara's favourite. She always wears it. Didn't you know?'

He'd looked cross and said, 'Is it? Don't open it then. Give to her as a gift. From you. I'll get you something else.'

Her eye was caught by a flash of colour on the expanse of blonde-wood floor by the window, and she noticed that a small tubful of Lego pieces had not been cleared away when Max had finished playing. She got up quickly and hurried across the room towards them, looking for the tub which must have slipped somewhere out of sight, and just as she was about to reach them, the telephone rang with a sudden violence that shattered the silence.

Caitlyn stumbled with surprise and stood hard on several small pieces which cut through her fine socks and dug into the sole of her foot. 'Ouch! Bloody hell, that hurts!' She reached the side table where the phone was still bright, flashing up the caller ID and singing out for her attention. She scooped it up. 'Hello, Patrick?'

'Are you all right? You sound like you've been running.'

'No, I'm fine, just stood on some Lego. Where are you?'

'On the M4 in a cab. The traffic's not too bad considering.'

'How was the flight?'

'Fine. Nothing to report. I'm looking forward to getting home, though.' Patrick sighed. 'It's been a long weekend.'

'Max was sorry to miss you.'

'I know. Rotten timing.'

'What time do you think you'll be home?'

'It'll be an hour at least. I'll keep you updated.'

'I'll get supper going. Do you want porchetta or salmon?'

'Oh. Oh God, I don't know. You decide.'

'All right.' She felt a tiny droop that he didn't seem excited by either option when she'd gone to the trouble of stocking up on both. 'See you later then, darling.'

'Wait, Caitlyn . . .'

'Yes?'

'How's Sara? Have you heard from her?'

'Sara?' She blinked, surprised. An image of Sara flashed across her mind: long russet hair, upturned grey eyes, khol'd into Cleopatra almond shapes. 'How funny, I was just thinking about her. She's fine, as far as I know.' She paused and then said slowly, 'Why?'

'Caitlyn, there's something I have to tell you. About Sara.'

A sudden wariness filled her. 'What? What about her?' A silence. Now he had her attention, he didn't seem to know what to do with it. A nasty sensation of fearful suspicion began to swirl in her stomach. 'Patrick . . . what do you want to tell me?'

The connection between them crackled with static.

'Are you there, Patrick?' She heard his voice. He was speaking but it was broken up by interference. 'I can't hear you. You're breaking up . . . Patrick!'

His words came in chopped and random. 'Sara . . . she said . . . explained . . . you . . . threatened . . . important . . .'

'I can't hear you! Stop talking, it's no good!' She began to turn about the room, hoping somehow that she could retune him into clarity by moving around. Now his voice was almost entirely lost to the hiss of static. 'This is hopeless.' She was about to end the useless call, when his voice suddenly bounced back into vivid clarity.

'Did you hear me?'

'No, no, I haven't heard anything you've said! There's too much noise on the line.'

She caught something in his voice. Was it desperation?

'I need to tell you before she does. Listen—'

Then it came. A noise like no other she'd ever heard: a fierce, vastly loud mechanical roar and crunch, with a great screech underneath. Then, abruptly, silence.

'Patrick? Patrick! Speak to me!'

But there was nothing. The phone was unconnected to anything or anyone. 'Patrick?' she whispered. There was no reply. She was talking only to herself and the empty room.

Chapter Two

January 1947

'Don't be silly, Harry, take it all down. All of it!'

Tommy stood in the hall in her fur coat. She hardly took it off at all these days, and certainly put it on to go from room to room in the house. Standing here on the cold stone flags, shouting up the stairs, she wished she had her hat and muff on too.

'All right. If you say so.' Her son Harry was on the first-floor landing taking the swags of ivy from the carved oak stair spindles. It had dried a little in the chill air and bits of stalk and crisp green leaves floated downwards as he tugged at the long ropes of greenery.

'No, don't just pull! You'll need to untwist it – look how it's caught in the spirals. Show him, Antonia.'

Her daughter, two years older, and finding her dignity at almost eleven, was descending the stairs ahead of Harry and pulling out the pine cones they had stuck into the ivy at intervals. Tommy had been particularly proud of the pine cones: they'd dunked them in a glue paste and then into salt to frost them, and used twisted wire to give them stiff tails that could be pressed into wreathes and garlands. Some, left untailed, were scattered on chimney pieces or arranged in a bowl to decorate the table. But that had all been before Christmas, when the excitement lay ahead, and the decorations had seemed glittering and magical. Now it was long over, and well past the time the decorations should have been taken down, and the sparkling baubles were just dried-up old cones that shook showers of salt everywhere when they were moved.

'I can't show him,' Antonia said, a touch primly. 'I'm full. Where shall I put these?' She pulled out her jumper to show that she had a load of pine cones in the front.

'By the fireplace in the drawing room. We'll burn them tonight. It'll be fun – the salt will make the flames change colour.' She glanced up at Harry who was tugging hard on a rope of ivy. 'Stop that, you chump, you'll cause an injury to the staircase! Just think how awful it would be if you snapped something. Come on, I'll help untwist.'

She ran lightly up the stairs as Antonia stomped off towards the drawing room, stopping to pull down some bits of holly from the top of picture frames and toss it over the banister to the floor below. It was already so littered with bits of foliage, the holly wouldn't matter. 'Here, I'll start and you follow me down.'

'Antonia had better get back in a moment,' Harry grumbled. 'I'm not doing all this by myself.'

'She will,' promised Tommy, though she had a feeling Antonia might have taken advantage of the situation and hopped it. Nobody was quite as keen on taking down as they had been on putting up. 'Come on, we'll be done in no time.'

As they untwisted the ivy, sending down showers of dry stalk and leaves, Harry said idly, 'Did Daddy like Christmas?'

Tommy stopped still for a moment; the children occasionally talked of Alec, but it was always a shock when they did. She'd get the same inner thud at the mention of him, and need a second to recover from it. 'Yes, of course,' she said. 'He loved it.'

'I wish I could remember him,' Harry said mournfully.

'I know, darling.'

'Mummy, can we look at the photographs later, please?'

'Of course we can.'

It was a little ritual they went through every now and then. She'd pull out the pile of snaps from the old biscuit tin and they'd go through them, the children asking hundreds of questions about their father, while she looked into that face again: Alec's dark eyes, his black hair and moustache. There he was on their wedding day, tall and handsome in uniform, while she stood – so very young – beside him, pale and wide-eyed, in a froth of falling veil and white silk. There was his studio portrait, making him look like a film star, with his chiselled features and smooth skin and straight dark brows; and all the records of the babies' arrivals, holidays, parties and celebrations.

'Tell us, Mummy,' they would beg, and she would have to tell them the stories again – about meeting Daddy and marrying Daddy, and having Antonia and Harry, and how happy they'd been in their little house. The only story they didn't want to hear was the one about Daddy dying. He had to live for them, just for a moment, their wonderful hero father, whom they'd never known.

And they never will.

'We'll get the photographs out after tea,' she promised him. That would give her a few hours to steel herself for the ordeal.

Ada Thornton came in, drying her hands on the large striped apron she always wore over her dark brown dress.

'Oh my, this mess! It looks like a forest floor in here.' She tutted. 'I'll tell Thornton to come and sort it out. You should have said, he'd have taken all this down.'

'I'm sure Thornton has plenty to do without taking down the Christmas decorations,' Tommy said with a laugh. 'We're fine, Ada. We can do it. I'll send Antonia to get the broom. If we ever see her again.' She was tempted to shout for her daughter, but she knew it would be useless. Even if Antonia were in earshot, she could simply pretend she wasn't. 'We're almost finished anyway. What is it you need me for?'

'I said I'd need to be off early today, miss.' Tommy would always be miss to Ada, no matter how long she'd been married. 'And it's Clara's day off so the dinner is in the range. You'll need to put the potatoes in at seven o'clock, and the greens should boil at a quarter to eight.'

'Thank you, Ada, I'm sure I can manage,' she said, tugging out a last bit of ivy, but Ada still looked worried. She knew only too well from Tommy's previous efforts that she would struggle with eight of them to feed, now that Roger's friend was coming.

'I could stay behind if you'd prefer . . .' Ada said.

'Don't be silly, Ada. I'll cope, I promise.'

'Very well, miss. The bedroom's all made up for the visitor.'

'Did Clara set the fire? The radiator never gets warm in there. Too far from the boiler, perhaps.' Tommy had no idea what might cause a radiator to be colder than it was supposed to be, but this sounded plausible.

'She did. And don't you forget to ask the gentleman for his ration book.'

'Of course I won't. Now off you go.'

'Very well, miss.' Ada, stout and walking with her toes turned out, went to take off her apron and put on her huge green wool coat and the small brown hat she always wore with it. Tommy tried to remember if Ada had said where she was going that day – perhaps it was the doctor; there was something of the sufferer in her general demeanour. Maybe her rheumatism was playing up in the cold. *That reminds me, I must get Thornton to chop more wood.* Something else to be done. Always a million and one things to remember, and never a pen and paper to write them down. *I must be more organised.*

Now Tommy regarded their handiwork; all the great skeins of ivy were on the hall floor. 'We just need the broom, and we can sweep all this up. It'll make very good kindling now it's so dry. Where is that wretch Antonia? And look at me, I'm covered in bits.' She brushed ineffectively at the holly leaves embedded in the rich brown fur of her coat, and then yelled as loudly as she could, 'Antonia! We've done all the blessed work. Antonia! Where are you, you lazy good-for-nothing?'

At that moment, the front door swung open and her brother Roger came in, exclaiming, 'What a racket! What on earth's going on?'

19

Someone else was just behind him. The two men looked similar in their dark overcoats and hats, but Roger was shorter, his face paler and pudgier than his friend's.

'Well, what are you doing coming in at the front?' demanded Tommy crossly, embarrassed to have been caught yelling. 'Close that door, can't you, there's a horrible draught coming in and it's cold enough already in here.'

'I thought it might be nice to show our visitor in the formal way,' Roger said. He glanced down at the strewn floor. 'But I see you've decided to create some kind of woodland effect in here.' He turned to his friend. 'Sorry about this, Fred.'

'I don't mind at all,' said his friend, his mouth curving upwards into a half-smile. 'I don't need a grand entrance, you know that.'

'No, but ... well, dash it, I did want to give a good impression of the Gainsborough.' Roger gestured up at the painting in pride of place on the wall opposite the front door, and the two men looked up at it. Tommy couldn't help turning to look too, even though she'd seen it thousands of times: the full-length portrait of a sad-faced woman with soulful dark eyes, standing beneath an oak tree, wearing gauzy white muslin, her white-grey powdered hair dressed high with soft curls falling over her shoulder.

'It's very fine. I'll have a good long gaze later,' the visitor said, taking off his hat as he stepped out into the hall from behind Roger. 'You must be Roger's sister. How do you do, Mrs Eliott.'

He put out his hand, and Tommy took it. 'Yes, that's right.

But please call me Tommy. And you're Mr Burton Brown, aren't you?'

'Yes. Fred.' He smiled at her. He was gaunt, she noticed, his cheeks sunken under high bones, his nose beaky and his eyes – green or blue, she couldn't quite make out – seemed deep in his skull. *But that's not surprising, I suppose. After all, he's been ill.* He turned to Harry who was standing quietly, his arms full of ivy, watching everything. 'And who is this young fellow, looking like a pageboy at a Bacchanalia?'

'My son, Harry,' Tommy said. 'Say hello to Mr Burton Brown, Harry.'

'Hello,' Harry said obediently.

'I suppose you're back at school now?' Fred asked him in a friendly tone.

Harry nodded. 'We have been for ages.'

'Where are you?'

'Spring Hall prep.'

'Do you like it?'

'I s'pose so. But it's jolly cold at the moment and we all scramble to sit on the radiators at lunchtime. I've been on one all week,' Harry said proudly.

'Survival of the fittest,' remarked Fred.

'You like school perfectly well, don't you, Harry?' Tommy said. 'And you'll find my daughter Antonia is floating about somewhere.'

'The lazy good-for-nothing,' Fred said solemnly.

'What? Oh yes. I was shouting for her.' Tommy laughed lightly. 'Please excuse our informality.'

'It's just what I want.'

'Enough chattering.' Roger grabbed his friend's arm impatiently. 'Come on, Fred. I'll show you around.'

'This really is a beautiful house,' Fred said, looking about. 'Seventeenth century?'

'Bits of it are,' Roger said importantly. 'This bit is sixteenth. Good Queen Bess. It was built as two separate houses, but connected. My mother lives in the smaller one these days. There are some later additions, though we think the barn is a medieval tithe barn, you must see it. But first, I'll show you the panelling. It's Jacobean and quite stunning.'

'I was hoping to look at the painting a little longer,' Fred said, gesturing over at it.

'Yes, but really it's too dark now for a proper examination. You can hardly see it hanging in the shadows at this time of day. We'll have a closer look in the morning. But you must see the panelling.'

'Where are your bags?' Tommy asked as Roger pulled his friend across the hall and towards the drawing room.

'We left them in the motor. Get them brought in, will you? Come on, Fred.'

Mr Burton Brown allowed himself to be led away, sending a look of mild amusement at Roger's enthusiasm over his shoulder to Tommy. She watched them go, feeling suddenly like a fool, standing there in her leaf-littered coat, her hair a mess and looking a fright. It hadn't always been like this. Once she'd cared about how she looked and had taken pains over her clothes. She'd lived a life of carefree gaiety, when she'd worn long dresses and waltzed in the arms of young men in candlelit ballrooms. Then, after she'd married, there were dinners and parties and dances. She remembered being in Alec's arms, his breath rich with tobacco, smelling the pomade he used to dress his moustache, her slender hand in his large one, his other palm heavy on her waist. He'd held her tight and controlled the way she moved about the dance floor, pressing against her from chest to ankle, turning her as he murmured in her ear promises for later, when they were alone . . .

Tommy shivered now just thinking about wearing a silk gown and very little else, and pulled her fur more closely about her.

That's all over now. It died with Alec. It's finished with. For good.

Chapter Three

From the first day, Caitlyn knew everyone was waiting for something: a breakdown of some sort. A huge emotional reaction. A response to the earthquake that had shattered her life. It hadn't come. Instead it felt as though someone had scooped out everything from inside her and left her functioning quite normally on the outside, but hollow and empty within. It was useful in some ways: it meant that she could cope, and get everything done that needed to be done.

She had already been thinking about that when she'd answered the door to two officers, the fluorescent flashes on their clothes and hats shining in the light from the hall.

'We've got some news about your husband, Mrs Balfour. Could we please go inside and sit down?'

She'd nodded. *They're going to tell me he's dead now. Poor things. I bet they dread this.*

A police sergeant and a woman constable, both solemn-faced, sympathetic through their well-cloaked discomfort. They made her a cup of tea, though she didn't really want one.

The words came like something she'd heard in a play or a film. She already knew them; they were familiar and completely expected. First one spoke and then the other – 'unfortunate road traffic accident' . . . 'ambulance' . . . 'hospital' . . . 'extensive injuries' . . . 'most likely instantaneous . . . no suffering' . . . 'our deep condolences.'

'I see. Thank you for telling me. What exactly happened?' she said, icy calm.

'We don't know yet. There'll be a full investigation. But preliminary reports are that a lorry went into the back of your husband's taxi, which went into the car in front, and caused several other collisions of varying severity.'

'How many died?'

'Your husband and the taxi driver are the only fatalities at present. But there are casualties in a serious condition.'

'Oh. That's awful.' She thought of the way the phone had cut off with a snap, from live to dead air, just like that. 'You think he was killed at once?'

'I'm afraid we can't confirm those facts at the present time. A full investigation will endeavour to answer all your questions.'

Police-speak. A whole different language. She imagined Patrick over her shoulder laughing at it. *Christ, where do they learn it?* she could almost hear him say. *Does someone actually teach them to talk that way?*

The officers refused to go until she had telephoned someone to come and keep her company. She said she would call Maura but as she went to the phone she pictured her sister and brother-in-law Callum asleep in their bed, great bulky lumps under a duvet, prodded awake by the ring of the phone. She saw Maura's dark hair askew, her blinking eyes, mouth agape as she reached for the handset and the horror and anxiety on her face as she heard the news. She'd drop the receiver and start to get dressed, panting and panicked. 'Holy shit, Callum, Patrick's been killed. I've got to go to Caitlyn right away. You stay with the kids . . . make sure they get to school in the morning.'

Why make that happen, when they could go on, blissful and untroubled till morning?

So instead she dialled Sara's number and waited for her to pick up the telephone.

Sara was not asleep. Of course she wasn't. She lived the adult hours of the childless, able to suit herself.

'Caitlyn? This is very late for you. Is everything okay?'

'Yes, fine,' Caitlyn said automatically, then saw the two police officers watching her solemnly and remembered. 'I mean . . . No. Sara, can you come round?'

'Now? Oh God. Is it Patrick?'

Caitlyn was too surprised to speak at once. *How does she know?*

In the silence, Sara spoke again. 'What's he said? Caitlyn? Are you okay?'

The policewoman came up, put her hand on Caitlyn's shoulder and nodded encouragingly.

Her voice returned. Sara didn't know. How could she? 'He's dead.'

'What? *Dead?* What? I don't understand . . .' Her voice

faded. Sara – always so composed, unflappable, confident. Suddenly speechless.

'His taxi crashed. On the motorway. On the way back from the airport.'

Sara was still silent, then words came in a rush. 'Oh my God. I'll come now. I'll be there as soon as I can.' And the phone went down.

'She's coming,' Caitlyn said to the policewoman. 'You can go now.'

'We'll wait.'

Then Caitlyn seemed to crumple down inside herself and her knees buckled. The policewoman reached out and caught her before she could fall, then helped her to the sofa by the window.

'I'm sorry,' she said, breathless. 'It's just ... my son. I'll have to tell my son.' And, suddenly, with Max's face in her mind, it felt as though her heart were bleeding.

Sara arrived thirty minutes later. She must have driven fast, Caitlyn thought, to get here so quickly. Once she was there, the police went, leaving grief-counselling leaflets and the case number for whatever would happen next.

Sara was pale, her face bare but for some smudges of the day's khol and mascara under her eyes, and her red hair was pulled back into a rough ponytail.

Yet she still looks like a Pre-Raphaelite beauty about to sit for her portrait. Caitlyn wondered how she could think such things with Patrick only just ... *Say it. He's dead.* Now that she stared into Sara's oval face, something came into her mind. It was her conversation with Patrick in the minutes before the crash, but his words, all that she could hear of them, were swirling around her head, refusing to make sense.

What did he say?

As the front door closed behind the departing police officers, Sara turned to her, hugged her and burst into tears. She was speaking, but her voice was a distant sound as Caitlyn strove to remember the words that Patrick had said just before the impact.

He said . . . he said . . . she threatened something. But what? What was it? Did I hear it? Or not? Patrick's words were sliding out of her mind even as she reached for them.

'Oh God, Caitlyn, I'm so sorry! This is such an awful, awful thing. I can't believe it! I can't take it in!' And then another tight hug, a cheek on her shoulder, the faint damp of tears on her shirt.

She put her arm around her friend's shaking shoulders. 'I know,' she said. 'I can't take it in either.'

'You're in shock!' Sara pulled back to examine her anxiously, wiping her tears and sniffing. 'Of course you are. You need a drink. Do you have brandy?'

And she was gone, heading upstairs in search of Patrick's drinks cabinet. Of course they had brandy. They had the finest Napoleon cognac. She heard Patrick's voice in her head: *Doesn't she know me by now? But ask her for the Glenmorangie, you know you prefer it.*

'Patrick,' she said out loud, and felt the first bitter burst of pain at her loss. Not Max's but hers. So much was gone. Just like that. 'Oh Patrick.'

Sara was coming down the stairs and towards her, two glasses of rich brown brandy in her hands.

'We need this,' she said, and smiled wanly. Her large grey eyes were reddened and her lower lip shook. Then she began to weep again. 'It's so fucking unfair! What are we going to do?'

Caitlyn stared at her, feeling for a moment as though she were looking at a stranger.

Patrick, what were you trying to tell me? And why can she cry when I can't?

Sara pressed the glass of brandy into her hand and wiped her eyes. 'Come on, drink it.' She drained her own in a gulp and then regarded the empty glass. 'I should have brought the bottle. I'll go and get it. And I'm not leaving you tonight. Understand? I'm with you every step of the way.'

Whatever it was, Caitlyn realised, it didn't matter now.

The enormity of Patrick's death blotted out everything else.

The next morning, as Caitlyn lay awake in bed, staring unseeing into space, gripped by an evil sense of sick dread and trying to grasp that Patrick was not coming back, she heard the front door slam. An hour or so later, Sara returned, then brought her a cup of coffee, knocking timidly at the bedroom door.

'Did you manage to sleep?' she asked, setting down the coffee and sitting on the bed.

'Not really. A bit.' Caitlyn remembered a blur of intense dreams. In them she'd experienced storms of passion, screaming, crying, maddened emotions, but she'd woken to the same

29

dank and bitter coldness within. It was a kind of icy horror that froze her in a state of fearful emotional paralysis.

'I've been home to get some things. I'm going to stay with you. You shouldn't be alone.' Sara smiled down at her, and put her hand on Caitlyn's. 'You need me.'

Caitlyn looked up at her, surprised. She had never known Sara like this. Their relationship usually involved Caitlyn providing the emotional support, the stability through times of crisis, the caring and nurturing. It was very odd to see Sara taking that role.

Sara stood up. 'I've put my suitcase in the spare room. I'm going to unpack. Come down when you're ready.'

'Yes. Thank you.'

Sara smiled again. Her grey eyes filled with tears. 'It's the least I can do, darling. The absolute least.'

Sara was as good as her word. She stayed by Caitlyn's side at almost every waking moment, through the horrible phone calls Caitlyn had to make: to Patrick's family and colleagues, to her own family, to Max's housemaster.

'Please don't tell him, Mr Reynolds. I'll do that. But just so you know what's happened.'

'Of course.' Mr Reynolds' voice was redolent with sympathy. 'How terrible. I'm so sorry, Mrs Balfour. Please accept my deepest condolences. Poor, poor little Max.'

The mere mention of Max's name could send a sudden shimmer of grief through her, and trigger a desperate need to weep, though she could manage to control that within a few moments. The sadness she felt for herself had burrowed itself down somewhere inaccessible, leaving her able to function but on a kind of autopilot. Instead she felt the burden of everyone else's shock and despair at what had happened.

'Oh God, Caity, we're so sorry,' Maura said, hugging her tight, her eyes pink around the rims and her skin blotchy. She had come over as soon as she could. 'I can't believe Patrick's gone. It's a bloody tragedy. You poor, poor darlin'.'

'Thank you,' Caitlyn said, thinking how Maura adopted Callum's Irish accent at moments of intensity.

Maura gave her a worried look. Then, over coffee at the kitchen table, she said, 'What are you going to do about Max?'

'I'm going down tomorrow first thing to tell him. I would have gone today but I can't quite face it yet.'

'Shall I take you? I can get compassionate leave from work. Callum can look after the kids.'

Caitlyn had a sudden flash of her sister's home: disordered, chaotic, but warm and loving, full to the brim with four children, an Irish wolfhound and two cats. Maura was their lynchpin, the creator and organiser and sorter-outer, ferrying kids to sport and music, conjuring up meals and clean washing. They needed her.

'No thanks. It's okay. Sara's going to drive me.'

Maura looked over to where Sara sat on the sofa at the other end of the room, talking intently into her mobile phone. Her expression was wary. She had never liked Sara, guessing, rightly, that despite being scrupulously polite, Sara looked down on her. 'How long has she been here?'

'Since I found out. I called her. She insisted on staying.'

'You didn't call me?' A wounded expression crossed Maura's face.

'I didn't want to bother you.'

'Bloody hell, Caitlyn, I'm your sister! What kind of bother did you think it would be?'

Caitlyn felt guilty, instantly seeing why Maura was hurt. 'I . . . sorry. I just thought Sara didn't have family commitments.'

'No.' Maura looked repentant. 'I'm sorry, I shouldn't have snapped. You should do what you think is right. It's what you want, darlin'. But if you need me to drive you to Oxford, just say.'

'It's okay, honestly. Sara will do it.'

But when they were flying down the motorway towards the school, Caitlyn wished she were with Maura after all. She'd forgotten how Sara liked to drive with her wrist balanced on the top of the steering wheel, the other hand gesturing as she talked, the speed dial climbing. She couldn't help thinking of Patrick, similarly oblivious to the danger as he talked to her on the phone, and then suddenly – boom. Gone. Dead.

The thought made her shake with fear. *I can't leave Max. I'm all he's got now.* Her voice came out in a kind of roar. 'For God's sake, slow down, Sara! Please! *Please!*'

Sara braked, surprised, and slipped the car into the middle lane. 'Sorry,' she said.

Caitlyn was shaken, panting and trembling. 'Don't you understand? Max needs me!' she said, and burst into tears. Sara pulled off into the nearest layby while Caitlyn wept, then, when the car was stopped, turned to her, stricken.

'I'm really sorry! I didn't mean to upset you.' She struggled to lean over and embrace Caitlyn but it was too awkward so she patted her shoulder instead, while Caitlyn cried. Sara started to cry as well, fat tears welling up and spilling down her cheeks – picturesque even in sorrow.

'Oh Caitlyn,' she said, wiping tears away. 'We loved him. We're going to miss him so much, aren't we? What are we going to do without him?'

Chapter Four

Roger took Fred Burton Brown away for the entire afternoon of his arrival, enthusiastically showing him everything. Tommy was glad to see Roger full of energy again. She'd been worried about her brother ever since his return from the army: he'd been so low, and getting lower, sunk in private misery. When Fred's letter arrived, Roger had smiled for the first time in an age.

'It's Burton Brown,' he'd said over the breakfast table, the letter clutched tightly in one hand. 'You remember Fred, don't you? From Cambridge?'

'I don't think so,' Tommy said, trying to recall. The days when she'd visited Roger at his college were so long ago now. Before the war. Before she and Alec were married. A different life, peopled by madcap, happy strangers, now just a blur in her mind's eye. 'Did I meet him?'

'How should I know? Perhaps. Anyway, it makes no odds. He wonders if he can come and stay. He's not long back from convalescing and he says his flat has been bombed out of existence. Poor chap.' Roger frowned, lost in a memory for a moment. 'What a shame.'

'How long?' Tommy asked, scooping out the last of her boiled egg.

'He doesn't say. A few weeks, I'd guess. He says he's still recovering, but not from what.'

'Of course he can come.'

'Yes.' Roger glanced again at his letter, frowning, then slapped it down on the table. 'Well, I'll just say he can come for as long as he likes. It'll be good to have him here.'

'Yes. It will,' Tommy said warmly, happy to see a light of enthusiasm on Roger's face. She'd grown so used to seeing him dull-eyed, his complexion pale and pasty, his hair carefully combed to hide the fact that it was already thinning although he was barely thirty. 'It will make us all a good deal chirpier, I should think.'

'What will?' asked her sister, coming into the dining room slowly and sightlessly, her nose buried in a book. Her spectacles suddenly popped up over the top of the cover, wide blue eyes behind them, blinking and curious.

'You'll get hurt doing that,' Tommy observed. 'You'll walk into a pillar and brain yourself.'

'No I won't,' Gerry said. 'I can see and read at the same time.' She put her book on the table, tossed her long dark plait of hair back over her shoulder and looked over at the chaffing dishes on the side. 'It's very tantalising to put those things out when there's nothing in them. It makes me think of bacon and kippers and kedgeree, and all the things we used to have.'

'There's porridge. Or an egg.'

Gerry went over and lifted a lid to peer at the grey, pasty sludge underneath. 'It's not the kind of porridge I like. What's in it? Dust? The sweepings from the stable?'

'Don't be disgusting. You know Ada does her best with what there is.' Tommy pushed her silver egg cup away. 'Have some porridge, Gerry, there's a dear. I don't want her to throw it away.'

'It feeds the hens, doesn't it?' Gerry said, lifting a solid scoop of it up with her spoon. 'I'm not entirely sure this is fit for human consumption in any case.'

'Please don't say that when Ada can hear you,' Tommy said quickly. 'Now, here's some good news. Roger has a friend coming to stay with us. A friend from Cambridge.'

Gerry looked interested. 'Fresh blood? Oh goody.'

Roger said proudly, 'He's rather a brilliant scholar. He gained a double first in Classics.'

'Really? Perhaps he can advise me on universities then.'

'I could do that,' Roger said, looking hurt.

'But you don't want me to go to one,' Gerry remarked.

Tommy said hastily, 'You'd better write to warn him about the cold, Roger, he might not be used to it. Tell him to bring the warmest things he can. He'll need all of them.'

Now, while Fred Burton Brown was getting the full tour, Tommy went in search of a broom so that she could sweep up the fallen greenery. She found one outside in one of the old stone sheds attached to the house. It was icy outside, the world chilled to its depths, and her feet were numbed almost at once from the iron cold of the ground that made even the stone-flagged hall seem cosy by comparison. At least sweeping would keep her warm. The fires would not be lit till later and the central heating was only switched on for an hour in the morning in the hope it would warm the house enough for the entire day. But even so, the boiler simply ate up coal, and there was the range to keep going, or there would be no hot food. Thank goodness there was plenty of wood for the house fires, or the coal would never last at all.

And now there's someone else here, another room to heat, more food to find. I must remember to ask Mr Burton Brown for his ration book or Ada will be cross.

As she swept the rubbish into a bucket, she wished she'd asked him to bring a hot water bottle. In fact, as many as he could get his hands on. The old rubber ones were perishing and there were no more to be had, so they were having to dig out clay ones. The other night Tommy had even filled a warming pan with hot coals and swept the children's beds to get some warmth into their clammy cold sheets. She was pretty sure the pan hadn't been used since last century.

I expect he's used to city life, she thought now, hauling up the bucket and heading out for the back door. *Hot radiators and endless steaming water. I hope we don't kill him. After all, he is convalescing.*

She left the bucket in the passage by the drawing room and took the broom back outside.

'Thomasina! What on earth are you doing?'

Tommy turned to see her mother, enveloped in a large tweed coat, a headscarf wrapped around her hair, with rubber boots on, come marching up, her two slender black labradors trotting at her heels. She looked disapprovingly at the broom Tommy was holding.

'Just sweeping up, Mother. I'm putting the broom back. We've taken the decorations down.'

'At last! It should have been done weeks ago.'

'The children didn't want to see them go so I thought it would do no harm to leave them. But with the visitor coming, it was a little too eccentric to have them up. They made a frightful mess to clear up though.'

'I can see that.' Mrs Whitfield looked peeved. 'But why are you sweeping? Where is Clara?'

'Day off. And Ada's gone too.' Tommy spoke lightly, brushing off the disapproval as she always did. She'd grown used to the idea that nothing she did would ever please her mother. The harder she worked, the more her mother disliked it. 'Roger bowled up with Mr Burton Brown about half an hour ago, and is now taking him on a guided tour of the house. He seems very nice. I'm sure you'll like him.'

'As long as he makes Roger happy. That's the most important thing. And you must tell the children to keep quiet – he won't want to be bothered with them and their racket. Please, Thomasina, tidy yourself up before dinner. You look a perfect savage. Come, Hebe, come, Hermione.'

Mrs Whitfield turned and headed for her front door, the black dogs following her obediently. Tommy watched her go, half relieved and half irritated.

Never a word of thanks. Never an acknowledgement of the work I do. Roger was sent to Winchester and Cambridge to prepare him for running this place, and he does nothing. I got piano lessons and French conversation, and I've run the whole show for years. Not that Mother has ever appeared to notice.

Tommy sighed. There was no point in dwelling on it. The truth was, she'd loved taking it all on, even if she never felt quite up to the task. It had given her a purpose and a refuge, and a place to raise the children.

Besides, there's no time. I shall have to start on the dinner soon, if we're going to eat anything at all tonight.

There was quite an air of excitement in the house with the new arrival. The children, who had been in a state of crotchety lassitude since Christmas, were noticeably more fizzy and excited. They were allowed to stay up late for dinner in honour of the new arrival.

'My goodness, what a treat, pheasant!' Mr Burton Brown said as they sat down to casserole with boiled potatoes and boiled winter greens. 'I haven't had it since before the war.'

'Pheasant again!' groaned Antonia. 'I hate it. When I grow up, I'm never going to eat pheasant again as long as I live.'

'What spoiled rotters you are,' Tommy observed. 'Just think of all the poor children in London not able to have delicious fresh pheasant whenever they want.'

'I wouldn't mind,' said Antonia mulishly.

'Nor would I,' declared Harry. 'I'm sick of it.'

'Careful,' said Tommy with a warning look, and both of them settled down at their places, suppressing their irritation. 'Excuse my horrible children, please, Mr Burton Brown.'

'Everyone must call me Fred, I insist.'

'All right, Fred,' Antonia said at once.

'Fred, Fred, Fred,' chimed in Harry.

'Children!' Mrs Whitfield looked scandalised and Tommy sent them another stern look.

'Mr Burton Brown to you, children. For now.' She smiled at Fred. 'Until we know you a little better.'

Fred looked even thinner and more angular now that he had discarded his great coat and was wearing a dark suit that had no doubt once fitted. She noticed his extremely long and slender hands, and the way a lock of dark hair fell over his broad, high forehead. He looked intelligent, she thought. But restrained. He had nothing about him of Alec's rich sensuality, that dark desire for life that had possessed him. Fred was outwardly serene and appeared to have a calm nature.

'Then I'd better get to know you all quickly,' he said, 'or I'll be Mr Burton Brown for far too long.' He began to tell them a few things about himself: how before the war he had worked at the BBC in London, which fascinated the children, then how he had joined the army and gone to fight in Africa. 'But just before the end of it all, I managed to get badly burned in an accident. Not even fighting, I'm afraid. And I got sent back to recover, to a place by the sea. But when I was well enough to go home, I found I had no home to go to. I'd heard my place had been hit in the bombing but I didn't know it had been obliterated. Octavia kept that from me.'

'Octavia?' Tommy asked. She'd been listening intently, although the story had been told for the sake of the children. They had all finished eating while listening to Fred and even

Gerry had come out of her own little world to attend to him.

'My sister,' said Fred. 'She stayed in London right through, working as an air-raid warden. She knew my place was gone but didn't let on. She said it would only depress me and there was nothing to be done. She scratched about in the rubble for anything that might be saved and picked up a few odds and ends. But most of it was turned to dust.'

The children stared, trying to picture a world where things could be transformed from solid to dust in an instant.

Thank God we had this place to come to, and I could spare them that. Tommy looked down at her plate to hide her expression in case she looked too sombre.

Harry asked, 'Have you seen it now? Your old house?'

'Yes, I have. It was quite a sight. When something's been bombed, you imagine it to be wrecked, but somehow the same. But to see the real damage . . . well, it's just a heap of rubble and timber, and you can see the insides you'd never usually know about – the ends of pipes hanging out, and wires, and the plaster ripped from the battens. Not that there's even that much of my old place. The whole building and the ones either side have gone, leaving a horrible, ugly gash in the street. It's a ruin. That's what London feels like now. It looks like a mouth where half the teeth have been punched out.'

'How awful,' Tommy exclaimed. 'To lose everything like that!'

'Luckily I'd sent quite a lot of things down to my parents in Kent beforehand to be on the safe side. That's why I still have some clothes to stand up in.'

Tommy thought of everything precious, of all the treasures in their house, vanished in one sudden flash of destruction. Not just the furniture and china and all that – *the blessed Gainsborough. Imagine* – but the mementoes of the children's babyhoods, the sentimental jewellery – not expensive but dear to her. It was a horrible thought. But she knew that as long as the children were all right, she wouldn't mind about the rest.

'Mother, may we go to London and see the bomb holes?' asked Antonia eagerly.

'Maybe one day we'll go. When it's warmer. But I don't know about inspecting bomb sites. It sounds rather depressing to me. Perhaps they'll all be gone by the time we get there.'

'I doubt it.' Roger shook his head. 'It'll be years. Decades probably. If ever.'

'Then,' Tommy said, 'perhaps I'm better off not seeing London again. It can live on in my mind as it used to be.'

'Never go to London again?' Gerry said. 'I'll believe that when I see it. You love London, Tommy.'

'Do I?'

'Well, you used to. You longed and longed to go. You said you'd never live anywhere else.'

'That was then,' Tommy said, with a shrug. 'Before everything. The war. And everything else.'

'Gerry, please clear the plates,' said their mother. 'Children, you can help her. If you're careful.'

Tommy noticed Fred was regarding her with an expression that she couldn't quite decipher. Was it sympathy? *Why should he feel sorry for me? I suppose Roger told him about Alec being killed.*

'Is there any pudding?' asked Harry. 'That isn't bottled plums?'

'No, sorry,' Tommy said, standing up to shake off the feeling of being observed. 'It's bottled plums all round. But Ada's made some sort of custard, so cheer up, Harry. It'll be delicious, I promise.'

She was glad to be able to escape to the kitchen, away from Fred's gaze and the sense that he could see the things that she was trying to hide.

I don't want that. That must never happen.

Chapter Five

Breaking the news of Patrick's death to Max had been the hardest thing in Caitlyn's life. She'd held him as he absorbed it, and began to cry bitterly, hiding his head in her shoulder. Then he had come home with her and Sara, until he felt ready to go back to school.

The following day, Sara had gone out to see clients and Max had wrapped himself in his duvet and watched hours of cartoons on the downstairs television, as though trying to shut out the fact of Patrick's death with bright colours and raucous sound.

Restless, Caitlyn wandered through the house, up the stairs, into rooms, inspecting them. Everywhere was immaculate as usual, just as Patrick liked it. 'Your perfect world,' her sister Maura had called it with a laugh. It was true this was a well-feathered nest, quiet and orderly and kept under strict control. Caitlyn had grown so used to the neatness and calm that she now found it difficult to be in her sister's home for more than a few hours, before she began to feel breathless and anxious to escape.

The effect of living with Patrick all these years.

She was in the drawing room now, standing there gazing at the beautiful, calm decor. It had all been Patrick's design. The colour scheme of the house – deeply serene, cool shades of chalky blue, calm greys and white – was his, and he had even designed the conversion of the basement into a gym, laundry and cinema space, complete with a double-height glass window that stretched from the ground floor kitchen down into the basement, providing a light well. Caitlyn remembered the havoc the delivery of that mammoth window had caused. There had been a vast crane truck to lift it over the roof of their terraced house and drop it into place, with dozens of workmen to guide it. The whole street had been closed off for the day and there had been many deliveries of flowers to the neighbours afterwards. But it had been worth it. The house was beautiful; interior-magazine perfect. From the giant modern chandeliers in milky glass and copper that hung like angular stars from the drawing room ceiling to the perfectly filled bookcases and the designer glass coffee tables next to the antique marble fireplaces, the house was a joy to look at. There were rules to keep it like this: no shoes in the house. No animals or pets. No dirt of any kind allowed to linger. No disorder or toys left out. The house's calm serenity was the result of constant vigilance, the permanent low-level hum of activity – picking up, putting away, folding out of sight, wiping down, clearing up.

When Caitlyn's family visited, Patrick took measures, hiding anything breakable, putting down mats and locking doors. The dog was forbidden or, if absolutely unavoidable, was confined to the garden. Patrick would wear an expression of determined forbearance, a smile glued to his lips no matter what, and even though the family were usually well behaved, the simple fact of so much anarchic presence in the house sent stress levels high.

Despite the tension they brought with them, Patrick liked Maura and Callum, and would often sit around with his brother-in-law listening to whatever was on Callum's mind that day. Caitlyn suspected that Callum thought Patrick was the easy-going one, and she was uptight. Last time he'd been here, he'd plonked himself on the sofa and bellowed at her, 'Come on, Caity! Come and have a bloody large drink. Let it all hang out. Relax a little.'

She'd grinned and said, 'In a bit. When I've got the potatoes in.'

But it had deflated her somewhat, making her wonder if he thought she was a controlling perfectionist with all the joylessness that seemed to imply.

After lunch, Maura had helped her clear up. The children had been sent off to the park with the dog, a football and ice-cream money, Max thrilled to be at home for the weekend with his cousins; the men were watching the England–Ireland rugby match on the big screen, Callum yelling for Ireland over cans of Guinness, Patrick with a glass of Puligny-Montrachet.

'Is everything okay?' Maura had asked, bringing over a pile of gravy-smeared plates and starting to stack them in the dishwasher. 'I mean, with life.'

'Yes, of course. Why wouldn't it be?' Caitlyn smiled stiffly, watching as Maura loaded the plates. She found it very stressful, having got so used to Patrick's ways. She was afraid that Maura would do something stupid, like slinging in wooden bowls or razor-sharp Japanese chopping knives or silver cutlery, and Patrick would be furious.

Maura frowned as her gaze swept over Caitlyn's form, dressed as usual in slim blue jeans, white shirt and an artfully sloppy grey cashmere jumper. 'Have you lost weight?'

'No! I don't think so. I haven't weighed myself.' Caitlyn shrugged. 'I'm pretty much the same, I think. I don't pay much attention.'

Which is, of course, a terrible lie.

She thought about her appearance all the time. She wished she could be more like Maura, who seemed to go through life untouched by the same anxiety. She was well upholstered, almost always bare-faced, her brown hair filled with silver-spun threads that glittered under the kitchen spotlights.

As though she doesn't care. What must that be like?

Maura said, 'Well, you seem a bit downbeat, that's all. What's up?' She put the plates down and leaned against the counter, watching her sister carefully.

'Nothing. Max is still finding it hard to settle at school . . . Patrick's so busy, travelling a lot . . .' She trailed off vaguely, hoping this would satisfy Maura.

'What about your plan to go back to work? Have you gone any further with it?'

'Oh. Well. Yes . . . I'm throwing out some lines of enquiry . . . Something might come of it.'

'You shouldn't waste that mind of yours. I wish I had

your education. You can't waste an Oxford degree, you know.'

'I do know. You've said so before. Often.' Caitlyn smiled in mock reproof. 'I just want to be sure Max is happy before I go back.'

'He's eleven years old and he doesn't live here during the week,' Maura observed, heading back to the table.

Caitlyn flushed and her skin prickled. 'Actually he's home for over half the year, and he has an exeat every few weeks. His terms are much shorter than yours, you know that.'

'Hmm.' Maura had her back to her as she picked up glasses. There was a pregnant pause, full of the remembered discussions about what Maura had thought of the decision to send Max away to prep school. 'Well, I think going back to work might be good for you. Keep at it, I say.'

'Yes. I will.'

'And Patrick – everything's all right with him?'

'Of course.'

Maura made a face as if to imply that it was a miracle. 'You're good at keeping in line, Caity. Just don't give in to him all the time, will you? You need a bit of yourself too. I'm worried that he keeps you on a short leash.'

'I don't know what you mean. We're perfectly happy.'

'Well, something's making you miserable. I wish you could tell me about it.' Maura shot her another sideways look. 'It's not your friend Sara, is it?'

'Sara? No.' Caitlyn laughed but it sounded forced. 'I know you don't approve of her but—'

'That's an understatement,' muttered Maura. 'I certainly don't think she's any good for you.'

Caitlyn hesitated, remembering the last time Sara had been here, drifting about the house, examining it, and asking her if Patrick minded that she'd gone up a dress size. Caitlyn had barely touched a carb – or any food at all, come to that – since then. 'I like her,' Caitlyn said firmly. 'We share a lot of history. She doesn't do me any harm.'

'If you say so,' Maura replied. 'But you know my thoughts on that piece of work.'

'Mmm.' She knew that Sara always had been rather standoffish when she met Maura. 'She's all right when you get to her know her, honestly.'

'I'm not so sure,' Maura had said. 'I don't like the way she's so hungry for everything you've got.'

Now Caitlyn thought over Maura's words while she took a bath, hoping that might help some of the cold tension at her core unfreeze. Why would Maura think that Sara was no good for her?

And hungry for what I've got? What does that mean?

The memory of her last conversation with Patrick swirled mistily through her brain. *What did he say?* She wished she'd written it down. Words formed in her mind – *threatened . . . important . . . tell you . . .* – but she couldn't pull it all together.

She swirled the warm water around herself, letting the bubbles melt on her skin. Already it felt as though Patrick were far away, out of her reach. How could he vanish so quickly?

49

I loved him. I miss him. What am I going to do without him? Then she heard an echo in her mind, and realised that Sara had said almost those exact words the previous afternoon in the layby. *We loved him. We'll miss him*, she'd said. *What are we going to do without him?*

We?

She heard Maura's words again: *she's so hungry for everything you've got.*

The water seemed suddenly chilly, and she got out.

That evening, when Max was asleep and supper was over, Sara opened a bottle of wine and poured them both a glass. They went up to the sitting room and sat down on opposite sofas, facing one another over the large glass coffee table stacked with glossy art books.

'I'm glad Max is home,' Sara said. She had curled up, her legs tucked underneath her. Her red hair glowed against the muted colours of the drawing room. They complemented her perfectly. 'You shouldn't be alone right now.'

On the opposite sofa, Caitlyn caught a glimpse of herself in the mirror over the fireplace. Next to Sara's vibrancy, she looked washed out: pallid and stringy haired, the highlights in her light-brown hair dull. Her eyes had a deadness in their hazel and blue depths, and her skin was puffy and grey. *It must be what grief does.*

She glanced away quickly so she wouldn't have to see herself. 'I'm used to being by myself. I was often alone with Patrick travelling so much.'

'Yes. He was away a lot, wasn't he?' Sara sipped her wine. 'How were things between you . . . at the end?'

'They were fine.'

Sara stared at her and blinked in that way she had: slow, feline. 'I'm glad. You'd had your rough patches.'

'Had we?' Already her marriage was in the past. A thing that used to be. She felt almost panicked at the idea that it would begin to slip away, out of her memory. Before it was a living thing with a future. Now it only had a past.

'I only know what I saw. Patrick liked to control things. Sometimes . . .' Sara hesitated and looked pained. 'I don't like to say it, with Patrick barely cold. But we can't pretend it was all sweetness and light, can we?'

'What relationship is?' Caitlyn replied. 'Of course we had our problems.'

'I thought you did an amazing job, considering,' Sara said firmly.

'Considering . . . ?'

Sara took a long drink and refilled her glass. 'It's the wrong time to talk about it. You're in shock still. I am, too.'

'I want to talk about Patrick,' Caitlyn said. 'I don't want us not to speak about him, as though nothing has happened.'

'Of course. But I don't know if it's right, because we can't sanitise everything even if we want to remember the good stuff.'

'Like what? Sanitise what?'

Sara paused, then said, 'Patrick could make you very miserable too, don't forget. You said yourself that he took every decision, ruled your life. He could be tyrannical. We both know that.'

'Well . . .' Caitlyn felt ashamed of her disloyalty. Any previous unhappiness seemed like nothing now, the petulance of a spoiled wife. Patrick had given her so much – a life she couldn't have had without him. He'd loved her too. What more, exactly, had she wanted? 'I know I complained sometimes.'

Sara nodded. 'I saw it. I know what it was like.' She took a long draught of her wine. 'To be honest, I don't know how you stood it. I didn't like the way he treated you. He could be so . . . inattentive. Couldn't he?'

'I suppose so.'

'He walked all over you,' Sara said, then smiled sympathetically. 'Sometimes.'

'Is that how it looked?'

'It's how it was. Don't forget. I saw it. It used to worry me, if I'm honest. Patrick was a handsome man. A sexy man. He must have had offers all the time. Do you think he ever cheated?'

Caitlyn blinked in surprise. 'I don't think so.' That was one thing she had never suspected. Patrick was many things but she had never thought he might be unfaithful. She remembered a party where one of the women had got drunk and thrown herself at Patrick, who had completely ignored her. He'd danced with Caitlyn instead. And with Sara. Caitlyn had a sudden flash of memory, of Patrick and Sara dancing together at that party, Sara murmuring in his ear while she did that slow, cat-like blink of hers. And they'd laughed together. 'Do you think he might have cheated?' Caitlyn asked.

'Hmm.' Sara frowned and looked up at the ceiling, then said, 'I don't *think* so. Not from what I saw.'

Caitlyn thought of how much Sara had seen since they met as students: the dating disasters, failed romances and, of course, Patrick. And Caitlyn had been there to witness Sara's dizzying life: her first marriage which, like a firework, burned brightly and exploded rapidly; and the longer, more painful death of her second marriage. A sense of unease came over her, and Patrick's jumbled last words echoed again in her mind, just out of reach.

Is Sara hinting that she knows something?

She looked across the table at Sara, at the familiar china complexion, the slanted grey eyes and the cascade of russet hair and thought, *I'm being crazy. It's Sara. My friend. We've been through so much. What don't I know about her?*

But Patrick had wanted to tell her something she didn't know.

What did he want to say? Even now, as she and Sara sipped their wine together, ideas flickered through her mind. *That they were having an affair?*

She dismissed it at once. The idea was too ridiculous. Patrick had known Sara for years. He met her before he'd proposed to Caitlyn. He was most certainly immune to Sara's charms. That had been one of the things that drew her to him in the first place.

If there was one thing I was sure of, it was that Patrick was not interested in Sara. And Sara would never do that to me. I know she could be badly behaved sometimes, but she never set out intentionally to hurt me. She wouldn't have dreamed of betraying me like that. Whatever Patrick wanted to say, it wasn't that. And it was probably nothing. I'm sure it was nothing. Some silly discussion they'd had. But now she had an opportunity to ask. She hesitated and then said, 'Sara, had he said anything to you recently?'

Sara put her head on one side, her expression mildly interested. 'Like what?'

'Oh, I don't know. About anything. How he was feeling. What he was up to. About me.'

Sara drank another mouthful of wine before answering. 'No. I hadn't seen him for ages. We hadn't spoken since that time I came over here for dinner. Why?'

'I . . . I just had the impression he'd been in touch with you, that's all.'

Sara's eyebrows lifted gently. 'Why did you think that? What did he say?'

'He said . . . you know what, I can't remember. It was nothing. I probably misunderstood.' Caitlyn sighed. 'I suppose I'm worried that he might have confided something in you – about not being happy.'

'He was happy,' Sara said simply, 'I'm sure of it. You don't have to worry about that. He liked his fun and games, didn't he?' And she took another sip of her wine. 'You were the one, Caitlyn. The one who wasn't happy.'

Chapter Six

Tommy marched across the great hall, sighing with exasperation. Her meeting with Mr Spottiswoode that morning about the estate income and the repairs had gone badly. Now that the men were coming back and taking up their old jobs, the estate manager seemed to think it was perfectly fine to ask for higher rents, which had been frozen for the duration. But Tommy didn't know how she could look the tenants in the face at church on Sundays if she demanded more money.

'We'll wait until the next quarter,' she'd said with finality. 'Then we can think again.'

'And what does Mr Whitfield say about this?' enquired Spottiswoode. 'There are many urgent repairs to take care of. The Charfield barn . . .'

Tommy had been irritated. 'You've dealt with me for the last three years, Mr Spottiswoode, and that's how it will continue until my brother is well enough to resume work. He's still recovering, as you know.'

'Of course, of course, Mrs Eliott. And it's a pleasure to

work with you.' Spottiswoode had smiled but Tommy knew what he really thought. The sooner Roger was back, the better.

The truth was that ever since Roger had inherited Kings Harcourt Manor a few years before the war, he'd never managed to take charge. Spotty had been left to his own devices, which was clearly the way he liked it. Once Tommy had arrived with the children, she'd seen at once that Roger would never be able to run the estate effectively. It wasn't in his bones. *Or not, perhaps, in his head. Whatever it is, it's always been there. It's not the war, even if that made it worse.*

Everyone had pretended that Roger was making the decisions, or that her mother was the arbiter, but, invisibly, unacknowledged, Tommy had taken on the burden and had shouldered it as well as she could, even though she felt ill equipped for the task.

And I think I managed it. We all came through. We're still here.

That was why it infuriated her to be patronised by Spotty, whose flat feet and short sight had made him unfit for army service and allowed him to lord it over those here at home.

Horrible man! I wish I had the confidence to let him go. But I suppose I need him. She flung open the drawing room door and went in, saying, 'Oh, damn it all!'

'Hello there.' Fred was standing at the piano by the silver-framed photographs that sat on its polished surface, his expression quizzical. 'Are you all right?'

Tommy stopped short, flushing pink with embarrassment. 'Goodness, I am sorry. Please ignore me. It's nothing.'

'I'm sure it's not,' he said, 'but I wouldn't dream of prying.'
He gestured to one of the photographs. 'I was admiring this.'

Tommy saw that he was indicating a studio portrait taken
at the time of her engagement. 'Well . . . thank you. It was a
long time ago now.'

Sometimes she could hardly believe that the perfectly
complexioned, full-lipped girl was her, with the soulful eyes
and dark hair set in immaculate waves, a strand of pearls
glowing on her pale silk dress. That morning, looking in the
glass, she'd despaired of the state of her hair, and used a tiny
amount of the lipstick she had left. Before the war, she'd
never have left the house without her hair perfectly done,
and powder, rouge and mascara. Now she was eking out her
supplies and doing her best with what was left.

But there were other reasons why she hated to look at that
photograph.

'I don't think you've changed at all,' Fred said gallantly.

Tommy laughed. 'I was only eighteen then. Two children,
ten years and the war! I've changed a little. We all have.'

'Perhaps you're right.' Fred smiled at her. 'I really came
down to look at the Gainsborough. Roger said it was best in
the morning light. I rather hoped you might explain it to me.'

'Yes, of course. I'm no expert, but I'm happy to show it to
you.' She turned and headed back out to the hall, gesturing to
Fred to follow her.

'Why is it tucked away like that? In the dark?' Fred asked
as they skirted the stairs to face the portrait in its shadowy
home. The murky light could not conceal its beauty. 'She

should be over the fireplace, instead of that collection of swords you've got there.'

'It's because she was in the attic for so long. The swords went up when some martial ancestor fancied a nice, warlike display, before the painting was discovered.'

'In the attic!' exclaimed Fred, astonished. 'A Gainsborough?'

'It's rather a sad story. The woman in the painting died at the age of twenty-two, not long after this portrait was painted. She was perfectly fine one day, then found dead in bed the next, for no reason they could discover. Her name was Venetia. Such a pretty name. It makes me think of Venetian glass, which seems appropriate – beautiful but fragile. I wanted it for Antonia but I was afraid of bad luck. Her husband, one of our ancestors, was so heartbroken he couldn't bear to look at her portrait, and put it away in the attic. It was only brought down a few generations later and hung here. I've often wondered why they didn't put her back over the fireplace, but she's been in the shadows ever since, even though it's our best picture.'

'Yes. It's very fine. Very.' Fred stood close to it, gazing up into Venetia's mournful grey eyes. 'She looks like a living ghost, with her powdery grey hair and white muslin dress. And yet she's also completely alive.'

Tommy came and stood beside him. 'I suppose it was love that made her husband put the portrait away.'

Fred glanced at her. 'What else?'

'There are other reasons why we can't bear to be reminded

of the dead, aren't there? Guilt, for example. Self-reproach. Despair.'

'They can all be mixed up with love, can't they?'

'Yes. I suppose so.' Tommy stared at Venetia. As a girl, she had always wondered what the portrait would say if it could speak, sure that there was a story behind those sad eyes. Now she didn't know if she could bear to hear it. There was already too much sadness in the world. 'I love this painting, but sometimes I wish we could turn it into money.'

'Sell it?'

Tommy nodded. 'It's a horrible thought but it would save our bacon. We sold a lot to pay off the duties when Father died. We're stony broke. I expect Roger's mentioned it.'

'I'm afraid he hasn't,' Fred said. 'Roger doesn't talk about things like that.'

'I don't think he even considers them.' They stood for a moment in silence in front of the beautiful young ghost on the canvas and Tommy said cautiously, 'I . . . I wanted to ask you about Roger. Do you think he's all right?'

Fred frowned and pursed his lips. 'Truthfully, I have no idea. He can seem perfectly fine and then not himself at all. He's very blue. I don't know why. He doesn't like to think about life and what he should do with his future.'

'His future is here,' Tommy said. 'At least, that's what everyone expects.'

'Yes. That may be the problem.'

'Really?' She was surprised. 'I thought it was the war that changed him.'

'I think the war has changed us all.'

'Yes. Of course. But . . . I don't know, he seems more shut off than he once was. Or maybe I'm imagining it.'

'He's always had a strong streak of melancholy. I don't think that the army was ever going to be the right kind of place for him. He'd have been better off serving some other way, but there's no explaining that sometimes.'

'Was it the right place for you?'

'I knew what had to be done,' he said after a moment. 'And I could bear it. But I wish it hadn't been necessary. There are things – horrors – that I'll never unsee. It's changed me fundamentally. It's no wonder Roger couldn't cope.' He looked at her with that sympathy she'd seen before in his eyes. 'He told me your husband was killed in the war.'

'That's right. In the first year, in France.'

'I'm very sorry to hear that. It must have been terrible.'

'Thank you.' *I ought to feel something. Everyone thinks I do.* Tommy said, 'You're very kind. But plenty of people lost someone. I'm hardly unique.'

'That doesn't make it any easier to bear, does it?'

'Oh, I don't know. I think perhaps it does.'

'How did the children take it?'

'They barely knew their father before he left, they were just babies. They've never known a life with him in it. They talk about him, but don't truly miss him at all. It might sound awful but they don't.'

'But you must miss him.'

She paused for a moment and then said lightly, 'Of course. It gets easier, though. And we all get our fair share of suffering.'

'Yes. That's true.' Fred gazed at her, his face even more

angular with the way the morning light cast shadows on him.

'Haven't you lost someone?'

The expression in his eyes was unreadable. 'Only friends. I haven't lost a lover, the way you have.'

She wanted to put out a hand and touch his arm and say urgently, *Oh, he wasn't a lover. I've never lost a lover because I've never had a lover. It wasn't like that at all.*

The door to the passage opened and the children came racing in, shouting about a fox in the garden, and the next moment, Tommy was being pulled by both hands to look through a window and see it. When she looked back over her shoulder, Fred was gone.

Chapter Seven

Patrick's family came over from Australia for his funeral, people so different from Patrick that it was difficult to believe they were his close relatives, except that his brother shared the same striking green-grey hooded eyes. Caitlyn had found Patrick's eyes so attractive, almost disconcertingly beautiful, lending a softness to his face. It was strange, painful, to see them again in his brother's rounder, tanned visage. But otherwise his family didn't remind her of Patrick at all. They only made her think of how hard he'd worked not to be like them in any way.

His mother, too tanned with bright blonde short hair, was loud, strident, her Australian accent so broad it was hard to believe she'd been born in Britain and only moved to Australia as an adult when she and her husband decided to seek the good life in the sun with three-year-old Patrick. His brother and sister had been born afterwards, in the new country. Now his mother had all the zeal of the convert for her adopted homeland, and was always astonished that Patrick had left.

The truth was that Patrick's whole existence had been

dedicated to removing himself from his family and embracing a self he carefully constructed. He had become the educated, cultured Englishman; there was no trace of a twang in his perfectly pronounced upper-class accent, and he barely acknowledged the years he'd spent in Australia or even mentioned the place. For him, life had started when he'd taken up his place at university in London, and he had quickly absorbed everything he needed in order to blend in to his surroundings and become a success there.

As they stood in the church on the corner of Kensington High Street, Caitlyn glanced along the pew at his family and couldn't help thinking how much Patrick would have disliked having them there at his funeral. He wouldn't have liked his mother's black dress or the fussy veiled hat she'd put on, and he would have loathed the way she sobbed into a ball of tissue throughout the service. He would have hated that his brother read out in a flat, heavily accented voice a poem chosen by the family from Winnie-the-Pooh – *Christ*, she could hear Patrick snap, *I'm not a bloody child!* He'd have been glad that Ryder, his best friend, did the eulogy in precisely the kind of restrained, English way that Patrick adored: elegant, unsentimental, with a touch of wit and a moving conclusion. He would have liked Ryder's Savile Row suit, and the vicar's address, with its tribute to Patrick's attendance at the church and his many generous gifts to it, and to its charities.

It was hard to stay focused during the funeral; Caitlyn was so aware of Patrick's mother and her heaving shoulders and his father patting her arm in a weak, ineffectual way. When she wasn't trying to shut them out, she was thinking of Max, who stood beside her white-faced, still dazed and uncomprehending, his hand clutching hers. He went up on his own when the vicar beckoned, turning to face the congregation, standing in front of his father's coffin as he read out the piece by Anne Brontë that she had chosen. His high voice sounded pipingly sweet as he said the words. They had rehearsed them so often that Caitlyn knew them off by heart and they chimed in her head as Max said them. Then he came back and stood beside her, looking up for her verdict. She smiled and whispered that she was very proud and so was Daddy. They sang the last hymn and it was over; they were stepping out into the bright spring sunshine, blossom whirling through the air on the breeze currents. The coffin would be taken away for an unwitnessed cremation. Later, there would be ashes to collect. She would think about that another time.

The procession went up the hill to the hall she had booked for the wake. Waiters carried trays, serving out tiny sandwiches, miniature quiches and sausages on sticks to the guests. A table of full wine glasses awaited them. Caitlyn took a glass of water and watched Max run off with his cousins, the gravity of the funeral forgotten. He couldn't stay sad for long; his childish optimism and interest in life couldn't be kept down. But when the sadness did come, it fell on him like a great weight, smashing him down, flooring him. Gradually, she knew, the weight would lessen. It would never go away but it would become easier to bear. She almost envied him the simplicity of the process: grief for his loved one followed by an eventual recovery. He was on his way to finding a peace with it. When would hers ever come?

Maura came up, looking unusually solemn in her black skirt and jumper. Her wild dark hair had been tamed into a neat ponytail. *She always wears colour. I'd never noticed*, Caitlyn thought as she returned her sister's hug.

'How are you?' she asked, gazing anxiously into Caitlyn's face.

'Fine.' Caitlyn smiled. 'I'm glad it's over.'

'It was a lovely service, darlin'. Patrick would have loved it.'

Caitlyn nodded. 'I know he would.'

Mourners were circling her discreetly, wanting to say their words of sympathy, and she geared herself for the job of receiving them. 'I have to mingle,' she whispered to Maura.

'I'll be right here if it gets too much. Just catch my eye and I'll rescue you.'

Caitlyn nodded, comforted, and turned to talk to the head of Patrick's chambers, who was evidently anxious to be on his way back to court.

She was talking to his clerk Stacey, who was asking about what to do with the contents of Patrick's rooms, when Patrick's mother came up. They hugged stiffly, both aware of their lack of real familiarity with the other.

'Thank you for that very nice funeral,' his mother said, her tone subdued. 'It did justice to Pat.'

'Thank you, Aileen, I'm glad you liked it.' It always jarred when they called him Pat, but it was their name for him, much as he'd detested it.

'We'll be heading off soon.'

'You're welcome to come back to the house . . . ?'

'Oh no, thanks. We're going to drive off this afternoon and we can be at my cousin's for dinner.'

Caitlyn nodded. She'd invited them all to stay in her house but they'd declined, and booked a place through a website instead. More relaxed, Aileen explained. Caitlyn understood. There was no way they would ever feel at home in Patrick's house. Now they were going to tour the country seeing relatives. No point in wasting the air fare after all.

'So,' Aileen asked, 'what are your plans?'

'I don't know really. I haven't thought. It's all so soon.'

'One thing's for certain, you'll be taking Max out of that snotty school of his, won't you? I never approved of him going there. Put a little boy in boarding school? I don't know what Pat was thinking of. He got some very strange ideas in his head at times but that was positively evil.'

Caitlyn was possessed by a sudden hatred for Patrick's mother and her certainty in her own judgement. What right did she have to decide what was best for Max? She didn't even know him. She hadn't bothered to come and visit her grandson, even when he was newborn. She just moaned and made Patrick feel guilty that he hadn't gone out there, with his infant son and postpartum wife. Phone calls always included her complaining that she didn't see them enough, even though Patrick had taken Max out for two long stretches when he'd been only little and again when he was eight, for a whole month. But she'd never once come over herself – 'I don't want to go all that way at my age' – until now. When Patrick was bloody dead. And still nothing was good enough.

'No, actually.' Caitlyn's voice was cold, her hands tightly gripped to hide their shaking fingers.

'What?'

'No. Max is staying at school. This is the worst possible time to move him. I'm not saying it's been easy but in many ways he's happy at Spring Hall. And it's what Patrick wanted for him.'

Aileen blinked at her. Her eyes were hooded like Patrick's, but without the green beauty. 'Staying at that school? While you're here in London?'

Caitlyn sensed an attack. 'No. I'm selling the house. I should have said. I'm moving to Oxford. Max will go as a day boy and live with me there.'

Aileen's lips and a nostril twitched as though she wanted to sneer but didn't quite dare. 'I see. You've kept that quiet, haven't you?'

'I don't see how it affects you one way or the other.'

'He's my grandson.'

'You live on the other side of the world. It's just a case of sending his birthday card to a different address.'

'He should be in a normal school with normal kids, not with a load of snobs. You'll ruin him at that place with all those stuck-up people.'

'You know nothing about it. You've never been there, or met any of the other children. If anyone's being a snob, it's you.'

'What?' Aileen looked disgusted. 'How dare you talk to me like that? I've just lost my son. Pat would have wanted us to be involved in his son's life. We have the right to have some input into what happens to Max.'

Caitlyn wanted to laugh at this. It was entirely the opposite of the truth. *Patrick would be happy if Max never saw you again.* She longed to say it. But she didn't care enough, and was bored at the thought of the tantrum that would surely follow. Instead she said coldly, 'I'm his mother and I'll decide what's best for him.'

Aileen stared at her, eyes narrowing, and she opened her mouth to say something, just as Maura swooped in and said, 'Mrs Balfour, hello! I'm Caitlyn's sister, my name's Maura. I want to say how sorry I am for your loss. Can I get you another glass of wine?' and she expertly steered Aileen away from Caitlyn, who stood staring after her, seething and yet suddenly certain.

Yes, that's what I'll do. I'll move to Oxford with Max. He doesn't have to leave school. Which, of course, she'd been thinking would happen. Her vague plan had been to stay in the house and move Max to a new school close by. But when she'd suggested it to Max, rather than being delighted to leave Spring Hall, he'd seemed reluctant. Now she'd found the perfect solution, allowing her to stay true to Patrick's wishes while keeping her and Max together. *It isn't Spring Hall that's the problem. It's being away from home. I don't want to take him away from his friends and lovely Mr Reynolds, not now when he's lost his father. And I was happy at college in Oxford. Maybe I'll be happy there again.*

Real life had started there: her first love affairs, her first steps into the adult world, her first experience of so many things. She credited Oxford with making Patrick fall in love with her. Not long after they'd started going out, they'd gone for a romantic weekend in the city and she'd taken him round her old college: the beautiful quads, exquisite gardens, the magnificent dining hall lined with ancient portraits. He'd been so impressed. It was everything he loved. The traditions, the grandeur, the effortless hauteur of the place, and its sense of exclusivity all spoke to him.

'You must have had a marvellous time!' he'd said.

'I did. It was wonderful. I loved it.'

He'd looked at her with new eyes after that, as though she carried some of that grandeur inside her permanently. Even recently she'd heard him say proudly to someone, 'Well, my wife was up at Oxford . . .' and knew that he felt it almost gave him the same cachet.

Yes, we'll go to Oxford.

'Caitlyn?' It was Ryder, Patrick's best friend. He had already spoken to her but now he had come to say goodbye. 'You don't mind if I head off, do you? Got to get back to the office.'

'Of course. Thanks for coming. And for that beautiful eulogy. It meant so much to us.'

'It was the least I could do.' He kissed her on the cheek. 'Poor Patrick. I still can't believe he's gone.'

'Neither can I.'

'I know this isn't exactly appropriate . . .' Ryder leaned in to her conspiratorially. 'But you'll forgive me, won't you? I wanted to ask you about your gorgeous redhead friend. Sara, isn't it?'

Caitlyn followed his gaze. Sara was standing talking to one of the lawyers from Patrick's chambers, looking chic in a black suit edged with white, and high heels. Her red hair fell in a torrent of curls down her back. Ryder had met her before at their house but now that he was divorced, he clearly thought he might be in with a chance. 'That's right.'

'Is she single? I saw her having lunch with Patrick a while back and thought I ought to look her up. I've got a thing for women who look like Julianne Moore.'

'Lunch? With Patrick?'

'Yes, at that place we always take our clients. I was with a rather important judge, so I couldn't go over and chat. It was just a week or two before the accident.'

'Really?' Caitlyn blinked at him, stunned. *But she said she hadn't seen him.*

'So . . . is she single?'

How many times have I been asked that by an eager-faced suitor? 'I don't think so. Sorry.' She wasn't sure one way or the other. Sara generally had a man in tow. But, in any case, she liked Ryder too much to put him in harm's way.

Ryder looked crestfallen. 'Shame. Oh well! Back to Tinder. Bye, lovely. I'll be in touch soon.'

'Yes, of course.' She watched as Ryder made his way through the remaining guests to the door. Then she looked over at Sara. *Why didn't she tell me she'd had lunch with Patrick?*

Sara seemed to sense her gaze and glanced over. Then she excused herself from her conversation and made her way to Caitlyn.

'Hi. How are you?' She embraced Caitlyn hard. 'You've been so brave.'

'I'm coping. That's the main thing.' Caitlyn stared at her, holding back the impulse to ask about the lunch. *How strange not to tell me. When I asked her particularly if she'd seen him.*

Caitlyn appreciated that Sara had given up her own time to stay with her, keeping her company in the evenings after work, but her presence was becoming suffocating. Perhaps it was the way Sara made herself perfectly at home, subtly changing things for what she thought was the better, whether it was which side of the stove the knife block was on, or the way the framed photographs on the bookshelves were arranged. She always seemed to be on the lookout for something, and Caitlyn sometimes came into a room to find Sara with her nose in a cupboard or looking in a drawer. She always had a reason, and was never disconcerted, but even so, Caitlyn found it odd. One afternoon, Sara had asked if she could have a meeting with potential clients for her interior design business in the drawing room and Caitlyn had agreed. Walking past the door, she'd heard Sara's voice floating out.

'Yes, this house is all my work. I think you'll agree it's been a success. The clients wanted a very soothing ambience, with a classic mixture of old and new. I chose the colour scheme, fabrics and fittings, with some input from the man of the house who had absolutely magnificent style and taste.'

Caitlyn had frozen at the foot of the stairs. *She didn't do any such thing!* She remembered Patrick poring over paint charts, ordering fabric samples, directing carpenters and workmen. He'd loved all of it. Perhaps it was harmless enough, to claim credit for the house and its exquisiteness.

But why would she lie to me?

Now, among the muted hubbub of the mourners, Sara said, 'Isn't it wonderful how well Max seems to be coping? In some ways, he seems more carefree now.'

Caitlyn snapped, 'What do you mean? That he's happier now Patrick's dead?'

'No! Of course not.' Sara looked hurt. 'I'd never say that. Just that he's doing well now. Better than he was.'

'Actually, I've come to a decision. Something that will help both Max and me.'

'Oh yes? What's that?'

'We're moving to Oxford.' There. She'd said it out loud as a real plan, something she'd have to carry through. But it was good. It was right.

Sara looked astonished. 'What? Leave London?'

'Yes. I can be closer to Max that way.'

'But you'll be so isolated. You won't see Maura as much.'

'I'll probably see her more. Crossing London takes about as long as getting to Oxford.'

Sara frowned. 'I don't think you should go. Take Max out of school. Move him to that excellent boys' school in the City. It's not far from your place.'

'I've made up my mind, Sara.'

They stared at one another for a moment and then Caitlyn added in a quieter voice, 'And I think it would be best if you thought about going back home.'

'But I don't want to,' Sara said quickly. Then she seemed to take a breath and added, 'I mean, I don't want to leave you on your own.'

'You'll have to go at some point. And I think I'm going to sell the house.'

'You can't sell Patrick's house!' Sara said, her expression horrified. 'He put so much into it. He loved it! How could you even think about it?'

'I have to move on, Sara. I have to think about Max and me and the future.'

'But . . . the house is him. It's his vision.'

So it wasn't all your idea then? But she bit back her retort and said, 'I know. But he's not here and I can't keep it as some kind of very expensive memento.'

Sara's voice started to tremble, her eyes filled with tears. 'Don't sell it. Don't go. We can't lose him like this.'

Caitlyn looked at her friend with growing apprehension. *Everything I feel, she feels too. It's like she has an ownership of all of this.* 'Sara,' she said quietly, 'he was my husband.'

The words dropped into the air between them like stones.

'My husband,' Caitlyn said again. 'My house. My life.'

'Oh really?' There was almost a challenge in her voice. 'If you say so. Fine. Of course.' Sara's grey eyes grew stony. 'But Oxford, Caitlyn? I'm surprised you can even stand the idea, considering how miserable you were there.'

'What are you talking about?'

'Come on – you can't have forgotten how much you needed me to get you through it.'

'I don't remember that,' Caitlyn said slowly.

'What *do* you remember?' Sara said in a tight voice. 'That's the question, isn't it? Or what do you choose to remember? Is it because Nicholas is still there, is that it?' She looked away, and then returned her gaze to Caitlyn. 'All right. You go. I'll move out if you like. I've only been trying to help you, like I always have.' She leaned in towards Caitlyn and said, 'You'll never know how much I did to keep your marriage alive.'

Caitlyn gasped. 'That's a horrible thing to say! What do you mean, you kept my marriage alive?'

'I mean, there's lots about Patrick you never bothered to understand. And you ought to be grateful to me, that's all.'

Without another word, Sara turned on her high heels and walked purposefully across the room and out of the door without looking back.

Chapter Eight

Tommy lay in bed, not wanting to get up. It was still dark in any case, but the main thing was that she was warm, and outside the covers the air was sharp enough to freeze her breath. She knew without looking that the windows were laced with ice. Cold lay heavy on the house.

But I must get up. There's work to be done. And yet she couldn't bring herself to brave the chill. Instead she was suffused with a bleakness that she was afraid was close to hopelessness.

What will become of me?

During the war there had, at least, been a sense of purpose, a goal to be achieved. What land they had left had been turned over for agriculture, and empty cottages and lodging requisitioned for land army girls and women. Tommy had taken charge, striding about in her trousers and tweed jacket, giving orders and overseeing what needed doing. Her mother hadn't liked it but Tommy had driven the farm trucks, forked hayricks and learned to change tyres. She'd liaised with government officials and the Ministry of Food, done her bit volunteering with the WVS when she could. She'd taken a dozen evacuees for a long summer and for a couple of months the house had been like a chaotic, noisy boarding school. It had been wonderful to have so much to do, to be here safe with the children, feeling that she was contributing.

Food had obsessed them all. Tommy thought about little else almost the entire time: how to grow it, rear it, harvest it, cook it and preserve it. Thank goodness for Ada, who had the practical knowledge to feed them all, and for the gardens, woods and hedgerows. Compared to many, she knew, they ate richly, supplied by the kitchen garden, orchards, streams and a forest full of game. They had chickens, pigs and goats. There was even wine sitting in the cellars, bottles of it. Good or not, she couldn't tell, but it was there if they wanted it. One of her friends had discreetly hinted she might sell it on the black market for a nice profit but Tommy pretended she hadn't understood. She preferred to give it away as gifts and she sent boxes of bottles to hospitals and rest homes for the wounded soldiers.

There's still so much I miss. I want limitless tea, lashings of butter and . . . oh, for some chocolate!

Just after New Year, she'd driven to Bristol to collect a banana each for the children, fresh off the boat from the West Indies, and the smell of them alone had been divine, filling the car all the way back with their sweet, sunlit aroma. The children had eaten them with interest and enjoyment. 'Very delicious,' was Antonia's verdict. 'Nice,' Harry said. He left just enough in the bottom of the skin for Tommy to nibble, who let the soft pulpiness slip over her tongue and down her throat, the tiniest taste of a vanished time.

It had made her think of a night in London when she and Alec had gone to the Cafe de Paris and she had eaten a banana soufflé. At least, she'd had some and pushed the rest away. Imagine now – the sugar, the cream, the eggs, the exotic fruit; such precious rarities that she had pushed away without a second thought, like a jaded pasha!

But that was how life had been then. Rich but dangerous. Teeming with activity, full of brightness and colour, and yet empty and barren.

The necessity of coming home had been forced upon her. With the outbreak of war and Alec going off, the lease on the London house had been given up and Tommy brought the children to Kings Harcourt, back to the house she had once been desperate to escape. But she'd been so happy to return, to see her mother and Gerry emerge from the side to meet them, waving, dogs barking at their heels.

I'm safe here, she had thought. *Nothing too terrible will happen.*

The threat to them all was far away on the continent and she could sleep easy.

But now the war is over. Life has to start again. It can't go on the way it has. Roger is back. I have to find a new reason to go on. There's always the children, of course, but . . .

Ever since Fred had arrived, she'd felt as though a tiny rip had appeared in the fabric of her life, so carefully woven to protect her. He guessed something, and she was afraid that he would somehow tear away the veil and make her look at what was underneath.

The thought was enough to propel her out of bed into the freezing air, the cold biting at her feet as they touched the floor.

I'll think about that later.

After breakfast, Tommy took Roger to one side. 'Come to the morning room with me, won't you?'

He followed her in, huffing a little. 'Fred and I are walking the dogs this morning. Mother says it's too cold for her. We'll go over the fields to the village. Fred's just getting his coat.'

'Well, it won't take a minute.' She smiled to keep the conversation on an even keel. 'You like having Fred here, don't you?'

'Of course. It would be me and a houseful of women otherwise.'

'Yes. I suppose so.' She felt a little stab of hurt that they were all so easily dismissed. 'I can see it could be dull for you. How long does Fred expect to stay with us?'

Roger fumbled for his cigarette case inside his jacket pocket and took one out. 'I've told him he can stay as long as he likes. He's not fit to do anything at the moment, with his wound still healing. We're convalescing, you know.' He looked at his sister almost accusingly as though she might be suggesting they were malingerers. He pulled out his lighter, lit the cigarette in his mouth and exhaled a stream of white smoke. 'I think we've earned our time to recover, haven't we?'

'I wouldn't suggest otherwise.' Tommy went to the window of the morning room. Usually this was bright and welcoming at this time of day, the pinks and blues of the wallpaper and silk curtains cheerful and sunlit. But the iron quality of the day outside had leeched the sweetness out of the colours and they were dull and lifeless. The ash-coloured clouds, tinged with yellow, hung low in the sky. 'But we've got problems, you know. There isn't a lot of money left. When we had our Ministry of Food business, it was a help. But that's over now. We'll have to stand on our own feet.'

'I know that,' Roger said, irritated. He smoked in three rapid inhalations. 'What do you want me to do about it?'

'Well, I suppose the house is, in fact, yours . . .'

'So I'm told. But I've heard nothing but how marvellous you were while I was away, running this place. Everyone seems to prefer you in the job. You can just continue, can't you?'

'But that's the point. We can't just continue. Things are changing. We have to look seriously at the financial position—'

Roger went white. 'I can't believe you would do this to me, Tommy. You know how I am. I'm ill! Why would you torment me with these things? Everything will be fine if you just stop worrying me with it all!'

'All right,' she said hastily, holding up a hand. 'I'm sorry. Of course you're ill. We'll wait until you're better before we discuss it again.'

'Thank you. Now if you don't mind, Fred and I are going

out.' He marched to the desk in the window and stubbed out his cigarette in the ashtray there. 'I'll see you later.'

'Yes. Goodbye, Roger. Enjoy your walk.'

Roger and Fred didn't get back until after lunch, missing the pilchard and salad cream sandwiches Ada served up. Tommy suspected they had eaten hot pasties in the pub, which had no doubt been much nicer. She waited for her chance and when Roger went upstairs, she found Fred in the library with the newspaper, still wearing his coat and muffler.

'This cold spell doesn't seem as if it's going to pass anytime soon,' he said, looking up as she came in. 'It's bitter outside. And look at this.' He held up the weather forecast on the back page of the newspaper.

She looked at it blankly. 'I'm afraid that doesn't mean anything to me. It's just lines all over a map.'

'There's a huge amount of high pressure over Scandinavia. I mean, a really vast amount. Just sitting there.'

'What does that mean?'

'It's going to get colder.'

Tommy was shocked, and she pushed her hands deep into the silk-lined pockets of her fur coat. 'How can it? We'll freeze here.'

When they weren't at school, the children had been spending all their time in the bathroom over the kitchen, where the hot pipes from the boiler went up to the tanks above. They only came down for food. Mrs Whitfield had not come into the main house at all except for meals, staying by her cosy fire swathed in blankets. Gerry looked comical in her three jumpers and fingerless gloves, a scarf wound around her throat. How could they manage if it got colder?

Fred looked over towards the window. 'There'll be snow soon. Look at the sky. I know that yellow, it means we'll get a big fall.'

'We must have a look at the wood and coal stores,' Tommy said, suddenly serious. 'And I'll get Ada to check the larder. We've always had plenty to see us through the cold spells or the floods but we're running much lower than usual. At least we have your ration book now.'

'You do a magnificent job of feeding us,' Fred said quickly. 'I haven't eaten so well since before the war.'

'It's all down to Ada, really. I'm hopeless in the kitchen.'

'Then she'll look after us all. You mustn't worry.' He fixed her with a clear, candid gaze. 'What did you want me for?'

'How do you know I want you at all?'

He smiled. 'I guessed.'

She flushed slightly. She'd not been alone again with Fred since they'd looked at the Gainsborough together but their private few words seemed to have created a small, unspoken bond between them. She caught his serious gaze at meals and felt that, somehow, he understood her and was on her side. It was an odd but comforting feeling. 'Well, as it happens, I did want to ask your advice.'

'I'll be glad to help if I can.' He gave her a keen look. 'You're bearing quite a lot on your shoulders, aren't you?'

'That's the problem. Roger can't cope at the moment. I've tried to talk to him but it's no good.'

'He was always the same, even at Cambridge. He never could keep himself on track.'

'Well, it's worse now.' Tommy sighed. 'I can't bring myself to tell him how bad things are going to get without some money. We might struggle through this year, but next looks impossible.'

Fred said slowly, 'Then you won't have a choice. You'll have to sell the beautiful Venetia.'

Tommy felt a burst of frustration. It was an answer, but no answer. 'I don't see how I can! My mother would most certainly forbid it, and Roger won't do it either. He's too proud, and he'd never go against what Mother wants. She can't bear to see us lose anything.'

There was a pause and Fred looked thoughtful. Then he said, 'What if she didn't know you were selling it?'

'I think she might notice if it vanished!' Tommy said with a laugh. 'Rather hard to explain its disappearance.'

'Unless . . . it didn't disappear.'

'What do you mean?'

'One of my hobbies is painting. I don't have much talent of my own, and I'm completely bare of inspiration. But one thing I love doing is copying and, for some reason, I'm rather good at it. I could paint a copy of Venetia, and you could sell the real one. Your mother need never know.'

Tommy stared at him, astonished. Of all the solutions she imagined Fred might suggest, she would never have guessed at this.

'I know what you're going to say,' Fred went on quickly. 'It would be wrong to deceive her – and so it would. But look at it this way: you're going to sell it anyway when she's no longer here to forbid it. So what's the difference? You'll get the money when you need it, instead of when it's too late.'

'I suppose you're right,' Tommy said slowly. 'When you put it that way, it doesn't seem so wrong. But . . . could you really do it?'

'I could have a damn good try. And if my efforts aren't up to snuff, well, what have you lost? We don't do anything but consign the plan to the scrapheap and have a laugh about it. After all, we'll only be fooling your mother, not Sotheby's. We're not trying to commit an art fraud, not a real one.'

Tommy laughed suddenly. 'But that's just what it is! Fraud!' She stared at Fred whose expression was wary, as if he were half afraid that she would think him base for his suggestion. 'It's an extraordinary suggestion. I'll think about it. Let's talk again soon. Now I'd better go and check the coal, if you're right about the blessed weather.'

Chapter Nine

Standing in the sitting room of the rented house, barely able to move for boxes piled high into great manila mountains, Caitlyn was overwhelmed by relief. It had taken so much time and work to get here, but now here she was, with Max upstairs unpacking his box of treasures carefully brought on his knee in the car. It had been a gargantuan effort, and now it was all done. Her next task was to unload their life and set up home for the two of them. All the people she'd needed to help her were gone now. It was just her and Max.

Thank God. I need the peace and quiet.

She did. But she was half afraid of it too, fearful of what she might find out in the silence. Since Patrick's death four months before – *four months? Already?* – life had been full of noise and activity. After the funeral, all the admin of moving had begun. The house had been sold but she hadn't found anywhere she wanted to buy, so she had rented this little furnished cottage in Jericho. What would happen now it was all sorted out, and here she was?

Caitlyn went to the window and looked out onto the little

road outside. There was just a wall opposite and behind that, she guessed, the gardens of the large houses on the main road. It meant she had a pretty view of treetops and assorted greenery, which was part of what had decided her on this house. That, and its primrose-yellow facade and the white front door with a lion's head knocker. Surely it was only possible to be happy in a house that was so cheery looking.

Maybe that was why Max seemed to be coping so well. There had been no trouble with the school about his becoming a day boy, despite the usual requirement for a term's notice.

'I think this is the right thing for Max,' Mr Reynolds had said when she'd collected Max's trunk and cleared out his little cubicle at the end of the Easter term. 'He's never quite found his feet as a boarder. Some don't. He'll get another chance this way.'

Another chance. Caitlyn liked the sound of that. So the London house had been sold, along with many of Patrick's possessions, and the furniture put into storage. She had folded her life down from the four-storey London townhouse with a large garden to a small terraced cottage in a run of identical, candy-coloured houses on a dead-ended lane close to the river. She gave away Patrick's rowing machine and gym equipment, his bicycle, his skis, his expensive fishing gear and his golf clubs. All the accoutrements of his comfortable middle-aged life.

At least he enjoyed himself.

The wine collection went to auction. The cars had gone last month, causing a small ripple of excitement in the sale room and a good solid amount of cash that would go into Max's fund.

On moving day, Maura came over to help her sort through the final things. She'd looked around the kitchen, with its open empty cupboards and the piles of stuff and the half-full boxes on the floor. 'God, this place looks so different. I can't believe how much was in it. It's sweet of you to give me so many things.'

'You're welcome. I'll never use most of it anyway.'

It's odd, Caitlyn thought, looking over at her sister, who was now busying herself with filling the kettle for another round of tea. *For once, I wish the children were here, and the whole place was packed with noise and chaos. The quiet seems so oppressive now.* But they'd been kept away, and Max was with them at Maura's house, occupied with computer games while his old life was packed away for good. She glanced around. The house was almost empty and she felt freer with every box that was carried out of it, as though the great tyranny of its perfection was finally being lifted from her shoulders.

'When do the new people move in?' Maura asked, rinsing out mugs.

'Tomorrow,' Caitlyn said. *So strange. So odd.* Those were the words that floated around her mind all the time now. Her inner voice exclaimed them all the time in a tone of mild surprise, or confided little things to her: *Just think, tomorrow this house will belong to strangers! They'll live here! Isn't that bizarre?* Every day it said, *The strangest thing has happened. Patrick's been killed in a car crash on the motorway! He's dead!* And Caitlyn would feel the punch of his loss all over again.

Maura turned around with a look of concern. 'Are you sure you don't want to stay with us tonight? It's so late to head down to Oxford now.' She smiled tentatively. 'Come and stay, Cait. You know Max'd love it. Don't go off on your own, I'm worried about you.'

'Don't be,' Caitlyn said. 'We'll be fine. I . . . really want to get to the new place. Honestly. It's what I need.'

'Are you sure?' Maura came over, looking as though she wanted to hug her but didn't dare. 'I know it's still early days, but you really don't seem like yourself.'

Caitlyn smiled at her. 'I'm fine.'

'I don't know if you should be on your own. Where's Sara? She was living here with you, wasn't she?'

'She's gone.'

Maura looked at her searchingly. 'Is everything all right between you?'

'Well . . .' Caitlyn would usually confide most things in Maura, but this was not an easy one. She had spent years defending Sara against Maura's obvious dislike. If she reported what Sara had said to her at the funeral – *how I ought to be grateful to her for saving my marriage!* – she knew it would turn into a diatribe against Sara, rather than a calm discussion about what it all meant. 'I think we spent a bit too much time together. And she didn't want me to sell the house.'

'What business is it of hers?' Maura asked indignantly. 'Cheeky bint! You should have told her to get lost, it's your house, and your life, she can piss off.'

I knew it. She can't wait to disapprove. 'That's what I said, sort of. So she went off in a bit of a huff. I haven't heard from her for a while. I think she's gone to America on a job. She'll be in touch eventually.'

'Enjoy it while you can then,' Maura said with a laugh. 'Sorry. I know she's your friend.'

Caitlyn turned back to another box. She didn't want to think about what Sara had said to her, not now when there was so much to do. It was a relief that Sara had gone away. And, she realised with mild surprise, she was dreading her return. More than anything, she wanted to get to Oxford before Sara got back, so there was a good safe stretch of distance between them.

'I thought I might look up a friend of mine when I get to Oxford,' Caitlyn said as she packed in some mugs.

'Oh yes?'

'A guy called Nicholas. I haven't seen him for years but Sara reminded me about him. He's an academic now at my old college.' She scrunched up some packing paper to put around the mugs. After Sara had mentioned him at the funeral, Caitlyn had looked Nicholas up. His thumbnail portrait on the college website had shown a familiar if older face, and she began to remember how they had been students together. They had been close once, she recalled. *I wonder what he's like now.*

'That sounds like a good idea.' Maura smiled encouragingly. 'Well, that's nice. I'm glad you'll have a friend there.'

*

But even though she'd intended to, Caitlyn hadn't looked up Nicholas. The Easter holidays started soon after they arrived, and she and Max spent all their time settling into the new house and doing up his bedroom, choosing him a cabin bunk bed with a desk tucked beneath. Caitlyn reflected that Patrick would never have allowed the football posters that Max had tacked up, or the glow-in-the-dark stars to be stuck on the ceiling. Max didn't seem to mind that his new bedroom was much smaller than his old one, or that it lacked the muted chic. He spent hours there, assembling his football trading cards into teams, or curled up on his bed reading and listening to music.

One day, he hung about in the doorway of Caitlyn's room next door to his, and stared in as she sat at her dressing table, brushing out her hair. 'I like that you're so close, Mum,' he said. 'Not like it used to be.'

'Yes.' She smiled at his reflection in her mirror. 'It's nice, isn't it? Cosy.'

'But . . .' His face grew solemn. 'I miss Dad.'

'Me too, darling.'

'I wish he was here with us. Not in London. Here.'

She smiled at him again. 'Yes. That would be perfect.'

But they both knew Patrick would never have left London, and would never have lived in this house.

When term began, for the first time Max went to school without howling. He still stayed close and went very quiet, but when she said, 'I'll come and get you at five o'clock,' he turned and beamed at her, then trotted off into school with the others.

Caitlyn watched him go, her hands deep in her mac pockets, happy, feeling able to meet the eyes of the other mothers for the first time, as they herded in sons loaded with sports bags and musical instruments. In the evening, Max came out with the handful of other day boys, looking about for her, relief washing over his face when he saw her waiting for him. She drove him home, crawling back through the city in the evening rush hour but not minding because Max chattered about his day all the way back. Then it was supper, some television, some reading together, a bath and bed, tucked up on the top of his cabin bed, with the pale green stars glowing above him.

There was no doubt about it, this change suited Max.

'That's wonderful,' Maura said, when she called up for a face-to-face over the internet. She looked rather grey in the light from her kitchen, and a large glass of wine, too close to the camera spot, loomed in front of her with an unattractive greenish tinge to the liquid. 'And does he talk about Patrick?'

'Not much. Sometimes,' Caitlyn said. 'But it seems to be easier for him now.' She got the impression that Max dipped in and out of the pain of losing his father, as though he sometimes put it away to be taken out when he had more time to give it. His world was so full already, and Patrick had been – now she thought about it – quite absent from it anyway. Work, travel, outside interests had all taken so much of Patrick's attention, and he had administered decisions on Max's life from afar, like an emperor making decrees about some far-flung outpost of his dominions that he had never visited.

'Poor wee kid,' Maura said. 'He's only going to know what he's lost later on, isn't he? But what about *you*, eh? How are you getting on all on your own there?'

'I'm fine.'

'Have you met your neighbours?'

'No, not yet.'

'They can't be very friendly then. You've been there six weeks.'

'Our paths haven't crossed, that's all.'

'I'm worried you're lonely. Have you contacted that friend you told me about?'

'Not yet.'

'I think you should.'

'Maura, I'm okay, I promise.'

'I'll come to see you soon. All right?'

'Yes. Please do. We've settled in very well since you were last here.'

But she didn't really want Maura to visit. She had fallen into a quiet routine of solitude that she found comforting. In the morning, she tidied and shopped, and in the afternoon, she wandered through the streets of Oxford, walking past old haunts and noticing what had gone and what was still there. She drank coffee in the Queen's Coffee House on the High Street, and watched students come in armed with laptops and mobiles, groggy with hangovers or studiously intense, some of them mooning over each other, others in friendship gaggles, and she thought of her own student days. No laptops then, or very few. She remembered how, in their first year, she and Sara would come here and watch the door of University College opposite, hoping to see a boy Caitlyn had had a crush on. One night, they'd blagged their way into the college bar and he'd been there. Sara had made her go and talk to him, and at the end of the night, he'd walked her back to college and kissed her by the gates. They'd gone out for a week or two. But she'd introduced him to Sara, and then somehow he'd ended up going out with her instead . . .

Oh yes. I'd forgotten about that.

Sara quickly lost interest in him, as she always did, but when Caitlyn found another boyfriend – sweet, silly Charlie – she'd not introduced him to Sara. Just in case.

I forgave her, though. I always did.

She thought about it as she walked around Oxford, passing the hours until it was time to go and get Max from school. She walked the familiar route from the middle of town to the faculty, feeling herself crossing her old paths, and wondering what her eighteen-year-old self would make of this older, sadder person treading the same pavements and crossing roads at the same places. The students looked so terribly young, fearless in their ignorance of the future. She envied and pitied them simultaneously.

Sitting outside the faculty on one of the benches, she remembered how she and Sara used to sit here after a morning's work, deciding what to do with the rest of their day. There was usually something interesting going on, and if there wasn't, they could easily laze away an afternoon in one of their rooms, listening to music, talking endlessly, making plans for the evening. There was no shortage of activity. Sara would always have a clutch of invitations. They arrived in her pigeon hole in the porter's lodge, some from complete strangers asking her to parties and dinners.

'But they don't even know you!' Caitlyn would say, astonished at yet another card from an unknown student. 'Why do they invite you?'

'I don't know.' Sara tossed back her hair and shrugged, completely unsurprised. Once she said, 'I think they look at the fresher photos in the photographer's shop.'

'Do they?'

'Yes, they send invitations to new students they like the look of. Or they ask who you are when they see you round town. You know how it is. They all come crawling out of the woodwork.'

Caitlyn didn't know. It was all news to her. But she began to realise the power of beauty and its strange effect on men. It was clearly a prize. It made Sara valuable in a way other women were not. But why did it give men the courage to chance their arm with Sara, when it must be obvious to both parties that it was only Sara's outward appearance that drew them to her? It was nothing to do with her personality, wit or charm, but only how she looked. Caitlyn thought that even while it must be flattering, it was also a little insulting.

Or perhaps I'm jealous. I must be jealous in some way.

She didn't feel jealous of Sara, although she did wonder what it must be like to go through life so looked at. It must be like being born royal, or becoming famous, the way all eyes turned and followed Sara wherever she went. She knew it and was used to it, and had a certain way of holding herself in public, and an expression she adopted when she was out: a slight smile, a dreamy gaze that meant she could look disconnected while remaining highly aware of how many people were watching her.

No, Caitlyn wasn't jealous, but she was curious, fascinated by the power Sara wielded. Sara was quite used to finding flattering notes and poems in her pigeon hole, or stuck to her door. She was familiar with men coming up to murmur admiring comments whenever she was out, or the constant tooting of horns when she walked by the road. She was accustomed to finding bouquets outside her room or left in the lodge for her, and rarely bought herself dinner or drinks. She never said anything but it was unspoken between them that it happened to Sara and it didn't happen to Caitlyn, who had her admirers, but not in the magnetic, all-encompassing way that Sara did. Men liked her, but they liked her blue eyes, or her smile, or the way she chattered and joked. They didn't go weak at the knees when she walked into a room, even when she'd taken the trouble to blow-dry her usually straight hair into light brown waves and put on make-up and high heels.

Perhaps I ought to be more jealous.

And yet she wasn't, because she felt sorry for Sara, and vaguely protective. Sara's beauty also made her vulnerable. It seemed to give men the right to think they could approach her, talk to her in crude terms, show their appreciation in any way they chose. She was never left alone, wherever she went. Men appeared to assume that she craved their attention, as though it were a gift they were bestowing on her, and she must like having her conversation interrupted by a stranger. 'Sorry for coming over, I just had to say something – you've got the most beautiful hair I've ever seen.' Then they would smile moonily at her, as though expecting her to gasp and swoon at their compliment, as if she'd never heard that before, and fall into their arms. Some were sweet and well meaning, evidently having gathered their courage to approach. But other men could be predatory and strangely possessive. They acted as though Sara owed them something by being so attractive, as though she was an item waiting to be claimed. They treated her beauty like a provocative act carried out on purpose by her in order to stimulate them – and if she refused them, she was somehow cheating them. They could be angry, even vicious, if they were repelled.

And then there were the women. Sara had so few friends. It was part of what had drawn Caitlyn to her; she actually felt sorry for her because so many women disliked her on sight. She could see at once, from the first day of term, that Sara was having trouble fitting in. The men were too dazzled to be her friends, though a few of the gay ones were keen to get to know her. And a lot of the women just steered well clear, as though reluctant to spend too much time standing next to Sara's shining, perfect beauty. Others were nakedly hostile, even if they'd never spoken to Sara. That seemed just as unfair as men adoring her without knowing her.

But it wasn't just the way Sara seemed to be held hostage by her looks, Caitlyn thought. *It was something else. It was what they did to her. What they turned her into. How they hurt her. And she never saw it.*

She got up from the sun-warmed bench and started to walk back towards the centre of town.

But I saw it. I saw how, gradually, she let it destroy her.

Chapter Ten

The snow came in the night, just as Fred had predicted, and Kings Harcourt was immediately cut off. The children were thrilled to wake to a world of huge white drifts almost covering the hedges entirely. The lane was deep in snow and there was a strange muffled quality to the air.

'We haven't seen snow like this for a long time,' Tommy said, gazing out at it from the dining room. She had made the breakfast that morning as Ada hadn't been able to get to the house. Tommy was glad she had insisted on all the woodpiles being restocked the previous day, and all coal buckets filled. But she hadn't liked the state of the coal bunker, which was worryingly empty. She looked at Antonia and Harry. 'I don't think you'll be going to school for a while.'

'Hooray!' they shouted. 'No school!'

'You need lessons, you ignoramuses.'

Gerry looked up from her book. 'I'll teach the little darlings.' She gave them a sickly smile. 'Lots of lovely spellings and dictations and punctuation tests. I shall enjoy that.'

The children booed loudly.

Tommy said, 'I think that sounds like a good idea. You can go out and play in the snow for some exercise and then come back and have some lessons.'

Fred spoke up. 'I can do a little teaching if you like. I can rustle up some French grammar exercises. Make Harry run through his Latin declensions.'

'I'm not doing Latin yet,' Harry said quickly.

'Then you'd better start.'

Roger said, 'Fred will be an excellent teacher, Harry. You'll enjoy doing some Latin with him.'

Fred said, 'Antonia too, of course.'

Tommy looked at him, pleased. 'What a good idea. I always wanted to learn Latin and no one ever offered to teach me.'

Fred smiled. 'Then you should learn too. Lessons are in order. This afternoon is our first one.'

Tommy laughed disbelievingly. 'What? Me? I'm far too old.'

'I don't think so. Come and learn.'

'Well . . .' Tommy blinked at him, surprised. Then she said, 'All right then. I'll do it.'

'Me too,' Gerry said bouncily. 'Count me in. I'll set up the morning room as our schoolroom.'

Roger rolled his eyes and reached for more toast. 'Poor you, Fred. You're a braver man than I.'

They all went out to play in the snow after breakfast, then assembled after lunch for their first Latin lesson. Fred met them in the morning room, with neatly handwritten sheets to pass around. His pupils sat down with trays on their laps, paper and pencils.

Tommy examined the sheet she was handed. It was headed *The First Conjugation*.

'Now, we're going to start with verbs in the present tense. In this case, the first conjugation ends in *-are*. The verb we'll look at is *labare*, to work. Our word "labour" comes from it, of course. See the endings below – you take the stem and add an ending to conjugate the verb. I work, you work, he works . . .'

Everyone listened intently as Fred stood in front of the fireplace and taught them. The lesson was only an hour but it went by in a flash, and Fred told them their prep would be to learn the endings they'd looked at that day.

That evening the temperature seemed to fall even further. Before dinner, after the children had had their tea, they all pulled chairs around the fire in the drawing room, the curtains shut tight to prevent the draughts from the leaded windows, and the children and Gerry played cards while the others read and Tommy sewed. Eventually she said, 'Bedtime, please, children.'

They both wailed, and protested that it was far too cold to go to bed.

'You must have a bath to get warm,' Tommy said, 'and I'll put hot water bottles in your beds to make them nice and cosy.' She put down her sewing. 'Come on.'

'I'll help you,' Fred said, closing his book and getting up. 'Let me do the bottles while you do the bath.'

'All right,' Tommy said, surprised but grateful. 'Come on, chop, chop, you two. Antonia, run and start the bath, will you? Just a small one, mind, only to the mark on the side of the tub.'

When the children were tucked up with their light off after a story, Fred and Tommy met on the landing. Fred looked solemn. 'It really is jolly cold in their bedroom, you know.'

'I thought the same. But we can't have fires in the bedrooms, there isn't enough coal. We can't heat the house very well, the system is awful.' She bit her lip with anxiety. 'Do you think they'll be all right?'

'Yes, of course. They're warm now, and they've got plenty of blankets. But is it going to be tricky, if it stays this cold? What is the situation with fuel?'

Tommy put her arms around herself, and shivered slightly. Her coat was downstairs, left in the drawing room, and now she was cold. Fred was warmly dressed in thick tweed trousers, a shirt, jumper and jacket but even so, his hands were white and his face had the greyish tinge of chill. 'The coal ration is due any day now. I applied for it ages ago.'

'But we're snowed in. How will they reach us?'

'If it doesn't snow again, we'll be clear in a day or two. We've often been cut off in the past. People find a way in and out rather quickly, you'd be surprised.'

'Then let's hope it holds off.' Fred looked suddenly a little awkward. 'And I fear it means you're stuck with me for a while.'

'Well.' Tommy turned to go back downstairs. 'You're

earning your keep in the schoolroom now, aren't you? So it's all quits!'

It didn't snow the following day, and the tractors were out ploughing through the drifts and clearing the roads. But it took two days for them to make the road to Kings Harcourt passable.

In the meantime, they continued their lessons. Harry and Antonia had French and English with Gerry in the morning and after lunch there was Maths and Latin with Fred. Tommy skipped the Maths but she was keen to keep up with the Latin. At their third lesson, Fred propped up a large drawing pad on which he'd painted pictures of a small Roman boy, going about his everyday life, and underneath were simple Latin sentences.

'No textbooks, I'm afraid,' he explained, 'so I've improvised.' He pointed to an illustration. 'This is Quintus. You see? *Ecce Quintus. Quintus laborat in agricolum.* Who can tell me what that means?'

'This is Quintus. Quintus works in the fields,' Gerry said quickly.

Fred nodded. 'Very good. You might have to hold back a little, Gerry. I can see you're getting it fast but let's give the others a chance. Harry, why is it *agricolum*? Think about the nouns we've been looking at.'

'It's a first declension noun that goes like *puella*. It ends in -um so that's in the accusative,' Harry said, 'because it's the object, not the subject.'

'Excellent. You're quite right.' Fred gave him an encouraging nod. 'Well done. Now, Antonia. Your turn.'

After the lesson, Tommy lingered in the morning room as Fred tidied up his things. 'What a lot of effort you've gone to for us,' she said. 'Thank you.'

'It's not much trouble, really, when you're all doing so much for me. Besides.' He took down his drawing pad and folded back the sheets of paper. 'It was rather nice to use my brain again. My Latin is rusty but I found an old grammar in the library to help me remember it all. And as for Quintus and his friends—'

'And his *canus*,' put in Tommy brightly.

'Let's not forget his *canus*, Fido. A man's best friend,' Fred said gravely, which made her laugh. 'I've enjoyed coming up with his adventures.'

'Your pictures are wonderful. I don't care what you say, it's obvious you're talented.'

'Well . . . in the most modest way imaginable. Have you had a think about my idea?'

'Yes, I have, if you mean copying Venetia. I'm sorry I haven't mentioned it but I really don't know if it can or should be done.'

He leaned back against the table and looked serious. 'I know it sounds absurd but my feeling is that if you can get yourself a bulwark of cash, you should. I don't think Roger is well. He may need some care if he gets much worse.'

'He's ill?' Tommy exclaimed, shocked. Roger had joined in the children's snowball fights with some enthusiasm, and she'd been cheered by the sight of him full of energy and laughter. 'I thought he was getting better.'

'In his body, he's recovering well and getting fitter. But he's not as whole as I should like in his mind. He seems tormented by something, but he's not able to talk about it.' He put out a hand to her, resting it on the soft fur of her coat. 'Please don't worry too much. I'm only thinking of the worst happening. I hope he'll find the peace here helps him to recover. I know it's helping me.'

'You seem so well,' Tommy said softly. 'I keep forgetting you're not recovered either.'

'I'm healing all the time.' He smiled at her, and she felt suddenly and unexpectedly bashful. He took his hand from her arm and she started awkwardly.

'Well, you know, if you think it would be fun, then why not try a copy of the painting? It can't do any harm to have a go.' Tommy knew she was talking too loudly and too fast, to detract from her embarrassment and the heat on her cheeks. 'I'm not sure how you'll hide it from everyone, though.'

'I've thought of that,' Fred said, seemingly oblivious to her blush. 'There's no need to hide it. I'll just say I'm making a copy for my own amusement.'

'Yes. That's a good idea.'

'But first I shall need to go to Oxford, to get all the equipment. I know an excellent art shop. And I'll make an appointment to get my wound checked as well. I think it's healing all right, but it's as well to be on the safe side.' He smiled at her and a pleasant warmth stole over her skin.

'I'll ask the postman if the trains are running, once he gets through tomorrow. It's not a long journey but it will be easier by train. I'll come along with you, if you don't mind. I need to do some shopping and I could do with getting out.'

Fred smiled. 'I should like that very much.'

'Oh good. So should I.' Tommy found herself staring at the pattern on the carpet, and then she heard the bell echoing through the house. 'There – it's tea. We must go quickly. You know how Ada hates it when we're late.'

Chapter Eleven

The early summer sun fell brightly through the sitting room windows. Caitlyn was drafting an email to her old friend Nicholas.

Hi, do you remember me? It's Caitlyn Collins. I see that you're a professor now, that's so impressive. I've just moved to Oxford and wondered if . . .

She read it over and deleted it. *What do I really want to say? You used to be my friend and I could really use a friend right now. And you knew me and Sara when we were just beginning, and I want to know what other people thought of her, if I got her right or not . . .*

But he would probably think she was batty if she wrote something like that. All these years of silence couldn't be wiped away just like that. She had to observe the niceties. She started again.

Hi Nicholas, it's Caitlyn Collins. I'm living in Oxford and wondered if you'd like to meet up and reminisce about old times—

A knock at the door made her break off. Suspecting the postman, who often had letters for her that didn't fit through the tiny letter box, she went over to answer it, only to find a small woman in a blue boiler suit on her doorstep, her air wild and rather dirty, with something claggy sticking in it. She had an open, pink, freckled face and very mucky hands.

'Hi! Do you have some cling film?'

'Er . . . yes, I think so . . .'

'Can I borrow some? I'm clean out. I promise I'll replace it.' The woman had round blue eyes like two bright buttons in a heart-shaped face. 'Only I haven't got time to get to the shops. My clay will dry out.'

'Okay.' Caitlyn went to the kitchen and the woman followed her in.

'I'm Jen, by the way. Your neighbour. I live right next door. I should have come round before now.' She laughed. 'Sorry about that. I'm a pro at displacement. Always do tomorrow what I ought to do today, and you know what they say about tomorrow . . .'

Caitlyn lifted the roll of cling film out of the drawer. 'Here. Take it.'

'I only need a little.' She frowned at the roll and looked at her dirty hands which Caitlyn saw now were covered in the

106

grey-white residue of potter's clay. 'But it'll be tricky to take a bit. I'll take the roll and bring it back. Promise.'

'Sure. Here.' Caitlyn held it out.

'You're a life saver. What's your name?'

'Caitlyn.'

'You've got a little boy, haven't you?'

'Yes. Max.'

'Oh, great name. Really great. Love it. What's it short for?'

'Maximilian.' Patrick's choice. It had to be suitably imposing, the name of his son and heir. Regal. Imperial.

Jen laughed. 'That's cool. Better than Maxwell.' She looked around the bright little kitchen. 'You've made this nice and homely. It was a bit chilly when the Robinsons were here.' She gave Caitlyn a sideways look. 'Naturally we've all been wondering about you. You've kept a very low profile, everyone's fascinated to find out who you are. They're going to be furious that I've stolen a march and got in first.'

Caitlyn stared at her and Jen burst into a peal of laughter.

'Your face! You look terrified! And so you should be – you won't be able to so much as sneeze here without us all noticing. But don't worry, it has its upsides too.'

Caitlyn managed to muster a smile, though inside she was churning. In London, she'd been anonymous. She'd never even spoken to her next-door neighbours beyond a 'good morning' when they'd passed in the street. Here, people were interested in her. They wanted to know her story.

What will I tell them?

Jen said, 'Come over for coffee tomorrow. I'll show you my pottery. Shall we say ten? You're usually back by then from dropping off your son, aren't you?' She held up the roll of cling film. 'And thanks for this – I'll have your refill tomorrow.'

Caitlyn was unsettled by the morning visit, worried that there would be more neighbours knocking on the door, wanting to know about her.

I should just tell them the truth. I'm a grieving widow making a new life.

The words startled her as she thought them. Then she realised with a shock that she was just that. Not just a widow. But grieving.

I miss Patrick. I miss him so much.

She was desperately sad. She was lonely. She missed Patrick's voice and his laugh and his arms around her; his certainty and his ability to make decisions in an instant. She had always been confident that he was steering their ship. Now she'd had to take over the rudder with no experience and sail the little craft into the great ocean on her own. She still found it hard to believe he wasn't coming back sometime soon, the way he always had. He'd brought vigour, excitement and energy into her life. Without him, she realised, she felt as though she was dying too. Slowly. Bit by bit. And all the time, there were questions tormenting her, buzzing away in the back of her head even when she wanted to ignore them.

What did Sara mean when she said I was miserable in my marriage? Was I? I know Patrick was often hard to live with, and things weren't always easy, but I thought that overall, I was happy. But, she remembered, Patrick had had lunch with

Sara without telling her. Sara had said Caitlyn ought to be grateful to her . . . for what? The insidious hints were breeding anxiety that her grief was not real because she was mourning a man she didn't really know. The worst thing was that she felt she was losing Patrick, the man she loved and married and remembered. He was being replaced by someone different, someone who had secret lunches and something to tell her about Sara.

Sometimes, lying awake at night and thinking about it, she had the most horrible feeling that Patrick had not really loved her at all. She worried that he'd been confiding his unhappiness to Sara and that she knew the truth about what Patrick felt, and was on the brink of telling Caitlyn. That was what he had been trying to tell her the night he was killed.

If Sara was his confidante, it would explain why she kept trying to claim ownership of my grief. WE loved him. WE'll miss him. As though we were on an equal footing with him.

It was so difficult to believe, though. The Patrick she remembered would not have confided in Sara, she was sure of it.

Now she stood stock still in the sitting room.

I've got to find Patrick again. The one I knew.

She climbed the stairs to the spare room and opened the door. Inside was a mound of boxes, packed up against the bed. She half thought of this as Patrick's room, because all that was left of him was inside it. The boxes contained the clothes of his she had kept, his mementoes, anything that

Max might conceivably want later, and the things she had to keep: paperwork, records, certificates. During her interview with Penny Young, the solicitor dealing with Patrick's estate, she had been handed a sheet of paper.

'We're finding this more and more,' Penny had said. She had the perfect manner for dealing with this necessary unpleasantness: formal yet sympathetic. 'A lot of our clients are making this kind of provision in their wills. It's increasingly necessary, and it helps speed up probate.'

'What is it?' Caitlyn was looking down at a list of names in bold – *Bank – personal, Apple ID, Email, Bank – joint, Email – joint . . .* – and underneath little words of gibberish, scrambled letters and numbers.

'It's a list of the passwords to the different accounts. So that you can get access to all of Patrick's online activity. There's an addendum to the will that goes with it.' Penny handed her a printed letter signed at the bottom by Patrick in his flourish of a signature.

I hereby grant my wife Caitlyn access to all my online and protected accounts. She may use them as she sees fit, according to her needs. She will know what to do with what they contain.

She'd stared, surprised. Then she'd laughed. 'Of course. That's so Patrick. He always thought ahead. He always made plans.'

'Sensible fellow,' Penny said with a smile. 'I wish more people did the same.'

'Oh, there weren't many people like Patrick. He always thought of everything.'

Patrick had renewed their wills once a year but she hadn't known he'd made this provision. *Typical – he liked his games. He liked to spring surprises. I suppose he thought of everything, including this.* The life that was half lived in the virtual world was protected by the secrecy of the password. She'd never asked for his passwords. He had never asked for hers. They had a joint email account but it was rarely used. She didn't even know the pin code for his telephone, which he changed regularly anyway, to stop Max fiddling with it, he said. He'd had a private life all along about which she knew almost nothing and the door to it had banged shut the moment he had died – or so she had thought. It had occurred to her, as she arranged for his computers to be boxed up along with his tablet and telephone, that it was all useless now, dark and silent. It reminded her of how her mother used to say that all the appliances designed to save labour were so much useless junk once there was no power. That was why, in the home where she and Maura grew up, there was always a mangle in the shed, and a stove-top kettle, and a pile of wood by the fireplace. Just in case the power failed.

She'd supposed that Patrick's computers must be accessible by a technology expert, who could unlock it all and access what was stored on it. But why bother? And as for all the places Patrick might have accessed by a password … she would have no idea where to start. Until now.

She'd taken the sheet of paper and folded it up, tucking it carefully in the centre of her purse where the notes were stored. It had stayed there all this time, sometimes forgotten and sometimes throbbing like a hot little hidden heart.

Now she went over to the mound and pulled a box off the top. She had no idea what was inside, all the boxes were marked the same – *Patrick*. The one she had lifted down was quite light and she stared at the pale brown strip of masking tape that sealed it. Nervousness fluttered through her and her heart began to race.

What on earth am I afraid of? Patrick's dead.

'I've just got to get on with it,' she said out loud, and she got her keys out, sliced one into the masking tape and slit it open with one smooth movement. Cautiously, she lifted the flaps of the box and peered inside. She saw a collection of leather boxes that she knew well. They had always sat on top of Patrick's chest of drawers, holding his collection of cufflinks, shirt studs and collar stiffeners. He liked that kind of thing. He prided himself on having a set of tailor-made evening clothes, both black tie and white tie, all done in the old-fashioned way, with detachable collars and studded fronts, double cuffs joined by oval gold links connected by tiny chains. They would all go to Max, of course. So that meant she knew what was in this box: his dressing table things. The bone tray where he'd laid his watch every night, his bottles of expensive cologne and aftershave, the little leather-bound travel clock. And his collection of watches, come to that. She'd kept them for Max, not knowing if he'd prefer Cartier or Rolex or Dunhill. Later, he could take his pick.

Patrick loved the finer things in life. He adored them. If it was worth having, he wanted it. She used to tease him that he wanted to be James Bond, with the fancy cars, the suits, the watches, all the toys.

'I just want to be the best version of myself I can,' he'd told her simply, unsmiling. 'There are two ways to be in this world – just existing, satisfied with all right. And really living, demanding the best. That's me. And I've done it all myself. I've made myself who I am, and I worked bloody hard to get here.'

He was right, of course. He had made himself, completely and entirely. The ultimate self-made man, sloughing off his past, his family, his accent – anything that didn't suit him. And dressing up was part of that. He'd cared more about his appearance than anyone she'd ever met.

She opened one of the leather boxes on the top of the pile and stared at the carefully paired cufflinks, some initialled, some whimsical, some bought by her as a gift – though she'd always had to be careful in case she got the wrong thing. Patrick had been visibly irritated by presents that didn't strike the right note.

That's the thing I don't understand. With everything he wanted in life, with his incredibly high standards and his exquisite taste – why did he want me? How did I fit in?

As she thought it, she realised that this question had been bothering her for a very long time. Even before he died, she had begun to feel more and more out of place in Patrick's world, as though she wasn't quite the right partner for him, and that he thought so too. He had never said anything of the sort. He had told her he loved her, he had outwardly cherished her with gifts and consideration. And yet . . .

I always felt there was something going on I didn't know about.

And she had always known there was more to Patrick than he told her, even if she barely admitted it to herself.

Caitlyn lifted her gaze from the leather boxes and surveyed the mound in front of her. *Well, it's all here. He's given me the key. The question is, whether I want to open the box or not. Once whatever is inside is released, there will be no way to put it all back.*

She picked up her keys again.

But I have to know. I want the answers.

There was so much to look at that by the time she had to stop and go to get Max, she had hardly made her way through more than a few boxes. So much demanded her attention. She spent a couple of hours leafing through Patrick's photo albums, seeing him transform from skinny, tanned student to the handsome, hardworking young lawyer she'd fallen in love with, following him on his holidays and travels, recognising some friends and not others, and then she began to appear in the pictures. *I look so young!* Just his friend at first, lounging near him on a beach in Greece, sitting up behind him on a motorbike in Egypt, both with checked scarfs as turbans and face masks to protect them from the sand. Then, as they became more intertwined, they were pictured holding hands, snuggling up on a towel, sitting together at dinner. Their private snaps – she smiling up from rumpled bedsheets at him, her hair a bird's nest; Patrick standing bare-chested with only a towel around his hips, fresh from the shower.

It was magical. Falling in love with him. Our crazy attraction for each other.

She felt wistful, nostalgic and yearning, and a feeling of deep sadness soaked into her. The boxes were going to cause pain, she had to realise that. *I can't expect to deal with this without feeling anything.* She'd been working hard at not letting things hurt her. A tremor of fear went through her.

Am I going to have to face this alone? Without him?

He's dead, you idiot, her inner voice snapped back. *You are alone. Or haven't you realised that yet?*

Of course I have, she told herself strictly. But this room with all its boxes seemed suddenly like a repository of everything she had so far been most desperate to avoid: memory, pain and knowledge.

She put down the album, closed the box lid on top of it, and went to collect Max from school.

Chapter Twelve

The next day the postman reported that the trains were running to Oxford and the roads to the station were clear. There had been no more snow, but there was no sign of the cold snap lifting either. It was still impossible for the children to get to school, though.

For the trip to Oxford, Tommy looked out some of her old London clothes, and chose one of her best suits, a beautiful soft grey tweed. It might have the cut from before the war, but there was no doubting its quality. With it, she wore her grey gloves, and a black felt hat with three felt flowers with fake pearls at their hearts, and a string of the real things around her neck, and carried a little crocodile-skin box handbag. She was satisfied with her reflection. Perhaps not quite the girl in the photograph on the piano, but acceptable.

'Gosh, Mummy, you look pretty!' Antonia said when she came to kiss them goodbye while they were still getting up.

'Thank you, darling. I'm going for a trip to town with Mr Burton Brown. We shall be back when you're asleep, so be very good for Gerry today.' She hugged her daughter.

'Does that mean no Latin today?' came Harry's muffled voice from under his eiderdown.

'Yes. So enjoy your holiday.' She blew him a kiss. 'Be good, you horror.'

'But I like Latin,' said the muffled voice indignantly. 'And I learned my third declension last night as well.'

'Very good. Now get up and get dressed.'

'But it's too *coooold*!'

'Then do it quickly – it won't get any easier!'

Twenty minutes later she and Fred were in the car and Tommy was steering it out between the gateposts and onto the lane. 'Oh, this is good,' Tommy said happily as she began to motor down the lane at a careful speed, wary of the ice. 'I haven't been out for such a long time. I went up to Bristol but that feels like half a lifetime ago. Is it snow that does that, do you think? It's hard to remember a time when the world wasn't white and grey and slushy.'

'Perhaps it is,' Fred replied. 'But you're right. Charming as the house is, it is good to be out.'

'Yes. Isn't it?' Tommy was suddenly filled with good cheer and excitement. A whole day lay ahead, a day of travel and new sights and people, and, of course, Fred. To be alone together all day, without Roger's gloom or Gerry's piercing gaze, her mother's pained judgement, or the constant noise and chatter of the children ... *Well, it's as though I've suddenly remembered what it's like to be an adult again.*

The car jerked along the lane, grinding over potholes and salt, and Tommy's gaze slid over to where Fred was profiled against the whiteness outside. His beaky nose and high cheekbones were familiar to her now, and the cut of his lips and shape of his chin.

I'm looking forward to spending the day with him, she thought.

'Do you know Oxford well?' Fred asked suddenly.

'Yes, quite well. It's only twenty-five miles away so we often go for shopping. I was at school there for a while.'

'I've never been. I heard of the art shop from a chap I met in the war. He'd been up at Merton and we discovered we both painted. He told me all about it.'

'My friend Veronica's brother was at Merton. I don't suppose it was the same man, unless his name was Brian.'

'It wasn't, I'm afraid.'

'I thought as much. I wonder if Veronica is at home. She was at school with me and lived on St Margaret's Road.'

'You should have written to her and made a date.'

'Perhaps. But I'm perfectly happy with you.'

'Really?' Fred smiled at her. 'I'm glad to hear it.'

On the train to Oxford, Tommy and Fred were in a carriage with three old ladies and a vicar, who chatted together very amiably and without stopping all the way. Fred raised his eyebrows at Tommy and she got a terrible fit of the giggles, which she had to hide by taking a book out of her bag and pretending that she was laughing at that. Fred lit a cigarette and smoked serenely while he gazed out of the window, apparently oblivious to the chatter going on around him.

The journey was a short one, and from the station they

took a bus into the city centre. The weather was bitterly cold and Tommy shivered even inside her coat as they climbed out at the junction of George Street and the Broad, where the wind was whistling up Cornmarket.

'I'm looking for Ship Street,' Fred said. 'That's where my artist supplier is. I can buy what I need and ask him to hold it until we go.'

'Good idea. Ship Street is just down there, second on the left past the church.' Tommy looked over at the elaborate frontage of Elliston & Cavell with its huge plate-glass windows, scrolled ironwork and gold letters. 'I need to buy wools and silks for mending. And I'd like to go into Woolworths too. And I promised to get some cakes for the children.'

'Let's do our errands first and then meet for lunch at Elliston's at one. I'll see my doctor at two and we'll be all ready to catch the four thirty home.'

'Will that give you enough time?'

'Plenty.' He touched the rim of his hat. 'See you later.'

Tommy found herself alone, standing at the top of Cornmarket among the bustling crowds, and wondered what had happened to her pleasant dreams of spending the day with Fred.

Come on, Tommy. Shopping. Off we go. The sooner you're in the warm, the better.

The shops that once groaned with their supply of luxuries were barer now but it had been so long since the days of plenty that it was hard to recall them exactly, or to believe that they'd ever come again. Tommy even felt embarrassed to be in her best suit, despite its age, and her fur coat looked almost sinfully comfortable, when most of the people around her were distinctly shabby, their clothes worn and their faces tired. The euphoria of peace had been replaced by a weariness as the grind went on with no obvious end.

This cold weather isn't helping. She pulled her coat around her and tried not to meet too many eyes as she walked. *Surely things will get better in the spring, but it's only the end of January now. That seems an age away.*

Tommy found some good cheap cotton and soap in Woolworths, but decided to get her quality silks at Elliston's. Then she went into Marks and Spencer to see if they had anything her ration book would be good for.

She was browsing through the knitwear when she heard her name.

'Tommy, Tommy Whitfield – it *is* you!'

She turned and looked to where the noise was coming from, and saw two women nearby, one of them waving at her excitedly. She smiled and walked towards them, recognising the one in the headscarf and camel wool coat. 'Goodness, Veronica, I can't believe it. I talked about you only today.'

'What a coincidence, we were just talking about *you* – well, you know Barbara, don't you?' Veronica indicated the woman next to her, a thin pale-faced blonde in a large-shouldered navy coat, a plain brown hat and fur muffler.

'Of course I do,' Tommy said smoothly. 'But it's been years. Hello, Barbara. How on earth are you?'

'Just about bearing up,' Barbara said, smiling a small, tight smile. Her voice was high and girlish and her eyes a striking pale blue. She was elfinly pretty, her clear complexion only marked by a pale pink mole on her chin. 'I'm homeless but Veronica is kindly keeping me and my daughter while we get ourselves sorted out.'

'I'm sorry to hear that.' Tommy tried to look sympathetic but her mind was roaming back to the days at school when she, Veronica and Barbara had sat together in the same classroom. She remembered Barbara sitting behind her, and a small shower of ink-soaked paper pellets landing on her clean notebook, on her blouse and in her hair. But when she turned around, Barbara was innocently working away, engrossed in her lesson, holding her pen in such a way that her fingertips were hidden and any ink stains concealed.

'Do you have time for a cup of tea?' Veronica said eagerly. 'We can't let you go, just like that!'

'I'm meeting someone for lunch at one,' Tommy said, looking at her watch.

'Well, we've just got time if we go to the cafe at Carfax. It's only over the road. Come on.'

The next moment she was being chivvied out of the shop and across the road to the cafe. It was warm and steamy, fragrant with the smell of tea and toasted muffins. The waitress took them to a table and Veronica asked her to bring tea quickly as they were in a hurry, then told Tommy how she was putting up Barbara and her daughter Molly in her house off the Banbury Road.

'But I'm ever so guilty,' she said, 'because I can't keep her for long. Can I, Barbara?'

121

Barbara shook her head, gazing at Tommy. 'She's got her sister-in-law coming.'

'I can't manage too many people,' Veronica said plaintively. 'It's just too much. But Barbara has no family to go to.' She made a face of sudden inspiration and Tommy felt sure that it was something that had been on Veronica's mind since the first moment she had spotted her in Marks. 'But Tommy, you have an enormous house, don't you? You must have room for two little strays! Why don't Barbara and Molly come to you?' Veronica clapped her hands with excitement at the wonderful idea that so obviously let her off the hook. 'This is a stroke of luck, it's meant to be.'

'Well . . .' Tommy felt ambushed, caught suddenly in the invisible but deadly strong cage of manners. 'Of course we'd love to have you. But I shall have to ask my mother. My brother already has a friend living with us, recuperating from his war wounds. It might not be possible—'

'Oh surely,' cried Veronica, 'they're no trouble at all. Molly is like a little mouse and Barbara is such a help—'

Barbara put out a pale hand and rested it on Veronica's arm as if to restrain her, but her light blue eyes stayed fixed on Tommy. 'Please, Veronica, it's too much to ask Tommy to take us in. It's an imposition.'

'I . . . well . . .' Tommy stumbled, feeling even more constrained by the chains of her manners.

'Please,' Barbara said firmly. 'I won't hear of it. It's far too much to ask. Let's talk about something else.'

Tommy closed her mouth and blinked hard at the table,

then she murmured, 'Well, I shall ask my mother what she thinks.'

But Barbara wasn't listening. 'So who remembers that awful mam'selle and her terrible smell? I can't speak a word of French without thinking about it, even now!'

Tommy arrived a little late and saw Fred waiting for her in front of Elliston's, gazing anxiously up the street and smoking as he stood by the door. As soon as he glimpsed her, he threw down the cigarette and ground it out.

'Ahoy,' he cried, waving. 'I was afraid I had the wrong place.'

'No, no, I'm late, I'm so sorry. Let's go in.'

She was hot as soon as they were in the restaurant. *I went too fast from cold to warm to cold and now into the warm again.* Beads of sweat broke out across her nose. The anxiety at being late and at meeting Barbara had not helped. *So much for my powder. I suppose I look a fright now.*

'I say, are you all right?' Fred said, regarding her keenly after the waitress had taken their order.

Tommy picked up the menu card and waved it in front of her face, an improvised fan. 'I'm so terribly warm all of a sudden.'

'Days of freezing ourselves silly and now we're sweltering.' Fred smiled. 'Don't worry, you'll get accustomed to being indoors in a moment.'

'I suppose I'm in a slight state. I just met my old friend Veronica, the one I told you about, and she had this girl

Barbara with her, and Veronica as good as told me to have Barbara live with us.'

'Rather a cheek,' Fred remarked. 'On what grounds could she ask this?'

'I'm not entirely sure. Mostly because we have room, I suppose, which strictly speaking we do. But the house isn't exactly comfortable and I barely know Barbara.'

'You were at school together?'

'Yes. But Barbara . . .' Tommy felt helpless and she looked away, anguished. 'I never liked her. I just couldn't say it. I couldn't say I didn't like her! You see, I remember what she was like at school. Sly. She told lies. She sneaked on others when most of us would have taken the rack rather than do that. She wasn't exactly wicked . . .'

'Just a bad egg.'

'Yes.' Tommy took off her gloves. 'I saw her in London once or twice, and I liked her even less then. I don't know how to describe it – it was nothing I could put my finger on. She would greet me as though we were the best of friends, and seemed to want to worm her way into my life. She was blatant about asking to be invited to things. She did things like . . . help herself to bottles of wine on someone else's table. Oh dear, it sounds so lame when spoken out loud like this.'

'No. I know what you mean. She was on the make.'

'Yes. Then she got married and went to live in India. But really, she never did anything to hurt me.'

'Will you turn her down then?'

'I don't know. It seems rather harsh, and she has a little girl. She said her husband was killed in Burma, so she is widowed.

She's homeless, apparently.' Tommy felt a little ashamed. 'I shouldn't judge her on the past. I'm sure she's changed.'

'Perhaps. I suppose people deserve another chance. It is possible to change, especially when life provides challenges like those. Ah, here are our luncheons. Excellent. I'm ravenous.'

After lunch, while Fred was at his doctor's appointment behind a blue and brass door on St Giles, Tommy wandered up and down; she looked in a bookshop window and peeped down Little Clarendon Street.

'How was it?' she asked when he came out, walking a little gingerly down the front steps to where she waited on the pavement.

Fred lit up a cigarette and offered her one, which she took. They smoked together as they walked back in the direction of the art shop where Fred could collect his purchases. 'I'm healing all right. He took off my dressing and had a prod about. Rather painful but he said it looked fine.'

'What was your wound? I know it was a burn, but Roger never said exactly what happened.'

'A large and awful burn on my side. I got soaked in spilled petrol that ignited. It was a bad accident that could have been a lot worse. They did a big skin graft all around here.' He gestured vaguely at his side. 'It's not pretty. I had no idea how long burns could take to heal or what ghastly pain they could inflict.'

They were passing the Martyrs' Memorial and Fred pointed at it. 'It makes you think hard about what those poor blighters suffered, burned alive like that. They say that Ridley had the worst of it. Some relative tried to help by throwing on wood to make the flames burn brighter and only succeeded in making it more excruciating. They'd tucked gunpowder under his arms to take him off, but it didn't work.'

'How barbaric!' exclaimed Tommy. 'I don't know how they could stand to watch it.'

Fred shrugged. 'I would have thought so too once. Now I've seen worse. It only astounds me that we manage to live in peace at all.' He smiled at her. 'I count every day I don't see death as a good one.'

They walked on in silence towards Ship Street.

Chapter Thirteen

Caitlyn was awakened from a heavy doze by knocking on her front door. Crawling out from under the duvet, she saw her bleary reflection in the dressing table mirror and groaned. She was tempted to ignore it but the knocking went on, so she stumbled out of bed and downstairs to answer it. Her neighbour Jen was standing there, smiling brightly, dressed this time in jeans, trainers and a long, sky-blue polo-necked jumper.

'Hi! Ouch, you look rough. Heavy night, was it? I had a feeling you must have forgotten.'

'Forgotten what?' Caitlyn said, blinking in the morning sunshine that raked the street outside. She had been up late, looking through the boxes in the spare room, and after taking Max to school, she'd gone back to lie on her bed and had fallen asleep. She was still groggy and couldn't work out what Jen was on about.

'That you're coming to my place for coffee of course. Come on, it's ready. Follow me!' Without waiting for a reply, Jen turned and strode off.

Blast, she's right, I'd forgotten. There didn't seem much choice about it now, though. She checked she had her keys and then went after Jen, pulling the door to behind her.

Jen waited for her just inside the bright red front door of the peppermint-green house next door. It was a bit shabby on the outside, and even shabbier inside, but bursting with colour and innumerable objects.

'I'm a magpie,' Jen said cheerfully as Caitlyn came in, looking around her. 'I just love collecting things. I'm a vintage nut – anything Edwardian, Victorian or art deco . . . that's my bag. We'll have coffee in the kitchen, it's lighter there.'

Passing an open door, Caitlyn caught a glimpse of a small dark sitting room, packed with antique brown furniture and glinting with the jewel colours of Tiffany lampshades. The kitchen was brightly painted in egg-yolk yellow and adorned with handmade mosaics instead of tiles. On the scrubbed pine kitchen table were two roughly made mugs next to a cafetière. Jen ushered her to a chair and sat down opposite to pour out the steaming coffee.

'Milk? I like loads. Here, it's very good. Not pasteurised. Just as nature intended.' She sloshed milk into both their cups. 'So. Are you all right? You really do look a bit tired.'

'I'm fine, thank you. Sorry I forgot about our date.'

'Don't worry. Lots of people would have sat here, maybe getting angry, maybe worrying about how to handle it. But I'm not like that – never let anything stew, that's my motto. Just get it out there. If you'd said get lost Jen, I'm not interested in having coffee with you, leave me alone – well, that would have been fine. I'd have released you back into the universe and gone on my own path.'

'Okay,' Caitlyn said cautiously, half wishing she'd known that before now.

Jen leaned in towards her, looming through the steam rising from her cup. 'But I knew that wouldn't happen. I don't think that's your way, Caitlyn. And I can tell you're in a bad way. I think that's why you've ended up here.'

'Really? Why?' Caitlyn couldn't help smiling at Jen. Her face was childlike in the way expression flooded over it, swift and changeable. Her round button eyes and small rosebud mouth were earnest one moment and merry the next. Hers was the kind of face that could be any age between sixteen and forty, and would probably look no different at sixty: plump, heart-shaped with a soft, clear complexion.

'Because,' Jen said in a solemn voice, 'I can teach you, if you like.'

'Teach me . . . pottery?' Caitlyn said, half teasing and glancing down at her mug, with its slightly wonky handle and uneven lip.

'Well, I could if you wanted – that's my studio in the garden. You can probably see it from your kitchen window. But I didn't mean that. I am a bird of many feathers, if that's the right expression. I'm a potter in my spare time, but I'm also a counsellor, hypnotherapist and yoga practitioner.'

Oh God. Caitlyn felt her smile freeze.

'Don't worry, I'm not a weirdo! I'm not going to start oming or going into trances. The truth is, I can sense that you're in a bad place. Honestly, I can help if you want me to. Or not if you'd rather I didn't.' Jen sat back and regarded her, beaming from her round face.

Caitlyn was touched. It was a while since she'd felt such pure kindness and it was like a soft blanket falling lightly around her and comforting her. Everyone else's kindness – Maura's, Sara's, the rest of the family's, her friends' – seemed to be mixed with something that she'd identified as discomfort or fear, though she didn't know what they could be afraid of. Maybe that she'd start losing it, or go utterly deranged, begin screaming and tearing her hair out, and then she'd become their problem.

That's probably really unfair. Maura is always desperate to help me.

But she also knew it was true. And here was Jen, a stranger, able to offer her something sweeter and purer. She felt suddenly drawn to her, wanting to open out to her and win more of this comforting kindness.

'You're right,' she said slowly. 'I'm not in a great place. My husband was killed in a traffic accident several months ago. I've moved here to start a new life with my son.'

Jen's eyes went round again and her mouth made a small 'o' as she reached out a hand and put it over Caitlyn's. 'Sweetheart, that's awful. I'm so sorry.'

'Thank you. It was – it is – terrible. It was so random. A driver texting at the wheel of his lorry so he didn't see the traffic in front was stationary until it was too late, and . . . pow. Patrick was snuffed out, just like that. All his energy and power and life force and determination – it was all nothing in the face of that bit of random bad luck. If his flight had been

130

delayed by ten minutes, or he'd been in a different place in the taxi queue, he'd be alive. But everything that happened took him inexorably to that moment, that point, where he was the one in front of that lorry driver. And he was killed.'

Jen rubbed her hand over Caitlyn's. 'What an awful story. You're right. It seems meaningless and unfair.'

'So pointless. Such a waste.' Caitlyn shook her head sadly. 'Patrick was robbed of so much. I hate that.'

'Yes. And you and your son lost him. That must be very painful.'

'Yes. Very.'

Jen said gently, 'A lot of people believe there is a purpose, though. They think that maybe Patrick's journey was supposed to end that way. Maybe he'd done what he was supposed to do.'

Caitlyn heard her voice growing shrill. 'He was supposed to be killed and leave Max without a father? Really?'

'I'm not saying it's a good thing. But that it might not be as senseless and random as it seems.'

'Or maybe it is. Maybe it is just as senseless and random as it seems, and there's nothing at all that we can take for granted, or trust in, in the whole of our existence.'

Jen nodded slowly. 'I'd say that's possibly right. It depends what you expect from the world. It depends whether you want to control it, or surrender yourself to its mysteries.'

Caitlyn was silent, thinking of Patrick. He had certainly tried to control the world. Was that a crime? Did he deserve to be mashed out of it by a lorry?

'Some people call it karma,' Jen said softly.

'Yes, I've heard of it, thanks,' replied Caitlyn curtly.

'I'm sorry if I'm offending you. That's the last thing I want. I want to help you.'

Caitlyn took a breath. 'I know you do. I'm sorry too. I don't mean to be rude.'

'Don't be silly. Be how you want. I've talked to lots of bereaved people and there's no right way to act or feel. You just have to let yourself experience whatever it is that you need to experience.'

'Yes. Perhaps.' She took a gulp of her coffee. It was warm and fragrant, and it comforted her.

'Maybe it's not just sadness you feel,' Jen went on. She gazed solemnly at Caitlyn. 'Perhaps you're angry as well. It's normal to be angry with someone when they've gone and died on you.'

Caitlyn was thoughtful. Jen's words resonated with her. 'You're right, I am angry,' she said. 'I'm angry because he left without telling me the whole story. There's something more going on that I don't know about, and I'm not even sure if I want to find out what it is. And yet . . . I can't stop thinking about it.'

'You two had secrets?'

'I didn't think so. But the more I remember, the more I suspect that there are pieces to the puzzle that I haven't put together yet, some I haven't even found.'

'Is it important to know all of Patrick's secrets? Perhaps they were meant to go to the grave with him. We all have our unknowable sides, our hidden and private selves.'

Caitlyn frowned. 'It's just that I keep getting the strangest feeling that Patrick wants me to find out more about him. He never did anything by accident. He always foresaw every eventuality. Sometimes I thought he was psychic but he would just say "Strategy, Caitlyn, strategy. See it from all angles, don't assume anything, and do your research."'

Jen smiled. 'He sounds like an interesting man.'

'He was. Too interesting for someone like me.'

'I don't think that's true for a moment. You'll have found what you need in each other. Imagine two of him in a relationship?' Caitlyn laughed, and Jen said gleefully, 'See! It would never work! He needed what you had to offer him, so don't do yourself down. But the point is, do you truly think Patrick wanted you to know more about his life?'

Caitlyn stared down at the oil cloth on the kitchen table, tracking the patterns made by the cheerful polka dots. 'Yes,' she said at last. 'I do.'

'So,' Jen said, lifting her cup to her lips. 'There's your answer. Do your research. Don't assume anything.'

'And look at it from all angles,' finished Caitlyn. 'You're right.' She was thoughtful again. 'I need to keep thinking.'

Jen nodded. 'Thinking and looking and making connections. That was the secret to Patrick's power, right? So use a bit of that yourself and you'll start to find the answers you want.'

Caitlyn went for a long walk around the university parks and thought about Patrick's power and how to apply it.

What was it like between Sara and me once we left university?

They had moved to London, Sara into a house share in

Islington and Caitlyn renting Maura's spare room while she supported herself waitressing and tried to decide what to do next. Sara's housemates were grand and rich, and Caitlyn went there often. She got to know them, and when Sara went off to Glasgow to do a course in the decorative arts, Caitlyn sublet Sara's room, glad to be away from Maura who had just met Callum and was in full love-bird mode. With a slightly higher salary from her new job as an assistant in a small gallery in Cork Street, she was just able to cover the steep rent, and she felt almost as glamorous as Sara, with her smart address and her job in Mayfair. Life breezed by in a whirl of parties and gallery viewings, champagne and canapés.

'You're quite the It Girl,' Maura said drily. 'Didn't I always say that Oxford would make you too good for the rest of us?'

'That's not fair!' Caitlyn protested, but she knew that her life was far removed from Maura's flat in a grotty part of south-east London on a student teacher's salary. Sara went off to Italy to be an apprentice under a famous interior designer and sent her excited emails from villas in Umbria, *palazzi* in Venice or yachts in the Mediterranean. She was flirting with playboys and the heirs to industrial fortunes, partying with the offspring of famous dynasties. At any moment, Caitlyn suspected, she would hear of an engagement to a rich and handsome man who would fulfil all of Sara's dreams.

But it wasn't all fun and laughter. There were late night telephone calls from Sara, drunk, sometimes lost, sometimes afraid. She would talk about men following her, or people treating her badly, and beg Caitlyn to come to her. There were always threats and menaces surrounding her, unasked-for cruelty, horrible treatment, mostly from other women. Successful female designers hated her, were threatened by her and tried to undermine and destroy her. Caitlyn listened, comforted her and offered advice, sometimes planned to get the next flight out, but the next day, Sara would usually be normal again, able to cope, brushing off the horror stories of the night before and telling her not to bother coming, she was fine.

When Sara got back from Italy and found a new job as assistant to a famous and eccentric interior designer, she moved back into the Islington house. The way things worked out, Caitlyn was able to keep her room and Sara took over the large top-floor suite. It ought to have been great fun, but somehow it wasn't. Sara was single, as she so often was, but hungry for a boyfriend.

'And we need to fix you up with someone too,' she said to Caitlyn. 'I'm sure we'll find someone. Perhaps one of the guys after me has a friend who might like you.'

Caitlyn was surprised at the way she bristled at that remark. While Sara had been away, it had been a relief not to have the constant tiny pricks to her confidence, and now they started again. There was the night when Sara invited half a dozen men round. 'Likely lads,' she'd described them as. 'You should see if you like any of them.'

But the evening was a dismal failure for Caitlyn. Sara sat them around in a circle and then stood in the middle, holding court, almost basking in their round-eyed admiration. Meanwhile, Caitlyn was in charge of drinks and snacks and answering questions about whether Sara was single and what her phone number was.

This is useless. I'm never going to meet anyone this way – Sara's only introducing me to people who are already batty about her. I haven't got a hope.

When they went out on the town, Sara couldn't resist overtures from strangers. If she and Caitlyn were in a bar together and men came over to talk to them, she always started flirting and trying to get them to buy her and Caitlyn drinks. Caitlyn found it embarrassing. It wouldn't have been so bad if Sara's flirting had been subtle, but she would pull her skirt up her thigh while raising her eyebrows suggestively and tossing back her hair like she was in a shampoo advert. It looked, Caitlyn thought, so very silly, like a little girl aping what she thought were the ways of grown-ups. She would dread men coming over but it happened often. She and Sara would be having a perfectly nice evening and then Caitlyn would find herself talking to a stranger who was evidently depressed to have ended up with her, while his more attractive friend was flirting with Sara. Caitlyn was always polite and made an effort, particularly because once they'd accepted drinks from the men, she felt obliged at least to talk to them. Sara didn't even feel that, happily discarding them for fresh conquests when she wanted to move on. She was irresistibly attracted to money so it was no surprise when she started a relationship with a much older, married businessman she met in a fashionable nightclub, and disappeared off for days at a time, sending Caitlyn excited texts from Paris and New York.

Being a mistress was a thrill for Sara in a way that Caitlyn couldn't understand, except that she could see that in the permanent competition between her lover's wife and herself, Sara was always the glamorous winner. Sara was involved with her businessman for quite some time. That didn't stop her going on the pull, though.

And then there was Patrick.

It was a gloomy Sunday morning when Caitlyn came downstairs to find Patrick asleep on the sofa in their Islington house.

At first she just saw a large shape under a blanket and raised her eyes to heaven as she went to the kitchen to make coffee. Another stray following Sara home, no doubt. She'd heard some noise at around 2 a.m. when Sara got back from her smart dinner. They must have brought the party back – there were empty bottles and glasses on the coffee table and the room reeked of tobacco and cigar smoke.

She was just putting the milk in her mug when a low and rather scratchy voice said, 'I don't suppose there's enough of that for two, is there?'

She turned to see a man in the doorway, wearing just a shirt and a pair of boxer shorts, his light brown hair ruffled and stubble darkening his face. His eyes were bloodshot but still remarkable for their greenish colour and their beautiful, hooded almond shape.

'I think there is,' Caitlyn replied, trying not to look at the bare legs and boxer shorts. 'I hope you slept well.'

'I slept the sleep of the dead,' the man said. 'How do you do. I'm Patrick.'

'Hello. Caitlyn.'

'Sara's housemate.'

'How did you guess?' She looked at him appraisingly. 'Let me see if I can guess who you are. Sara's conquest's friend.'

'Very good. Yup. Rupert got lucky. I got the sofa.' He smiled at her. 'Though if I'm honest, I wasn't in the running. Sara's a wonderful girl. But she's not my type.'

'Isn't she?' Caitlyn poured him out a cup of coffee and passed it over. She didn't believe him. In her experience, Sara was everyone's type. This was just the bluster of the loser, she suspected. 'What is your type?'

'Someone sane,' Patrick said bluntly.

Caitlyn laughed. *Maybe he's not just a sore loser.* 'You can talk, standing there without any trousers.'

'True. Excuse me while I make myself more presentable.'

By the time he got back with his trousers on, he'd smoothed down his hair and his voice had lost its just-woken-up sound. Now, she noticed, he had a particularly beautiful voice – smooth, rich in tone, with perfectly annunciated words in a strong well-bred accent. She liked his turns of phrase, with their quaintness and his old-fashioned vocabulary.

'So you and Sara are chums?' he said when they'd sat down at the kitchen table and were eating toast.

'Yes. From Oxford. We were at the same college.'

'Really?' He raised an eyebrow. 'Brains and beauty.'

'Yes. Sara's very clever,' she said. 'People often don't believe she went to Oxford.'

'Not her. I meant you.'

She laughed disbelievingly and gave him a sideways look to see if he was teasing her.

'I mean it,' Patrick said, and bit down on a slice of toast and Marmite. He stared at her while he chewed, watching as she blushed harder and harder under his gaze. When he'd swallowed, he said, 'You don't rate yourself very highly, do you?'

'Don't I?' She was taken aback and slightly offended. 'You don't know me. As it happens, I rate myself perfectly highly.'

'Hmm. Maybe.' He changed the subject and asked what she did. He was fascinated by her work in the gallery and soon showed he knew a lot about art himself. They were chattering away about the Raphael exhibition at the National Gallery when Sara and Rupert emerged from upstairs, their post-coital aura worn with unconcealed pride.

'You two are getting on well,' Sara said, her eyes more feline than ever as she examined Caitlyn and Patrick, now on to fresh mugs of coffee.

'Not as well as you two,' Patrick said pointedly. 'Hello, Rupes, old mucker. Ready to make a move? We ought to be going.'

'Are you going?' Caitlyn asked, surprised to find how disappointed she was at the prospect.

'I'm afraid Rupert and I are due at his parents' house for lunch and it wouldn't do to be late as there is a dowager marchioness coming.' Patrick stood up. 'Come on, Rupert.' He turned to Caitlyn. 'Thank you for the toast and coffee. You've been a charming hostess.'

When the men had gone, Sara said, 'I think you're on to something there. With Patrick.'

'Really?' Caitlyn felt a lovely little burst of excitement explode in her stomach. 'Do you?'

'Oh yes. And he's quite a good prospect – a trainee barrister, got all the smarts. But not as good as Rupert, of course. Rupert's the real thing. Patrick isn't.'

'What do you mean?'

'Rupert is the nephew of an earl. His family have a house in South Ken and a place in Scotland. He went to Harrow and Edinburgh.' Sara shrugged lightly. 'The real thing. That's what I mean.'

Was that why I was allowed to have Patrick? Caitlyn wondered now.

Suddenly at this distance, she could begin to see things clearly. Patrick's death was shunting her whole life into focus. Before, stuck inside it, lost and out of control, she had been blind. And now it was becoming clear. But not quite clear enough, not yet.

In her own terms, Sara had done better than she would have by going out with Patrick. She had married Rupert after a whirlwind six-month courtship, and discreetly dropping her married lover. Her wedding had been exactly what she'd dreamed of: a glamorous society church, with titled guests in attendance, and a reception at the Carlton Club. If there had been Instagram then, it would have made wonderful images for her account, displaying her amazing life, marvellous taste and eligible husband for the world to see. As it was, it appeared in the society pages of *Tatler* and Sara and Rupert went off on their honeymoon to Italy looking destined for great happiness.

And at the wedding, Caitlyn and Patrick – the bridesmaid and the best man – had finally got together, after Patrick had played a long and curious game of cat and mouse with her, never quite making his move but never giving up his flirtation with her either. By then, she was hopelessly in love with him, and even more so because she knew that he was immune to Sara's charms. He didn't even seem to like Sara very much; he was always talking her down.

'She's mad as a box of frogs,' he used to say, and Caitlyn would laugh. But he always asked about her. He was always interested in what Sara was up to, and what she had said, though sometimes he raised his eyebrows at her snobbish remarks and the things she said to Caitlyn.

Once he said, 'I don't know what you get out of the friendship, Caitlyn. You give more than you get, that's for sure.'

'She's my friend,' Caitlyn replied stoutly. 'She always looks out for me.'

'Okay,' Patrick said, giving her an odd look. 'If you think that, then fine. I wouldn't want to come between you two if you really like her.'

'I do.'

She meant it. Yes, Sara was unpredictable and most certainly had her problems. She was needy, though once she was married the late night sob-filled calls stopped. But Caitlyn was always grateful for Sara's friendship, and the way she shared her glamorous life with her. When she and Rupert

141

bought a Chelsea flat, Sara wanted Caitlyn with her every step of the way while they furnished and decorated it. They had fun together. It was undeniable.

But the paint had been barely dry before the marriage imploded. Caitlyn had never really found out why it had failed so spectacularly, but Rupert was gone and the divorce underway before they had been married a year. Sara transformed from adoring him to loathing him with all her might.

'I'm sorry, you're caught between my best friend and your best friend,' Caitlyn said to Patrick, as she told him all the details she'd heard from Sara that day. 'I feel for you.'

'It's the same for you,' Patrick said.

'Not really. I never see Rupert.'

'I'll live. Don't worry about me.'

She was vaguely surprised but grateful when Patrick let his friendship with Rupert slide and barely saw him after the divorce. Sara remained in their lives, but Rupert did not. By the time Caitlyn and Patrick got married, in a gorgeous ceremony and exquisite reception planned entirely by Patrick, Sara was happily going out with Mark. After Sara married again, Caitlyn never gave Rupert another thought.

Isn't it funny – how Patrick chose her over Rupert? I thought that was for my sake. But . . . was it? The answer, she felt sure, was within her reach.

Think from every angle, Caitlyn. Do your research. Assume nothing.

Chapter Fourteen

Tommy was aware of a slight distance between her and Fred after the trip to Oxford and she wondered if it were her fault or his. And yet, even as they avoided each other it was obvious to her that it was because of a new intimacy between them that they seemed nervous to acknowledge. Things were serene enough when they were with everyone else, gathered around the fire in the drawing room or eating in the dining room, but they hurried past each other on the stairs and muttered hellos if they met accidentally.

Antonia and Harry still couldn't get to their proper schools as progress on the snowy roads was too slow, so Tommy arranged for them to go to the village school in the meantime, and even the Latin lessons were halted. The children said they missed them, but they were having a wonderful time being taken to school by Thornton on the pony cart. School finished early because of the cold, and they got back just as the dark was falling, tired from their journey, hungry and eager for warmth.

Tommy was going through the accounts that Spottiswoode

had drawn up for her and delivered now that he could drive through from his house on the other side of the estate when Fred put his head around the door.

'I'm sorry to disturb you. I'm going to set up my easel this morning. I thought we ought to get our story straight.'

'Oh yes, of course. Come in. Sit down.'

He walked towards her, smiling. 'You look rather formidable behind that desk.'

'Do I?'

'Yes. Like the young queen of some island nation, signing death warrants.'

'I would sign life warrants,' she said with a laugh.

'All effective queens must know when to send an enemy to their death.'

'Like Mary burning poor Ridley? And old Cranmer?'

'I was thinking of Elizabeth really. Sending Mary of Scots to the block. Perhaps you're right. Life warrants are better.' He sat down on the chair where Spottiswoode had been only the previous afternoon. The contrast made Tommy full of warmth for him, with his languid grace and wise humanity, and she wondered why on earth she'd been avoiding him.

'So,' she said. 'Are you really going to do this? Recreate Venetia in all her sadness?'

He leaned forward conspiratorially. 'If it's what your majesty wants, then that is what shall be. I believe this deception is for the good of the realm.'

'On your own head be it. If you're captured, I shall have to disavow all knowledge. For the good of the realm.'

'I'm almost ready to go. The easel is up in the hall. I said to

Roger I fancied my hand at doing a copy of the Gainsborough for my own amusement. He didn't think it was odd. He understands that sort of thing.'

'That's what we'll tell Mother too.'

'As your majesty wishes,' Fred said with a small bow.

'Listen, Fred,' she said awkwardly. 'It's fun to pretend but I don't think we ought to assume that we're going to substitute it for the real thing. That's just a silly idea, isn't it? I don't think I could really do it.'

'Of course,' he said easily. 'It's all a joke. Not a serious endeavour. Believe you me, I don't have the talent Gainsborough had in his little finger. But it will be amusing to see how well I can copy him. Now, I shall get on.' He got up and started on his way to the door. Tommy noticed at once that he was moving a little oddly.

'Fred, are you all right?'

'Oh yes. I'm fine.' He turned and smiled back at her over his shoulder. 'That doctor, the one in Oxford who prodded around and took a look . . . he's rather messed me up and it's got a little inflamed. I should have gone to my specialist really but it's such a bally long way to Kent. I'm sure it'll settle down in time.'

'Do you want medicine for it? We have antiseptics.'

'Perhaps. I'll let you know if I do.'

'Good.' She watched him go out of the door, then turned her mind back to the accounts.

The sight of Fred standing behind his easel sketching was of great interest to everyone.

'What is that young man doing, Thomasina?' her mother asked as she came through on her way to the drawing room. To save fuel, her fires were no longer lit in the evening and she was spending more time in the main house.

'He's trying out a copy of the Gainsborough. You know how amateurs like to have a go – sometimes I could hardly move in the National Gallery for easels. Perhaps once he's done that, we can get him to paint a picture of the house for us. What a nice memento of this winter it would be.'

Her mother shivered. 'I'm not sure I want to remember this awful winter. I've never known it so cold.'

The newspapers were writing about this terrible sustained cold spell. The snow was incredibly heavy in Scotland and in the north, and in Wales, the sheep were dying out in the great freeze. It was not moving on. It was not really thawing. So far there had not been a day without snow somewhere in Britain.

'It must get better soon,' Tommy said, following her mother into the drawing room. 'We'll be all right, if we're careful.'

Her mother settled down by the fire, drawing her shawl tightly about her. 'It's put me in mind of the Spanish flu that came right after the end of the last war. Just when we thought we were safe, that awful force of nature came to give us another bashing. This winter, this awful cold – it's like that.'

Tommy said comfortingly, 'It's just a question of hunkering down for a while. Hibernating like bears. We'll be all right.'

But privately she was worried. Her mother had got it right in a way – they were at their weakest, with so little food available already, and now this weather was going to punish them further. There was meat in the game larder but it would be harder to get more in this weather. Shooting and snaring would be impossible. And if the sheep were freezing in the fields . . . it made her sick to think about the waste of good meat. *Vital meat. As if we can afford to lose so much, when there's barely enough to live on as it is.*

Tommy knew they had been sheltered from the kind of want that others endured. Thornton kept a good kitchen garden for them, and he was handy with the shotgun, knowing how to lure ducks into his sights, and how to shake game birds out of cover and tempt rabbits into traps. But the terrible weather had the potential to remove their ability not just to look after themselves, but to get to the shops where they might supplement their natural larder.

She asked Ada to make a list of all the supplies they had left, and to stock up as much as she could from the rations, just in case.

'I don't know how Fred paints, with the hall so freezing,' Gerry said. 'Especially when it's going so slowly.'

'I hope you're not bothering him,' Tommy said sternly. She was waiting for the children to get back from school, worried by the lowering skies with their nasty shade of yellow that made her think of an aged wedding dress, gone from ivory to the colour of crackled cream. It meant fresh loads of snow would soon be released upon them.

'I'm not bothering him,' Gerry said, 'but Roger is.'

Tommy knew it was true. She had seen it for herself: Roger was orbiting around Fred like a moon around its planet, unable to leave him alone for long. When Fred was drawing,

Roger would observe and offer advice, or sit on one of the hall chairs, smoking and talking at great length about whatever he had read in the papers that day, or a book that had absorbed him. Politics was a favourite topic, and the future of the world now that the war was won. Tommy went through several times a day to see what the situation was and found that, with nothing left to talk about, Roger would read aloud while Fred drew. The painting was coming along at a snail's pace.

When Roger went upstairs the next evening to take his bath before changing for dinner, Tommy seized her chance and hurried to the hall. Fred was there, cleaning his brushes with rags and spirit.

'Oh dear,' she said, her heels tapping loudly on the flagstones as she approached. 'Are you getting anything done?'

'Not much,' he admitted. 'I've barely begun. I didn't take Roger into account. A mistake, I fear.'

'But . . .' Tommy gazed at him. 'Is he always like this with you?'

Fred wiped the soft top of a brush clean with his rag. 'Yes. He seems to need me to talk at, as much as to. I release something in him. Or else he can access something in himself through me.'

Tommy nodded. 'Yes, I see. Well, perhaps this idea is a no-go. I didn't think about Roger either, even though we all know how much he depends on you.'

'Don't give up. We might yet find a way. We could always explain to him what we're doing. Perhaps he would think it's a good idea.'

'I really don't think that Roger would ever understand it. It would run against everything he feels about keeping this place just as it is.'

'Yes, he's rather a conundrum. He's very keen on world socialism. He thinks Russia must be some kind of paradise on Earth and tells me often that he wants something of the sort in this country.'

'That's very odd,' Tommy said, 'because he doesn't show the slightest inclination to want to practise any kind of socialism in the house. He's quite the laziest of us all.'

'I think we should be grateful for that,' Fred said. 'Goodness knows what he might take it into his head to do.'

The next day, the weather was more oppressive than ever and the bitterness was back with a vengeance. The papers said more snow was coming, and when the postman arrived, he said the village school was closing because of the low temperatures.

'Closed till further notice,' he said almost proudly and shook his head at the state of the world. 'The way things are going . . . It's all the government's fault. They should never have thrown Churchill out, that's all I can say.'

'It's hardly the government's fault that the weather's so bad,' Tommy said, taking the letters he was holding out to her.

'No. But they're to blame for the lack of coal,' said the postman solemnly.

'No coal?' Tommy felt a stab of anxiety.

'That's right, ma'am. The deliveries are late, and if the weather gets worse, there's bound to be a delay. That's why the school is closing. They can't keep the heating going for more than a few weeks.' The postman touched his hat. 'Don't worry, ma'am, I'm sure we'll get our thaw before too long.'

'Yes,' Tommy said vaguely, trying to picture what was left in the coal bunker. 'I'm sure we will.' She looked down at her letters as the postman headed back to his van. One addressed in curling black handwriting was postmarked from Oxford. She opened it as she went back inside.

Dearest Tommy

Please forgive me, but I really can't keep Barbara and her daughter any longer. She has nowhere to go and I must throw her on your tender mercies as you have the room for two more. I'm so sorry but I simply can't think of an alternative. She promises me there is a cousin she can go to in a month or two, so it won't be for long. She is a dear, very easy to have about. I know you won't mind, as we were all schoolgirls together. She and Molly will be on the train to you on Friday so please arrange to have them collected at 5.05.

Do come for lunch when you're next in Oxford, I'd love to hear more of your news.

Lots of love,

Veronica

Chapter Fifteen

'You are joking, aren't you?' Caitlyn cried down her mobile phone. She was standing in the middle of the M&S lingerie department, and a lady rifling through the all-in-ones looked her way with interest. 'How can that be the case?'

'I'm afraid it's in the standard contract you signed,' said the estate agent apologetically down the line. 'You can be served notice anytime from five months, and then you have to leave by the end of the sixth month.'

'You're telling me I'm going to be served notice to quit?'

'On the next rent day. That will give you a month to make other arrangements. But I'm giving you a heads-up so that you don't get a nasty surprise.'

Caitlyn thought of the little sitting room, homely and cheerful, the sofa covered in a bright patchwork blanket and the vase of drooping pink tulips on the coffee table. She had begun to think of the cottage as home, and couldn't bear the thought of uprooting herself and Max again, not when they'd just settled in. 'You said it would be a long-term contract

151

because the owner had gone abroad for the foreseeable. Not six months!'

'The owner's plans have changed. I'm sorry, Mrs Balfour. There's really nothing I can do. But I can set up some viewings of other rentals on our books – we've got some really delightful properties ready to view—'

'No thanks, not right now. I'll call you back when I'm ready to do that.' Caitlyn clicked off the call and stood fuming by a stand of dressing gowns. A moment ago she'd been thinking about bras and pyjamas. Now she had to consider the fact that they were going to be homeless in less than eight weeks. Bang in the summer holidays, when she'd been planning to join Maura and the family on their trip to Cornwall.

Great . . . just . . . great!

She strode out of the shop, dropping her mobile into her bag and hardly seeing anything as she went. Out of Marks she turned right and a moment later found herself standing at the crossroads by Carfax, just up the hill from her old college. There it was, huge, golden and imposing, dominated by the great bell tower. Almost without thinking, as though following old song lines from her past, she started to walk down the hill towards it, past the queues of people in the bus stops outside its honey-brown walls, until she reached the cobbled ground under the great arch. Beyond the two enormous studded gates was the sunlit quad, its tended lawns like emerald velvet and a fountain playing in the centre. It hadn't changed a bit in all the years since she had last been here. It seemed an obvious place to come, and yet she hadn't made her way here until now. There were too many bittersweet memories to contend with inside the walls.

Shall I go in? She hesitated on the threshold, almost pulled forward into the old familiar place. Then on impulse she marched through the gate and into the porter's lodge. The porter looked up as she stood at the desk. 'Can I help you?'

'I'm looking for Nicholas Brooke, he's a fellow here—'

A voice came from behind her. 'Caitlyn! It is you, isn't it?'

She jumped and turned to look at whoever had called her and saw Nicholas coming towards her, beaming.

'I can't believe it!' He was already at her side, and had enveloped her in a tweedy hug, his jacket scratchy through her thin top. He kissed her cheek and stood back to look at her. 'Caitlyn Collins! You're exactly the same. What on earth are you doing here?'

'I came in on the off chance you might be here. I should have emailed first, I know . . .'

'Don't be silly. It's great to see you. Have you got time for coffee?'

She smiled at him. A moment ago, in her memory, he'd been about twenty, fresh-faced, with spiky black hair and dark brown eyes, a legacy of his Italian heritage. Now that image was rapidly being overwritten with the reality of a man of almost forty, with silver-grey in his dark hair, and wrinkles round his eyes and mouth, a dusting of grey and black stubble over his chin. He was a little heavier than he had been, but then, he'd been skinny as a young man and it suited him to carry a bit more weight. He had aged well. His olive skin was only a little lined and the wrinkles were from expression rather than age. And where once he would have worn jeans and baggy T-shirts, he was now in muted cords and a tweed jacket, a well-washed checked shirt underneath. 'I'd love that, thanks.'

'Come on, then.' He led her out of the porter's lodge and into the quad. 'What brings you here? Are you just visiting for the day?'

'No. I live here now,' she said, almost apologetically. 'We moved a while ago.'

'I had no idea. I don't do much social media or I probably would. I'm too taken up teaching the kind of bloody-minded, vaguely interested, lazy undergraduates that we once were. Well, I was.'

As he turned and led her down a small corridor and then up a winding wooden staircase, she was overwhelmed with memories. The sound of her feet on the wood, the dusty smell of the staircase, the echo of the stone walls transported her back in time twenty years while Nicholas was explaining how he'd gone to work in the City before feeling he'd missed his vocation and returning to academia. He stopped in front of a sturdy outer door with his name painted in white above it: *Professor N. C. Brooke.* He took out his keys and opened it, then the inner door that revealed the rooms within, and turned to smile at her.

'Come in. Excuse the mess.'

She followed him in, fascinated. She'd always known that there was far more to the college than she'd ever seen, more than her own rooms, her friends', the communal bits. There were hundreds, perhaps thousands of lives going on within its walls. Whole houses existed unseen inside the quads. There were hidden gardens, little-known staircases, secret libraries, invisible balconies, room after room behind stout locked doors, like a castle of secrets from a fairy story. She realised suddenly what a very little part of it she'd experienced. It was bigger and deeper than she'd guessed. And here was another part revealed: Nicholas's rooms.

'Aren't they lovely?' she said, as she came in, dipping her head beneath a low beam. Nicholas's rooms weren't on the grander lower floor, but tucked up towards the top, with high windows overlooking the battlements and the stately quad below.

He looked around proudly. 'It's bigger than you'd think up here. And as I'm stuck up under the roof, in the less desirable bit, they've given me a larger set than most. I've got two bedrooms, a kitchen, a bathroom and' – he led her through a dark oak door – 'of course, my sitting room and study.'

She almost laughed out loud as she looked around. 'It's perfect,' she said. 'Exactly right. I bet your students love it.'

It was a cosy room, with a low ceiling with ornate plastered squares, and a thick black beam over a fireplace where the remains of a log lay in soft white ash. The walls were lined with bookcases full of volumes and ornaments and pictures. Where there was no bookcase, there were panels hung with pictures, and one side of the room had deep stone window seats in front of two windows. The curtains were dark red tapestry, and green and ruby-red velvet cushions provided softness on the hard stone. A squashy green sofa and two armchairs draped in colourful ikat fabrics were grouped around the fire, and everywhere were more books, piled on the coffee table and beside the chairs. By the fire was a drinks tray, with large bottles of sherry, gin and vodka, tiny tins of tonic, and an ice bucket shaped like a golden pineapple.

'Sherry! I bet you hand out little glasses before a tutorial. You're a textbook Oxford don,' Caitlyn said, laughing properly now. 'Your students must be impressed.'

'Whatever it takes to make them happy,' he said. 'I hate to let the young people down.'

'It's wonderful.' She followed him as he led the way to his tiny garret kitchen. 'You should hire it out for films. Are you happy up here?'

'I am. It can be a bit reclusive. But I always get away during the holidays. I spread my wings and escape Oxford's little enclave, do some living. But I love coming back. It's a kind of home to me.'

'Yes. I know what you mean.' Caitlyn watched as he filled the kettle and set about making coffee. 'Ever since we moved here, I've felt as though I've come home. Which is odd, as I grew up in Southport. But there's something about this place, isn't there?'

'It stains you. Marks you. Like the ink hidden in banknotes to explode over robbers. You can't see it but it's there.' Nicholas grinned at her. 'But in my case, I grew up really quite close.'

She looked around the little set. 'And you live here alone?'

He nodded lightly. 'Yes. I'm single. It hasn't always been the way, but it is right now.'

'Oh.' She was wary of stamping over his life, asking questions when she so dreaded the same herself. Besides, how well had she really known Nicholas all those years ago? Did she have the right to make such personal enquiries?

They went back through to the study-sitting room and Caitlyn sat down on the squashy sofa. 'I feel as if I'm about to have a tutorial. I'm nervous. I haven't got an essay.'

'Do you mean to tell me, Miss Collins, that you don't have your essay with you?' Nicholas sat back in armchair. 'What's your excuse this week?'

'Ugh, that just gave me nasty butterflies. And I'm not Collins any more. I'm Balfour. I've even got a son, Max. He's eleven.'

'Ah. I've got a daughter. Twelve.'

'Really?' Caitlyn almost looked about as if she might spot a twelve-year-old girl hiding behind the curtains. 'Where is she?'

'She lives in the States with her mother, who is also an academic, at Columbia. That's where I go during the holidays.'

'Oh, I see.'

There've been twenty years of living since I last saw him. We both have our stories. She smiled at Nicholas again. 'It's so nice to see you. You've hardly changed.'

He ran a hand through his silver-streaked hair, his expression rueful. 'That's nice of you, but I have a bit. I'm getting on a little now.'

'We all are. What's nice is that we'll always remember how we used to be.'

'True.'

They looked at one another, and there was a moment of awkwardness as their gaze met. A memory swum into her mind but she rejected it before it had time to form properly. Nicholas glanced down into his coffee and Caitlyn, wanting to ease the sudden tension between them, found herself propelled up and out of the sofa. She walked over to his desk, a battered antique piled up with books and papers, and a green-shaded brass reading light. There were some framed photographs propped up on it, and her eye was caught at once by the picture of a merry young girl with long blonde plaits wearing denim dungarees and a stripy top. 'Is this your daughter?'

'Yes, that's Coco.'

'Isn't she pretty? She's so fair! Not like you at all. But she has your brown eyes.'

'Yes, her mother is Swiss German. She got the Nordic colouring from her.' Nicholas stood up and came over, looking fondly at the photograph. 'She's the light of my life. I miss her horribly when I'm over here. Thank goodness for technology, that's all I can say. We connect on the screen all the time. But we both count down the weeks until I can get there.'

'I'm not surprised you miss her.' Caitlyn looked back at the picture. 'There's no way she can live here?'

'Nope. None.' Nicholas sounded final on the subject.

God, listen to me. I'm prying. When I promised I wouldn't.

'So,' Nicholas said. 'What brings you to Oxford? Are you working here?'

'No . . . no. I used to work in the art world, assessing paintings for an auctioneer. But I'm not working at the moment. I don't know what brought me back exactly. It's close to my son's school, I suppose, but also . . . well, it sounds a bit odd, but I wanted to find out more about the past. To see if I'd remembered it correctly. I thought you might be able to help me with it, that's why I dropped by on the off chance you were here.'

'Okay,' he said. 'I'm happy to help.'

There was a pause, then he said awkwardly, 'And Max's dad? Is he with you?'

'No. No. I'm . . . on my own.' For some reason, she couldn't bring herself to say that Patrick was dead. Instead she said hastily, 'You remember Sara, don't you?'

'Of course I do. She was unforgettable. Trouble with a capital T. Do you still see her?'

'Oh yes. I do. Not recently, she's in America. She's a successful interior designer now.'

'Why doesn't that surprise me?' Nicholas smiled and raised his coffee cup to his lips.

'We're still close. She's Max's godmother.'

Nicholas looked embarrassed. 'I'm sorry, I didn't realise you two were still friends. Forget what I said about trouble, I was only joking.'

'No, I'm interested. Really. What do you remember about her?'

'Sara was great. Lovely, intelligent and fun, if a bit highly strung. And you two were best friends. I remember you sharing tutorials and being basically inseparable.'

'Yes.' Caitlyn knew that wasn't the real story but that she'd mishandled it and missed her opportunity to find out the truth. She would have to win Nicholas's trust to do that. She felt flustered, impelled to change the subject. 'Perhaps I can pick your brains about something else. I've had a rather frustrating piece of news. Just when I'd got Max and myself settled in town so I could be close to his school, the landlord has served notice on me. I've got to be out in a few weeks, right in the middle of the holidays, so I need some recommendations of places to live.'

'Where is he?'

'Spring Hall.'

'I know it. I went there myself, actually. It's not far from my childhood home.'

'Your childhood home? I don't suppose it's for rent, is it?' Caitlyn asked jokily.

Nicholas looked at her oddly. 'Well . . . as it happens, some of it is for rent. My great-aunt lives in part of it. But the other half is empty. She's let it out at various times, but it's vacant right now. There's plenty of room there.'

Caitlyn gazed at him, interested. 'Where did you say it is?'

'In a village not that far from Spring Hall – about ten miles the other side, twenty-five miles from Oxford. The house is called Kings Harcourt.'

'I don't know it.'

'Then why don't I show it to you? It has a famous painting you might be interested in, if it's in your sphere of interest. A portrait by Gainsborough.'

'Really?' Caitlyn was intrigued. 'That's my period, actually. I'd love to see it.'

'Good. I can show you the house at the same time. It could be just what you need.'

Chapter Sixteen

With the school shut and the children cooped up at home, Fred declared that he would resume the Latin lessons, but Tommy was too distracted even to thank him for the offer. No one seemed particularly bothered when she told them that Barbara Hastings and her daughter were coming to stay. Even her mother, whom she'd expected to complain, said only that it would be pleasant for Thomasina to have a friend around.

'I barely know her!' protested Tommy. 'I haven't seen her for years if you don't count last week.'

'If she's been living with Veronica Macintyre, she must be respectable.' Her mother was embroidering a cushion cover but her fingers were now become arthritic and her progress was very slow. She peered down hard at it as she moved her needle carefully through the fabric, drawing a long shiny thread after it. 'What do you know of her circumstances?'

'Only what she told me the other day. Her husband was in the army and they lived in India for a long while. Their daughter Molly was born there. He was killed in Burma and now she seems quite alone.'

'I'm surprised you don't want to help her then.'

'I do want to help her! But . . .' She stopped. There seemed no answer to it. Hadn't she opened her doors to a parcel of little evacuees, total strangers from goodness only knew what background? So why was she so reluctant to shelter Barbara and her daughter?

'It seems to me,' her mother said, 'that another woman who knows what you have suffered might be a comfort, not a hindrance.'

'Well, they're coming tomorrow afternoon and even if I wrote now, I don't suppose it would reach them in time.'

'You could telephone if you're determined to refuse.'

Tommy quailed at the thought of talking to Veronica and in any case, she knew exactly what would happen: she would back down and give in. 'No, it's all right. I might as well tell Clara to make up the extra beds.'

The one thing that cheered Tommy up was the sight of the coal man, his truck lumbering up the lane to deliver her ration.

'How do ye do, ma'am,' he said as she ran out to greet him.

'Well, this is very welcome!' she cried. The bright morning sun glittered on what was left of the previous fall of snow. 'You're just in time. We're nearly out!'

'I've got two ton for you.'

'Oh, thank goodness. We're running so low. But my ration is six tons. Is more coming?'

The coal man jumped down from the cab of his truck and began to haul the dirty sacks off the back. They left black and grey smudges in the snow, which looked even filthier against the white. 'I don't know about that. There's plenty who won't get their ration, not enough is coming through. And if you've got your boiler coke, don't waste it now. There's no more to be had.'

'No more?' Tommy said, dismayed.

'Not right now. If you'll excuse me, ma'am, I'll take these to your bunker.'

The arrival of the coal was a great relief but her two tons did not go far to filling up the coal bunker, and there was little clue as to when there would be more. They would have to be careful; there could be no relaxation in their vigilance.

I'm so tired of it all, she thought, putting on her hat in front of the mirror in the passage by the kitchen. *It's been so long since we were able to live without thinking about saving everything. Petrol, soap, clothes, food. On and on it goes. Never ending.*

She reached for her coat and was pulling it on when Fred came down the passageway looking anxious.

'What are you doing, Tommy?'

'I'm driving to the station to collect Barbara, remember?'

'I've just been listening to the wireless news and they are warning of severe weather conditions tonight. A frightful blast of snow and cold.'

Tommy sighed. 'Well, that's just wonderful. At least we got some coal before it arrived.'

'Are you sure you should drive to the station?'

'What choice have I got? I can hardly leave Barbara and

Molly to freeze on the platform, can I? They're coming and that's that.'

'Can't you telephone to Veronica and ask if they're on their way?'

'Oh, they will be, believe me. You've never seen anyone so eager to be rid of her guests as Veronica. I'm sure I shall be all right. It's not snowing yet and if it started now, I'd have time to get there and back.'

'I'll come with you,' Fred said. 'Just to be sure. I'll meet you at the car.'

Before she could say anything, he had hurried off to get his things.

Fred put a shovel and some blankets into the back of the car, and two stone hot water bottles wrapped in more blankets.

'Won't those be useless in no time?' Tommy said, coming out after him. 'Oh my goodness – it's so cold!'

The air had a hard bite to it, eating at her cheeks with icy fangs, and her fingers were instantly numb. It was already getting dark and trepidation filled her as her animal senses told her there was danger in the world tonight and that the safest thing was to retreat to somewhere warm.

'Go and change your shoes,' Fred said briefly, looking down at her sturdy leather lace-ups. 'Those won't be warm enough. Do you have anything else?'

'I've got some fur-lined boots,' she said.

'Put them on.' He grimaced in the gathering gloom. 'This is a fool's errand but we're in for it now. Shall I drive?'

164

'No, it's my car. I'll drive it,' Tommy replied quickly. 'I think I can manage a bit of cold. We'll be fine.'

Once they set off, though, she was shivering quickly. Beside her, Fred sat wrapped up in a blanket, his hat pulled low. 'We might warm up in here in a bit,' he said. 'The hot water bottles might do something.'

But their two bodies and the stone bottles seemed like nothing against the might of the cold. The roads were not too bad, though Tommy could sense a little slipperiness under the wheels. It felt like everything was waiting, anticipating whatever was to come.

It seemed to take forever to reach the end of the lane and then things became a little easier on the main road, where there were other cars and trucks. Very few people were out on the streets of the village, and lights glowed from behind curtains as darkness fell hard around them.

'What train are they on?' Fred asked.

'The 5.05.'

'We should be there in time, then. But it's going to be slow getting back.'

Tommy nodded and stared out at the darkness that awaited beyond the lights of the village. The station was still a way off, on the outskirts of the small town of Wedford five miles on from the village. She knew this road well: she had roared along it without a second thought many times. Now it was strange and perilous and she strained to see every familiar landmark.

Fred said quietly, 'I admire your courage, Tommy. You've got grit.'

She laughed lightly. 'I don't know what you mean. Driving a car is nothing. I'm sure you've seen real courage.'

'I've seen different courage, perhaps. But it's all from the same place. It's pressing on with determination no matter how grim it looks outside. That's what you're doing now. It would have been easier to call Veronica and cancel Barbara – is she your problem after all?'

Tommy tightened her grip on the steering wheel. 'You don't understand. I've taken the coward's way out.' She turned quickly to smile at him. 'You should try crossing Veronica, it's much more terrifying than this.'

Fred laughed. 'Even so. I admire it.'

It was a relief to see the lights of the town and the sign to the station. They were five minutes early for the train, and they stood together on the platform, stamping and blowing on their gloved fingers to thaw them. Fred offered her a cigarette and they stood smoking together.

'Is the Oxford train on time?' enquired Tommy of the stationmaster as he came out.

'As far as I know.' He shook his head gloomily. 'But who knows what waits for us tomorrow?' There was a click as the signals changed and the lights above them glowed green and red. 'Ah, here she is!'

The sound that was muffled at first grew louder as the train rounded the bend in the track towards them, a great black shape in the darkness with a bright yellow eye, then puffed to a stop with a shrill whistle and a release of steam. Tommy was both relieved to see it and filled with a sense of gloom that it was now inevitable. Barbara was here.

They waited until all the doors were open, watching for a woman and a little girl, and then there they were, Barbara unmistakable with the broad shoulders of her navy coat and her blonde hair falling long over her shoulders. She carried a Gladstone bag and a box tied with string. Next to her was a small girl well wrapped up against the cold, clutching a teddy bear.

Tommy waved, full of a sudden sympathy for the two figures that seemed so lost. *How horrible it must be to be homeless*. 'Barbara! Hello!'

Barbara spied her and waved back. 'Tommy. How marvellous to see you.'

Tommy and Fred went over to meet them. 'Barbara, this is Mr Burton Brown. Fred, this is Mrs Hastings.'

They said their how do you dos while Tommy said, 'Hello, Molly, how nice to meet you,' but the little girl said nothing, only gazed up at her from light blue eyes like her mother's. Fred arranged to collect the suitcases from the porter while the women made their way back to the car.

'It's absolutely freezing,' Barbara said, in her high, thin voice. 'Molly and I were huddled together all the way, and we were still shivering. The guard said there was warm air coming out of the vents, but we never felt it, did we, Molly?'

Molly shook her head and Tommy could see she was trembling with cold. 'You poor things. Let's get in the car. There are blankets and hot water bottles, though I'm afraid they may be only tepid by now. There are sandwiches too. Oh good, here's Fred with the suitcases. Now we can start for home, and the sooner we get going, the sooner we shall be there.'

The drive home was much worse than the one out. The temperature was lower than Tommy thought she'd ever known, and as they pulled away from the station, the first scattering of white fluff in the air, swirling in the beam from the headlights like large motes of dust, heralded the snow.

'It's here,' Tommy said, wide-eyed.

'Let's hope we get back in time,' Fred murmured.

Barbara started off by trying to talk in a jolly voice, but she soon gave up. All of them could only think about the snow which went in a matter of minutes from a light flurry to a thick blizzard of flakes, whirling around them. As they left the lights of the town, Tommy could see almost nothing in front of her and was forced to drop her speed to barely a walking pace as she tried to pick out the road in front of her through the spinning white. Outside the snow was settling fast. Within twenty minutes the ground was thickly blanketed and she began to feel real fear at their situation. In the back Barbara and Molly sat close together under the blankets, their anxious eyes gleaming in the darkness as they stared out at the wildness beyond the car.

'I think we're going to have to go faster,' Fred muttered. 'The roads are going to be impassable if it goes on at this rate. I think we've got about half an hour before we'll risk getting stuck.'

'Oh my goodness,' said Tommy, worried. 'The drive home is half an hour from here on a good day. But I'll do my best.'

'You're doing very well,' he said encouragingly. 'Keep going.'

Tommy began to gain some confidence as she went and her eye grew accustomed to making out the road between the larger banks of snow on either side so she picked up speed.

'That's it, that's the ticket,' Fred said. 'We're not too far from the village now.'

But it seemed miles and miles away as they crawled along the deserted road.

I don't think I've ever felt so tiny and alone in my whole life, Tommy thought. Huge forces were raging outside. What on earth were they doing, trying to fight them? *Well, there's no choice now. We have to go on. We can hardly go back.*

The snow was already a foot deep as they approached the village but the car was ploughing through the soft, hardly set layers. Nevertheless, Tommy could feel the resistance growing. It would not be long before they wouldn't be able to force a way through. And there was the awful cold too. Her fingers on the steering wheel were numbed and painful, her toes were impossible to feel. Only the adrenaline of driving was keeping her warm at all. She could sense Fred beside her, huddled down into himself, folding his slender body up to preserve warmth, fighting against the urge to shiver.

'Nearly there,' he said.

'Oh look!' Tommy said brightly. 'Look, Molly, that's the village, can you see the lights? We're nearly home!'

'That's good,' said the girl's small voice from the back of the car.

'What a relief!' Barbara said, and it was evident how worried she had been.

Tommy looked over at Fred, hoping she was conveying the thought that was now in her mind – that they were far from safely home. The hardest part was yet to come.

As they motored slowly through the village, Tommy wondered if they should take a wiser course and stop for the night somewhere. The vicar and his wife would surely give them shelter. The lights were on in the large house by the green where the Hendersons lived. But something in Tommy urged her forward and she didn't suggest that they stopped. As they left the shelter of the village, the snow grew much worse, the drifts against the hedges now higher than the car and the level of snow in the road approaching two feet. She pressed her foot down on the accelerator as the car nosed forward into the swirling blackness, and stared out through the moving windscreen wipers as hard as she could, trying to see the signpost that would tell her when to turn into the lane. All the familiar landmarks were lost in the dark and the blanket of thick snow. The snow falling on the car was mounting up and the bonnet was covered.

Fred turned to her, his face grey with cold. 'You'd better stop for a moment – don't switch the engine off. I'm going to clear the snow off the windscreen.'

She stopped obediently and he opened his passenger door. A gust of freezing snow came whirling in and then he was out and the door slammed behind him. She watched, shivering as he wiped away mounds of snow from the windscreen and bonnet with his arm, and then braced herself for the torrent of cold as he got back in.

'All done,' he said, and his teeth were chattering as he huddled back down. 'There's no time to lose, old thing. Put your foot down if you can.'

But when Tommy pressed on the accelerator, she could feel how much momentum they had lost by stopping. The car pushed against the snow and began slowly to move, but the pressure against it was growing at every moment. The engine whined as it struggled.

'How far do you think we are?' asked Fred in a low voice.

'We must be almost at the lane. From there it's half a mile or so to the house.'

'Half a mile.' He looked at her grimly and she could see his expression in the half-light. 'It's going to be tight. But we've got no choice. We can't walk in this. We'd be lost in no time.' He turned to look over his shoulder at the passengers in the back. 'We'll be home before too long, don't you worry.' Then to Tommy he said, 'Do what you can.'

'We'll get there,' Tommy said determinedly. 'I know we will.'

It was only by luck that she spotted the turn-off to the lane. The world outside was so changed that it was impossible to get any bearings. Turnings, hedgerows, familiar trees had all disappeared and there was nothing to tell road from field. But the beam of the headlights caught a bit of the sign not covered by snow and Tommy noticed the gleam long enough to recognise what it was.

'Here,' she said. 'We turn right here. We're not far away.'

'This blizzard is extraordinary,' Fred murmured. 'I've never seen anything like it. It's Siberian.'

'What will it be like in the morning?' Tommy asked.

'That's why we have to get back,' Fred said. 'Don't give up, will you?'

'I won't,' Tommy said, trying to force more strength out of the car, 'but the engine might. The tyres don't want to turn any more.'

The snow in the lane was deeper than on the road, for it had been blown hard over the fields to fill the gap between the low hedges. The level was almost over the bonnet.

'Oh Fred,' Tommy said, frightened now. 'I don't think we can get much further.' She turned to him anxiously. 'We must be close.'

'Go on as far as you can, every little counts.'

She pushed down, urging the little car on, and it fought forward a few more feet.

'I'll get out and shovel,' Fred said.

'You can't. It'll take far too long for you to make a path and the snow will fill it up as quickly as you do it. Come *on*.' She urged the car on and it made headway of another few feet, and then it would go no further. 'Oh dear,' she said. 'We must be a quarter of a mile from home.' The thought of Captain Scott and his men drifted into her mind. They had been so close to survival but a blizzard had stopped them from reaching supplies and so they froze in their tent. *Is that what will happen to us? Dead in our car, so close to food and warmth?* 'Fred. What shall we do?'

Fred turned to her, pulling the torch from his coat. He switched it on. His lips were pinched and blueish in the pale light that came from it. 'We could wait here. Till the snow stops.'

Tommy shook her head as she shivered. 'It might last for days. It will only get worse. We'll have to walk for it.'

'You're right, of course. It's a quarter of a mile. I'll take the shovel and make whatever path I can. You try and keep us on track. We must go as quickly as we can, especially Molly.' He turned in his seat so that he could see Barbara and Molly, quiet and frightened in the back. 'We're going to walk. Molly, you must stay close to your mother and right behind me. Tommy will have the torch. We'll go as fast as we can because we can't linger in this cold. Barbara, you must leave the cases here. We'll get them tomorrow.'

Barbara nodded and didn't demur.

She's got pluck, Tommy thought. *She must be terrified for Molly.*

'Let's get on our way,' Fred said with a smile. 'I don't know about you, but I'm dying for a hot cup of cocoa.' He passed the torch to Tommy and opened his door. The furious wind burst in again, bringing a flurry of snow. 'I'll get the shovel and you all get out.'

Tommy pushed her door open with an effort and struggled out into the freezing darkness, sinking immediately down into deep snow. *Thank goodness Fred told me to put on my boots.* But Barbara and Molly were not so lucky, their shoes and stockings disappearing into the drift as they climbed out.

'Follow me,' yelled Fred, his voice fighting against the howling wind, and he struggled forward with the shovel, pushing what snow he could out of the way. Tommy hustled Molly and Barbara in front of her, so that they were sheltered as much as possible, and urged them forward.

'Come on!' she shouted, chilled to the bone by the biting wind. 'We must press on as fast as possible.' And she threw out the beam of the torch as far as it would go into the tempest.

Fred tried to shovel but it was almost pointless. Soon he concentrated on fighting a way through the drift with his body, using the shovel more as a machete to chop and loosen snow than to dig it. The others pressed on behind him, their eyes scrunched against the whirl of wind and snow.

But where is the house?

Ahead seemed only blackness, full of storm-tossed snow.

It must be near. Why can't I see it?

She shone the torch as far forward as she could but there was nothing to be seen more than a few feet ahead. So she lifted the torch skywards and waved the beam upwards, then down, then up again. Every few feet, she did it again.

She could see Barbara shivering as she fought her way through the deep snow. 'Mr Burton Brown!' she yelled, thumping Fred on the back. 'It's Molly! She can't go any further. She's too cold and it's too deep!'

Fred turned to her and saw Molly, rooted to the spot and shivering uncontrollably. 'Tommy!' he yelled. 'You lead. I'll take Molly.' He lifted the little girl up into his arms, wincing slightly as he did, and Tommy plunged forward through the snow, taking the shovel.

I've never been so cold.

They seemed to have been walking for hours. She was exhausted, blinded by the snow, freezing to her marrow. But there was no way they could give up. They had to keep on. She could hear Fred grunting with effort as he carried the shaking Molly.

Could we really die out here? The possibility suddenly seemed closer than it ever had. Death was very near, she knew that. Life, it turned out, was fragile. Just a walk in the snow could snuff it out. And how long before it was a blessed relief to give up the struggle, and sink away from the cold and noise and fear into silence? *Stop it! I mustn't think that way.* She fought against the shivering and the pain in her hands and feet. *Come on, now, Tommy. Be sensible. Don't think about such awful things. We really must get home. But where is it? Why can't I see it?*

She swung the torch beam back up into the sky and then she saw an answering flash. Two strong points of light suddenly came to life just a little way ahead. 'There!' she yelled. 'We're nearly there, come on!'

With new energy, they battled on, and the lights grew closer until Tommy saw that they were lanterns, put up on the gatepost pillars.

'It's the last push!' she yelled, and then, to her great relief, she saw two figures bundled up in coats and hats, standing in the snow, waving torches desperately towards them.

'Over here!' yelled Gerry against the howl of the wind.

'We're coming,' shouted Tommy as they struggled the last few feet along the lane. She was almost weeping with relief. 'We're coming. We're home.'

Chapter Seventeen

Nicholas came to collect Caitlyn for their trip to the country, arriving just after she returned from dropping Max at school.

'I don't keep classic university hours any more,' he said as she made him coffee. 'I've got that middle-aged sense of time running short, so I get up early. Eat healthily. Go to the gym. Got to make the most of it.'

'Ouch, middle-aged,' she said. 'Surely not.'

'When you spend most of your time teaching students, you don't just feel middle-aged at forty. You feel bloody ancient!'

The sun was out, clouds scudding over the sky in little battalions, the treetops waving in the breeze. Nicholas had an open-topped MG sports car in bright green – 'All right,' she said with a smile, 'you win. You *are* middle-aged' – and they roared through Oxford, the wind whipping up her hair until she managed to tie it back with an elastic band she found in her bag. The city was not yet clogged with traffic and they were soon westbound on the A34, speeding along in the sunshine. Talking wasn't possible with the roof down, and she lost herself in the enjoyment of the ride, the wind battering the top of her head, the sun bright on her dark glasses. She didn't feel nervous as she had with Sara, despite the speed. In fact, sitting here with Nicholas, even though she'd not seen him in twenty years, felt absurdly comfortable and natural.

They followed the road westwards towards Wiltshire for half an hour, passing Spring Hall on their way.

'Nearly there,' Nicholas said as they drove into a market town, around its tortuous one-way system and out the other side, flying along country lanes. Suddenly they were in a pretty village of grey-stone houses and imposing gateways that obviously led to large mansions. A bright and lively looking pub flashed past, and then they were out the other side and turning up a long narrow lane. They went about half a mile along the lane until suddenly, almost magically, a beautiful house appeared, a seventeenth-century Jacobean manor house in mellow golden stone, with deep-set mullioned windows and a studded oak front door.

'Here we are.' Nicholas slowed down as they pulled up in the lane opposite it. The house, magnificent but not lonely in its isolation, overlooked a wonderful view of forests and fields, with the roofs of the village and spire of the church visible over the distant hedges.

'Your great-aunt lives here?' Caitlyn said, surprised. The house was enormous; she'd imagined they were going to a largish but sensible house, perhaps even a sprawling bungalow. A great-aunt had to be fairly old, after all, when Nicholas was nearly forty. Not a place like this.

'She does. Come on, let's get out and see how the old bird is doing.'

They left the MG as it was – 'It doesn't look like rain,' Nicholas said, squinting up at the sky, 'I think she'll be all right' – and crossed the lane to the house. Instead of going to the large front door in the central part of the house, Nicholas skirted down the side and knocked on a door at the back, in the west wing of the house. A flurry of barks greeted them and the sound of racing paws and panting excitement.

'Down, girls, down!' said a loud voice and the door opened to reveal three excited terriers and a stout red-faced woman with steel-grey curls wearing a large striped apron over her sensible skirt and jumper. She smiled. 'Well, hello, how nice to see you.'

'You did know I was coming, didn't you?' Nicholas said, going up the step and kissing one cherry-red cheek. 'I left a message on the answering machine.'

'Oh yes. Of course you did.' The woman's gaze turned to Caitlyn.

'This is my friend, Mrs Balfour,' Nicholas said.

'Caitlyn, please,' she said quickly.

'This is Renee,' Nicholas said. 'She helps my aunt in the house.'

Renee nodded, smiling. 'A little more than help, but yes. Glad to meet you.'

So this isn't his great-aunt at all, thought Caitlyn.

'Is she in the sitting room?' Nicholas asked.

'That's right, you go through. I'll make some tea.' She called to the dogs, 'Come on, girls, excitement's over. Back in your beds.'

Nicholas led her through a kitchen warmed by an old iron

range in the chimney breast and full of the comforting smell of a stew cooking. It was much smaller than Caitlyn had expected, what with the size of the house. It wasn't much larger than her kitchen in Oxford. The kitchen led straight into a sitting room, with low dark beams and a vast fireplace where a stove burned brightly, warming the room to a solid stuffiness. The wood-panelled walls were covered in paintings and prints, and the furniture was worn but comfortable-looking. There was, Caitlyn realised, nothing new in the room at all, including the piles of ancient magazines, and its occupant looked equally elderly; she sat dozing on the sofa, a book sliding off the rug that covered her knees, her white head nodding and her breathing heavy.

'Aunt Geraldine!' called out Nicholas, and the old lady jerked awake, blinking hard and looking about to find the source of the disturbance.

'What? Oh! Nicholas, it's you.' She blinked harder and then smiled to see her nephew.

'How are you?' boomed Nicholas as he bent to kiss her powdery cheek.

'No need to shout, dear, I'm not deaf,' she said, accepting the kiss.

'You are a bit deaf,' Nicholas said loudly.

'Well, a little, I suppose. Still, no need to yell at the top of your voice.' She readjusted the blanket on her knees. 'I'm fine, thank you, and very glad to see you as it means Renee will now be forced to minister to my needs and bring me a cup of tea.' Her bright eyes turned to Caitlyn. 'And who is this?'

'This is my friend, Caitlyn Balfour. I want to show her the house.'

'Well, I always do like to meet new people. It can get a little dull here, you know. How do you do, Caitlyn Balfour.'

'Very well thank you,' Caitlyn said politely, realising that she didn't know Great-Aunt Geraldine's surname, and so had no idea what to call her. Great-Aunt didn't seem entirely right, and Geraldine a bit too familiar.

'Please, sit down, both of you.' Aunt Geraldine frowned. 'Now, are you cold? Shall we stoke up the fire? It's been rather chilly lately.'

Nicholas said, 'Oh no, we're not cold. Quite the opposite. It's like an oven in here.'

'Is it?' Geraldine shivered. 'I don't quite feel it any more. This house was always so icy cold, I never seem to warm up. We're spoiled now – you should have been here when the winters were frightful. You wouldn't have believed it, the way we got snowed in. And when the rain came, well, this place was an island, cut off from everywhere by water right across the fields.'

Caitlyn sat down, thinking that being stranded in this cosy place seemed rather appealing. Nicholas sat next to his aunt and she asked him about Oxford life. A few minutes later, Renee came in with the tea and they were occupied pouring it out and handing it round. With focus off her, Caitlyn was able to look around, taking in the shabby but pleasing nature of the room. Still, it seemed far too small for the size of the house they had seen from the lane.

'So,' Aunt Geraldine said, after they'd drunk their tea.

'Caitlyn – that's a pretty name – do you live in this country?'

'Yes, I do.'

'Good. Nicholas's last lady friend lives in America. I'm glad that you don't.'

Caitlyn felt her cheeks burst with colour. 'Well—'

'Caitlyn's a lady and a friend – but not a lady friend in the way you mean,' Nicholas said with a laugh. 'She's married for all you know, anyway!'

Aunt Geraldine looked at her. 'Are you married, dear?'

'I . . . no. Not any more.'

'There you are – she's not married. So one can always hope.' Aunt Geraldine smiled at Caitlyn. 'I don't like to see him alone, and he's going to need someone to help him take this place on. It'll be his in a year or two.'

Nicholas said, 'Oh, I hope not, Aunt Geraldine. You've got some years ahead of you yet.'

'I'm eighty-five, and let's not pretend that's young. Someone called me late-middle-aged the other day. Can you believe it?' She pealed with laughter. 'I'm old, and that's a fact. And we might as well prepare ourselves for the inevitable.'

'Don't get morbid on me, now. I'm easily depressed.' Nicholas stood up. 'I'm going to give Caitlyn the tour. She's looking for somewhere to live and I thought this might be the place.'

Geraldine looked interested. 'A new tenant? That's a nice idea. This house always thrives on young blood.'

'Like a vampire,' Nicholas murmured with a sideways look at Caitlyn. 'Bleeds you just as dry financially too.'

'What did you say, dear boy?'

'Nothing, Aunt. We'll come in and say goodbye before we go.'

'Do. Enjoy your look around.' Geraldine waved them off.

Nicholas went over to a door near the fireplace and opened it, turning to Caitlyn. 'Excuse my aunt, she's not very subtle in her old age. This way.'

She followed him into a large long hall with a flagstone floor and a staircase to an upper landing. Now she could see the front door and realised that they'd passed from the west wing into the central hall of the house. It felt quite different: the cosiness and warmth was gone. Now it felt cold and un-inhabited, despite the furniture.

'Oh, I see how it fits together.' Caitlyn gestured to the door they had just come through. 'So your aunt lives in that wing?'

'Yes – the smaller part, designed as a complete house when this one was built, but for the younger branch of the family. This bit is empty now. No one here.'

'And you're really going to inherit it?'

'That's what Aunt has threatened.' Nicholas looked around. 'She's about to sign it over to me in the hope that she'll stay alive long enough to avoid the inheritance tax. I'd have to sell it then, no question. But' – he shrugged – 'the chances are it'll have to be sold anyway.'

'Really? But it's so beautiful!' Caitlyn looked around, wondering what it must be like to live here.

'It costs a bomb to run a place like this. There's no family money, there never was all that much. The estate relied on farming and tenancies, and the land all got sold over the years. So it'll have to be bought by someone very rich as

183

their country retreat, or turned into a hotel or something.'

Caitlyn looked about. The hall was not so large as to be imposing but full of grace and the grandeur of age. 'It seems a shame. It feels like it should have a family in it.'

'There'd only be me – and maybe Coco in the holidays. It needs more than I can give it.'

'I see that. I do.' Caitlyn's attention was grabbed by a large painting hanging in the shadows on the back wall of the hall. 'Goodness, look at that.' She walked towards it, staring. 'That must be the painting you told me about.'

'According to family lore, it's by Gainsborough himself.'

Caitlyn stood in front of the painting, enraptured despite the gloom in the hall. 'It's beautiful. She's so sad. A real Gainsborough?'

'Apparently.'

Caitlyn laughed. 'I can't believe it's hanging here in this deserted room. I hope you've got a good alarm system!'

'It's pretty secure here. The doors are thick, the windows are leaded, so very hard to break. And Renee sets the alarm every night. But you're right, it's a bit ridiculous to have it here.'

'Why don't you sell it? It would be worth millions. You'd be able to secure this place.'

Nicholas nodded. 'True. But I'm keeping it as a bargaining chip just in case I get hit with the death taxes. The revenue might accept it in lieu.'

'Oh yes. I see. Not a bad plan.' She looked over at Nicholas. 'Are you fond of this house?'

'I love it. My mother loved it too, though she said it could be deathly cold, and they all suffered freezing hands and feet all winter long. She ended up living in Cyprus where it was always warm – I'm sure it was because of this place – but she came back often. She couldn't stay away for long. She died a few years back. My uncle Harry was in line to inherit it but he died quite young, with no family of his own. Geraldine has been here forever. She taught French at Spring Hall for years and then became headmistress of a local girls' school. Somehow she kept this place going. And then she told me that I was the one who'd have to take the house on after she died. I know she wants me to keep it in the family – but I don't want to saddle Coco with it. The chances are that it'll be sold to a developer or something, and the money will get divided up between all the cousins that are left.' Nicholas shrugged. 'Sometimes things come to an end. I think maybe my family's time here is up, after six hundred or so years.'

'It seems sad somehow.'

'Do you want to see the rest?'

'Yes please.'

They spent an hour wandering around the rooms, most emptied of everything but their basic furniture. Nicholas told her that there were boxes and boxes of things in the attics. On one of the landings, Caitlyn stopped, her attention caught by some unusual plasterwork. Going up to examine it, she saw that it was a pattern of circus figures and dancers among swirls and dashes of decorative work. From a distance it appeared almost Jacobean but close up it was clearly more modern.

'Look at this, it's fabulous!'

'Oh yes. The result of boredom, I think. Apparently there'd been a fire and the old plaster was destroyed. This was done for fun during a very long and dull winter. It wouldn't be allowed now – just dolloping what you fancy on a wall. The conservation people would be right after you.'

'It's lovely. Very Bloomsbury.' Caitlyn examined the intricate figures, entranced by the details and the energy in them. There was a ringmaster, and a strongman holding his weight, and an acrobat on a wire. A seal balanced a ball on his nose and a lion sat on a little dais. Ballerinas spun and jumped. 'This is quite a treasure.'

'Do you think so?' Nicholas was surprised. 'I don't suppose it's by anyone famous.'

'I'm interested.' She took out her phone and snapped a couple of pictures of it. 'Do you know who did it?'

'No. But Geraldine might.'

Nicholas showed her the bathrooms and kitchen, apologising for their old-fashioned appearance. 'They haven't been done up for years. They function – they just don't look very smart.'

'They look amazing,' Caitlyn said, entranced by the huge old baths with their copper taps, the high-cisterned lavatories, and the old range in the kitchen, next to a newer electric stove. 'I really love it. I mean, it's huge and impractical but . . .' She looked at him with excitement. 'Would it really be possible to live here – even if just for a while?'

'Oh yes, I'm sure it would. But take your time. Don't rush into anything. Think it over first. You'd be out here on your own, you know, with only a nonagenarian for company – don't believe Aunt's nonsense about being only eighty-five!'

When they went back to the old lady's sitting room to say goodbye, she was sound asleep so there was no asking her about the frescos. Renee showed them out, promising to give her their farewells.

'I don't know about you but I'm starving,' said Nicholas as they stepped out into the open air. When she heartily agreed, he said, 'Good. Let's go to the pub in the village.'

They were finishing up their lunch when Nicholas said, 'You haven't really told me yet why you came to Oxford. Is it because you and Max's dad split up?'

Caitlyn had been enjoying the tales of Nicholas's life at the college, and was taken by surprise. 'No, not exactly. I should have said before . . . my husband died.' She smiled at him, to balance the look of concern that immediately crossed his face. 'I didn't mean to say it quite like that, but that's how it is. He was killed suddenly in a car accident. Max was already at Spring Hall, and I didn't want to move him. So I moved me instead. And it was a good thing to do. I had had enough of London. We needed a change.'

'I'm so sorry, Caitlyn,' Nicholas said in a low voice. He put down his fork, as though eating was now in bad taste. 'What an awful thing to happen. When was this?'

'Just over six months ago.'

He looked bewildered. 'So soon . . . ? You moved here in that time?'

She laughed lightly and said, 'London houses sell quickly.'

'I didn't mean that. I mean . . . I don't know. You changed your life so fast.'

'It had been changed for me. Nothing could be more elemental than losing Patrick. Moving house was child's play after that.'

'Of course.' Nicholas shifted a little awkwardly and bit his lip. 'Well. I'm very sorry to hear that.'

'Thank you.'

She could tell that he was uncomfortable now. She wasn't a divorcee on the lookout for another relationship – *if that's what he's been thinking* – but a widow reeling from her recent bereavement. It put a different complexion on things, she guessed. She wished she could have kept it secret, she'd been enjoying the light-hearted chat that Nicholas now probably thought was inappropriate.

Despite her efforts, they couldn't get back the easy companionability of before. They paid the bill, going halves, and went back to the car. Once they were on their way back to Oxford, the engine was again too loud for conversation, and she was grateful for it.

'Thank you for today,' she said as they pulled up outside her house. 'I enjoyed it a lot.'

'Me too.' Nicholas smiled at her, his brown eyes warm. He seemed to be over the awkwardness of lunchtime.

'I'm sorry that things got a little gloomy.'

'Don't be. And it's hardly your fault.'

'I know but . . .' She sighed.

'What is it?' he asked softly.

'I wanted this to be . . . well, not overshadowed by what's

happened. I carry it round with me all the time. And sometimes it feels good to put it to one side, just for a while.'

'I understand.' He smiled at her again. 'I want you to know that it would be great to see you again – as friends. We were friends once, weren't we, in the third year . . . remember?'

The words triggered something and a rush of memories descended on her, fluttering images that she'd thought were gone forever.

How could I have forgotten?

For the first two years of their time in Oxford, their paths had hardly crossed. They weren't tutorial partners; they didn't go to the same parties or do the same activities. Nicholas rowed for the college and that kept him busy on a different schedule to hers. She remembered going up to the college boat house to watch the races, sipping on Pimms and seeing him go past, his face a picture of intense concentration as he pulled on the oars in perfect time with his crew, their muscles hard and rippling. It had been the first time she'd thought how attractive he was.

'God, dishy rowers,' Sara had said. 'I'm on the pull later, definitely.'

Of course. Sara was there too.

Then, in their third year, living back in college, Nicholas had given up rowing to concentrate on his finals. They'd started to see each other in the library, sometimes sit together at lunch or dinner. Nicholas began coming round to her room after dinner, and she'd make coffee or open a bottle of wine and they'd talk for ages, and she'd feel herself sparkling under his attention. She would wonder if he was going to make a move on her, but nothing ever happened. After a while, he'd gather up his gown and say, 'Back to the grindstone!' and head off to his rooms. And she'd think, *Oh, he doesn't really like me. Not like that.*

But each time he came back to her room, she'd feel that hum of possibility, the sparking attraction between them.

Where was Sara? Why wasn't I with her in the evenings then? We were usually together. The thought floated through her mind, distracting her for a moment. *Of course. Sara wasn't there because she didn't do her finals. She didn't finish. She dropped out.*

'Caitlyn?' he asked, prodding her out of her reverie. 'We were friends, weren't we?'

'Yes,' she said slowly, 'of course we were.'

'Good.' He paused as though on the brink of saying something else, but changed his mind and said briskly, 'I'll drop you a line. And let me know what you want to do about the house when you've had the chance to think it over. I'll speak to Aunt Geraldine.'

'Okay.' She hardly saw him as she climbed out of the car, her mind was flooded by the rush of images. The memory she had suppressed was suddenly loud and clear in her imagination. 'I'll wait to hear. Goodbye, Nicholas.'

'Goodbye.'

As he drove away, she waved after him, only now able to remember why they had lost touch all those years ago.

Chapter Eighteen

The storm that night was the worst they had ever seen. The windows on the ground floor had new shutters of white, and from upstairs the view across the fields was almost unbroken white as though everything had been swallowed whole by a great white beast.

The wireless, in dramatic tones, reported that the country had been brought to a standstill, that most of England had been swathed in snow and that Scotland was entirely cut off. Temperatures had dropped to record lows, and already there were fears for people stranded in remote villages and hamlets, with plans being made to drop in supplies, for there seemed to be no sign of the cold weather lifting in the immediate future.

Tommy listened, nestling inside her fur coat, keeping as close to the kitchen range as she could while Ada bustled about making breakfast. Tommy had woken to find her bedroom cold, her breath coming out in clouds and the window panes lined with ice. She struggled out, gasping at the chill, and pulled on her clothes before hurrying to find the children.

'Come on, put on your warmest clothes,' she urged. 'And come downstairs as soon as you can.'

Thornton and Ada had not gone home last night as the blizzard had made it impossible so they had stayed over in the old housekeeper's rooms in Mrs Whitfield's house.

'I can't see us getting back today,' Ada said, worried. 'I hope Tatty will be all right.'

'Tatty?' asked Tommy, putting a saucepan of milk on the range to heat up, thanking her stars again that the coal had arrived just in time.

'The cat. She won't be happy that we didn't come home.' Ada shook her head. 'We shall have to see if we can get back today.'

'Have you looked outside, darling?' Tommy asked. 'It's got to be six feet deep out there. Thank goodness we got back when we did.'

'Yes, you were lucky,' Ada said solemnly, wiping her hands on her apron. 'Any longer and I dread to think . . . Your friend is upstairs, is she?'

'Yes. I'm sure she and Molly are still sleeping. It was quite a day for them. I put them both in the rose bedroom with fresh hot water bottles. We were all frozen to the bone. I hope Molly has recovered, I was quite worried about her.' Tommy looked back at the surface of the milk trembling as it warmed.

'They said on the news this cold will be here for some time. What on earth shall we do, cut off like this?'

'I'm sure we'll be fine, dear, don't worry.' Tommy hoped

she sounded certain of herself, despite the worry that was eating away at her.

Her mother came into breakfast and announced that she had decided to move back into the main house.

'It can't be right, heating my house as well. I know I gave up my evening fires, but if I move across, we'll save more fuel,' she said, sitting down at the table, twice her usual size with jumpers, cardigans and a raincoat on. The room was freezing cold, the windows frosted with icy patterns. Tommy wore her fur-lined boots but her toes were still numb and the children wore their outdoor coats and scarves as they munched on toast that had long cooled and gone stiff. Even the boiling cocoa had turned tepid as soon as it came out of the kitchen.

'Perhaps that's true,' Tommy said. 'But I thought the best thing would be for us all to move into your place, as it's so much smaller and cosier.'

'That's a good idea,' Gerry piped up. She had on a large woollen tartan beret and a scarf wrapped tightly around her neck and she held her cocoa mug with fingers wrapped around to extract all the warmth. 'I keep dreaming of the stove in Mother's sitting room.'

'But where would we all sleep?' Mrs Whitfield asked gravely. 'I don't have the room, not with Mrs Hastings and Mr Burton Brown as well. Perhaps we could have made do without them, but as it is ... and I don't know when the Thorntons will get back home.'

'Yes. We'll just have to cope in here. But ...' Tommy frowned. 'Gerry's right. Your sitting room is cosier. Let's close our drawing room and stop trying to heat it when it's so vast, and we'll keep your stove going instead. It's more efficient than the fireplace. It will be a squeeze but at least we'll have somewhere warm to go. And then you can stay in your bedroom, Mother, it'll be warmer than any room in this part.'

'Very well,' said her mother. She sighed. 'This weather is astonishing. I've never seen anything like it.'

'Can we play outside later?' asked Harry. 'I'm going to put grease on my sledge so I can go extra fast.'

'Perhaps.' Tommy looked over at the windows, piled high outside with snow so that only a patch of foggy grey sky was visible beyond. 'I wonder what state the car is in.'

'Perhaps you'll never find it again,' Gerry said. 'Or not till spring, when we'll find a rusted skeleton in the lane.'

'I hope not. And I'd like to find it before then – all of Mrs Hastings' things are in it.'

Roger came in, his face white with cold except for his nose which was pink, and he sniffed, slapping his sides with his arms. 'My God. Can't we switch on those blasted radiators?'

'They are on,' Tommy replied. 'At least they were, but you know how rubbish they are. I'm trying to keep them on to stop them freezing, but we need to save oil as well. So we can't turn them up.'

'This is inhuman.' Roger breathed out. 'Look at that! My breath is like smoke, here in the dining room. We'll all freeze to death at this rate.'

'No we won't,' Tommy said quickly, looking at the children's anxious faces. 'We'll be perfectly all right, especially with Granny's stove going.' She smiled at Antonia and Harry.

'Perhaps you can persuade Ada to let you make some toffee with her precious treacle.'

'Where's Fred?' demanded Roger, looking around.

'Still in bed. I think he was shattered after yesterday. And you know he hasn't been well since he saw that awful doctor in Oxford.'

'Oh yes. Oxford.' Roger made a face. He hadn't liked Fred and Tommy going off together one bit and had been in a sulk for days afterwards.

'I'm sure he'll be down soon. And you must meet Barbara. She's staying with us for a while.'

Roger grunted and sat down at the table. 'I expect the toast has turned to ice.'

'I'll get you some more,' Tommy said soothingly, and got up to go back to the kitchen.

Roger was crotchety and dissatisfied with everything, evidently missing Fred. Everyone was relieved when he decided to go back to bed.

The children went outside to explore this new, epic level of snow that made the previous fall look like a practice run. Tommy told them to be careful, as it was more than twice Harry's height and he could get buried if he didn't look out. So they played in the courtyard at the back of the kitchen, making tunnels and mazes and gradually clearing quite a large part of it. Tommy changed into her stoutest trousers and put on a woollen jacket over her jumper and a pair of shooting socks. Then she found her mother's old skis in the boot room, and took them outside.

'What on earth are you doing?' Gerry asked, her pink nose just above her scarf and blue eyes just below her beret, watching as Tommy struggled to put them on by the back door.

'I'm going to try and find the car,' she said, strapping her boots into the bindings. Then she pulled on her father's old fur-lined leather skiing mittens.

'It'll be buried,' Gerry said, jumping up and down on the spot.

'Maybe. I've got the shovel too.' She turned to show that she'd strapped the shovel to her back with a belt. 'And a rope to drag a suitcase back. You see, if I ski, then we can get to the village. Hasn't it occurred to you that we're now completely cut off? What will we do for milk and food?'

Gerry stopped jumping. 'I hadn't thought of that.'

'No. That's why I'm trying the skis. Look, I can get up here where the drift is low.' She took the poles and manoeuvred herself awkwardly to where she could walk sideways up the drift. 'My goodness, I haven't done this for years. I hope I remember how.'

Gradually she found the level. Her skis sank a couple of inches and then she was stable on the surface, with a new and unfamiliar view of everything. She could see how the snow had banked up against the garden walls and the barns, and now she was high, she could see the tops of hedges and the snowcapped forest, even over the faint outline of the church spire. But the air was foggy with ice and as she breathed she could feel the prickle of tiny icicles in her nostrils. 'I won't be able to stay out for long,' she said. 'But it can't hurt to have a go.'

Tommy set off, pushing herself along on the skis in the direction of the lane. It was hard work without a slope to go down and she was soon feeling warmer as she pushed herself along with the poles, sliding a few feet before she had to force herself forward again, although the exercise did nothing to warm up her hands and feet.

The car can't be that far away, she thought, keeping an eagle eye out for it. She was soon used to the movement of the skis, her old knowledge coming back to her, and she felt confident of being able to move easily. *It must be completely buried. Wait – what's that?*

Tommy caught sight of some blackness in the snow, and as she approached, she saw that it was the roof of the car. The wind had blown the snow over it, leaving a small part exposed. She came up to it, and put down her poles, so she could scrape away some of the snow.

Thank goodness we didn't stay in here. I'm sure we would have frozen to death.

She snapped off her skis and promptly sank through the snow to find herself standing on the back of the car. She pulled out her shovel and started to clear away the snow from around the car. It was hard work and she was at it for some time before she was able to move safely to the back where the suitcases had been put. Thank goodness Fred had thought to move them from the boot to the back seat when he collected the shovel.

Tommy managed to get the back door open and pulled out

one of the cases. There was no way she could manage two of them, one would be hard enough, so she chose one and left the other there. She would have to come back for it. Then she prepared herself for the journey home, this time with a large case to pull behind her.

'The lake is completely frozen,' Tommy said, coming back into the kitchen, breathless. 'I could see it from the top of the lane. It's beautiful out there but . . . oh my fingers!'

'Did you really manage?' Gerry said, excitedly jumping up from the table. 'The children and I were just planning our rescue mission. Hermione and Hebe were going to pull the sledges.'

'We were going to mush them,' Antonia said. 'Like Captain Scott's pack of dogs pulling them to the South Pole.'

'Mush, mush, mush, all along the lane,' Harry added. 'But we weren't going to eat them.'

'But,' Antonia said sadly, 'you're back.'

'Sorry to thwart your mission. At least you're defrosted from this morning.' Tommy looked around. 'Where is everyone?'

'Thornton is trying to make a path back to their cottage – he's ever so cross that his last one's been covered up. Ada is out looking for her cat. Granny is sewing. Mr Burton Brown isn't up yet.' Gerry tapped off the household members on her fingers. 'Roger went back to bed in a grump because it's so cold. And your friend Mrs Hastings came in for something on a tray for her daughter, and then disappeared again. Goodness, she's pretty, isn't she?'

'Yes, I suppose she is. I'll go and find her. I've got her case.'

The advantage of being out all morning was that the house felt quite warm in comparison, even if it was still very cold. Tommy went upstairs with the suitcase and knocked on the door of the rose bedroom, so called after the Victorian printed wallpaper in a trellis of roses all over it – on the walls and ceilings, with a matching fabric for the curtains. A bit much, Tommy had always thought, like being smothered in blossom, but it had its charm.

Barbara answered the door.

'Good morning,' Tommy said, smiling and holding out the suitcase. 'How are you? Look what I've got.'

'Goodness me, however did you get it?' Barbara said, looking down in astonishment. 'I've seen the snow out of the window. Has someone towed the car back?'

'Oh no. I went and got it.'

'On your own?'

'Yes. I'll get the other one later.'

Barbara looked bemused. 'How extraordinary.'

'Are you all right? How is Molly?'

'Recovering. It was rather an ordeal. I'm going to stay with her until she's ready to come down.'

'Of course.' Tommy peered past her into the bedroom but couldn't make out anything in the gloom beyond. The curtains were drawn. Barbara seemed to be unaffected by the previous night; her clothes looked neat and tidy despite the walk through the snow. Her golden hair was carefully combed and tied back and she wore bright red lipstick that made her pale eyes even more piercing.

'We'll be down for lunch. What time will it be?'

'Oh, it's all a bit ramshackle today with the snow. I expect it will be sandwiches at one o'clock in the kitchen.'

'I see. Thank you.' Barbara went to close the door, then hesitated. 'I do appreciate this, Tommy, really. I know you didn't want to have us. And now you've got us until this snow clears. I'm grateful.'

'Oh.' Tommy felt at once embarrassed. Barbara was no fool, but she felt compelled to do as she always did and say what was expected. 'On the contrary. We're happy to have you. Come down when you're ready.'

She paused for a moment on the way back downstairs, looking up the passage to where Fred's bedroom door remained closed. It wasn't like him not to come downstairs in good time. She hadn't yet known him stay in bed so late. Wondering if she should go and knock on his door, she paused on the landing.

He's probably just tired out from last night. It was quite an evening.

If he didn't come down for lunch, she told herself, she would go and check, just in case.

Then she went downstairs to start on the sandwiches.

Chapter Nineteen

The day after the visit to Kings Harcourt, there was an email from Nicholas in Caitlyn's inbox.

> Thanks for coming yesterday. I really enjoyed it. I've sent a letter to Aunt Geraldine (the phone's no good, she's too deaf) to ask her if she'd like to rent the main house to you, but my guess is, she'd be delighted. She always prefers it when there are people there. I'll let you know when I hear back from her. Maybe we can meet up and discuss it. Drop me a line if you've got any questions . . .
>
> Nicholas x

Caitlyn read it through twice. It was a perfectly nice message – friendly, normal, kind.

Can I accept an offer to rent the house? she thought anxiously. *I mean, it's wonderful. I loved it and so would Max. It's a bit remote but for a summer while I look for somewhere to buy, it would be perfect.* She imagined Maura and the family coming to spend the long summer holidays, with

201

Callum joining them at weekends, the children playing in the gardens and in the fields, barbecues on the terrace . . . Nicholas had said there was even an ancient swimming pool.

But how can I? After all, he turned out to be like all the rest, unable to resist Sara. All the rest except Patrick.

She closed the message and put him out of her mind. There were plenty of other things to think about, after all. It was almost half-term and Maura had suggested that Max come and stay with her and the family for a few days, if Caitlyn wanted some time to herself.

Time to myself! I'm alone so much.

But actually the prospect appealed to her. She wanted Max to enjoy being with his boisterous cousins, but it wasn't something she could yet handle. Her days were usually so framed by his needs and his timetable that, if she was really going to have to pack up the house again and prepare to move, it would be good to have a few clear days. They arranged for Maura to drive up on the Friday, collect Max and take him back to London.

'Hello, you're looking well,' Maura said as she came into the cottage.

'Am I?' Caitlyn flushed. 'I haven't done anything different.'

Maura smiled and tossed her coat down on the sofa. 'I'm really glad. Oxford obviously suits you. I always thought you were a little bit lost in your old house. This is not so smart as you were used to – but it's more you.'

'I suppose it is.' Caitlyn looked around. There was no pale

blue or grey to be seen. The exquisite perfection of her last home had been replaced with piles of books on tables, cups on the draining board, a mishmash of cushions squashed wherever they'd last been sat on. It would have driven Patrick nuts.

I suppose without him, I'm slipping back to my ordinary old self.

It gave her a pang to think about it: the years with Patrick which at times had seemed oppressive but were also so full of beauty, sparkle and glamour.

She pushed the sadness away by telling Maura about the notice to quit.

'What?' Maura exclaimed. 'But you've only just got here!'

'I know. The timing's rubbish. I'm looking for somewhere else. Somewhere in Oxford, I suppose. Unless I move closer to the school.'

'Wouldn't you be bored to tears in some dead-end village?'

'Maybe.' Caitlyn smiled. 'Or maybe I need to get away from Oxford. Too many memories.'

'I thought you loved it here when you were a student.'

'I did but . . . you know. It wasn't all good.' She thought of Nicholas, then said quickly, 'Anyway, how are the kids?'

After a good long catch-up, Maura took an excited Max away with her, leaving the house calm and quiet. Caitlyn went to the mirror over the fireplace and gazed at her reflection. She was thinner, definitely. More hollow-cheeked. After all those years of worrying, she'd not thought about her weight for ages and this was the result. But without Patrick to cook for, she barely ate in the evenings and rarely drank.

But I look so old, she thought, pinching her cheeks to smooth out the line from her nose to her mouth. *Old and tired*. There was a broad line of dark roots at her parting. Her golden brown highlights had not been topped up since before Patrick died. Grey wisps floated over her ears and sprang up around her hairline. *Well, I'm not eighteen any more, and that's that. I'm not that girl any more. I might as well leave it all in the past, just as Nicholas has.*

But the memories of what had once almost been were too strong to resist.

The exams were over and at last Caitlyn could relax and celebrate. The college threw them a special finals dinner. They'd dressed up: black tie for the boys, evening dresses for the girls, all wearing their gowns over the top, the dark cotton flapping around them like bats' wings. A scholar's gown for her, falling to her ankles, framing her black velvet dress, because she'd won the scholarship, the one that Sara had told her so confidently that she – Sara – was going to get. They'd assembled in one of the grand college rooms for drinks beforehand. She remembered Nicholas now, so very handsome suddenly in his dinner jacket, his bow tie at a slightly jaunty angle, making her want to reach out and straighten it, though she didn't dare. They'd drunk champagne with their tutors, all chattering away, almost dizzy with relief that the exams were over and now they were free of the burden of finals hanging over their heads. They'd talked about their future plans and what awaited them after the summer. And all the time, despite spending ages with Dr Yates, she'd been aware of Nicholas, always close.

Maybe tonight, she'd thought. *Maybe.*

They'd gone to the Senior Common Room dining room for dinner, a place they'd never seen before and never would again – *but Nicholas must go there all the time now* – and dinner had been served, five courses on shimmering antique golden plates with the best wines from the college cellar, and then coffee in the drawing room.

I'll never do this again, she'd thought, telling herself to enjoy every moment, but all she could really think about was Nicholas. *Because it's our last chance.* Even if they kept in touch, this was the last time they would be here, belonging to this place and everything it had meant to them. Sometimes she'd glance at him and find his eyes on her, and a pleasurable rush would zoom through her, the tingle of anticipation flooding out to her fingertips. *It's got to be tonight.*

And, inevitably, they had gravitated together. When the tutors had bidden them farewell, congratulated them on three years well lived and wished them luck for the results that would soon be posted, they had strolled out together into the dark quad, stars glittering overhead and a great silver disc of a moon glowing above the bell tower.

'Let's go to the garden,' Nicholas said, and they walked through the echoing hall where the staircase led up to the dining room, and then out over the crunching gravel to the wooden door in a wall that led to the garden. Inside, he lit a cigarette and exhaled a plume of dark grey smoke into the navy-blue night. They hardly needed to say a word to each other. They knew what was going to happen.

In the darkness of the garden, the richness of fine red wine flowing through them, they turned at last to one another and he pulled her to him, throwing down his cigarette and kissing her hard. He tasted of smoke and honey, and the exhilaration of the kiss, and all its utter rightness, flooded through her. The long, long build-up, the weeks of low-level flirtation, and the mutual craving came together to intoxicate her beyond anything she'd yet known. The clumsy kisses and the silly sweet ineptness of Charlie – long gone, sometime in her second year – and anyone else she'd dallied with . . . all of it was like a necessary prelude to this, the real, grown-up version of what she'd been looking for.

They kissed for long minutes, then Nicholas pulled away and said breathlessly, 'Let's go to my room.'

'Yours?' He was a dark shadow in front of her eyes, the wind blowing her hair in finely whipping strands over her face.

'It's closest.'

'Yes.' He had a room tucked away from the main quad, the staircase almost invisible if you didn't know it was there. They had passed it on their way to the garden. She thought of strange little practicalities, things she needed if she was going to stay the night in his room. She wanted it to be right, not a scramble of embarrassment. She was aware that she had cinched herself in with an ugly elasticated support thing and knew she didn't want him to see it. 'I'll go back to my place first.'

'Really?' He dropped his smoky velvet-soft lips on hers again. 'You don't need to.'

For a moment she was tempted. What did it matter? But then, she realised, she'd been dreaming of this moment, fantasising about it. She wanted it to be right.

'No. I will. I'll be back. I promise.'

'Okay. I'll go to mine.' He kissed her and smiled, she could feel it under her own mouth, then murmured, 'Don't be long, will you?'

'Of course not.' She left him at the echoing staircase, and walked along the deserted quad, elated and rejoicing. Something wonderful was waiting for her, a glorious adventure was about to begin, one that she had known was coming and had wanted for so long. But now, it was all perfect: the time was right and they both knew it.

She saw no one on her return, though lights were burning in rooms all over the quad where she lived. She sang to herself, almost floating. *Too much of the college wine. But I don't care. I'm glad.* At the door to her room, she fished her key from the little evening bag she was carrying, and opened it.

'Caitlyn.'

She turned to see Sara stepping out of the shadows. 'Oh . . . hi! What are you doing here?'

'Have you had a good time?' A bitter look twisted Sara's beautiful face. 'I don't suppose any of you missed me.'

'Of course we did.' Sara's presence had a drenching effect on her happiness. Why did things that were fun, light-hearted, innocent, become something else when she was around? It shouldn't be true, when Sara loved parties and playing so much. But it was. She reached for a white lie. 'We all talked about you. How much we missed you, and wished you were there.'

'Really?' Sara looked wistful, then suddenly harsh. 'Well, fuck them all. I don't give a shit! I hate Yates. I'd still be here if it weren't for him telling me I couldn't cope. It was his stupid fault. Tosser.' She gazed at Caitlyn, poised at the door of her room. 'Shall we go in? Have you still got that vodka?'

'Well . . . I . . .' Caitlyn dropped her gaze, suddenly nervous.

'What?' Sara pounced like a cat on a fluttering moth. 'What is it? Are you all carrying on the party somewhere else?'

Caitlyn felt wretched. She was sorry for Sara, sympathetic to the fact that she hadn't been able to carry on the course. The tutors had told Sara frankly that she couldn't manage the workload, even if she did the work, which she didn't. She had been asked politely to leave. She had managed to blag staying in her college room until the end of term, and had been wafting about pretending nothing had happened. But even she couldn't get an invitation to the finals dinner. This evening was for them, the ones who had gone every day, twice a day, for a tortuous week to sit those examinations, and who had survived the process. Whatever else she'd suffered, Sara hadn't done that. She couldn't join that club. It was the first time ever that Caitlyn felt she had something that Sara did not. And whereas in the past Sara had always made the most of any situation to make Caitlyn feel inferior, Caitlyn felt it was the last thing she would ever do to Sara. She couldn't rub it in, or gloat, however casually. But she wanted to get away from Sara as quickly as she could, before the joy of kissing Nicholas and the delightful anticipation of being with him began to diminish.

'Sorry, you can't come in,' she said quickly, almost breathlessly.

'Why not?'

'I'm . . .' She wanted to lie but had paused too long and now couldn't. 'Well . . . I'm going to see Nicholas.'

Sara's eyes narrowed. 'Really? Why?'

'Because . . .' She took a deep breath. 'I think we're going to spend the night together. But take the vodka if you want it, I'll get it for you—'

Sara laughed, a bitter, harsh little sound. 'Oh. So that's his game.'

Caitlyn was` wary. 'His game?'

'He said he might have a crack at you. I told him you were too intelligent to let him get away with it.'

Caitlyn felt her stomach churn with something nasty. 'What do you mean – have a crack at me?'

'Oh, come on, you must have guessed something was up. He's been playing you. All that coming up after dinner, spending hours talking to you and never making a move.'

'How did you know about that?' Caitlyn's heart was beating faster, her mouth dry. She almost knew the answer already. But she had to hear it.

'He told me.' Sara put out a hand to her shoulder. 'I'm sorry. I really am. I would have said something before now but I assumed you must be wise to him. And just in case you weren't, I didn't want to distract you from your revision. I know how important it was to you.'

'I see.' She looked down at the wooden floor, noticing all the thick wads of dust that lay between the boards. *How long have they been there? They might be Victorian.* 'So what did he say?'

'Just that he thought you might be up for some fun. No strings. He told me tonight was the last chance to get into your pants.'

Hurt prickled all over her. 'Really? He said that?'

Sara shrugged. 'He's like that, I'm afraid. And believe me, I know.'

'How do you know?'

'Because he's been after me of course.'

Of course, Caitlyn thought dully. *I should have guessed.*

Sara went on: 'He's been trying his luck for ages. He's been round at my room nearly every night. He got drunk in the bar last week and he was all over me – ask Robbie, he saw it all. I had to fight him off. Honestly, I almost had him reported for harassment. You've only seen one side of him. There's another side – and not a nice one.'

'What were you doing in the bar?'

'Well, now you're so diligent and keen on revision, you're not about any more, are you? So I went down there with Robbie and his pals.'

'The rugby lot?'

Sara nodded. 'They're a laugh.'

Caitlyn blinked at her. The image of the rugby boys leaping to Sara's defence to ward off a lecherous Nick seemed topsy-turvy somehow. But she felt the dull thud of defeat, knowing that if anyone had to pick between her and Sara, they were

210

going to pick Sara. It was always the same. Nick would be no different to any of the others. He thought she, Caitlyn, was desperate enough to be easy, and Sara was the prize he really wanted.

Of course. He was probably laughing at me behind my back all the time. Wondering how long he'd have to butter me up before I succumbed.

'There's a party in Robbie's room,' Sara said with a shrug. 'I came over to see if you wanted to go to it. It's going to be wild.'

Caitlyn said nothing, a weight of misery descending on her.

'You're not still thinking of going to see Nicholas, are you? You must be insane. He's using you! Come on. Come to Robbie's. We'll have fun. Come on.' Sara took her hand and wheedled. 'Take off the stupid gown, get the vodka and come and party. For me? I'm only looking out for you, you know.'

There was a long pause. Then Caitlyn said, 'Okay. I'll come.'

But the party was grim and she hated it. After two hours of loud music and hot bodies dancing and drinking, she slipped away, leaving Sara writhing about with Robbie. In the cooler air of the quad, she wondered about going to see Nicholas.

But what's the point? He wants Sara, not me. And it's too late now anyway.

So she went back to her room to go to bed. She didn't see Nicholas again after that, and at the end of term, everybody went their separate ways.

Chapter Twenty .

Barbara was quiet and polite and made no trouble, just as Veronica had said. Over their sandwiches on the first day of her visit, she'd charmed Mrs Whitfield, who was evidently pleased with the good manners and elegant femininity of their guest. Tommy felt the contrast, as she was still wearing her stout trousers and thick knitted jumper, and her hair was in a state from the hat she'd worn while collecting the suitcase.

She had a sudden vision of the classroom of their Oxford school and recalled that Barbara had been the same then: beautifully turned out, very self-possessed, somehow a little distant as though she wasn't quite as involved in the messiness of everyday life as the rest of them were.

'I'm just going upstairs to check on Roger,' Tommy said, and left them all to their sandwiches.

From behind Roger's door came the rattle of a snore so she went along the passage and across the landing to Fred's door. There was silence from the room beyond.

She knocked lightly on the door. 'Fred?' After a moment, she tried again. 'Fred, are you there?'

There was a groan from within. Worried, she called louder. 'Fred, please let me know if you're all right.'

Another groan came and she couldn't stop herself any longer. She opened the door and let herself into the room, which was dark and very cold. She could see that in the four-poster bed that dominated the bedroom a shape lay large and still. Going over, she could make out Fred and as her eyes adjusted to the light, she could see that his face was covered in sweat. He appeared to be asleep.

'Fred, it's me, Tommy. Are you sick?' She put out a hand and touched him. His skin was fiercely hot. 'Oh my goodness. You're the only person in this house who's warm. You shouldn't have come out last night. You've got a fever.' Tommy wondered if it was anything to do with his wound, and if she should try and examine him. But it seemed far too intimate an act. It would mean pulling back his blankets and lifting his pyjama top. She couldn't do it. Instead, she stood and regarded him, feeling helpless. Then she went downstairs to find Ada. If she couldn't look at the wound, she could at least do whatever else was possible to make him comfortable.

When Fred woke up later, Tommy was sitting in the corner of his room, reading in the lamplight. A fire burned in his grate and the room was warmer than before. At his feet was a hot water bottle, one of the last rubber ones, and a jug of water was next to him on his night table, along with a cup of hot water and honey.

As soon as she saw he was awake, Tommy got up and went over to him. 'You must drink this,' she said firmly, lifting up the drink. 'It's not exactly hot now, but it's got aspirin in it. Are you in pain?'

Fred blinked and winced. 'Yes. My wound. It's inflamed.'

'I can tell – you're running a temperature. The aspirin will help a little. I don't know what else we can do at the moment.'

Fred, still a little groggy, tried to sit up and grimaced again at the effort. 'We should try and clean it, I think. The blasted doctor must have infected me somehow when he prodded around. The main thing is that I don't get blood poisoning. That could do me in pretty quickly.'

'Do you in?' Tommy echoed, shocked. 'But I thought you were almost better!'

'Infection is the killer,' Fred said. 'I've seen men die in hours from septic shock.' He sat himself up. 'Can you take a look?'

'Of course,' Tommy said, suddenly wishing she had taken up nursing service during the war, instead of running a farm. *If only I knew what to do.*

Fred pushed back his blanket and lifted his pyjama top. Underneath was a dressing taped to his side, a large white square that covered most of his torso. Tommy bit back a gasp at the sight of it.

'Have you been looking after this on your own?' she asked.

He nodded. 'I have plenty of dressings and I've been changing it regularly. I didn't want to worry you all with it. I'd almost run out which is why I went to see that quack in Oxford. I think we must clean and re-dress it.'

'Yes,' Tommy said, trying not to show her apprehension. 'I'll get some warm water and clean cloths.'

214

'I've got some antiseptic,' he said. 'We must put plenty on, to minimise the infection.'

'I won't be long.'

Tommy was back five minutes later with water that had boiled in the kettle and some freshly cleaned cloths.

'I don't know how sterile they are,' she said, 'but they're all we have.'

'They'll do.' Fred smiled at her. 'Thank you, Tommy.'

'Don't be silly, as if I wouldn't help you. Let's see to this wound.'

She had to hold back another gasp after she had lifted the dressing from Fred's side. Beneath was a huge patch of angry red and purple skin, raw in places, puckered at the edges and, in the middle, covered with a sticky whitish yellow film.

'That's where the infection is,' Fred said, looking at it. 'The idiot stuck his finger in my side. He must have transferred something nasty there.'

'Oh Fred. It looks painful.'

'It is. I can't deny.'

'I'll do my best not to hurt you.'

Tommy dipped a cloth in the warm water and gently began to clean the wound, stopping when Fred's wincing and gasps of pain got too much, then starting again when he'd recovered. Gradually, she worked over the great red stain. Then she soaked another cloth in the antiseptic from the bottle Fred pointed out on the chimney piece, and covered the wound with it. 'We'll let it soak in,' she said. 'Does it sting?'

'Rather,' he said in a tight voice. 'But I know it's good pain. So I can bear it.'

'A bit like having a baby,' Tommy said with a laugh.

'I imagine that might be a bit worse than this.'

'At least you know a baby will be over within a few hours. How long have you been suffering like this?'

'A while. My last doctor said that my diet wasn't providing enough vitamins to encourage healing. But we are all in the same boat.'

Tommy said crossly, 'I've been an idiot. I'd forgotten you needed nourishment. You're an invalid, and that's all there is to it. You'll have soup, good soup, and plenty of the fruit that we bottled in the summer. Why didn't I think of it before? And coming out in the freezing cold last night was the last thing you should have done.'

'Don't be silly. You needed me.'

'I suppose I did,' she said softly. 'And now you need me.'

For the next two days, Tommy was a nurse. She and Ada boiled up a ham bone and made a nourishing barley soup and plied Fred with it, along with bottled cherries and peaches from the larder, but he had little appetite. His temperature stayed high, so she carried on giving him water and aspirin, keeping the room warm, and trying to find whatever they might have in the medicine cupboard to help drive a fever down and keep infection at bay. She was reluctant to reopen the dressing, thinking she should leave the wound alone to heal without disturbing it.

Fred drifted in and out of sleep, his skin sometimes flushed and hectic, sometimes beaded with sweat. He groaned from time to time, and muttered when he was in the grip of the fever, occasionally talking and laughing so clearly it was as though Tommy was hearing only one side of a mystical conversation.

She disconnected from the life of the house while she was looking after Fred. She knew that Roger had emerged from his room and was drifting about disconsolate, cross at being forbidden from Fred's sick room, but Tommy had decided that Roger's presence wouldn't help.

Gerry took over the care of the children, overseeing their mealtimes and bedtimes, taking them out to play in the snow and teaching them lessons in the afternoons. They had cautiously accepted Molly, who recovered quickly from the ordeal of her journey, and she joined in their games and lessons. Tommy wondered how Barbara was getting on, but she saw little of her. Gerry told her that she spent most of the day with Mrs Whitfield, the two of them staying close to the stove in her sitting room, listening to the wireless reports of the extreme cold and its effects on the country.

Outside, the snow that lay on the ground froze and more squalls brought fresh falls to lie on top of it and freeze again. The second suitcase remained uncollected in the car in the lane, and Tommy rang the next-door farmer to ask if the car could be dug out and towed back by the tractor. He said he would see what he could do, but the blasted weather was hampering everything and his sheep were freezing to death in the fields.

When she wasn't ministering to Fred, she was worrying

about their situation. There was enough wheat flour left for Ada to bake a loaf of bread or two, but no one liked the stuff, which was grey and mealy and tasted dusty. All they would have for milk in a day or so was a tin of powdered skimmed milk that Tommy had bought on rations a while ago in case of an emergency like this, but it wouldn't last long. They had plenty of cocoa but their tea supplies were not very good. They had Barbara and Molly's ration books now, it was true, but they would be useless as Barbara was probably registered in Oxford and anyway, how much in the way of supplies could have got to the village shop in this weather? There were eight adults, including the Thorntons while they were here, and three children to feed.

We've got plenty of potatoes and oatmeal, and lots of stored root vegetables, and thank goodness for our pigs and chickens. I'll get a pig butchered if we have to, and hang the government – they can have their half if they want to come and get it. We have the eggs that Ada has stored as well. But milk and bread and butter and tea and sugar . . .

One of the problems was solved when Ada went out to feed the chickens and came back in to the dining room where they were all having breakfast, weeping, saying, 'Poor little things! I should have thought.'

'What is it?' Tommy asked, anxious.

'The hens!'

'Oh, don't tell me the fox has been in! I suppose he must be starving too, but still – all the chickens?'

'Not the fox. They've frozen to death! All of them, cold and stiff.' Ada sniffed and wiped her eyes. 'I should have brought them inside in their boxes at night. It never crossed my mind.'

'Well, let's look on the bright side. At least we can eat them now, which we couldn't have if the fox had got them, and they'll keep if they're frozen. Let's put five in the meat safe and prepare one for dinner. They weren't laying anyway. Now we can have our egg ration back too, and get chickens again in the spring.' Tommy smiled, staying as cheerful as she could under the worried gaze of the children and Gerry. 'And for goodness' sake, let's check on the pigs!'

The pigs, though, were perfectly all right, lying in a mountain of hay well mixed with their ordure, kept warm by virtue of the fact that their sty backed onto the kitchen wall where the boiler was situated. They seemed content to lie there all winter, munching on kitchen scraps and slurping warm water from a bucket.

Barbara came to her afterwards and asked for a quiet word. They walked together away from the rest of the family, into the hall. 'I'm sorry, we're going to be such a burden on you,' she said quietly.

'Don't be silly,' Tommy said assuredly. 'It will be perfectly fine. We'll be all right, and I'll get to the village tomorrow for more milk.'

'Yes, but I know very well that our ration books are useless for a week or two. And our entitlement for these weeks will have run out by then. So you're stretching all you have for two more mouths.'

'We're good at stretching. And we have rabbit and pheasant in the game larder, vegetables in storage.'

'Perhaps that's true, but even so.' Barbara looked serious. 'If I can help in any way . . .'

Tommy sighed and said, 'Actually, it's Fred who is my real worry. He isn't getting better. His fever dies down, then springs up again. My aspirin supplies are nearly depleted, and I've nothing to reduce inflammation but the antiseptic.'

'He has an infected wound?' Barbara looked about, as if worried someone might overhear them. 'Then perhaps I can help. I have some penicillin tablets.'

'What?' Tommy was shocked. 'How? I thought all the supplies were with the army.'

'I have some . . . that a doctor friend gave me when Molly was very ill last year. She had meningitis, it was her only hope. He . . . agreed to help me. He gave me more than I needed. I kept them of course. Just in case. Perhaps they would help Fred.'

'I'm sure they would,' Tommy said, and looked away soberly. She was certain that Barbara was telling her the drugs had been obtained illegally. How could they not be? It hadn't been possible to get penicillin whenever it was wanted, not with wounded soldiers taking priority. *But does it really matter? Fred is ill and getting worse. And he was a soldier when he got hurt.*

She had looked at the wound that morning, and even before she uncovered it, she could see that the skin all around it was red and angry, the vivid colour creeping over his whole stomach and round his back. He'd been half conscious, hot and drenched in sweat but shivering. She'd known they needed the doctor but when she tried to call, the lines were down. Now here was Barbara offering exactly what was needed. Perhaps even more than the doctor could offer. *I can't hesitate.*

'I'll take them,' she said quickly. 'Can you give them to me now? The sooner Fred gets his first dose, the better.'

Chapter Twenty-One

Caitlyn received a letter from Geraldine the next day, a polite, old-fashioned note offering her the opportunity to rent Kings Harcourt for six months and promising complete privacy. The handwriting and the address brought the house right back to life in her mind. She had begun to dismiss it as perhaps not as lovely as she remembered, but now she saw it afresh.

Oh, I would love to live there, just for a while. Imagine – a Gainsborough in my hall! Patrick would have adored it. And now – well, it's obvious the old lady is expecting me. I'd feel awful letting her down.

Nicholas hadn't been in touch, though, and she still didn't want to contact him while the memories of their younger selves were so fresh. It felt almost bizarre that they had spent a whole day together without mentioning it, as though nothing had happened.

How could I have forgotten?

Ill at ease with the way her mind could play such tricks on her, she went up into the spare room and looked at the mound of Patrick's boxes she had yet to open. She had been avoiding it, she knew that, but now thoughts of Sara were swirling again through her mind.

They have been ever since I got here. She's what drew me to Nicholas. I suppose all along, deep down, I must have wanted to find out the truth from him, about what happened between the two of them. Just like I do about her and Patrick. I feel as though she's always been there, in all the important relationships of my life.

Caitlyn opened the nearest box and began to look through it. This one had files of old bank statements and insurance policies, and she flicked through them. Patrick had kept that kind of administration away from her, which had added to the stress of selling the house; she'd long forgotten the rigours of forms and small print. One file was an account at his private bank – nothing High Street for Patrick – and scanning through a few months' worth, she noticed that a large monthly payment went in that was quickly reduced to almost nothing by the end of the month. The names he was paying money to meant nothing to her, though they came up again and again. Campanilo Media was one name. Fortescue House was another. Rose Yard Flowers appeared several times. But the largest payment went out every month to Allegra Communications.

Have I heard of them? It rings a bell somehow.

Caitlyn put the file back in the box. She knew that Patrick did a lot of entertaining and gift buying as part of his job. Perhaps this account was for that. In fact, his financial arrangements were vast and complex, and she couldn't begin to understand them. She had put them all in the hands of

Theo Ronson, his long-term accountant, and asked him to sort out whatever was necessary so that she had the funds she needed and had paid whatever had to be paid. Theo had been happy to help and had arranged it so that she had a monthly payment into her account and a large sum invested to provide an income, as well as establishing a trust for Max. She knew that she wasn't poor. Patrick had done all the right things. His insurance payout and the compensation claim that was in hand would more than provide for them. It was typical of him that he had thought of every eventuality.

I suppose I ought to wise up and start learning how to manage. I can't go on relying on Patrick and all his minions any more. But Allegra Communications. Where have I heard that name before?

She turned back to the boxes but the two she opened were more of the same admin. She read through the papers until the printouts were swimming in front of her eyes, then closed them up. There were still more boxes to go through.

Somewhere in them is the truth about Patrick. I'm sure of it.

Caitlyn was in a supermarket the next morning when her phone went, and she fished it out of her pocket and answered it without looking at the caller ID.

'Caitlyn, hi, it's Nicholas.'

'Oh . . . hi.'

'You gave me your number, remember? Is it okay to call?'

'Yes.' She was flustered, not sure of how to act with him now that she had recalled their parting all those years ago. 'Sorry. I'm out shopping.'

'It's a bad time?'

'Well, no, it's fine. If you don't mind me talking while I shop.'

'Are you busy today?'

'I . . . No.' She was never any good at the direct lie. *Evasion I can manage. But not lying.*

'Good. Let's meet up. It's a beautiful day. Shall we go to the Botanic Gardens?'

'Oh. Yes, all right.' There was no way to get out of it. She would have to see him.

'Great. See you outside at two. We can talk about Kings Harcourt.'

Nicholas was waiting for Caitlyn outside the gardens, the tickets already bought. He looked different from when they had last met, less tweedy and donnish, in a thick navy jumper and jeans. It made him look younger, more like the man she remembered. He'd always been attractive, and he still was.

'Hi.' He greeted her with a smile and a kiss on the cheek. 'I'm glad you could make it. I hope you like rockeries, and glasshouses, and hardy perennials. Actually, this is a wonderful time of year to visit – it reminds you that summer is ahead of us now.'

'I don't know much about gardens,' she said apologetically. 'But I like looking at them.'

'Come on then. Let's go in.'

Yes, he definitely looks younger. And handsome. Those dark eyes of his. I used to want to drown in them.

Caitlyn pushed that thought out of her mind, but as they

wandered around the gardens together, she began to recall more vividly the way he had once made her feel. At first, she'd been rather in awe of him, hardly daring to talk to him. He was evidently brilliant, with a healthy streak of self-confidence and a touch of youthful swagger. She'd wished she could have a bit herself; she was still astonished to find herself at the college, with a much-sought-after place, and still fearful they might tell her it was all a mistake and she must pack her bags and go home. Nicholas hadn't seemed plagued by such doubts. And, of course, he'd been good-looking too, with that dark Latin colouring and an allure she wasn't immune to.

And here we are, all these years later, walking around the Botanic Gardens.

She relaxed as they strolled together, Nicholas talking without any awkwardness, and when they sat down on a bench to look out over a sea of purple Alpine flowers pouring over rocks, she had almost forgotten that she had been dreading seeing him.

Nicholas said, 'Did Aunt G get in touch with you?'

'Yes, yes. She wrote a very nice letter. It seems like a done deal as far as she's concerned.'

'She did seem very keen on the idea. And not just because she wants the rent. She liked you when you met.'

'I'm flattered. I liked her too.'

'Good. So. What do you think? Would you like the house?'

Caitlyn thought for a moment. She'd been looking at places for rent online, and none of them had appealed. Certainly none were as nice as her little Jericho cottage, and all of them carried the same risk that in six months, they'd be turned out.

This way she could have the summer to look for a place to buy, where they could really begin to settle. And to live in that house, to enjoy the garden, in the ripe green months of summer . . .

Patrick would have said go for it. He would have liked the idea of Max roaming free in such a magnificent place. And if I don't find anywhere to buy, we're still close to the school.

'Yes,' she said decisively. 'I think we'll take it.'

Nicholas smiled. 'Good. Then I'll set to sorting out all the boring stuff, and send you a contract.' He paused and then said, 'So Caitlyn, why have you been so elusive? I've got the feeling you've been avoiding me.'

She felt a flush climb over her face. 'I haven't . . .'

'Yes you have. You changed in an instant when we got back from the house that day. One moment you were laughing and chatting, the next you froze up and dashed away. Then you never got in touch. I'm not daft. What's behind it all? Have I offended you?'

She bit her lip, embarrassed. 'No.'

'I must have done something,' he said gently.

'You didn't.'

'So, come on. What was the problem? I always thought you and I got on well.'

'We did.'

There was a pause and then he said, 'We got on very well, didn't we? Towards the end. And then . . .'

She said nothing, lost in awkward confusion. So he hadn't forgotten at all. He remembered it too. She felt a dash of indignation that he'd brought it up at all, considering how he'd treated her.

Nicholas said, 'And then ... you bailed out, without a word. Just when we were on the brink.' He stared at her, waiting for her to say something, and when she remained silent, he said softly, 'I was in love with you.'

She almost trembled, feeling crosser even while she was afraid of what he might say next. 'I don't think you should say that.'

'Well, it's true. I thought you felt the same. And that we had a future.'

She shook her head in an involuntary, quick motion. 'I wish you wouldn't say this!'

'I'm sorry. I know in lots of ways it's not right to talk about it, considering what you're going through. But we can't just ignore what happened. And that's how it was.'

Caitlyn felt something snap and flicker inside. It was anger and resentment, sparking back into life after decades buried beneath the ash of forgetfulness. 'It isn't true, and it wasn't true. I don't know why you pretended then. You don't need to pretend now!'

Nicholas held up a hand, his expression wounded. 'Whoa. Wait a moment. What do you mean, pretend?'

She looked over at him, staring into his brown eyes. 'It was all fake.'

'What are you talking about?' he said, looking bewildered. 'Have you forgotten about the finals dinner? About what happened then?'

'No. I remember it,' she said. She turned to watch the little Alpine flowers nodding in rippling waves of purple.

'You never came back,' he said. 'Even though you promised you would. I waited for you. I went to your room and knocked. You weren't there.'

'I went to a party with Sara.'

There was a long pause, and he said in a matter-of-fact voice, 'Look, Caitlyn, I know this was all a very long time ago. I know that the activities of a bunch of silly drunk kids doesn't really matter any more. But I still want to understand why you didn't return. I thought that we connected that night. I'd hoped we could make something of it. I've always wondered what might have happened.'

She shrugged and pulled her cardigan a little tighter around her. 'Sara told me the truth about you. She said that you'd been desperately chasing her for months. You only wanted me for a bit of amusement, because you couldn't have her.'

Nicholas stared at her, his mouth open. '*What?*'

'That's what happened,' she said, almost obstinately.

'Wait. Back up. *Sara* told you this?'

'After I left you that night, I met Sara and she told me how you had been chasing her – coming on to her in the bar. The rugger boys had to fend you off. She was the one you were interested in.'

He laughed but in disbelief. 'No. No! That's not how it was at all.' He twisted so that he was facing her. 'I can't believe she told you that. But then . . . I could hardly believe it when you told me that you're still friends. It was obvious to everyone what was going on between the two of you.'

'What do you mean?' She felt chilled suddenly. 'What was going on?'

'A weird push me-pull you relationship. You thought she was great. And she was bloody jealous of you!'

Caitlyn laughed and shook her head. 'I don't think so. What did she have to be jealous about?'

'This is crazy. She said I was after her? That's the exact reverse of the truth.'

His brown eyes were almost pleading with her.

Nicholas put his hand on her arm and said intensely, 'You've got to believe me. Sara had been plaguing me, turning up at my room off her head, begging me to sleep with her. It'd been going on for a year or so – me sending her away or walking her back to her room. She'd be all over me, trying her best to seduce me, practically prostrating herself . . . and I did my best to let her down gently. Then, in the bar that night . . . God, I can remember it so well. She came up to me, three sheets to the wind as usual – the poor kid had a problem, anyone could see that – and announced that it was my last chance with her. I told her kindly but firmly that I wasn't interested. And she started . . . I don't know . . . she lost it a bit. She started getting angry with me, asking me what I wanted if it wasn't her. She asked if it was you – and when I didn't reply, it seemed to push her over the edge. She started to go nuts, shouting and crying and spluttering. Saying you were a little nobody. A nothing. The rugby boys . . . yes, they were there, they saw it all. They took her off me. They steered her to another table and calmed her down, distracted her, and I left. That was the last time I spoke to her. I never wanted to go near her again, in case she began accusing me of stuff I hadn't done. I knew she was crazy enough for that.' He shook his head gravely. 'I didn't hate her. I was more worried for her than anything. She was eaten up with sadness. And what I really couldn't understand was why you spent so much time with her, when it seemed to me that the thing she most feared and resented in life was you.'

Caitlyn remembered how topsy-turvy Sara's stories so often were. She could see her behaving just as Nicholas described. And yet – she'd seen the evidence of Sara's irresistibility with her own eyes. She'd had it happen before; the men wanted Sara. That was why it had been so horribly plausible. 'So you weren't after Sara?'

'Never.'

'No hanging around her, pleading with her, chasing her, telling her that you just intended to toy with me?'

'No!' He laughed, almost helplessly. 'It was the other way around – she wouldn't leave me alone! The more I told her I wasn't interested, the more persistent she got! And I never talked to her about you. She'd be the last person. I knew she couldn't be trusted.'

It was strange how everything could turn around so fast. She believed him. The image, flipped over, looked right, when it had never been entirely convincing the other way. Of course . . . she could see Sara now, in full seduction mode, fired up by the unaccustomed rejection, intent on having what seemed unattainable.

'She wanted to spoil it for us,' Nicholas said softly. 'She wanted to make sure that you and I wouldn't be together.'

'But . . .' Caitlyn shook her head, frowning. 'I don't understand! She could have had anyone! She had so much!'

'It seemed like it.' Nicholas sat back against the bench. 'But despite everything, she was one of the coldest, emptiest people I ever met. All she ever wanted was what she couldn't have.'

'Oh my God.' She blinked at the little flowers nodding in the breeze.

'Caitlyn, why are you still friends with her?' Nicholas gazed at her earnestly. 'You don't need her. You never did.'

'But she *is* my friend,' she said slowly. 'At least, that's what I've always believed.'

'Come on,' Nicholas said, getting up and holding out his hand, 'let's go back.'

'Yes.' Caitlyn stood up without taking his hand. 'I think I'd like to go home.'

Chapter Twenty-Two

When Tommy went up with Barbara to give Fred the first penicillin tablet, he was in a worse state than before.

'Oh Fred,' she cried, rushing over to where he lay, soaked in sweat, murmuring. Barbara joined her and looked at him critically.

'Not a moment too soon, I would say. I'll get the stuff right now. It's in my bag. Luckily you chose the right suitcase, or it would be frozen solid in the lane.'

She was back in moments, holding a small glass bottle full of pills. Tommy had propped Fred up so that he was half sitting, though she could hardly bear to see the pain on his face as she moved him.

Barbara shook out a pill into her palm. 'Have you got some water?'

'There, on the table.'

'We'll have to make him swallow it.'

'We can grind it up if we have to.'

'Hold his head back.'

Tommy tipped Fred's head back and spoke to him gently,

'Now, Fred, dear, you have to swallow a pill for me. Will you do that? It will make you better, I promise. It will kill all that terrible infection in your blood. But you have to swallow it first.' Barbara passed her the pill and she placed it in Fred's mouth, pushing it in between his teeth. She was worried he might spit it out but he didn't, although neither did he swallow it. She picked up the glass of water from his night table and pressed it to his lips, tipping it over his tongue.

At first it dribbled from his mouth and then he swallowed a little, leaving the pill still on his tongue.

'That's right, Fred, swallow it for me, there's a dear. The thing in your mouth – let it go down your throat.' She tried to sound coaxing and comforting at the same time, keeping up her murmur into his ears as she tipped more water into his mouth. Suddenly he seemed to realise that his thirst was being assuaged and he gulped the water, taking with it the little pill.

'He's swallowed it,' she exclaimed happily.

'Good.' Barbara examined the bottle of pills. 'There are plenty left. But you're just in time. I've seen infections like this – left much longer, there is no way of saving them, penicillin or not.'

'Thank you, Barbara.' Tommy smiled over at her and Barbara's pale face with its thin, pink mouth smiled back. *She's been kind. Perhaps I've misjudged her.*

'I'll go and tell Roger, he's worried sick. I only just managed to persuade him not to come here.' Barbara pulled her cardigan around her. 'He seems to think you're keeping Mr Burton Brown all to yourself for some reason. Naturally I told him he's being very silly.'

'Yes, thank you. Tell him Fred will be up for visitors soon, if all goes well.'

'I don't think I can remember a time when the world wasn't white,' Gerry said thoughtfully, sitting on the window seat in the sitting room of her mother's house.

They had all taken to spending as much time as they could there, soaking up the warmth before returning to the icy main house where the fires were no longer lit and the radiators were on low to stop the pipes freezing. Only Fred still had a fire in his room, while he recovered. Tommy had taken the children to sleep in her bed, pooling their blankets and eiderdowns on top, and closing the heavy tapestry curtains that hung from the four posts. She felt stupid that she'd only ever considered them decorative; now she realised they had an important purpose, creating a tiny warm room within the larger cold one. The children had stopped shivering in their sleep, which was a good thing.

Those Tudors and Stuarts knew a thing or two, she had thought, climbing in between their two warm, slumbering bodies. *Sharing beds and lots of curtains is definitely the only way to survive the winter.*

'Perhaps,' Gerry said now, turning back to look at Tommy and her mother, 'we shall never see anyone else as long as we live.'

'I do hope not,' Tommy said. She was pulling on her shooting socks in preparation for the trip to the village. Her mother watched her, still stitching away with her silks.

'I don't know why you're bothering,' Mrs Whitfield said in a gloomy voice. 'There won't be anything there to buy.'

'You, Mother, are to stop listening to the wireless, do you hear? You believe everything they say.' Tommy stood up and tightened her belt. 'Time for me to get into harness. I'm rather looking forward to this, if you can believe it.'

'Ration books?' asked Gerry.

'Check!'

'Cash?'

'Plenty.'

'Compass and torch?'

'I don't really think I need them but yes, I've got them. Just in case. But I'm not taking anything else, it's really too much to haul.'

Mrs Whitfield said, 'I'm not exaggerating, Thomasina. The army is being called out. The Thames is frozen. And there's no end in sight.' She shook her head. 'To think we survived the war to be defeated by this awful weather.'

'We won't let it defeat us,' Tommy said. 'We won that, and we'll survive this too.'

Mrs Whitfield sighed. 'We shall probably freeze if we don't starve first.'

'She's such a harbinger of doom,' Tommy said as she and Gerry walked to the back door. The children were there, excitedly examining the sledge she was going to take with her, attached to her belt with two ropes. Molly was standing nearby, her face pinched and pink with cold, watching the two others jumping round the sledge pretending to be dogs.

She didn't seem quite able to join in. 'Please don't let her talk like that to the children.'

'I don't think they hear her,' Gerry said. 'Lucky, merry little things. But I wonder if she's not right this time.' She turned to her sister. 'Don't you think there's something a little apocalyptic about all this? I mean, if you take out the hellfire in the Book of Revelation and replace it with snow and ice – well, it feels a little like the end of the world.'

'Your imagination!' scolded Tommy. 'We can't afford to give in to all that. We have to stay strong. It's a horrible cold spell. It will pass. Just like the war.'

'But think how many died in the war,' Gerry said. Her chin sunk into her scarf and she said sadly, 'If there's anything we learned, it's that no one has a right to survive.'

'All the more reason to stay cheerful while we're here,' said Tommy. Then she advanced on the children. 'Right! Who's ready to watch me set off?'

Just then there was the slam of the back door. It was Barbara, running swiftly down the steps, wearing a pair of trousers under a long coat, and a bobble hat. 'I thought I'd come along and give you a hand,' she said, pulling on a pair of gloves. 'Roger says there are spare skis.'

'Yes . . .' Tommy said, surprised. 'I suppose there are.'

'Good. Then I'll use those.'

'I'll show you where they are,' volunteered Gerry.

They disappeared, to return a moment later, Barbara carrying a pair of skis over one shoulder. She put them on as the children ran around excitedly, working out how they might harness two people to the sledge instead of one.

'Easier with both of us,' Barbara said as she snapped on her skis and let Antonia tie the rope connecting the sledge onto her belt.

A few minutes later, they set off, pushing themselves up along the snow drifts that were now hard under their skis after nights of freezing temperatures. The sledge bounced around behind them until Tommy announced that this was no good, and took over pulling it on her own, which was much easier. The snow had kept on falling and had compacted, so now it was possible to ski over the tops of hedges at many feet above the level of the ground, with the roofs of the village in the distance looking almost at the same height, although they were little more than misty shadows through the grey fog around them.

'I feel as if it's days since we last saw the sun,' Tommy said.

Barbara pressed on beside her, panting with the effort. 'This is not exactly skiing, is it? More like walking and sliding.'

'Yes. Come on, we're not so far now.'

As they approached the village, there had obviously been efforts to clear the snow along the main street and up to the houses. People were out and about, well wrapped up, walking carefully on the icy paths, and children were playing in drifts. A variety of snowmen dotted about showed their previous efforts, still solid and bearing their pebble buttons and stick arms.

Tommy skied down a drift to ground level, Barbara close behind her, and they took off their skis so they could walk along the main street to the village shop, where there was already a queue of women holding baskets.

'Morning, Mrs Eliott,' called one as Tommy joined the line.

'Morning, Ruby. How are you?' Tommy wiped her forehead which was damp from the effort of their ski.

'Very well, thank you, ma'am. Did you come on those planks all the way from the house?'

'It's the only way. We're snowed in.'

Ruby turned to the woman next to her. 'Didn't I say?' She made a knowing face. 'I said you'd work out a way to get over here, you've always had a way with working things out. Whether they've managed to get through from town is another matter. The ploughs have been out clearing the way and we've heard the army have been dealing with the railways, scraping off ice so the trains can get through.'

'Prisoners of war,' put in Ruby's friend. 'Doing a bit to earn their keep, I'm glad to say.'

'So there's no milk or bread?' asked Tommy.

'Not yet. But they're due at ten.' Ruby stamped her feet. 'It's cold work, waiting, though!'

At that moment, Mr Trent, the owner of the village store, came out and started handing out slips of paper with numbers on them. 'Come on, into the shop all of you. This will ensure you don't lose your place in the queue. But you can't wait out here, you'll all freeze.'

They went in gratefully, and Tommy and Barbara found a corner to rest against.

'Queues, queues, all through the war, and still we have to

wait,' Tommy said. 'I believe it's even worse than it used to be.'

Barbara said quietly, 'You don't always have to wait, you know.'

'What do you mean?'

Barbara looked around to make sure no one was listening, then murmured, 'Veronica didn't wait. And she got as much milk and butter and cheese as she wanted.'

Tommy frowned. 'The black market, you mean. I don't think there's much of that round here.'

'There will be, you just haven't seen it. If you've got the money, you can get whatever you want. I'm sure there are ways to find out.'

'No thank you,' Tommy said coolly. 'We do very well without that. And I couldn't look Ruby and Edith and Elsie and all the others in the face.'

Barbara laughed. 'You can be sure they're at it. Everyone is. You needn't be so holier-than-thou. We mostly stick to the rules, but the occasional sin doesn't make us criminals.'

Tommy flushed. 'No. Of course not. I wasn't being a prig—'

There was a sudden murmur of excitement and a rush to the windows as the noise of a grinding engine grew louder. 'They're here!' shouted one woman and they all rushed outside to see the supply truck making its lumbering way down the main road. When it finally drew to a halt outside the shop, the driver leapt down from the cab and took off his cap to wipe his forehead. 'We set off at five o'clock this morning and it's

240

taken us all this time to get here.' He shook his head. 'I've never seen drifts like it. And the bus has been left abandoned in the road; we had to drive around it, that wasn't easy.'

His mate had already begun to uncover the load and everyone cheered to see crates of milk bottles packed with hay against the frost, and boxes of supplies, while Mr Trent began bustling about, organising things.

When it was finally Tommy's turn to claim her ration, there was no moving Mr Trent over the issue of Barbara and Molly's ration books. 'If they're not registered, I don't have anything for them,' Mr Trent said firmly. 'It'd be taking it out of the mouths of others, you know that, Mrs Eliott.'

'Yes, of course,' Tommy said sheepishly. 'I didn't think of that.'

'The only thing you're allowed is their tea ration. That's all I can do for you.'

'That's something, I suppose.'

'I'll register them now and you should be able to claim the next lot, if the post is running,' Mr Trent said, and went to fetch his registration book.

Nevertheless, the amount they returned with still seemed like plenty compared with the bare cupboards at home. They had bread, milk, margarine, butter, cheese, sugar and tea, as well as rice, biscuits and tinned tomatoes and beans, and some jam as a treat for the children. Tommy used her saved points for tins of meat and fish, cereal, oats and biscuits, and bought as much off ration as she could. The sledge was satisfyingly full of boxes as they prepared for the journey home.

'You see, it's not so bad,' Tommy said, as they strapped on their skis.

Barbara prepared to help pull the sledge. 'Of course, you have so much already.'

'We're very lucky,' Tommy said again. *Is she telling me off? Is she saying that it's easy to be good when your need is not so great?*

On the way back, they went more slowly because of the loaded sledge and the awkwardness of pulling it between them while they half skied, half walked along the mountainous drifts of snow, packed hard and frozen almost solid. That meant they could talk and Tommy asked Barbara about her life after they had all left The Grange School.

'I went to be a secretary,' Barbara said. 'I ended up working in Whitehall for the civil service. Just typing, you know, but it was fun. I loved it. I lived in a boarding house in Battersea run by a barmy old lady, one of those places for single girls. Stockings and underthings drying on the banisters. Rather shameless but a laugh. We'd go out dancing in the evenings, they'd take me places I never would have known about otherwise. It was a happy time. I saw you a few times then, remember? Then I met my husband, Duncan, and we were engaged. He was in the colonial service, and not long after we were married, he got the chance to go to India. Well, not many wanted to go, with things there so tricky, but Duncan thought it would be a good opportunity. So off we went.'

'What was India like? I've always wondered.'

'Hot,' Barbara replied flatly. 'Sticky. Infuriating. Awful

creatures – the flies and mosquitos and snakes and things. Pig-headed people. But it was also wonderful. We lived very well, there's no denying it, in a big bungalow with lots of servants. As long as one could keep cool, it was rather lovely, with an endless stream of boys to fetch and carry, and women to tend to one. But Duncan didn't much like the work and it was obvious the way things were going. We had to struggle with the blasted independence fighters, who want us all gone. Some even set fire to one of our neighbours' places. Thank goodness they all got out. The British will be thrown out before too long, you'll see, but it made life . . . annoying. Still, the social life was good fun.'

'What an experience it must have been.'

'Yes. Splendid parties. Elephant rides in the hills. Polo. I didn't lift a finger the whole time we were there.' Barbara sighed. 'Then the war came, and it was all over. Duncan volunteered, and Molly and I came home.'

'How terrifying,' Tommy said. 'Weren't you afraid of the U-boats?'

Barbara shrugged. 'You take your chance. Not every ship went down. I had a feeling we would be all right. But when we got here – my God, this place! So grey and dull and deprived after India.'

'Deprived!' Tommy laughed. 'Surely not.'

'But yes. The rations, the lack of anything lovely. I've never been so miserable as when we landed here to the rain and gloom and nothing nice to eat and drink. I longed to be back in our old life so much I could hardly stand it.' Barbara paused as she struggled up a drift and they stopped on the top to look at the view of foggy white and grey, the house looming larger beyond them. She turned to look at Tommy. 'And I still hate it. But I have no choice now. Duncan is dead, and I have to make a life for Molly and me. All I can do is make the best of it.'

The two of them were greeted like returning adventurers from the lands of plenty, their boxes and packets oohed and aahed over as if they were exotic treasures from beyond the sea.

'We'll eat like kings,' Gerry exclaimed, going through the shopping. 'Oh, biscuits, how wonderful.'

'Jelly,' sighed the children.

Ada was more interested in the sugar and butter, but Tommy said there was something for everyone and they were just to be grateful that the trip had proved a success. After all, perhaps there would be no more snow and things could start to get back to normal. But that afternoon, another storm blew up and brought more whirling whiteness.

'What's going on downstairs?' Fred asked when Tommy went to see him with hot soup, bread with a scraping of dripping over it and a chopped tomato from that morning's shop. She also had another pill for him.

'You are much better if you're even vaguely interested in what's going on elsewhere. Only yesterday you barely knew where you were.' Tommy smiled at him as she put the tray on his lap. 'I'm happy you're so much better.'

'Thanks to you.' He smiled back at her. He looked ruffled from his days in bed and the tossing and turning during his fever, and his jawline was dark with stubble. 'You've looked after me so well.'

Tommy shrugged. 'I did what I had to.'

'I'm embarrassed you've had to nurse me like this.'

'Don't be. Besides, it's thanks to Barbara you're well again. She had some medicine that's done the trick. Talking of which, take this pill, will you?'

'How are Barbara and Molly getting on?' Fred asked.

'Very well. But I feel sorry for Barbara. She's so alone in the world, with her daughter to look after.'

'You're widowed, too, with children.'

'But I've got all this.' Tommy gestured to the house. 'Barbara has nothing.' She straightened his bedcover and said strictly, 'Now, when you've eaten that, I'll come to take the tray away. And I think you'll have a visitor this afternoon. I can't keep Roger out now he knows your fever has broken.'

'I'd love to see him,' Fred said sincerely, then gave her a conspiratorial smile. 'But thank you for holding him off while I was ill. He's a good fellow but . . .'

'Say no more.' Tommy winked at him. 'Now eat up and get your strength back. We need you downstairs, it's far too female down there.'

On the stairs, she met Roger, who was obviously on his way to see Fred. 'Roger, dear, I don't think you should disturb Fred, he's eating. Why not go in later, when he's finished?'

Her brother shot her a sour look. 'You can't keep him to yourself forever, Tommy. I won't allow it. You've shut me out without a word!'

And he pushed roughly past her, leaving Tommy looking after him in surprise.

Chapter Twenty-Three

Caitlyn had not heard from Sara since the funeral, and that was an unusually long time to go without hearing anything. When Sara was away working, she could go silent for long stretches but that was not normally for more than a few weeks.

She thought about it as she began sorting through Max's things, packing some away in preparation for the move to Kings Harcourt. In normal circumstances, Caitlyn would be aflutter with anxiety, wondering what she had done to offend Sara and how she could make amends; she'd be inviting her for lunch or dinner, or offering to meet in one of Sara's favourite bars for cocktails. Sara would reject a few dates and then graciously accept, arriving with a hint of frostiness around her. But a few drinks, some well-placed questions about her work and social life, and Sara would begin to relent. By the end of the evening, things would be back to normal, Caitlyn's sin forgotten. Never had she left it like this, waiting for a breach to be healed by Sara.

Now, though, she didn't want to talk to her. Sara had said

those awful things to her at the funeral. And according to Nicholas, even twenty years ago, Sara was trying to undermine her and sabotage her relationships.

So what were you really up to with Patrick, Sara? And what are you doing now?

On impulse, she went to her bedroom, picked up her phone from the bedside table and opened up her Instagram app. She didn't post herself, but Sara had urged her to install it so she could look at all of her latest projects. For that reason, Caitlyn hadn't bothered with Sara's account very much, as it was mostly a shop window for her design business, mixed with a healthy dose of 'my perfect life' that infected so much of Caitlyn's friends' social media. Alongside pictures of her projects at various stages, Sara also had plenty of glamorous selfies, showing her looking beautiful in gorgeous locations, being served impossibly artful meals or sipping drinks in front of sunsets. Even the *Oh God, I look rough!* shots showed her tousled and still lovely. The Sara Caitlyn knew at the end of a hard night – bleary, slurring, red-eyed, shabby – naturally never appeared.

She clicked on Sara's account and began to look through it. The latest batch of photographs were no different: shots of an amazing beach house in the Hamptons, Sara – neatly businesslike but stylish and slim in tight white trousers, ballet pumps and a blazer – pointing out work to builders, excitedly sharing the mood boards of colours and fabrics, or snapping *the perfect chair – love, love, LOVE!!* – confiding that *my client's favourite tweed is ideal for this wonderful sofa* and tagging her stockists who then liked her pictures in a mutual love-in of joy at everyone's genius. Then there were selfies of Sara looking great on a sun lounger in a bikini and a sun hat, with a self-deprecating excuse for showing it: *Pity us poor redheads – hats and suncream needed!* Or there was an innocent pleasure in her good fortune to conceal the showing off: *Sundowners in the Hamptons by the pool – I'm just the luckiest girl in the world #lovemyjob.* There were endless shots of cocktails, bead-dappled wineglasses, flutes of champagne, with warm little comments: *End of a hard day. My reward!* or *Cold white wine, sunset – what could be more perfect?*

It all left a bitter taste in the mouth, Caitlyn found. It was pretend. It wasn't real, of course, even though it was strangely seductive to believe in it all. She knew what the reality of it would be, because more than once she'd been there, watching Sara being rude to some clients and sucking up appallingly to others, flirting with workmen or condescending to them, depending on their attractiveness. She'd seen Sara throw awful tantrums when things didn't go the way she wanted. And she knew that at the end of any working day, Sara would be drinking. Whether it was billed as a reward, a treat or an adventure, it was all the same stuff in the end. The same that the alkie in the park was drinking. The same stuff the kid in the hospital bed with liver failure was on.

She manages to dress everything up and make it look pretty, no matter what a sordid mess it is underneath. And she's the living embodiment of it. She's peppermint sweet on the outside but the reality is something else altogether.

She closed the app and stared at her phone, unseeing for a moment. Then she dialled Nicholas's number and waited for him to answer.

'I've not got the paperwork for the tenancy agreement ready yet, I'm afraid. But it's on its way, I promise,' Nicholas said.

They had met at the gates of the college and gone for a stroll along the river, watching the tourists having a go at punting. They'd talked easily and he'd evidently been relieved that they hadn't fallen out after the meeting in the Botanic Gardens. They didn't refer to their previous conversation at all, but had gone back to Nicholas's rooms high up in the quad. Caitlyn liked being tucked away from everything, invisible to the crowds on the streets outside and the visitors milling around the college.

'That's all right. But I've been thinking – I'd like to move sooner than I'd previously planned. Do you think your aunt would mind?'

'I'm sure she'd be delighted. Do you mind if I ask why?'

'I don't know really. Max's term ends in four weeks or so. We should go then, if not before. It's not just that I'd like to get settled and enjoy the house during the summer.' She sighed. 'I feel as though I'd like to get out of here. Away from Oxford.'

'Too many memories?' Nicholas asked softly.

'Something like that. I've been thinking so much about Sara after what you said.' She saw the expression on Nicholas's face and said quickly, 'I completely believe your version, there's no question about that. It's just a shock, to realise that she could do something like that to me. And yet, it's not exactly a surprise.'

He looked over at her with a questioning expression. 'How do you feel about it?'

She sat back against the squashy cushions of the sofa. 'I don't know. Not good.' She frowned. 'Ever since Patrick died . . . well, I feel as though my life has shifted focus and I can see everything differently. And after you told me about what happened between you and her . . . it's made me think about our friendship and why she wanted to thwart things for me.'

'Caitlyn,' Nicholas said solemnly, 'the miracle to me was that you were ever her friend in the first place. The way she treated you depressed me.'

'I don't understand that. We had lots of fun together.'

'Did you? Really?'

'Yes!' She thought back to the student days, with their parties and balls and nights out. 'We went everywhere to-gether.'

'Yeah. Like a countess and her lady's maid.'

'What?' Caitlyn laughed uncertainly.

'You let her boss you around, and talk down to you. I heard her do it. She was always ramming home the message that she was the real deal and you, poor thing, weren't quite it. She was the most appalling snob. Once in the bar she told me to imagine what it would be like if I took her home to meet my family – what would they all think when they saw someone like me with someone like her?' He laughed. 'I think she assumed that I was brought up on some rough estate somewhere. And I bet she thought you were bloody lucky to be allowed to hang out with her.'

Caitlyn opened her mouth and shut it again. This was what she had begun to realise herself. But had it been so evident to everyone else?

Nicholas went on, 'But you're not innocent in this. You let it happen. You let her do it. You ran around after her, riding on her coattails, letting her believe she was amazing and you weren't.' He fixed her with a stern look. 'Why did you do it?'

Caitlyn was indignant but embarrassed. 'Come on, it wasn't that bad. I was her friend! She didn't have all that many friends. She needed me.'

'Why do you think she didn't have many friends?'

'Other people were jealous of her.'

'That's what she wanted you to believe. But maybe she didn't have any friends because she wasn't particularly nice.'

Caitlyn stared at him.

Nicholas warmed to his theme. 'I think you've fallen for a rather nasty lie. Remember Hattie Harris? She was a stunner.'

'Of course I remember her.'

'She had plenty of friends, male and female. Men adored her, and she had loads of girlfriends.'

'That's true, she did. But she wasn't like Sara.'

'No, she wasn't – that's just the point. You seem to think that Sara was the ultimate woman. There were plenty of gorgeous girls around. She wasn't the only one.'

'Everyone fancied her!'

'No, they didn't. I didn't.' Nicholas leaned towards her, his dark brown eyes intent. 'Sure, she could be dazzling. She could turn heads. But she attracted people like her – cold, snobbish and vain, or else idiots who couldn't see past a pair of beautiful eyes and a mane of red hair. You weren't like that, but you were all over her like a rash. So what did you get out of it?'

'I suppose . . .' Caitlyn went quiet, thinking back, trying to be honest with herself. 'I suppose I hoped that some of her sparkle might rub off on me. And I found her world a bit intoxicating too. I thought it was glamorous. It *was* glamorous.' She felt suddenly ashamed, as if she'd revealed something ignoble. 'I suppose I . . . used her too.'

'But what a price for a few parties,' Nicholas said. 'I hoped you'd escaped her years ago. Maybe you need to tell Sara that you've moved on. Friendships can end, you know. Like love affairs. There's no rule that says they can't. And if your life is better without Sara in it, then maybe you should do the right thing and tell her it's over.'

'I think you're right. That's what I need to do,' Caitlyn said slowly. 'I can see that now. The miracle is that I never saw it earlier.'

Nicholas walked her back to the college gate through the bright morning sun.

'Your son is back today, isn't he?'

Caitlyn nodded. 'My sister's bringing him back after lunch.'

'I'd like to meet him one day.'

Caitlyn turned to look at him. He was looking at her with warmth and a tiny amount of anxiety. 'I don't know . . .' she said uncertainly.

'As your friend. Nothing else.'

'I know. But Max might not think that. It's so very soon.'

'I understand.' Suddenly he took her hand. It felt startlingly warm and alive on hers, the smoothness of his skin almost shocking her. 'It is soon. I don't want anything from you, please believe me.'

Caitlyn was touched by the kindness in his voice. She felt almost choked. 'I'd like us to be friends,' she managed to say.

He smiled at her. 'Me too. Goodbye, Caitlyn. I'll be in touch. Let me know if you decide on a date to move into the house; it's ready when you are. And don't forget, you are in charge of your relationships. If you don't want someone in your life, just tell them to go.'

Maura brought Max back that afternoon and they had a few hours together before she headed home, taking her excitable brood with her. Caitlyn felt better. It was good to see her sister, even if only for a short time, and Nicholas's straight talking had helped too. She felt supported on both sides, and that soon she would be ready to start taking baby steps forward into the future on her own.

I think I'm beginning to accept that Patrick is really gone. And I'm working at discarding what isn't good in my life. I must filter out what's harmful and leave the positive behind. I know it's just the start of the process.

She was serving Max his supper at the table in the tiny garden when she heard the rapping on the front door. Leaving Max to his baked potato, she went to answer it.

'Surprise!' Sara whipped off her sunglasses and stood there, beaming. 'Glad to see me?'

Chapter Twenty-Four

It was two weeks since the great storm and there was no hope of post, and the telephone lines were still down.

'I expect they have better things to do at the moment than fix the telephone,' Tommy said, and they all gathered around the wireless to listen to the news. It was February now and there was no sign of the weather letting up. If anything, it was colder.

'How long can it go on?' Gerry said, looking pinched and tired.

The children were listless and stir crazy. They ran around screaming and shouting until Tommy shushed them, worried that they were disturbing Fred.

'We're bored, Mummy,' Antonia said.

'Can we have lessons again?' asked Harry.

'Aunt Gerry is still doing French with you, isn't she?'

'But we want Latin too,' Harry said. 'Molly wants to do it too, don't you?'

Molly nodded. She seemed to be improving despite the bitter weather; her cheeks were pinker and her pale blue eyes sparkled. 'I want to do what you're doing,' she said to Antonia, who she clearly admired.

'When Mr Burton Brown is well again, perhaps he'll start up the lessons. We'll see. But keep quiet upstairs, can't you? He still needs his sleep.'

But Fred was on the mend and with less to do in his sickroom, Tommy discovered that Barbara had, unobtrusively and unnoticed, made herself a part of the household. She was always beautifully turned out, in expensive clothes and neat shoes, her hair coiffed and her pale face brightened by make-up. Her scarlet lips were vivid in her paper-white complexion, her small pink mole the only other touch of colour. Occasionally Tommy would walk into a room to find Barbara already there, quietly examining things: pictures, photographs in their frames, a china dish or a silver tray. But most often she was to be found with Mrs Whitfield, sorting silks and separating threads for the old lady's embroidery, keeping her company.

'What do you think of Barbara?' Tommy had asked Gerry idly as they went down to the kitchen for tea. She had said nothing of her own feelings about her before Barbara's arrival in case she was being unfair.

'Oh, I think she's splendid. She takes all the burden off me. I don't have to do all that boring silk sorting and needle hunting that Mother likes to inflict on me. More time to read in the bath.'

When Gerry wasn't minding the children, she was in the warm bathroom, curled up with a book lying in the bath in her coat and beret, a stone hot water bottle under her toes.

'So you like her?'

'Not exactly *like*. She's rather a cold fish, isn't she? Though I'm rather obsessed with her face – that whiteness and that pink mole, she makes me think of a naked baby mouse.'

Tommy had laughed. 'Well, she's certainly being nice to Roger, and that's good of her. It takes the heat off Fred.'

Barbara, away from Mrs Whitfield, was often with Roger, who had been lost and miserable during Fred's illness. Now he seemed to be becoming as dependent on Barbara's company as he had been on Fred's. Tommy, while she was nursing Fred upstairs, would hear Roger's voice floating up as he and Barbara meandered around the ground floor now that it was so difficult to walk outside.

'You see, Barbara, what we have now is an opportunity. We were at loggerheads with Russia for so long but the war has brought us to a point where we can start to understand each other and perhaps our government will begin to see that there really is only one way to go if we are serious about improving society . . .'

Then Barbara would murmur a response and Roger would start again.

She's being so kind to Roger. It's helping him too. I do believe he seems happier. It was a blessing after all that she and Molly came to the house. What a crew we are, stuck up here in this great freezing place, nowhere to go, just concentrating on survival.

Only Ada did not seem won over by Barbara's charms. She was prickly whenever Barbara went into the kitchen but Tommy didn't ask what it was that riled her. Thornton had, over the last few days, dug a long tunnel through the snow to their cottage and it was with relief all round that the Thorntons went home to their own hearth and the cat.

When Tommy went up with Fred's lunch and the last of the tablets from Barbara's bottle, she found him restless after more than a week in bed.

'I'm better,' he said bluntly. 'I need to do something. I have to get up.'

'Let's check your wound,' she said, 'and see if you're up to it.'

The wound had calmed down and was healing, but it was far from better. Fred still winced when he moved. 'I'm dying of boredom,' he complained. 'I've only been as far as the bathroom and back for days.'

'Yes, but you're lucky you can even do that.'

'Please, Tommy. Be a brick and let me out. I'm itching to work on the painting. When I was ill and floating in and out of dreams, I had the most extraordinary visions of it. That sad beauty kept coming and talking to me about her tragedy. It was rather magnificent being in her presence. I must paint her now.'

'Very well . . . but should you be in the freezing hall in your state?'

'Then let's move it. Put it somewhere warmer – it'll be easier for me to see as well if I'm closer to it. I still doubt it will be terribly good, though, even with my fever-induced inspiration.'

Tommy laughed. 'So much for saving the family fortune

with your masterpiece! Thank goodness I never expected we'd actually see it through. Come on, I'll help you up.' She went over and he put out his arm. She grasped his hand and he leaned on her so that he could turn around to climb out of bed. He was heavier than she expected, when he looked so slight, even more so since his illness. But he was broad of shoulder and muscled, from his army service, no doubt. When he pulled on her arm, she was taken by surprise and was unable to resist his force, so that she fell forward and, putting her arms out to stop herself, she landed across him, almost embracing him.

Fred groaned.

'I'm so sorry,' she said, flustered, looking up to find herself gazing straight into his eyes. 'Have I hurt you?'

He said nothing for a moment, regarding her intently with a strange softness on his face, then said, 'No. Not at all. Not really.' The next moment he leaned forward to kiss her, his lips brushing hers and then pressing harder. She let it happen, feeling the rush of joy as he touched her, and then she pulled rapidly away.

'Oh no,' she said, panic-stricken.

His expression changed immediately. 'I'm sorry, Tommy. How awful of me. I thought—'

'No, it's not you at all. I . . . it's my fault. But . . . I can't. I wish I could. I can't.' She took several steps away from him as if afraid that he would lunge for her and she hated to see the mortification on his face as she did so. She longed to explain, but that was impossible. Her panic had subsided to be replaced with embarrassment. 'I'm sorry, Fred. Really, I am. You

258

must come downstairs as soon as you like.' Then she hurried out of the bedroom, closing the door behind her and rushing to her own room where she lay down on her bed and stared at the wall, her heart racing with a mixture of fear and longing.

Now, more than ever, Tommy was grateful that she had Barbara to keep the eyes of the others off her. She was sure that her inner agitation, sparked by the brief but intense moment of her kiss with Fred, would have been obvious to them all otherwise.

She couldn't understand why she had reacted so strongly to it, but it had shaken her deeply, causing her pleasure and pain in equal measure, along with a large dose of confusion. Having previously visited Fred several times a day, she stopped abruptly, unable to bring herself to see him.

Instead, whenever she could, she escaped to her bedroom, where she drew the curtains around the bed to make a dark cave, and lay in there thinking.

This wasn't supposed to happen. I told myself I would never let this happen to me again. What have I done?

And yet, when she thought about it, she could see that all along she had been walking the path to the moment that Fred would kiss her. She had made it come to pass by removing him from everyone and keeping him to herself – *No, that was his illness . . . or did I use his illness as an excuse?* – which had intensified their relationship. *But I don't want him! I don't want any man. That's what I decided. And that's how it must be.*

And so, to punish herself for her secret desire for Fred, she shunned all contact with him. Whenever she felt the yearning for Fred's company, or remembered with a burning thrill the moment their lips had touched, she shut it firmly away.

No. It can't happen. I promised myself. Never again.

Tommy told Thornton to take Venetia down from the hall and move her into the library. The fire that had been set in Fred's room while he was ill would now be lit in there, so that he could paint without freezing.

Fred got up at last, thinner and weaker, dressed himself as warmly as possible and vanished inside. Tommy knew, as she walked past the library door, that he was in there, sketching out the form of the painting on the stretched canvas. But she didn't go in, and now she only saw him at mealtimes, although she found it hard to look at him. When she did glance over, he was rarely looking at her. Despite polite conversation, there was very little interaction between them.

I've offended him. It's awful. Why have I spoiled everything like this? It was so nice before – and now it's all ruined. It hurt her horribly but she felt that she was to blame for it all.

At dinner the day after Fred had rejoined them, he barely looked at her and she only stole glimpses of him while talking to the others. Then, looking up, she found Barbara's gaze on her, her expression knowing and faintly amused. From Tommy, she looked to Fred and then away.

It was nothing, and yet Tommy couldn't help feeling a little afraid.

Barbara always liked to stir things up. Perhaps she hasn't changed so much after all.

Roger, delighted that Fred was back, spent long hours in the library, talking while Fred painted, but in the afternoon, when Fred went to rest, he resumed his walks with Barbara, round and round the ground floor in a slow promenade.

Tommy was on the upstairs landing on her way to the stairs when she heard Roger's voice say sharply, 'Do you really think so?'

She stopped suddenly as Barbara said, 'It's as plain as day, darling.'

'I suppose, now you say it, it makes sense.'

Tommy realised she was eavesdropping, but she couldn't move. She stood still, letting the voices from below rise up to her.

Barbara went on: 'Just think about it. She kept you away from him all that time when he was ill, even though you would have done him the world of good. I saw it at once – remember what I told you at the time? You knew it was true. And now, when you're with him while he's painting, she's gets terribly agitated. Well, doesn't she?'

Tommy's mouth went dry as she realised that Barbara was talking about her. She heard Roger say slowly, 'Why doesn't she want me close to Fred?'

'I should think she's jealous of your friendship. And she knows Fred has your best interests at heart. And those aren't Tommy's interests, I'm sorry to say.'

'What do you mean?'

'The house, darling. The estate. She wants to stay in charge. She's dividing to rule.'

'I never thought of that,' Roger replied.

'Of course you didn't. You're far too pure of heart. But I hate to see you being manipulated . . .'

The voices faded as Roger and Barbara walked out of the great hall and away. Tommy stayed standing there, her heart beating rapidly. *What are you doing, Barbara?*

Tommy felt a coolness prickle over her skin. She remembered the day at school that Arabella Guthrie's fountain pen had gone missing. Everyone had been stood at the front of the schoolroom to swear on their honour in front of Miss Bates that they hadn't taken it. Barbara had been as convincing as the rest of them, wide-eyed and innocent. And then Tommy had seen it glint with an ebony shine from the inside of Barbara's desk that same afternoon. At least, she'd thought she had, though she didn't want to believe it.

What's your game?

Chapter Twenty-Five

Caitlyn stared at Sara who stood on her front step with a suitcase and hand luggage next to her. A rush of confusion and shock raced through her. But, she realised, she was also afraid. *Afraid of her, and afraid of myself and the way I act around her.*

'Glad to see me?' Sara said brightly. She was looking good, a touch of Hamptons golden sun on her usually pale skin, her red hair twisted up in a thick ponytail.

'Er . . . I'm very surprised!'

'That's the idea. Can I come in?' Sara peered over her shoulder into the cottage gloom beyond.

I ought to tell her to go. But the reality of Sara, so insouciant, acting as though everything were completely normal, was hard to confront. 'Of course.' She stepped back and a moment later Sara was standing in her sitting room, looking around, the suitcase and hand luggage by the door. She was somehow too large for the space. 'Your house is really sweet. So different to your old place. Where's Max? Call him in. Max! It's your godmother!'

Max came running in from the garden. 'Hi, Sara!'

'You've grown, young man.' She gave him a kiss, then fished a large bar of chocolate out of her bag. 'Here, this is for you. Eat it now if you like.'

'Oh, wow! Thanks!'

Caitlyn said, 'He's about to have his supper.'

'It's a treat! How often does he see me?'

Max turned pleading eyes to her.

'All right,' Caitlyn said, not wanting to let him down. Two seconds in the house and Sara was already steamrolling over her.

'Now,' Sara said, taking off her jacket and tossing it onto the sofa. 'I could kill for a glass of wine. What's in the fridge? I've got duty free if you haven't got anything.'

Caitlyn went to the kitchen, feeling helpless. *So much for my new-found bravery.* 'Why are you in Oxford?' she asked as she looked in the fridge for the bottle of white wine chilling there.

'I got a call just as my job in the Hamptons came to an end. A boutique hotel is being completely refurbished here and they just lost their project manager and designer, so they asked me if I could take it on at short notice. Isn't that great? We can hang out when I'm not working!'

Caitlyn poured two glasses of wine. It was, she could now see, typical of Sara to act as though nothing had happened after no word for months. As she went back through with the glasses, her gaze fell on the luggage by the door. 'Are you planning to stay here?' she said with a hint of trepidation in her voice.

'Well . . . if I can. Just for a night. I can move into the hotel tomorrow. Just say if it's a problem, I can find somewhere else. I should have called but I didn't want to ruin the surprise.'

Caitlyn knew she should say that it was a problem and Sara should go to the hotel right now, but she wasn't ready for a battle yet, and Max was here too. *Just one night. I can handle that. She'll go in the morning and I can get myself organised.* Sara had sat herself down on the sofa and Caitlyn took her place opposite.

'How did the Hamptons project go?' she asked.

'Brilliant. They loved it. Did you see the Instagram posts?'

'Yes. It looked amazing.'

Sara nodded. '*Amazing.* They want me back to do the place they're buying in Colorado. Now I've got this hotel to sort out – only because the owner's been left in the lurch. It's a really lovely project, an old house on the edge of town.'

Sara chattered on about her job, her feline gaze sliding about, taking in all the details of the new house. She subtly looked Caitlyn up and down, noting what she was wearing, how she looked, the style of her hair. Caitlyn felt a sensation she had not experienced since Sara left: that she was being examined and found wanting.

Caitlyn wanted to get to her feet and say, *That's it! It's all changed now. You can't sit in judgement of me any more. Go away. Patrick's gone, and losing him has cut the cord between us too.*

Instead, she lifted her wine glass to her mouth and gulped the cool liquid, her hand shaking lightly as she thought, *I mustn't let Sara see how I'm feeling. I don't know why . . . but I mustn't.*

Sara stayed where she was, drinking and flicking through magazines while Caitlyn sorted Max out and put him to bed. When Caitlyn came back down, Sara had opened a fresh bottle and was ready to chat.

'There you are! You've been an age. How is he? Asleep?'

Caitlyn nodded as she sat back down. 'Getting there.' While she'd been upstairs with Max, she'd taken the chance to think over her strategy. She wouldn't provoke a reaction right now. Sara could stay tonight but after that, Caitlyn would take a stand and tell her that things weren't going to go back to the old ways. And she'd also gone into the spare room and pushed all of Patrick's boxes against the wall and covered them up with a cloth. Then on top of that she'd piled books and old box files. It was hardly Fort Knox, but at least Patrick's things weren't quite as obvious now.

Sara had switched on the lamps now that the evening sun had moved to the other side of the house. She gazed over at Caitlyn with a laugh.

'Goodness, what would Patrick think if he could see you now?'

'What do you mean?'

'You've let yourself go a bit, haven't you?' She smiled to take the sting out of her words. 'When did you last get your hair seen to, or have a facial?'

'I don't know. It hasn't seemed important.'

'Patrick would not like that one bit,' Sara scolded. 'You need to keep up standards, just like he did. Remember?'

'Of course.'

'I can't pretend I'm not disappointed to see how much you're changing now he's not here. The house is sold, all his stuff gone, and now you're reverting back to the little plain Jane I rescued at university.' Sara took another sip from her wine glass. 'Patrick was the making of you, darling. Before him, you were absolutely hopeless, don't you remember? One disaster to the next, getting laid by anyone who so much as smiled at you. No wonder you were so miserable! I know, darling, because I held your hand so many times.'

'That's not how I remember it,' Caitlyn said slowly.

Sara didn't appear to hear her. 'And then, when I found Patrick for you, you weren't happy either. I think, really, he was too much for you, don't you? He was just a different calibre, wasn't he? More like me, in a funny way! Obviously you were his wife . . . but I was definitely a kindred spirit. We were very alike, him and me.' She sighed. 'I know he made you wretched but I always seemed to touch a chord in him.'

When she took a drink, Sara's grey eyes flicked up at her over the rim of the glass.

Caitlyn blinked at her, biting her tongue. So it was no accident that Sara was back, she had plenty of venom to disperse. She must have been waiting until she could return here and get her teeth into Caitlyn. Perhaps she'd been laying her plans all these months. Caitlyn watched Sara as she drained her glass and poured another. The second bottle was almost empty. She remembered what Nicholas had said about Sara's drinking.

She actually has a problem. I never noticed it before. How did I not realise?

'A party animal.' That was what Patrick had called Sara. 'She doesn't have limits,' he used to say. Sara's second husband Mark had been the same. They had lived only for entertaining, parties and buckets of booze. Dinners at their house were marked by wonderful food and the way they went on until the early hours, fuelled by rivers of champagne and ice-cold vodka shots. Sometimes, Sara brought out wraps of white powder and chopped them on the coffee table, sharing the lines with anyone who wanted one. Caitlyn didn't and refused shyly, while Patrick simply laughed when Sara offered them to him.

'No thanks, darling. As a barrister, I'd better not.'

But they drank with the others, because that's what they all did.

When Caitlyn announced her pregnancy with Max, the first thing Sara said was, 'Oh my God, no booze for nine months! What will you do?'

'I know! Awful!' Caitlyn said, but in the event she couldn't stand the thought of it anyway. She craved soft sweetness: elderflower, diluted cranberry, fizzy apple. The hard medicinal reek of alcohol turned her stomach. Suddenly the dinner parties that had been such fun and so enjoyable became marathons of tedium. The first hour was great, the second okay and from then, she found it increasingly boring and bewildering, as people lost their trains of thought, yelled loudly across one another, screamed with laughter at the smallest and dullest things, or argued, or starting singing and dancing.

'Let's go home,' she would beg Patrick, desperate to sleep, and after a while she refused to go altogether.

'You've become so boring,' Sara would say accusingly, sunglasses hiding her hangovers, 'and that's why I'm never having children.'

She was mildly irritated by the reality of Max once he arrived, and the way his needs took priority over everything, even though she cooed and smiled and demanded to hold him. She was thrilled to be a godmother, but uncomprehending of the fact that a baby needed constant attention. For a while, Caitlyn saw much less of Sara and Mark, and she was able to concentrate on motherhood and her beloved boy.

But when she and Mark began the descent towards divorce, Sara was back, regaling Caitlyn with stories of his treachery and unfitness to be her husband. It was, Caitlyn realised, a story she had heard many times before. It was identical to her break-up with Rupert. And all the others, before and after. They were not up to her high standards and, it turned out, they were not her equals. Even Rupert, the nephew of an earl, had a mother whose roots were – Sara's nose wrinkled as she said it – 'rather common'.

Mark was revealed to be the same: an upstart who didn't deserve a thoroughbred prize like Sara.

And of course, the trauma of her break-up meant Sara needed to drown her sorrows in drink. Plenty of drink.

Why didn't I see it before now? Caitlyn wondered again, as

Sara took another gulp. *She's a functioning alcoholic, and she has been for years. Did Patrick know? He must have. Nothing escaped him. She must be drunk now, she's had most of two bottles at least.*

'So you and Patrick were kindred spirits?' she said casually.

'I think so,' Sara said, with only the slightest slur in her voice. She could obviously hold her drink, no doubt used to it.

'Did he . . . reach out to you? Confide in you?'

'Caitlyn, anything I did, I did for you.' Sara leaned forward in her chair. 'I always had your best interests at heart, you know? I always have.' She sighed heavily. 'God, don't you miss him?'

'Of course,' Caitlyn said. Her heart began beating faster.

'So do I.' Sara sighed, her eyes suddenly dull, as though the cumulation of two bottles of wine was finally telling. 'I miss him so much.'

'Why do you miss him, Sara?' Caitlyn asked. All these years she'd been Sara's confessor, listening to the baring of her soul. Why stop now?

Sara rolled her eyes up to Caitlyn and smiled. 'Wouldn't you like to know?'

'So you were close. You used to meet up with him without telling me.'

Sara shrugged. 'Oh, sometimes. If he needed a shoulder to cry on. I suppose he didn't tell you about it?'

'No.'

Sara smiled, her lips twitching as though she couldn't quite resist showing her pleasure at this. She twisted her glass between her fingers, watching the last of the shimmering liquid as it swayed inside. Then she said quietly, 'He understood me.'

Caitlyn felt as if they were trembling on the edge of some kind of revelation, as long as she went carefully. She spoke slowly so that she didn't give away her racing heart and quaking voice. 'Did he? In what way?'

'He knew how I ticked.' Sara frowned. 'I liked that. It wasn't always the most . . . flattering thing in the world. He'd tell me off. Did you know that? Men don't usually tell me off! Patrick did.'

'When did he tell you off?'

'When we talked.' Sara lifted her wine glass up to drain the last rivulet, then put it back on the table.

'How often did you talk?'

'Quite often. Emails. Chats. We were in touch.' Sara smiled at her. 'Friends.'

'Of course. Friends.' Caitlyn could see that Sara was having a little game with her, dangling something just out of reach. She was sober enough to know exactly what she was doing.

'A special . . . friendly relationship.' Sara sighed again, almost luxuriously. 'He knew me. Inside out.'

'I had no idea,' Caitlyn said. 'He never said.'

Sara blinked her slow blink. 'No,' she said, 'you didn't.'

Caitlyn didn't know how she got through the next few minutes, as she stood up and said she was too tired to talk longer, and showed Sara, swaying on her feet now, the way to the guest bedroom. Inside, she was shaky, almost tearful, but she managed to hide it until she was safely inside her bedroom with the door shut.

In her bathroom, cleaning her teeth, she saw her own frightened gaze staring back at her.

My God, she wants me to believe that she had something going on with Patrick. The thought was devastating. It was everything Nicholas had said about Sara, and more. *She wants to undermine me, demean me, frighten me. Why would she do that? I know he didn't desire her, I know it.*

It had been such a pillar of her life that Patrick had not been attracted to Sara that she felt everything would collapse if that were not true. But was he such a good actor that he could have concealed it? Over all those years, could they have been hiding something from her? She had never doubted him.

But I know that she had lunch with Patrick and he didn't tell me. He gave me her favourite perfume as a gift – was that a mistake, or was Sara's hand behind it, giving me a little clue that she was with him when he chose it?

An image played suddenly in her mind, of the bank statements she had looked at and the payments that had been made. Something chimed, two pieces of a puzzle that un-expectedly connected. Caitlyn pulled out her phone and went with shaky fingers to Sara's Instagram account. There they were – the many photographs of her perfect life and the gor-geous projects she worked on, with their chirpy comments and shout-outs to the people involved.

Caitlyn scrolled back through the images she had looked at just the other day, and found what she was looking for. It was a photo of a large and exquisite bunch of tulips so dark they were almost black.

Beautiful bouquet arrived for me today – I'm a lucky girl. I loved being bunched!

So gorgeous #RoseYardFlowers

The text swam in front of her eyes and she squinted to be sure she was reading right. *Rose Yard Flowers. I've seen that name before. On Patrick's bank statements.*

Then it's true.

Chapter Twenty-Six

Tommy sat in the window seat, a blanket round her fur coat, her fur hat on, and stared out at the endless whiteness. The others had abandoned the ice-cold drawing room but Tommy went there when she needed a respite in a place where she wouldn't run into Fred. It made a change from the darkness of her bedroom, at least.

She sighed and wrapped her arms tightly about her knees. Such moments of peace were rare. There was always so much to be done, keeping order in a house that was occupied at all hours of the day by the whole family. Sending the children out to play meant coats and boots and socks to dry out, and hungry, cold people to restore to warmth. There was housework, laundry and mealtimes to manage too. Ada couldn't cope alone and Clara would not be seen until the thaw came. They all had to muck in, which in practice meant Tommy, while Gerry was on child patrol.

It's so odd that Barbara spends so little time with Molly. She's a sweet little girl, quite merry now she's come out of her shell, and yet Barbara ignores her almost entirely.

She hadn't been able to look Barbara in the eye since she'd overheard the conversation with Roger, but she was more alert to the way that Barbara fluttered around her brother like a butterfly round a flower, attending to his needs, listening to him, flattering him – *fawning, almost* – and while Roger clearly enjoyed the attention, he didn't seem much happier. All he really wanted, Tommy thought, was to spend time with Fred, discussing the evils of capitalism and the joy of collectivisation.

And Roger's cooler with me too, I'm sure of it. If Barbara wants to put a wedge between us, she's succeeding. Oh, I wish I could talk to Fred about all this. But I've ruined everything.

Feeling dog-tired and depressed, Tommy hauled herself out of the window seat to make her way back to the kitchen to start on tea. As she went by the piano, she stopped suddenly, frowning. There was an empty space where a silver filigree bonbon basket had once stood. She looked around the room for it, and quickly noticed that there were several other empty spaces. A trio of china pillboxes and a Dresden shepherdess had gone. The silver candlesticks from the glazed cupboard had vanished too, and so had a gilt-framed watercolour that was usually almost concealed from sight by the standing lamp in front of it.

Has Ada taken them for cleaning? wondered Tommy. But she never had before. Why would she start now?

She went quickly out of the room, across the hall and over to her mother's side of the house. Listening at the door, she could hear Mrs Whitfield's voice talking at length and mur-mured replies from Barbara. Tommy darted away, back into the hall and up the stairs. She went swiftly along the passage to the rose bedroom and quietly opened the door, her heart racing. Then she slipped inside and stood looking around at the gloomy room.

It glittered like a treasure cave. Everything she had noticed missing was there, and much more besides. The ornaments had been carefully placed around the room to dress it in a lustre of richness. The silver candlesticks stood on the dressing table on either side of the Dresden shepherdess, and the painting hung on the wall, alongside other small pictures taken from around the house. Some of the family photographs, including one of Roger taken in a photographer's studio in Oxford, were on the chimney piece, as though they were Barbara's own family. Going towards them, Tommy noticed a glint of something in the silver bonbon basket which sat on an antique demi-lune table. It was a sapphire ring that belonged to her mother.

'This is outrageous,' Tommy said out loud. 'She's been stripping the place bare while we haven't been looking!'

Despite her outrage, she was nervous of being discovered, and didn't dare risk staying any longer. Her palms prickled and her pulse was racing like the clappers as she tiptoed back across the room and out onto the landing.

'Tommy?'

She gasped and jumped violently. Fred was standing there. 'You frightened me!' she cried, clutching at her chest.

'I'm so sorry. Are you all right?'

'Yes, yes, but . . .' She beckoned to him. 'Follow me!' She went hastily into her room, held the door open for him and shut it behind him when he was inside. 'Fred, it's dreadful. Barbara's been taking things from around the house. She's got loads of it in there! It's like Aladdin's cave. Do you think she's been stealing?'

Fred looked surprised. 'Stealing? I shouldn't think so. She's just borrowed it, no doubt, to cheer up her bedroom.'

'Then why not ask?' Tommy shook her head. 'It looks very sly to me.'

'If she were stealing, she'd have hidden it all under her bed in a suitcase. And Ada goes in there to clean, doesn't she? So it's all quite obvious.' He looked amused. 'You're imagining it, Tommy.'

'Maybe. But I think it's distinctly odd, especially after what she said to Roger about you and me.'

Fred fixed her with a candid look. 'What did she say?'

Tommy began to blush hard. 'Only that we were friends.'

'We are . . . aren't we?' he asked. A shadow passed over his face. 'At least, I thought we were.'

'We are,' she said stammeringly, 'only . . .'

'For God's sake, Tommy,' he burst out, 'it's killing me! The way you're ignoring me! I'm sorry, I truly am. I trespassed unforgivably on your kindness, and you've a perfect right to cast me into outer darkness. But I'd do anything if you'd only forgive me.'

She stared at him, mortified. 'No . . . no . . . you're wrong. You don't understand!'

'You're grieving,' he said. 'Of course I understand that. It's too soon. Your husband—'

'Stop it!' Tommy cried sharply. She put her hands on her

ears. 'I don't want to talk about him. I don't want you to either!'

Fred looked shocked, then said, 'Of course not, I'm being horribly clumsy. Tommy . . . I'm so sorry . . .'

Tommy curdled inside, with embarrassment and something else that was horribly, shiveringly intense. 'I can't talk about it. I'm sorry, Fred. Please. I must get on now.'

It took all afternoon to overcome her emotions and go back downstairs for dinner. Fred was there, and the chasm between them seemed wider than ever. He looked worn and sad, his expression defeated. He was polite but remote, and she felt wretched.

Why is it so hard to tell him the truth?

But she had locked it away so deeply in her own heart, she could barely admit it to herself.

As Barbara passed her a serving dish, Tommy noticed a mineral glint on the other woman's earlobes and saw she was wearing large diamond earrings that Tommy had never seen in her ears before.

'Here you are, Tommy. Carrots,' Barbara said, then turned to murmur in Roger's ear.

Tommy stared at her. *Where did those diamonds come from?* Such rich jewels didn't seem to sit very well with Barbara's portrayal of herself as a desperate poor widow supporting a young child alone.

Mother's got studs like those – but there's no way Barbara could have borrowed them, not the way she's borrowed the other things. But then, there's the sapphire ring. That certainly came from Mother.

She eyed Barbara across the table, watching as she talked to Roger, laughing and murmuring under her breath. Her blonde, pink-and-white beauty had something jagged and bloodless about it. Tommy could see sharp collarbones protruding beneath the white cashmere jersey, and the long thin fingers deftly manoeuvring cutlery in elegant, minute movements. Occasionally Barbara's pale blue gaze would flicker up at Tommy and then away without expression.

Why is she watching me? Then Tommy caught herself up. *Why am I watching her?*

She had the uncomfortable feeling that they were each a threat to the other, and that they'd been locked in a battle for some time that she was only now becoming aware of.

She is slowly but surely taking over. I can feel it.

She looked over at Gerry, who was frowning at Barbara, and guessed that her sister knew it too.

But how will we stop her?

The next day, Tommy took the opportunity of Barbara going on her promenade with Roger to visit her mother, who was sitting by the stove in her sitting room, the dogs curled at her feet.

'Thomasina, hello, how nice of you to come by,' her mother said with a touch of sarcasm, as Tommy came in. She was stitching away at her cushion cover with lime-green silk.

'Well . . . I've been rather busy,' Tommy replied with a

laugh. 'Ada has had me cleaning cupboards this morning. It's quite an education.'

'I've no doubt. But you needn't obey her orders, you know. She is paid help. You are not.'

Tommy sat down in the flowered chintz armchair opposite her mother. It was pleasant to be in the fuzzy warmth emitted by the wood-burning stove. 'We're all mucking in, you know.' As she said it, she knew it was untrue. That great Marxist socialist Roger never lifted a finger. Barbara was nowhere to be seen when there was work to be done. Fred hardly could, even if it occurred to him that laundry and cooking weren't done by magic. Her mother was not to be moved from the warmth and comfort of her sofa. That left Ada, Gerry and Tommy taking care of the house, while Thornton did his best to clear snow outside.

'Mother,' Tommy said, taking a deep breath and pushing away her resentment. 'I want to ask something. About Barbara. Have you been giving her jewellery?'

The skein of lime-green silk stopped in mid-stitch, then her mother said, 'I have lent her one or two pieces. Why is it a concern?'

'It's not a concern, I simply wanted to make sure that you knew she had your sapphire ring and, I think, your diamond earrings.'

Mrs Whitfield's mouth stiffened as she slowly drew the thread through her canvas. 'Are you calling me a fool, Thomasina?'

'Of course not! Why would I?' Tommy was confused. 'I just want to be sure you know what's happening.'

Her mother put down her sewing and fixed Tommy with a cold stare. 'Of course I do. I know exactly what's going on.'

Tommy frowned. 'What is?'

'Don't pretend you're not up to your old tricks.' Mrs Whitfield was clearly seething, and had been since before Tommy came in. 'I'd hoped you'd learned your lesson. But obviously not. You come in here with your nasty insinuations about an honourable woman when you ought to ask yourself why it is that you haven't turned out more like Barbara Hastings.'

'What do you mean?' Tommy said, hurt.

'She's so elegant. Always perfectly turned out, and with such beautiful manners. She's a support to us all, without trying to take over, and she retains her dignity. She doesn't try to be a skivvy. Besides which, she made a very proper marriage.'

'I see,' Tommy said icily. Hurt burned in her chest. 'You mean she hasn't put herself forward like I have.'

Her mother sighed again, picking up her sewing once more and staring at the stitches so she would not have to look at her daughter. 'I think you know what I mean.'

'Say it, why don't you?' Tommy said, her breath coming faster and her fists clenching. 'You want to, you always have. I've felt it for years. You want to, you say it in a hundred different ways every day.'

'I don't know what you mean,' her mother replied testily.

'Yes, you do! You mean that my marriage wasn't entirely *proper*, don't you?'

'Well, it wasn't,' said Mrs Whitfield flatly.

'Do you think I don't know that?' hissed Tommy. 'Don't you think I paid for it?'

'I have no idea, I'm sure.'

'Well, I did, in ways you can't imagine.'

'Don't be disgusting.'

'Oh . . . go to hell!' cried Tommy, turning and running out of the room, bumping into Barbara as she did.

'I'm sorry,' Barbara said silkily. 'I was just getting . . .'

But Tommy didn't stop to talk to her, rushing away into the hall instead, to stand alone in the dark under the stairs so that she could control her trembling lips and the tears that flooded unwanted down her cheeks.

I want comfort. I can't bear all this alone. But I have to be strong.

She straightened her shoulders and prepared herself to face everyone as normal.

I want Fred.

She suppressed the thought as soon as it came into her mind. Fred was dangerous, and that was that. The safest way, the only way, was to cope with it all on her own. That was the promise she had made to herself and she intended to keep it.

Chapter Twenty-Seven

As soon as Sara had left the next day, Caitlyn ran up the stairs to the spare room and uncovered the boxes. She tugged a few down onto the floor, yanking open their lids and pulling out the contents. The box she'd opened before was now at the bottom but she found what she was looking for, lifting the bank statements out with shaky hands. Yes. Here it was. Every month, there was a payment of hundreds of pounds to Rose Yard Flowers.

She went back to Sara's Instagram account. The date of the photograph was the day after a payment to Rose Yard Flowers of £125.

Oh no. Surely not. Please . . . not that.

She called Theo Ronson, Patrick's accountant.

'Well, Caitlyn,' he said when she'd explained what she wanted to know. 'I'm not sure there's much I can tell you. Patrick said that this account was for his private use.'

'So not a business account? He didn't reclaim what he spent as expenses?'

'No, he didn't. Sorry I can't be of any further use.'

'That's fine, really. You've been a help,' Caitlyn said wretchedly. So her theory had been wrong. It wasn't business. *Pleasure, then. Oh God.* 'I'm very grateful.'

When she'd put the phone down, she went back to Sara's Instagram account. Now the pictures filled her with violent distaste. She scrolled through, going back years, recognising some outfits she'd seen Sara wear, some of the locations, and even some of the parties.

Then she saw it. A photograph of a hand and wrist wearing a watch she knew well, resting on a table by a Martini glass. The caption said: *A preprandial with a handsome man with exquisite taste #luckygirl #shyclient.*

Fighting an urge to be sick, Caitlyn texted Nicholas.

Can you come up here? I really need to talk to you. C

Nicholas arrived a few hours later, when his tutorials were finished, clutching a bag of croissants.

'I thought these might be welcome,' he said, holding them up with a smile, then he saw her face. 'What's up? You look awful.'

'It's Sara.' Caitlyn's eyes filled with tears. 'She turned up here yesterday out of the blue.'

'What? Sara's in Oxford?' Nicholas looked bemused. 'The two of you, both back at the same time? That's weird.'

'It's worse than that. I think she's come back on purpose to play games with me. And the awful thing is that I'm pretty sure she was having an affair with Patrick.' It sounded so grim spoken out loud like that, and the same stomach-dropping mixture of betrayal and despair plummeted through her.

'Let's sit down and you can explain it to me.'

As Nicholas made a pot of coffee, Caitlyn tried to recount as clearly as possible what Sara had said last night, but her words kept coming out jumbled and Nicholas would make her go back and tell him again as slowly as she could. 'And then on the way home, I remembered something to do with her Instagram – and the name Rose Yard Flowers.' When she told him how she had found that name in Patrick's bank statements, Nicholas's expression grew solemn.

'Okay. That's not good.' He put a cup of coffee in front of her.

'That's not all. He also had payments to a place called Fortescue House. And look.' Caitlyn got out her phone and opened the Instagram app. She put it in front of him so he could see the picture of a smart hotel room on Sara's page, with a caption underneath it.

Love this hotel, so chic and stylish. Real inspiration here. Thanks for a marvellous stay @FortescueHouseHotel

'It matches the date of a payment by Patrick to the same hotel.' Caitlyn lifted miserable eyes to Nicholas. 'It's not even that far from his chambers.'

'Oh shit.' Nicholas gave her a sympathetic look. 'That's hard to explain away.'

'And then there was this.' She scrolled to the picture with Patrick's hand in it. 'You see? That's him.'

'Are you absolutely sure?'

'Of course I am. That's his hand.' She couldn't help her voice coming out shrilly. 'I think I would know my own husband's hand. I know that watch, it's upstairs if you want to see it!'

Nicholas looked at her anxiously. 'It's okay, I believe you. I just wish I could say I'm surprised. It's what you'd expect from Sara, isn't it?'

'But . . . not from Patrick,' she whispered, desolate. 'I trusted him. He never gave me any reason not to. And it must have been going on for a while. Look at how long ago these pictures were posted! Two years ago, more for that one.' She took a deep breath and tried to speak coherently so that Nicholas would understand. 'He . . . rang me, the night he died, and tried to tell me something about Sara but I couldn't hear what it was. There were just a few words I could make out – I heard "threatened" and "important". And he said he wanted to tell me, before she did.'

There was a long pause and then Nicholas said, 'I am so sorry, Caitlyn.'

She felt a stab of agony. 'So you think it's true?'

'I would say it's fairly conclusive that Patrick and Sara were having an affair.'

Heat rose up in Caitlyn's chest and into her face. Hearing it like this from Nicholas, even though it was the inescapable conclusion, was more horrible than it had been on her own lips. Boiling tears stung her eyes and she felt her shoulders shake.

'Oh Caitlyn. I'm really sorry. This is just terrible. To find out like this . . .'

'I can't . . . I can't believe she would do that to me. Well . . . I can now. Now that you've told me what she was like, what she did. But . . . not him. Not my Patrick.' She began to weep, seized by an awful grief. 'He . . . he died . . . and my old life and everything I believed in died too – and what have I got now? It was all . . . all a lie.'

'Come on.' Nicholas got up and lifted her coat to her shoulders. 'Come on, we're getting away from here. Right now. Where's Max?'

'Next door, doing pottery with Jen. He's with her all day.'

'Good. We're going to escape for a few hours.'

She cried as he led her to where his car was parked, put her in the passenger seat, and then switched the engine on so that it roared into life.

She sank down into the seat and wept as he drove, aware vaguely of the wipers going as the rain came down. At last she said, 'Where are we going?'

'We're going where I always wanted to be when I was most miserable. Back home.'

The rain had stopped by the time Caitlyn and Nicholas reached King's Harcourt. It was surrounded by a riot of blooms, its ancient stones golden and dappled by sunshine, rambling roses climbing up around the ground-floor windows.

'It's so incredibly beautiful,' Caitlyn said, as they got out. She was calm now. 'I can see why problems seem to melt away here.'

'There's a serenity,' he said. 'And it always helps put things in perspective.'

They stood together gazing at it. 'You shouldn't lose this place, if you can help it,' Caitlyn said softly. 'It's too precious.'

They said nothing for a while, soaking in the house's ancient beauty. Then Nicholas said, 'Come on, we won't go in just yet. Let's walk for a while.'

They wandered around the house and through the gardens at the back, walled quadrangles leading into one another, each with a different style of planting.

'That's a bowling green,' Nicholas said, pointing to a velvety square of lush grass.

'Francis Drake style?' she asked.

'That's right. Come on. Through here.'

He led her through crumbling brick arches with bright pink and white daisies growing in busy profusion from cracks in the mortar. From the formal gardens, they walked through a shaggy paddock fenced off for ponies no longer there, and then out to the woods. As they crunched under the trees, Caitlyn saw a large wire enclosure.

'What's that?' she asked, pointing,

'Feeding pens for the pheasants.'

'Is there shooting here?'

'I think Aunt Geraldine lets a local farmer set up shoots.'

'Oh.' Caitlyn pursed her lips. 'I don't know how I feel about that. Shooting's cruel, isn't it?'

Nicholas laughed as they went past the pen. 'Look.' He pointed at drums with small trays at the bottom and water dispensers. 'If I could come back as a pheasant here, I wouldn't be too unhappy. Food and drink on tap, protection from predators and a lovely wood to roam in. Encouraged to breed as much as possible. A couple of times a year, some guns take aim at you and if you're terribly unlucky you might get shot but most don't. If you do, you get put in the pot. You get eaten. You have had a much nicer existence than just about any supermarket chicken that can be bought. So . . .' He shrugged. 'Is that cruel?'

She laughed. 'You've converted me. And you're clearly a lot posher than you ever let on before.'

Nicholas shrugged. 'I don't know about that. But it's amazing how many people want to be your friend because of somewhere like this. I preferred to keep it quiet.'

'From people like Sara,' Caitlyn said, and her spirits swooped again as she remembered.

'Absolutely.' He smiled at her. 'If Patrick really wanted her, and risked his marriage for her, then he wasn't the man he must have been when he married you.'

'But you think that's exactly what he did.' She looked at him anxiously.

'I think that's how it looks. But there's still doubt. And he's not here to confirm it.'

'She is.'

'You can't trust her,' Nicholas warned. 'Don't forget that. She's not to be trusted. If she thinks it'll get a response, she'll say anything. She loves to stir. Creating waves is all she really cares about.'

The walk soothed Caitlyn's mind a little and helped her through the pain of what she had learned. They talked about the past, their student days and everything they remembered, except for the last time they had seen each other.

When they reached the house again, she was calm and ready to have a cup of tea with Aunt Geraldine. The old lady looked as neat and well presented as last time, her snowy hair set in waves and a string of pearls at her neck tucked under the silk collar of her blouse.

'Well, this is a nice surprise,' she said. 'How very pleasant to have you back here.' She raised her eyebrows at Nicholas.

'Caitlyn's still just a friend,' Nicholas said, as they settled down by the stove for their tea.

'This is the most beautiful place,' Caitlyn said, wanting to change the subject. 'I can't wait to move in. It feels as though it must be impossible to be unhappy here for long.'

'I'm afraid that's not true. It's possible to be very unhappy even here. My poor dear brother was the proof of that. And then there's Venetia.'

'Venetia?' asked Caitlyn, taking the cup of tea that Nicholas offered her.

'The lady in the Gainsborough portrait. My sister Tommy was quite entranced by her and often used to talk about her story. She died young and suddenly – Venetia, I mean – found dead in bed in the main bedroom upstairs, and left her husband heartbroken. He didn't look at the portrait again. So you see, even here, unhappiness can persist. Although perhaps it's easier to bear life's challenges when you're surrounded by beauty.'

'Poor girl,' Caitlyn said, filled with melancholy thinking of the young beauty in the painting. 'That's awful.'

Aunt Geraldine leaned towards her. 'I think you're carrying a grief like that. Something very heavy. It's weighing you down awfully.'

'Auntie,' Nicholas began, looking embarrassed, but Caitlyn stopped him with a smile.

'It's fine,' she said. 'Yes, you're right. I lost my husband very suddenly. I'm still coming to terms with it. In some ways, I still feel as though Patrick is just away, and that he might come back through the door at any time. And the longer he's away, the crosser I get with him. I know I ought to feel sad, and I *do* feel sad because I miss him all the time. But . . .' She frowned. 'Oh, I don't know how to explain it. It's like he's playing hide and seek with me and I keep expecting him to pop up again. And more than anything, I want him to come back and explain things to me. But he's never going to do that.'

'The answers are always there, if you look for them. But often, they are inside yourself. That's what I've found anyway.' Aunt Geraldine looked at her over the top of her spectacles. 'But I also believe happiness can be a choice. And so can unhappiness. The will is a powerful thing, but you do need to learn how to use it, and how to battle with others who want to use their willpower over you when you don't want them to.'

Caitlyn nodded thoughtfully.

'You're quite the oracle today, Aunt,' Nicholas said with a laugh. 'Very Delphic pronouncements.'

'And you are too cheeky by half. I think Caitlyn knows what I'm talking about.'

'I don't think it can always be chosen,' Caitlyn said. 'And besides, don't we need sadness? If something awful happens, if we lose someone we love, don't we need to feel grief?'

'Of course it's natural to mourn, and mourning often never ends,' Aunt Geraldine replied. 'But it must be encompassed into life, folded into it, alongside all the other emotions of existence. As we live, we layer our experiences one over the other, learning as we go. When I say one can choose to be happy, I suppose I mean that you have to recognise the point at which you allow sadness or rage or despair to infect you so thoroughly that it overwhelms everything else, rubs it all out.'

'People with depression don't "allow" themselves to feel it, do they?' Caitlyn asked, frowning. 'Most loathe it, in my experience.'

'Of course there are gradations, and things outside one's control. You must decide if it is beyond your scope of choice or not.'

'I see,' Caitlyn said slowly. 'At least, I think I do.'

Geraldine smiled at her as she picked up a digestive biscuit. 'Oh good, dark chocolate. My favourite. Renee got milk last time. Filthy!'

Before they left, Aunt Geraldine said to Nicholas, 'So, boy, why don't you spend more time here?'

'My work's in Oxford.'

'Terms are eight weeks long. Three terms a year. That's less than half the year,' said his aunt sternly.

'I will definitely visit more often,' Nicholas promised, kissing her cheek.

'I suspect you will, once Caitlyn's here.' When Caitlyn bent to kiss her farewell, Aunt Geraldine said, 'Come as soon as you like. I'd like to meet your boy.'

'I will,' Caitlyn said. 'Max will love it here.'

'Nicholas has a daughter, you know. He called her Coco. So funny to me. We used to drink cocoa all the time. Not rationed, you see. I got to like it without sugar as well. But nice as it was, I'd never call a child after it!'

Chapter Twenty-Eight

'You'd better look the candles out,' Gerry said to Tommy, coming into the kitchen. 'We've just heard it on the wireless. They're going to ration electricity. Gas too.'

'What?' cried Tommy, dismayed.

Gerry nodded. 'It's the shortages. We've got to turn the electricity off for five hours every day. And they're stopping the television broadcasts and cutting down the radio transmissions.'

'Oh my goodness. It's really very serious,' Tommy said. 'I mean, we knew that. But still.'

They all gathered around to listen to the next broadcast, the grown-ups solemn as they realised that the crisis was becoming a desperate emergency.

'Luckily we don't have a television so it doesn't matter to us if they turn it off,' Gerry said cheerfully, but no one smiled. The newsreader went on with the litany of woe: transport across the country was at a virtual standstill. Coupled with fuel shortages, the result was that industry was seizing up, leaving thousands unemployed. Coal could not get to the power stations, and without that, there could be no electricity.

'This smacks of incompetence,' Fred said gravely.

'But what are they do to, with conditions like this?' demanded Tommy, looking at him furiously. He looked sadly back, and she flushed, turning her face away.

'I shouldn't think this happens in Russia,' Roger remarked.

'I imagine it's probably worse,' Tommy snapped. Her nerves felt frayed and her ability to cope was wearing thin. But she knew that the tension she felt came partly from this unbearable situation with Fred, and partly from the way she could feel Barbara burrowing into their lives. At some point, Barbara had turned from an admittedly cool friend to foe, and she didn't know when or how it had happened. She didn't even understand what Barbara hoped to achieve. 'I'm going to get out the old lamps and see if we have any spirit left. Otherwise it's candles for us during the day.' She sighed. 'I thought things couldn't get any harder. Thank goodness for our coal.' She shuddered, thinking of what life might have been like but for their delivery. 'Well, chin up. It has to be done. And it can't last forever.'

'How will you finish your painting?' Gerry said to Fred. 'You can't do it by candlelight, can you?'

'It's coming on very well,' Fred said lightly. 'I'm almost finished and I'll use the few hours of daylight we get. If I move the easel to the window, I should be fine.'

'What are you painting?' Barbara asked, and Tommy realised she must never have been in the library to see what Fred was up to. For some reason, she was not very bothered with

Fred. It was noticeable that she had a harder tone when she talked to him, quite unlike the soft, winsome girlishness of her conversation with Roger.

'I'm making a copy of the Gainsborough portrait. Just for my own amusement.'

'Really?' Barbara blinked at him slowly.

'That's right,' Fred said politely. 'It helps pass the time.'

'Are you a painter?'

'Only in the most amateur way.'

'I see.' Barbara nodded and looked over at Tommy. 'Isn't he clever?'

'Very,' Tommy said. She didn't look at Fred again. 'Now if you'll excuse me, I must go and look out those candles.'

Tommy was in the storeroom, scrabbling about among all the old items in there, sure she had seen an ancient bottle of spirit for the lamps, when there was a sound behind her. Before she could turn around, she heard Fred's voice.

'Tommy . . . are you all right?'

'Yes, yes . . . Oh, where are the blasted things?' She stumbled over a box of rubbish and banged her head on the shelf. 'Ouch! Oh God.' She rubbed it and, to her horror, burst into tears.

'Tommy.' He was at her side in a moment. 'Are you hurt?'

'No, not really, but . . .' Now that she had allowed the tears to come, they fell fast. 'It's all so terrible! The cold, the blasted awful cold . . . and the struggle to feed us all and keep warm, and now there'll be no electricity. Oh God, I can't bear it.'

Fred hugged her, pulling her to him, and for a moment she

let herself lean against him, feeling the scratchiness of his overcoat against her cheek. Then she pulled away, sniffing.

'I'm sorry. I'm being pathetic.'

'No. You carry the worry for all of us,' he said quietly. 'I can see that. Everyone relies on you. It isn't fair.'

'It's perfectly fair. It's what I'm for.' Tommy wiped her eyes. 'Please forget you saw me give in like that.'

'I'm glad I did. It makes me realise you're only human, like the rest of us.'

'Of course I am,' she said with a small laugh.

'I shall stop painting at once,' he said gravely. 'I came to tell you. We can't light the fire in the library just so I can dab away with my paints. And I won't be able to see much without the lights anyway. The daylight is too gloomy.'

'I miss the sun,' she said with a sigh. 'Do you think it'll ever be warm again?'

'You said yourself it had to end sometime.'

Tommy was overcome with a tremendous sense of exhaustion. The struggle was so hard and so ongoing. Tomorrow she'd have to try and get to the village again, and the snow had fallen once more last night. She couldn't sleep for fear the pipes would freeze and there would be no water.

'Tommy,' Fred said quietly. 'What happened between us . . . you've barely spoken to me since—'

'Please don't,' she said quickly, flushing. She looked away, embarrassed.

'I have to talk to you about it. I know you've found it hard to forgive me, but please . . .'

'Forgive you? Of course I forgive you.'

Fred looked at her, puzzled. 'But I must have offended you very badly.'

She shook her head. 'But that wasn't about you at all. It was about me. I daren't be around you, I can't trust myself.'

He stared at her, absorbing what she had said. 'But—'

'Don't you see?' she said, suddenly sharp. 'I'm the one at fault, not you. And it's better for you if I simply stay away. I'm sorry, Fred, but it's for the best. Now, I'm going to ask Ada if she and Thornton want to move back in during the cuts. If you want to help, you could see if you can find the spirit before we turn the lights out.' She made her way past him, and hurried away, hoping he hadn't seen the pain on her face.

They turned the lights out that afternoon at exactly two o'clock on the grounds that they might as well get used to it and start saving power right away. It seemed such a strange idea, that the lights going out in a house in the middle of nowhere would contribute something towards resolving the crisis.

'I suppose it's like everything during the war,' Tommy said, as she went around switching off lamps and lighting candles, Gerry helping her. 'It's all the little, individual efforts that seem like nothing but put together with thousands and thousands of others make a difference.'

'It's wonderfully eerie. We should tell ghost stories,' Gerry said, not listening.

'I suppose so. That reminds me, don't let the children have candles at night. It's far too dangerous. We can put the lights on again at four, but we should leave them off as long as we can.'

'Yes, ma'am.' Gerry saluted her. 'You run a tight ship.'

Tommy laughed. 'What else is there to do?'

They went back to Mrs Whitfield's sitting room where Barbara, Roger and their mother were playing cards. Fred had taken the children off for a drawing session, and the room was quiet, lit by candles and the glow of the stove. Tommy sat down in an armchair and picked up a book but couldn't concentrate on it. Gerry settled on the hearthrug and stared at the trio playing cards. Eventually she said, 'That's a pretty brooch, Barbara.'

Tommy looked over and saw that on the lapel of Barbara's jacket shone a large diamond brooch.

Gerry went on: 'It looks just like one of Mother's. She has a lover's knot like that. Almost the same, in fact.'

Barbara looked over from her card game. 'Oh, it is the same.'

'Really?' Gerry asked in surprise. She turned to her mother. 'Is it yours, Mother?'

'It's a very sweet little loan,' Barbara said quickly. 'Isn't it, Nancy?'

'No it's not,' Mrs Whitfield said in her most imperious tone. 'It's a gift. I've given it to Barbara. She's been such a help and support to me over these difficult times.'

Tommy looked again at the glittering jewel. Barbara had sat next to Mrs Whitfield and had her ear bent, and folded silk into neat figures-of-eight, or split threads. For these arduous duties, she had received a family jewel. Tommy, on the other hand, slaving to protect the estate and worrying how to feed them all and keep them warm, had barely received a kind word.

Gerry looked scandalised. 'Mother, you can't give away your

possessions! They're family things. They belong to the house!'

'They certainly do not,' Mrs Whitfield said. 'They are mine and I shall do what I choose with them. I choose to give this to Barbara.'

Roger spoke up, as he examined his hand of cards. 'I think it's a very good idea. I can't imagine them looking finer anywhere else.'

Tommy turned to him, astonished. She had never heard anything like this clumsy gallantry from him before.

Barbara said demurely, 'You're too kind, Roger.'

Gerry looked over at Tommy and mouthed a word that no one else could see.

Trouble.

Tommy gave her a warning look and Gerry, with obvious effort, said no more.

Tommy had gone to the dining room to set the table for dinner when Gerry came to find her as soon as she could escape from the sitting room.

'What's Mother playing at?' Gerry demanded. 'She can't just give away those things. That brooch was Grandmother's. It ought to go to you, or to me. That's what Father would have wanted. Now it belongs to Barbara?'

'It's not the first thing.' Tommy loaded a tray with cutlery. 'Barbara has a ring and earrings as well. I can't help feeling that Mother is trying to get at me. But Barbara said she considered it a loan, so no doubt she'll give it back.'

'I'm not so sure. She's wearing it so the rest of us can see that she's claimed ownership, I bet. And if darling Barbara is such a help, why isn't she here with us, instead of sitting in the warm with Mother?' Gerry started distributing the cutlery from Tommy's tray. 'And what about Roger taking her side like that?'

'They all like her,' Tommy said. Her spirits were low and she felt as if all the fight had gone out of her. 'I thought you did too.'

'I did at first but now I don't,' Gerry said. 'Do you know how much notice she takes of Molly? Almost none. Ever since I've been minding the children, it's quite clear that Babs doesn't give a toss about poor little Molly. She's never there at bedtime. I think it's wonderful for Molly to be here, if I'm honest.'

'So do I,' Tommy said, cheered a little. 'She's a sweet little girl, quite different from my two with that quiet thoughtfulness of hers.'

'Yes. We love her, and she gets friendship from Antonia and Harry, and attention from me. She's quite blossomed since she's been here, even though she never sees her mother. Barbara's always somewhere else, oiling up to Roger or Mother. She's got a plan and I don't think I like it.'

'I think you could be right. But what I don't understand is what she hopes to gain.'

'As much of our loot as she can pocket probably.'

Tommy stopped short in the middle of placing a knife. 'Is that it?' she asked. 'Just simple, vulgar theft? I find it hard to believe, but you must be right.' She told Gerry about the things in Barbara's bedroom.

'There you are. Proof,' Gerry said darkly. 'She strikes me as the kind of person who looks out for herself, and has the audacity to get away with whatever she wants.'

Tommy thought of Arabella Guthrie's pen. Audacity was right. Barbara had got away with so much. Many times, at school, she'd caught Barbara out in some tiny act of selfishness. She'd always taken the largest serving, or ensured she was first in line, or helped herself to things that weren't exactly meant for her. *One can't help but see a pattern. And she has no qualms about buying things on the black market.*

'As soon as this weather is over, she'll leave. She can't do much harm in that time.'

'I think she should know we're on to her. Come on, while she's busy with Mother and Roger.'

Gerry hurried out of the room and Tommy put down her tray and followed. Upstairs, Gerry went straight to Barbara's room and flung open the door. Going inside, she stopped short, gasping in surprise. 'Oh my goodness – the nerve!'

Tommy followed her and saw that there were even more of their possessions scattered about than there had been. 'She's taking advantage of the fact that we're not using the drawing room. Look, all the snuff boxes are here now. And the painted miniatures from the cabinet.'

'How dare she!' exclaimed Gerry furiously. 'Come on.' She started to go about the room, picking up ornaments and silver and stuffing them in her pocket. 'We'll put it all back. She can hardly complain. And perhaps it will stifle her kleptomaniac tendencies for a while.'

Tommy followed her, taking up more of the borrowed possessions. 'Unless she's given more by Mother.'

'We'll see about that,' Gerry said sternly. 'I think it's time we stopped dear Barbara's tricks. And as soon as the weather turns, she'll be out on her ear.'

Tommy was walking slowly up the stairs later that afternoon when the sound of her name being spoken made her turn around. Barbara was standing there, on the cold stone flags of the hall, her breath coming out in clouds of steam.

'Tommy, you've been in my room.'

'What makes you think that?' Tommy said, outwardly calm but wishing Gerry was there.

'You know very well. You've taken things your brother said I could have.'

'Have or borrow?'

Barbara shrugged. 'A little of both.'

Tommy was outraged. 'Roger can't simply give away the things in the house! Does he really know how much you'd smuggled upstairs?'

Barbara smiled thinly. 'Careful, Tommy. I don't like your language. I think you'll find Roger can do what he wants with his possessions.'

Tommy gaped at her. 'This is extraordinary. I've welcomed you here, as my guest. Have you forgotten that this is my house, and my family?'

Barbara smiled coldly. 'It's not your house. It's Roger's. And I'm Roger's guest – you'd do well to remember it.'

'If you think you can turn my family against me, you're wrong.'

'We'll see,' said Barbara. 'I think you'll find you're already on the back foot.' Then she turned on her heel and stalked away.

Chapter Twenty-Nine

Once she was on her own, Caitlyn found it impossible not to think about Patrick and Sara and the serenity she had felt at Kings Harcourt evaporated. The thought of them grew and possessed her mind like a virulent infection. As soon as Max was in bed that evening, she went back to the boxes and spent hours going through all of Patrick's financial paperwork; but there was nothing else that she could find to give her the kind of concrete proof she wanted.

She sat on the wooden floorboards of the spare room, surrounded by mountains of Patrick's files, and said despairingly, 'Oh Patrick. I wish you could just tell me the truth. Were you having an affair with her?'

She tried to think back over the years and all the things that Patrick had said to convince her that he really didn't think of Sara in that way. She had never caught him out in any suspicious behaviours or unusual activity. She could barely remember seeing him on his own with Sara. But then, why flowers? Why a hotel?

What are the chances I would catch Patrick anyhow? He

was far too good for that. He was an absolute master of himself.

Patrick had control. He steered his own life with precision and determination, and refused to let anything undermine him or push him off course. And he liked to control those around him too, she knew that. Right from the start, he made it clear that she would have to abide by his rules and that he would be making the decisions. He didn't impose it on her; he made it clear that it was the only way they could be together, and she, wildly in love, agreed.

Besides, he made me feel so safe. So protected and looked after.

She had a sudden image of the pheasant pens at Kings Harcourt: the fat happy birds in their cage, eating corn and kept coddled until the day they were flushed out and forced to fly for their lives.

Was that me? Never really safe at all, but just getting closer to the day when I'd have to face my greatest fears.

'Tell me the truth, Patrick!' she shouted, and then bit her lip, appalled by the sound of her voice in the silence and worried that she might wake Max. *I should go to bed. I'm tired. My vision is blurring.* She would open one more box and that would be it. Selecting one near the back of the pile, she pulled it out into the middle of the room and opened it. Inside was a jumble of electrical equipment, cables and chargers. Almost on top, in its black leather case, was Patrick's tablet. It was so familiar that she felt a jolt as she saw it again. She lifted it out carefully, and opened the case. It was out of power and so she took it downstairs to plug into her own charger while she got the list of Patrick's passwords out of her purse, then waited for the tablet to get enough power to start up.

She waited, her stomach churning, the passwords in hand, the same thought passing through her mind over and over.

Perhaps he wanted me to know his secrets.

The next day, after dropping Max at school, Caitlyn walked into town, the tablet in her bag. She'd stayed up for another hour searching through it but had found nothing out of the ordinary in Patrick's email accounts. She'd searched for Sara's name and the messages that came up were completely innocent, usually confirming arrangements that Caitlyn remembered making or thanking Sara for dinners and parties she remembered attending. The tone was what she would have expected: friendly, casual, familiar. There was nothing like the intimacy that Sara had been hinting at, or evidence of their being kindred spirits. It had been enough to make her doubt the fact of their affair again.

She'd finally gone to bed, exhausted, and fallen into the kind of deep sleep that meant she could barely wake up when the alarm went off at seven. With the help of a mug of strong coffee she'd managed to get Max to Spring Hall, and the journey had shaken off her fatigue. Now she wove her way through the crowds milling along Cornmarket, heading determinedly for the college.

'I'm here to see Professor Brooke,' she said to the bulldog in his bowler hat as she went through the gate, and hurried along the quad and into Nicholas's staircase. She bounded up the stairs. 'Come any time,' he'd said. 'My third years are revising, all my tutorials are done this week.'

There was his door, the last one on the staircase. The outer oak door was open and the one inside was slightly ajar. She strode over and pushed it open.

'Nicholas, are you there?' she called. 'I need your help.'

She walked in and stopped abruptly. Nicholas was staring at her from his armchair and opposite on the sofa, turning to look at her from behind a curtain of red curls, was Sara.

'Well, well,' Sara said, with her slow blink, 'fancy seeing you here.'

Caitlyn gaped at her, unable for a moment to take in what she was seeing.

'So, naughty, naughty!' Sara said sweetly. 'You didn't say that you'd been meeting up with Nicholas.' And then she turned to Nicholas. 'You dark horse, you. Why didn't you tell me you two are back in touch?'

Nicholas looked guiltily at Caitlyn. 'It was a real coincidence. Sara and I bumped into each other in the street. Completely unexpected.'

Sara cooed, 'He insisted we come back here for a proper catch-up. He's been telling me everything he's been up to since I last saw him. A professor.' She turned to smile at Nicholas, leaning towards him. 'What an amazing achievement. You must be so proud.'

'Well . . .' Nicholas looked embarrassed.

Caitlyn was dumbstruck. She had assumed that Sara and Nicholas would not meet. She was not going to tell her about him, and she was sure that Nicholas had no desire to see Sara.

So why had he invited her here to his rooms? But here she was, talking in that soft syrupy way that Caitlyn knew so well.

A sick feeling rolled through her, and she realised that she was afraid.

She's doing it again. Invading my life, coming into my space. There's nothing I have that she doesn't want a piece of. Why did I ever, ever think we were friends?

'Do you want a cup of coffee?' Nicholas said, standing up, still shame-faced. 'Come and join us.'

'No, no. I . . . I'm busy. Sorry. I can't stay.' She turned on her heel and hurried away, running down the stairs as fast as she could, panting and shaken, and not stopping till she was out of the college and halfway up the hill. Then she began to walk and went home slowly, feeling as though she had been hit over the head.

When Caitlyn arrived back at the cottage, she was overcome with exhaustion from her late night. She climbed the stairs, each one feeling twice its size as she dragged herself up. As she lay down on her bed, her phone beeped and she fished it out of her pocket. A text from Nicholas popped up:

I'm really sorry. She ambushed me in the street and made me take her back to college. She's gone now. Give me a call. N xx

Caitlyn almost laughed. As usual, Sara was unstoppable. No one could say no to her.

She threw the phone down and closed her eyes. A moment later she was asleep.

Two hours later, she woke, rising groggily from her unconsciousness, woken by a beep from her mobile phone. A text from Sara was on the screen.

You kept that in the dark!! Why didn't you say? N is quite the silver fox now, isn't he? What's the situation? Do you have some gossip to share??? Come on, spill! He's dishy, quite fancy him myself xx

Caitlyn read it over twice, her spirits sinking, recognising Sara's modus operandi: she would ply Caitlyn with questions, demanding answers and worming information out of her with persistence. Usually Caitlyn would squirm but surrender the details Sara wanted.

Not this time.

She deleted the text, and sat back with a sigh, one thought possessing her mind.

I want to be out of here. Somewhere Sara can't find me. What better place than that beautiful house in the middle of nowhere? And when I was there, I felt, weirdly, like I belonged there, even though it's nothing like where I grew up.

Caitlyn had been raised in a terraced house in Southport, a comfortable but modest dwelling kept in good order by her house-proud mother. Patrick had never criticised it openly, but tiny pointed remarks about the decor told her that he considered it an inferior place. She forgave him because he talked the same way about his own background: the home in Australia that he hated and the way he felt compelled to become everything that was its opposite. As a result, their homes were always beautiful. Perfect. Nothing jarred. Everything flowed.

The only imperfect thing in them was me.

The thought broke in on her with the force of a revelation.

I've always been afraid that I wasn't good enough for him. I was the odd thing out in his collection of beauty, and his pursuit of perfection. That's why I can believe that something in him wanted Sara, with her beauty and class. I was crazy about him. But what did he get from me?

Even when he'd proposed, going down on one knee in the Bois de Boulogne in Paris, she'd accepted rapturously and then said, 'Are you sure, Patrick? Do you really want me?'

'Yes,' he'd said, kissing her lazily. 'I really do.'

'Why?'

'I love you, you silly sausage.'

'Good. I love you too.'

He'll keep me safe, she had thought then. *And he knows exactly what to do in life. He'll steer us in the right direction.*

Perhaps Patrick had thought she was malleable enough to be made into his creation. Maybe he witnessed the way she submitted to Sara and he guessed that she would submit to him too. And she did. She let him mould her and form her. The power of his vision of how life should be was so powerful there was no resisting it, and she found his certainty comforting. He knew what was right, and she relaxed in the knowledge that he would lead the way, from the decoration of their house to the kind of glassware on their dinner table. From where they went on holiday to the sort of Christmas cards they sent. Every decision was Patrick's, and he chose always with the skill and taste of the connoisseur.

I worked so hard to be what he wanted! Caitlyn remembered the hours she had devoted to keeping herself fit and slim, to maintaining her looks. Patrick had chosen most of her clothes; he saw the subtle variations in style that crossed the line between acceptable and too flashy or try-hard. He disliked both the ostentatious newness of the way some of her friends looked, and the striving for a kind of vintage dream of how things once were. He could be trusted to get it just right, and some of their happiest times were when he took her out to dress her, spoil her and style her.

But there was the other side to Patrick, she mustn't forget that. He liked games. He was mischievous, and a tease. He liked to fool her, or lead her on silly errands or treasure hunts. His Christmas treasure hunts were his favourite thing of all. Her gift would be hidden somewhere and she'd have to interpret the clues in order to find it. He'd follow her about as she deciphered them, gleeful when she worked one out, unbending when she didn't.

'You need to find your own way there, Caitlyn,' he'd say firmly. 'It's only worth having that way.'

The clues could lead her anywhere – once even to the church down the road where she was astonished to discover that he had clasped a necklace around the neck of a statue of the Virgin Mary and a pearl bracelet around the wrist of a funerary angel.

311

'Thank you, you nutter, but anyone might have taken them!' she'd laughed, delighted.

'Sometimes people don't see what's in plain sight. Or they can't distinguish the really precious from the simply flashy,' Patrick had said, helping fasten the necklace on her. He'd bent down to kiss her softly. 'Don't forget that you're the precious one,' he'd murmured. 'Remember that, Caitlyn. Now we'd better get going, they'll be arriving for the big service any minute now.'

She remembered it now as she stared into space. *Maybe he was unable to resist Sara's allure, and the thrill of playing the game. Of hiding the affair from me.*

But that's between Patrick and me. I need to get Sara out of my life. But how?

Chapter Thirty

The prolonged cold had created a strange atmosphere of half-wakefulness in the house, perhaps because of the almost constant darkness. Outside, there was no sign of the sun, just a paling of the darkness to a weak, foggy grey that lingered a few hours and dissolved back into night. The candles about the house glowed, casting out their small golden aureoles and making the shadows around them even blacker.

The children were muted, and had lost much of their urge to go out and play in the snow. The novelty had worn thin and now they were tired of the grey-white world outside and the constant, unrelenting cold. They craved warmth like little cats, and now were most often to be found in their grandmother's sitting room, toasting themselves by the stove while they played cards and board games and read books. There were plenty of logs, thanks to Thornton's efforts before the snow, and the coal was now saved only for the boiler and the range, for there was no knowing when the thaw would come.

This weather could go on until March. Perhaps even till April, Tommy thought. It seemed impossible, but it wasn't.

The wireless was quiet most of the day now. Even if there had been electricity, there were no broadcasts. When it was on, it was to report more of the calamitous effects of the weather: there were shortages of everything, not just food now. More stringent regulations were imposed, along with harsher penalties for breaking them.

'Would they really put us in prison for using electricity?' Harry asked, looking worried.

'I suppose only if we kept doing it when we were told not to,' Tommy told him. 'But we don't do that, so it's perfectly all right.'

Tommy spent a lot of time in the kitchen with Ada, going through the food in the cupboards, the meat safe and the game larder. It helped divert her from the deep sense of depression that threatened to engulf her. She was fairly certain that they could manage, though she hadn't been able to summon up the strength to get to the village lately, and she suspected there would be no milk if she did. They had milk powder, though, and that would see them through a little longer. There was a little butter left, and quite a big stock of margarine as Ada used her large store of cooking fat accumulated over the last year, most of it from the last pig that was killed, and from the goose they'd been given for Christmas by their farmer neighbour. But the only eggs they had left were the ones stored in the big crock in the larder, covered with water that had isinglass dissolved in it.

'We must all eat a little less, that's all,' Tommy said. 'I don't need so much. The children must have what there is, then the men, then the rest of us.' Her great fear was that lack of food and nourishment would mean the children wouldn't grow properly and it would be her fault. But so far there seemed to be no ill effects, and their appetites appeared to be satisfied. What they really longed for was sweets and chocolate and limitless cake. Those, she supposed, would not contribute so much to their growth, while the good rabbit stew, boiled up with carrots and oatmeal to bulk it out, and served with their own cauliflower mashed to be a little like potato, would fill their stomachs and provide goodness.

Fred now refused to have the fire lit in the library, but he still painted for a few hours in the morning when the light was at its best. He came to find Tommy, who was reading with the children in the morning room.

'Hello, everyone. This reminds me of our Latin lessons. We ought to start them up again.'

'I think we'd all enjoy that,' Tommy said politely.

'Yes.' Fred went to the window. 'It's going to snow again, I think. There really is no end to it.' He looked back to Tommy. 'I wanted to tell you, the painting is almost finished.'

'Well, it hardly matters as we're not going to do anything with the copy. You must take it with you when you go.'

'I will. It will be rather amusing to hang it in whatever little place I end up in. But I've thought of something else I'd like to try my hand at.'

'Yes?' She looked at him, feeling a sudden longing to jump up and ask him to put his arms around her again, and give her that solid, silent support that had helped her for that brief moment in the store cupboard.

315

'I couldn't help noticing the bare patch in your plaster upstairs, on the landing near my bedroom.'

'Yes, it's been like that for ages. There was a fire decades ago and they hacked away the bits that were damaged but never mended it.'

'Well, I might have a go at patching it. Would that be all right with you? I've always wanted to try plasterwork.'

'Of course. Please do.'

Harry looked up from the book and said, 'What will you put on the wall?'

Fred smiled at him. 'I don't know. What do you suggest?'

'The circus,' Antonia said eagerly. 'Do the circus!'

'Now that's a good idea. The circus it will be.'

Fred began work at once on the design for the plaster on the landing, first making his drawings on paper and then working out ways to turn them into little moulds for plaster. He began whittling away at pieces of wood, but nothing came out quite to his satisfaction.

They had eaten a frugal lunch of soup and a kind of oatmeal cake invented by Ada, topped with slivers of cheese for flavour, and Tommy was planning to make the children do their reading, when Roger asked if he could talk to her privately.

'Of course. Let's go to the library.' She led the way down the passage, pulling her fur coat tightly around her. Weeks of little heating had made parts of the house feel as cold as the outside.

In the library, Fred's copy of the Gainsborough stood almost complete upon the easel. Roger saw it as he went in. 'Well, I must say, that's rather good, isn't it?' He pointed at some of the more finished work. The loveliness of Venetia, particularly the sadness in her eyes, had been captured wonderfully well in the fluid, feathery strokes so like the original. 'Excellent likeness, not easy to tell it apart from the real thing at a glance. Very good indeed. Fred is so talented, isn't he?'

'He is indeed,' Tommy answered casually.

'I'm very lucky to have him as my friend. He was quite brilliant at Cambridge. Everyone looked up to him. He was a leading light in our debating group, rather dazzling in fact. I'm sure he's destined to go far, once he's recovered and this frightful winter is over.' Roger gazed longer at the painting. 'Though he's got to put this painting lark behind him and knuckle down.'

Tommy was surprised to hear Roger talk like this. 'I thought you were rather keen on painting,' she said.

'Well, in a way. But really I need to concentrate on what needs doing here. On the house and the estate. I need to get on with managing my inheritance.'

'I see.' Tommy tried not to sound as astonished as she felt. Roger had never shown the slightest interest in managing anything. 'Is that what you wanted to talk to me about?'

'Yes. I know you had to be in charge while the war was on – that was only right. A lot of women did a fine job while we men were fighting. You are certainly one of them. But the place is in a bad state, Tommy. You said so yourself. So it's time I took over.'

Tommy sank down into one of the chairs by the fireplace,

now cold but full of ashes from the last fire. It looked dirty and depressing. 'You're going to sort everything out?' she asked in a neutral tone.

'Yes. It's incumbent on me. This place is mine, after all.'

'Of course. But we – Gerry and I – we think of it as our home as well,' Tommy said carefully. She didn't want Roger to say anything regrettable that he might feel obliged to carry through.

'Of course. There will always be a place for you here.'

'That's . . . kind.' Tommy fought a rising panic within her: a few minutes ago, it had never occurred to her that she and the children had anything other than a permanent home at Kings Harcourt. Now, just by confirming it, Roger had raised a doubt in her mind that what she believed was so. *He's telling me that our presence here is in his gift.*

Roger went on: 'Perhaps I didn't see it before, but now I do. I must secure my birthright. So from now on, Tommy, you don't have to worry. I shall take up the reins and sort it all out. Just point me in the right direction, and off I'll go.'

Tommy ran upstairs and knocked on Fred's door, hardly waiting for a reply before bursting in. He was sitting at his desk, drawing by the light of a candle, muffled up in his coat and soft woollen hat with a bobble on the top of it, wearing a pair of fingerless gloves. He turned as she came in and smiled.

'Ah, I'm glad you've come to see me, Tommy, I wanted to show you my sketches of the circus figures.' He held out a piece of paper just long enough for her to notice some roughly drawn seals and ballerinas but she wasn't interested in them now.

'What have you been saying to Roger?' she demanded angrily. She put her hands on her hips. 'What nonsense have you put in his head?'

'I really have no idea what you're talking about,' Fred said, evidently bemused by her reaction.

'You spend half the day with Roger, talking, talking, talking,' Tommy went on, 'and he's just come to me to tell me that he needs to take on the running of his inheritance. He was practically on the brink of telling me that my job was done and I could now move out! As though this isn't my home as much as it is his!' She shook her head furiously. 'And I'm the one who's kept it running until now! I've looked after it, managed it, made it into a successful food-producing enterprise during the war. I've fed us all, and anyone who came here. I know it's Roger's house by the terms of my father's will but he's done nothing to deserve it except be born a man. It's as though everything I've done is invisible and has to be invisible to save Roger's face, and now that he wants to play squire for a while, I have to retreat into the shadows, or take my children and make myself scarce – though goodness only knows where on earth we would go!'

Fred stood and put up a hand. 'Wait, don't be in a fury with me. I haven't said anything of the sort to him. I'm not likely to either. Not so long ago, the thought of taking this on was depressing him so badly I was seriously worried for his health. He's been more obsessed with selling the place and giving the money to the cause of international socialism than he has with putting on tweeds and opening the village fete.'

'That's what I don't understand.' Tommy began pacing

about, her hands deep in her pockets. 'He's tried to avoid this place, if anything. And he hasn't the slightest idea what it all entails.'

'Sit down, Tommy, you're making me nervous.'

She went over and perched on the side of his bed, and Fred sat back down at his desk, looking like the leader of a mysterious underground movement, with the candle glimmering behind him, and his bulky outdoor clothes making him appear as though he was about to go on the run at any moment.

'I have no interest in Roger taking on this house. And I haven't encouraged him to do so. The opposite, if anything. But someone in this house might have a very good reason for urging him to take up his inheritance.'

Tommy laughed bitterly. 'It's like a murder mystery. One of us had to have done it and there aren't many suspects. Of course. It's Barbara.'

Fred nodded. 'Your friend Mrs Hastings has had plenty of time for him and, probably, quite a lot to say to him.'

Tommy knew he was right. 'She's been playing him. Swindling us. She as good as threatened me if I stood in her way. But what I don't understand is what good it will do her if Roger chucks me out.'

'You can't be that dense, can you, dear Tom?'

'You mean . . .' She stared at him and then laughed again, now with disbelief. 'Oh no. She hasn't set her cap at Roger, has she?' She thought of Barbara, so pretty and sophisticated, with her marriage and her life in India. She had imagined that, back in London in the spring, Barbara would reinvent herself somehow and find a rich husband, someone suave and well dressed with excellent taste. Perhaps she'd be the second wife of a successful widower, a businessman or a banker, and host charming weekend parties with bridge and croquet and quiet talk of deals over port and cigars. 'She can't want Roger! I thought she was after jewellery and gewgaws – not Roger!'

'Why not? She's desperate, anyone can see that.'

Tommy thought back over what Barbara had said to her that day when they'd skied to the village shop. 'She told me that, in so many words. That she and Molly are alone, and she has to make a life for the two of them. She obviously doesn't have any money.'

'I should say she doesn't.'

'But she can't be in love with Roger!' Tommy exclaimed. 'I know he's my brother, but I'm sure he has no sex appeal, not for someone like Barbara. She's pretty and stylish and desirable. She can't be attracted to Roger.'

'She wouldn't be the first pretty girl to marry a house.'

'But this place is falling apart! There's hardly any money. Why? I don't understand, why would she waste herself here, if it's money she wants?'

'Perhaps what seems like a falling-down house to you is security to her. What looks like no money to you is actually diamond brooches and a Gainsborough to her.'

Tommy was abashed. 'Of course, you're right. I spend so much time thinking about what we don't have, I forget what we do – how fortunate we are. But . . .' She flushed slightly. 'I never thought that Roger was . . . the marrying type. He's never seemed very keen on women. He certainly has never fallen in love as far as I know. You've known him since Cambridge. Has he ever fallen in love with a woman?'

Fred said slowly, 'Not with a woman, no.'

There was a pause and she said, 'Oh. I see.'

'He's never said anything, not directly. Nevertheless, I've always felt his desires lie in a different direction. I believed it was one of the things that made him miserable. Not his desires in themselves – I met plenty like him at Cambridge, believe me – but the effect they would have on others. His family. This house.'

Tommy nodded. She was not surprised. She had always sensed that Roger had a deep romanticism but that it was not directed towards women. 'Do you know if Roger found . . . like-minded company at Cambridge?'

'I believe he did. But he never found love, at least not with someone who felt the same way he did.'

'I see.' She felt sorry for her brother suddenly, that he was not able to live openly the way he was. *We're all so boxed in. So confined. Who decided that we all had to live and love a certain way?* 'Well then, Barbara is on a hiding to nothing, isn't she? If you're right, then she's wasted her time.'

'That's what I assumed.' Fred looked thoughtful. 'But perhaps what you've just heard from Roger means she's making more progress than I suspected she might. You need to keep an eye on it. For Roger's sake.'

Tommy said, 'I don't believe she loves him. Not for a moment.'

'No. I don't believe she does either.'

Chapter Thirty-One

Max was upstairs doing his homework that evening, and Caitlyn was tidying up the sitting room when there was a knock at the door. A nasty tremor went through her. Was it Sara, come to conduct an interrogation on the subject of Nicholas? She was surprised at how viscerally she felt that she did not want Sara in the house. She could hardly bear the thought of her anywhere near her or Max.

She went to the door and said loudly, 'Yes? Who is it?'

'Caitlyn, it's me, Nicholas.'

'Oh. Right. Hold on.' Slowly she opened the door. Nicholas was standing on the doorstep, his expression repentant. 'Hello,' she said coolly.

'Caitlyn, please,' he said in an agonised tone. 'Don't punish me. It wasn't my fault. Let me explain.'

She paused for a moment and then said, still cool, 'All right then. Come in. But quickly. I don't want Max disturbed.'

'It was complete chance that I ran into Sara,' Nicholas said, standing near her in the kitchen as she went about making tea for them both. 'She was coming out of that stupidly expensive decorating shop, you know, the one with the tiles handcrafted by Moroccan princesses or something. I was on my way back from Somerville, and I almost ran right into her. I recognised her at once and as soon as she saw that, she got who I was too. I think she might not have noticed me if I hadn't looked so damn guilty.'

'I suppose she is rather unmistakable.'

'And she's got a sixth sense. She could tell I didn't want to talk to her, and that set her juices flowing. She wasn't going to leave me alone after that. You know what the born seductress is like – she can't rest until she's won over everyone in the room. She insisted on coming back to the college to see my rooms.'

'That is what she's like,' Caitlyn agreed. 'Within certain parameters.' She sighed. 'I just felt so invaded, to see her with you in college like that. After everything you'd said about her, and all the advice you'd given me to get her out of my life. There she was – right back there, with you.' They went through to the sitting room and sat down, Caitlyn on the sofa where she curled her legs up under her as if for comfort. 'I can't understand why she's turned up here. Taking over a project manager's job just isn't her usual thing – far too lowly.'

Nicholas fixed her with a keen look. 'You don't understand because you don't think you're important to her. You don't know why she'd bother.'

'You mean she came here because of me?'

'Of course.'

Caitlyn thought about this. 'I thought it was just coincidence.'

'No! She still wants to go on the way things were.' He leaned towards her, his dark brown eyes earnest. 'That's what I've been trying to tell you. You've never understood that you are important to her. She needs you.'

Caitlyn shook her head. 'She doesn't need to cannibalise my life. Hers is more glamorous and exciting than mine any day.'

'But that's the point. She wants what you've got, like a vampire craves the warm blood of a mortal. She always has. My theory is that Patrick wasn't really what she wanted, even if she was sleeping with him – and we don't know that. It's all about her relationship with you.'

She stared at him for a moment. 'But she's always trampled all over me. What does she get from it?'

'Recognise your power,' Nicholas said. 'She wants your life force, of course.'

'You do sound batty!' she said, and burst out laughing. 'Vampires, life forces. What next – possession? Stealing my spirit?'

'I'm glad to see you laughing,' Nicholas said, smiling at her. 'I'm explaining it in dramatic terms, but it's simple: she wants to control you because she's jealous that you know the secrets of life and love, and she doesn't. She'll take away whatever you want, because if you want it, it must be worth having. But I'm not going to fall for her routines, you don't need to worry about that. You've got my loyalty. I've proved it once already, remember?'

She stared back at him, unable to speak for a moment. 'Thank you,' she said quietly.

'Friends again?'

'Yes. Friends.'

*

Caitlyn did not answer Sara's text about Nicholas even though she knew that would stir her into action, like laying a scent trail for a hound. A hint of anything being held back and Sara would be after it. She tried to imagine simply facing Sara down, demanding answers about the flowers and the hotel and just asking her straight out: *Were you sleeping with my husband? Did the two of you betray me for all those years when we were supposed to be friends?*

All the evidence seemed to point to the fact that they had, and yet there was not enough proof. She couldn't be certain.

A few more texts followed from Sara, asking what Caitlyn was doing and why she hadn't been in touch. Caitlyn stared at them, wondering if she should reply, but every draft she wrote, she deleted. Anything she wrote would open up the channels of communication and at the moment, she just wanted them closed. But she knew that Sara wouldn't be satisfied with silence for long.

Caitlyn found that she couldn't stop tapping on Sara's Instagram account and looking at the photographs there. More were being added: pictures of the hotel renovations along with the usual gushing captions, and, Caitlyn saw with a jolt, one of Nicholas's rooms high up in the college.

Wow, my friend is an actual real Oxford academic! Can't believe I'm back at my old college like this – feels like a tutorial #nervous #wheresmyessay?

Or, Caitlyn thought cattily, *How clever I am to have gone*

to Oxford and don't I have interesting friends #admire me.

Seeing Nicholas's rooms on the account made her feel discomforted. She scrolled down quickly but always stopped at the photograph of Patrick's wrist on that table in some unknown restaurant. The shy client. She could just imagine him telling Sara firmly that he didn't want his photograph taken while she giggled and cajoled, then took a sneaky snap anyway.

She was always telling me to look at her Instagram. It was entirely possible I would have seen this. Even if she didn't have an affair with Patrick, she doesn't mind making me afraid that she did. And that's reason enough to cut off contact. A few weeks and her project will be done and then maybe she'll leave me in peace. Perhaps she can find someone else to torment instead.

Caitlyn's phone rang when she was in the chemist's in town. It was Nicholas's number and she answered it with a chirpy, 'Hello, stranger! Have you got my paperwork for Kings Harcourt yet? I'm nearly packed up.'

'Caitlyn, where are you?'

'Shopping on Cornmarket.'

'Okay. Will you go to that upstairs cafe in the covered market, the one where we used to get hot chocolate after tutorials? I'll be there in about five minutes.'

'Sure.' He rang off before she could ask any more, so she paid for her purchases and wandered out to the covered market to find the old cafe. It was still there, much the same, but now with USB ports by every table, about ten types of coffee and a range of gluten-free cakes and pastries. Caitlyn ordered two cappuccinos and sat down to wait for Nicholas. When he came in, it was with an almost furtive air and as he sat down, he looked anxiously over at the stairway up into the cafe.

'Are you all right?' she asked. 'Here's a coffee I ordered for you.'

'Oh, thanks.' He looked at her a little distracted. 'Yes, I'm fine.'

'I wondered when you'd get in touch. I want to sort a date for the move.'

'What? Oh yes. I don't think I told you, but Coco's arriving today. Her holidays have already started. But that shouldn't be a problem, we can both help you move. But that's not what I want to talk to you about.'

'Oh?'

Nicholas shook his head. He looked, she thought, absurdly young today, though his silver streaks gave away his age. His Italian looks had matured well and his dark brown eyes had kept their rich hue. He leaned towards her over the pine table. 'I don't want to sound crazy . . . but I think Sara might be stalking me.'

Caitlyn frowned. 'What?'

'Yes. I keep spotting her all over the place. She's bumped into me *accidentally* several times since she came to my rooms. I mean, it's weird. I was getting a sandwich in Gloucester Green – and there she was. That's miles from where she would normally be, isn't it? Where is this hotel of hers?'

'Out on the Banbury Road, I think.'

'Exactly! So why is she popping up in a sandwich bar near the bus station? If I thought it was because she has a thing for their pastrami and Swiss cheese rye bread sandwiches, I would rest easy – but I suspect it's not that.'

Caitlyn shook her head in disbelief. 'You think she's up to her old tricks?'

'It would be funny if it weren't so creepy. Twenty years later, and she's sneaking round the quad, keeping an eye on me just like she used to. I suppose I ought to be flattered.'

Caitlyn said flatly, 'She thinks we might be involved.'

'That did cross my mind.'

'That's it. It's pure Sara. Don't you see? It's a rerun of what she did before – she's probably laying the groundwork for a full seduction attempt just in case.' Caitlyn laughed bitterly. 'I can't believe I never saw it at the time. It just makes it more likely that she was having an affair with Patrick.'

'Hold on.' Nicholas put a hand on her arm. 'It's a kind of proof – it suggests that she might have *tried* to have an affair with Patrick, not that she did.'

'So she sent herself flowers and put herself up at the hotel? And somehow got the payments on Patrick's bank statement?'

Nicholas frowned. 'Okay, that would be hard. But you know what, she's so creepy, I wouldn't put it past her. I just actually sneaked out of college by the back gate and made a run for the alley. I still wasn't sure she wasn't on my tail.'

They looked at each other and the comical side of Nicholas, a middle-aged don, running out of the back of college in case Sara was chasing him, struck them both at the same time and they started to laugh, but Caitlyn's quickly died away.

'What shall I do?' she asked. 'I keep getting texts from her about meeting up for drinks and dinner, asking me why I'm not replying. I don't know what to say. I don't want to see her.' Caitlyn stirred her coffee until the foam top had vanished into its milky depths. 'I hate the way she's changing how I think and feel about Patrick.' A sudden wave of rage burned through her. 'She's destroying my marriage in retrospect, making me distrust my husband, suspect him now he's dead, when she could have left me in peace! If Patrick did – if he *did* – well, that's a whole other issue that I'll have to come to terms with, but she wants to make sure that I suspect it.' She lifted an agonised gaze to Nicholas. 'Why would she do that to me?'

'I don't think you can expect normal standards of behaviour from her. She doesn't work that way. That doesn't mean you excuse her – it means you get her poison the hell out of your life, and you go on without her. She needs you, Caitlyn, that's why she can't leave you alone. But you don't need her.'

'You're right. I have to be strong.'

'Yes. Ignore her. She'll get the message in the end. I'll avoid her wherever I can, and we'll just wait it out. She'll get bored and then get lost.'

Nicholas smiled at her and she felt comforted. She had someone to help her this time, someone she could trust not to give in to Sara's wiles.

Nicholas took his hand away and said more seriously, 'Have you been through all of Patrick's stuff then? That might give you the answers you need.'

Caitlyn shook her head. 'There's a lot of it. And it's a very emotional process. I feel both close to him and so very far away. I'm always floored by the emotional impact after I've opened a box. He kept so much and I didn't throw away any of his papers. One night I ended up reading through all his school reports from his nursery onwards. I was up nearly all night, and cried just about the whole time.'

'It must be heartrending.' Nicholas looked sympathetic. 'But the more recent stuff – the electronics, the emails – you've been through all of that?'

'Just the tablet so far. It's got all his email accounts on it. Well, the ones I know about. There are some perfectly inno-cent emails between him and Sara, but nothing more as far as I can see, but I'm not an expert on that kind of thing. He could have a whole other hidden email life for all I know.'

'Whatever he had, it will be there, frozen, ready for you to find. And he gave you all his passwords?'

She nodded. 'He made a stipulation that in the event of his death, I was to get access to all of it. He told me' – she frowned, remembering – 'that I could access everything and use it as I thought fit.'

'All of it,' echoed Nicholas. He made a wry face. 'Most men might think twice before they let their wives onto their elec-tronic devices.'

'Really?'

'Well, you know . . . stashes of dirty pictures. Visits to porn sites. The odd video download.'

'Oh. Of course.' Caitlyn blinked at him, embarrassed. A

slight flush crept over her cheeks. 'I suppose so. Is that what most men have?'

'A lot. I'm told. But you didn't find any evidence of that with Patrick?'

Caitlyn shook her head. 'I wasn't looking for it, but no. I didn't. He thought internet porn was incredibly vulgar. I think he was appalled by how cheap they all looked. I can just imagine him being horrified at the women's nails and bad hair and fake breasts. Not his bag at all. He preferred the real thing.' Her blush deepened to scarlet as she realised what she'd said. 'I mean, real life! I mean . . . well . . . not that, not internet stuff!'

Nicholas looked away gallantly, and said, 'I'm sure he had no need whatsoever to get stimulation elsewhere.'

They both started laughing again at the awkwardness of it all, then Nicholas said more seriously, 'I think you should keep looking. Maybe he expected you to.'

'Maybe.' Caitlyn sighed. 'I will, when I can face it. But I do want to move to Kings Harcourt sooner rather than later. The agents won't care when I go as long as I pay the rent to the end of the contract. I've found some local movers who can pack me up and get me out as soon as I like. By the end of next week even. So I thought I might go over with Max tomorrow, and give him a tour of his new home, if you think that would be okay?'

Nicholas thought a moment, then said, 'I don't see why not. I'll check with Aunt G. I'm collecting Coco this afternoon from her godmother, who brought her over from America. Why don't we pick up you two tomorrow? I was thinking of taking her to a theme park but this would be much nicer. We can make a day trip of it.'

'Okay. Yes. That's sounds lovely, I'd like to meet Coco. And I'll book the movers, if you're sure that's okay. I just have the strongest feeling that it's best if Max and I leave Oxford as soon as we can.'

Chapter Thirty-Two

Tommy couldn't stop watching Barbara. She saw clearly what she had only half noticed before: Barbara concentrated her entire attention on Mrs Whitfield and Roger. She didn't do it showily and draw attention to it, but Tommy now saw the intensity and dedication of Barbara's actions.

At every meal, Barbara was at the side of one or the other, most often Mrs Whitfield, with whom she talked easily, and who she made sure was supplied with anything she needed. Then there were the long afternoons she spent at the old lady's side.

While Gerry or I look after Molly.

In the morning, Barbara took tea to Roger and walked with him around the house, Roger sometimes declaiming as he went, and Barbara murmuring, one slender arm tucked through one of Roger's meatier ones. But what amazed her most was that Roger seemed to be so susceptible. Now that she was observing properly, she realised that Roger was eager to be given attention and listened to, and that Barbara was the only person in the house to give him that.

Tommy was writing letters in the morning room, though there was no hope of posting them. She looked up as Fred came in, his expression excited.

'There's a movement in the lane. It looks as though the men have been out digging the roads clear and they're finally reaching us.'

'What?' Tommy dropped her pen and jumped up. They hurried upstairs to look out of the upper window over the landing. There, across the field of white, they could see the slowly moving dots of black and behind them a vehicle breaking through where they had cleared.

'Oh my goodness,' Tommy said, thrilled. 'They're coming towards us. That means we'll be able to get out soon. Perhaps the thaw is coming!' She turned to Fred and without thinking threw her arms around him. 'This is marvellous!' Tears of delight sprang into her eyes. Now that the end might be in sight, she realised what an awful strain this long period of isolation had been on them all. The constant darkness and the battle to stay warm and fed had depleted and depressed them all, but only now did Tommy realise how much it had been oppressing her.

Fred returned her hug and they almost jumped up and down with the childish glee of seeing escape.

'I'm sorry – your side!' Tommy said, pulling away.

'It's much better. It's almost healed.' He smiled gently. 'I don't mind you hugging me one bit.'

She gazed at him, her heart suddenly racing, and the next moment he had pulled her into his arms and was kissing her hungrily. 'Tommy,' he murmured between kisses, and she found she couldn't fight any longer. She had to give in to everything she had been feeling, for all these long days and nights. She didn't have the strength to keep her promise to herself any longer. It was bliss to surrender to it at last. The warmth of his body and mouth, the woody fragrance of his skin and the need she felt in every kiss were like a healing balm. She closed her eyes and gave herself up to the whirling pleasure.

This isn't like before, with Alec. Perhaps . . . She allowed herself to feel a tiny bit of hope. *Perhaps it will be all right.*

'Tommy,' he murmured. 'I can't think of anything but you. I'm in pieces. Please . . .'

'Yes,' she whispered between kisses. 'I feel the same.'

He kissed her again deeply, his hand in her hair, the other arm pulling her close with a ravenous tenderness.

The sound of footsteps on the stairs made them pull apart, awkward, struggling to seem normal. Barbara was standing there, assessing them with a cool gaze.

'Hello,' she said. 'I hope I'm not interrupting anything.'

'Of course not,' Tommy said, trying to conceal her breathlessness. 'We've just seen the men clearing the road. Isn't it marvellous, Barbara? We'll be able to get out of here.'

'Yes, that's wonderful,' said Barbara, but Tommy got the distinct impression that Barbara was not in the least pleased that the outside world was arriving at last.

Now, Tommy found she had the curious sense of being observed herself. On the one hand, she knew that Fred was watching her, the power of their recent kiss shimmering in the air between them, trying to read her reaction to it. And on the other, there was Barbara. The tables were turned, and now the cool blue gaze was directed at her, watching and waiting.

'Come on, Roger,' Fred said when they all gathered to share the news of the approaching rescue. 'We should go out and do what we can to meet them.'

'All right,' Roger said, unable to resist the infectious enthusiasm around him. 'I'm sure we have enough shovels.'

'Then we'll all go,' Gerry said in excitement. 'Come on, children, shall we start digging and see how quickly we can reach them?'

Tommy knew they'd make no more than a few feet of progress through the enormous drifts outside, and that, with the best will in the world, they were still at least a day away from being dug out. But everybody's spirits were lifted and it was good to see the children scampering about, getting ready to go out and help.

'Perhaps there really is an end in sight to this ordeal,' Mrs Whitfield said. 'I would help myself if I could.'

'There's no need for you to risk your health,' Barbara soothed. 'We'll do more than our bit getting ready to warm them all up when they get back in. And I think we can now put the lights on and spare your eyes, Nancy, dear.'

She went over to the light switches near the door and flicked them. The bulbs flared into life.

Tommy gasped. 'You can't do that, Barbara! It's against the rules. We can't have lights on till twelve.'

'You can see for yourself they're clearing the road. If they can be bothered to try and get here, they must have opened the bigger routes all ready. You'll see, the electricity cuts are no longer needed. I'm sure they've only been imposed so the government can pretend it's doing something about the crisis. It won't do any good. We might as well have light if we want it.'

'But it's against the law!' Tommy retorted. 'There's a hundred-pound fine if we're caught! Prison!'

'I won't tell if you won't.' Barbara walked coolly to the sofa and sat down next to Mrs Whitfield who was suddenly concentrating hard on her cushion cover. 'Can I help you, Nancy dear?'

'That's not the point,' Tommy said, walking over and standing in front of her. 'We all have to abide by the rules, until they're lifted.'

Barbara fixed her with a piercing blue gaze and said in a low voice, 'You weren't so particular about following the rules when you took my penicillin. Where were your high moral standards then? You didn't mind getting Fred out of trouble when it suited you, even though you knew that those pills weren't exactly above board.'

Tommy stared at her, dumbstruck. *She's right. Damn it, why did I take those pills?* But she knew she had no choice, when it came to saving Fred. 'That was another case entirely. A matter of life and death. And as long as I'm in charge here, we will have the lights off until instructed otherwise.'

Her mother looked up, and said, 'Thomasina, I think it will not hurt to leave them on. Just this once. Barbara is right – it spares my eyes.'

Tommy stared at her mother in surprise. Then she saw Barbara's expression. It was one of pure triumph.

You see? it seemed to say. *I am the one in charge now.*

Everyone came back in hot from their exertions and full of high spirits. They had made good progress considering, and cleared a fair few feet down the lane. In the afternoon, once their lessons were over, the children amused themselves by sitting in the window upstairs and watching the black dots get closer.

'Will they be here by teatime?'

'By supper?'

'By bedtime?'

'When we wake up?'

'They'll be here soon,' Tommy said, when she kissed Antonia and Harry goodnight. They talked about all the things they would do as soon as they were free to go out and about. Even school seemed like the height of excitement after so much restriction.

Tommy shut the bedroom door quietly as she went out, and walked along the passage towards the stairs. The day had been stressful in a new way. The situation with Barbara was more worrying than ever. Her act of switching on the lights had been about power in more ways than one.

She wanted to show me that she can do what she wants. And Mother chose to side with her, not with me. And that's the strange thing. Mother would never usually break rules. And yet she wanted to show me that being on Barbara's side was more important than that.

But there was also the fact of her kiss with Fred. She kept allowing herself to think about it so she could experience the giddy rush of excitement that the memory brought on. They had not been able to speak together since, but she had felt as though they were communicating with one another all the time. *Soon*, they seemed to be saying silently. *Soon we'll be alone again and then we can share that wonderful thing again.*

As she walked along the passage, she was startled when someone jumped out in front of her, but saw immediately that it was Gerry.

'I've been meaning to talk to you all day,' Gerry said. 'About the dreaded Barbara.'

'Shh,' Tommy said, looking about in case Barbara was nearby. 'She might hear you.'

'I'm really worried, Tommy. She's up to something, and I'm afraid it's Roger she's set her sights on. He's changing, haven't you noticed?'

Tommy nodded. 'Yes ... but don't worry. He's not interested in her, not like that. She won't succeed that way. My feeling is that she'll get Mother on side and do her best to worm what she can out of her. I believe it's money she's after, as much as she can get before she moves on.'

Gerry looked anxious. 'Mother's not so batty she would let Barbara fleece her, is she?'

'You don't have to be batty to be dissatisfied with your own family, and liable to be gulled into thinking that other people are much more appealing.'

'But,' Gerry said, pained, 'why should she be dissatisfied with us? What have we done to disappoint her?'

Tommy took her hand and said, 'Oh darling, it's not you. It's me that let her down. And she's never forgiven me for it.'

Tommy sent Gerry downstairs, and went over to the window to look out into the blackness. She thought for a moment that she could see lights glowing in the distance over the fields, but then she couldn't. The fog that descended at night was too thick for light to penetrate at that distance. She stood by the window and lit a cigarette, one of the last in her only remaining packet. She smoked rarely but tonight, she felt as though she needed the dark rasp of smoke in her lungs, the adult taste of it, and the sense of being a grown-up who could make her own decisions. Perhaps it was also the effect of the red wine they'd had at dinner. Lately, Roger had been going down to the cellar every evening and coming up with more bottles from the supply down there. Now her head was slightly fuzzy. It reminded her of the old life, the one in London. There had been lots of drinking there. In the drawing room of their small London house, there had been a well-stocked drinks tray where she learned to mix a good Martini and other cocktails Alec liked. She had often drunk one or two before they sat down, and then a couple of glasses of wine at dinner. It had all helped to numb her against reality. When she and Alec went out, they'd end up at a nightclub, usually the Cafe de Paris, to drink until the early hours. She'd tried to be the perfect wife, she really had. She'd spent hours on her appearance, bought the best clothes she could afford. Once, passing a table on the way back from the ladies' room in the Cafe de Paris, she'd heard someone say 'Tommy Eliott is so awfully elegant, isn't she?' and she'd been childishly happy, but just for a few moments. Because the only way to cope, she found, was to shut her heart, put it away. Only the children could bring her joy. They'd become the only things worth living for.

And now, here was Fred, making her experience all kinds of new emotions. It was terrifying and exhilarating. She blew out a stream of smoke and stared out at the winter night. *This freeze has done something nothing has succeeded in so far. It's made me stop. It's forced me to do little more than think, for hours. I don't think I can resist coming back to life, even if I want to. The pull is too great.* She took the last inhalation from her cigarette and turned to go back downstairs to join the others. *But what will I do if he hurts me? I couldn't bear it.* A small, high-pitched sound, throbbing and repetitive, came down to the landing. Tommy turned and listened and realised that it came from the room where Molly slept. Barbara had long since moved her daughter out to a smaller room along the passage. Tommy went quickly to the door and stood outside; the noise resolved itself into sobs. She opened the door and went in to the small dark shape huddled under the covers of the bed. Molly was shaking as she cried, clutching her pillow over her face to muffle the sounds.

'Molly, darling, what is it?' Tommy asked, sitting down beside her and putting an arm around the girl's shoulders. 'Why are you crying?'

It took a while before Molly could speak, but then she said, 'Because they're coming.'

'Who are?'

'The people who're going to get us out. With the tractors and ploughs. They're going to come and take me away.'

'What? Of course they're not!'

'They will! We've been safe here while there was snow. But now . . . I'm going to leave you and I've been so happy here.' She sobbed again. 'Mother is happy too. I don't want us to leave, and be alone, not knowing where to go or where we'll stay.'

'Oh Molly.' Tommy was full of pity, and torn between her desire to see Barbara gone and the wish to care for Molly, whom she'd grown to love.

'Can I stay here, with you? I want to be with Antonia and Harry. I want to stay. Can I?' Molly asked in a whisper, gazing up with wet, pleading eyes. 'Please?'

'I don't know. I don't know what will happen. But I'll make sure you're all right. I'll not desert you, Molly. I promise.'

Chapter Thirty-Three

Back at home, Caitlyn found the conversation with Nicholas echoing in her mind. Patrick had invited her to go through his most private world when he gave her his passwords. She had thought it was simply a practical step, so that she could access bank accounts, administrative info and the apps that ran their home. Perhaps it was more than that. She remembered the treasure hunts he used to set for her. He would always tell her to keep her eye open for clues, and to stay alert.

'Sometimes you're too blinkered,' he would scold her. 'Always think about what you're seeing and why.'

I'm missing something. I'll look again.

After Max was in bed, Caitlyn went to her bag and took out Patrick's tablet. She typed in the password. The tablet sprang into life, the screen glowing blue, its neat rows of apps like little doors promising entry into other worlds. She ran her finger over the display, scrolling through the screens. There were the standard applications – nothing mysterious about those. She noticed again the backgammon app that he used to play in the cinema while they waited for the main film to start. He hated adverts but he also had to arrive early, so he needed the distraction. There were other games too: a fantasy cricket game, spider solitaire and snake, the old-fashioned computer version where the snake is made to eat apples, growing longer with each bite so the challenge is to avoid it meeting its own tail. There were his favourite news apps, his stocks tracker, his Spotify.

Caitlyn went back to his email account. It gave her a horrible sick sensation to see the last one he sent, on the afternoon of the day he died. It can't have been that long before he decided to call her. It was to Stacey in his chambers, reminding her to bill a client for Patrick's hours.

Caitlyn thought of those last moments again, picturing Patrick in the back of the taxi, talking in the darkness, not expecting the lorry speeding towards him. She thought of the impact. Patrick's inquest had gone into detail about his injuries and the way his body had torn and shattered under the force of the crash. She believed them when they said it must have been instantaneous: a moment of surprise and then doused, like a candle snuffed. From light to dark, in one violent second. He would have been dead before he felt any pain, and that was a comfort. She thought of his telephone that had connected them both at that moment of elemental transition. It was amazing really that his phone was not more damaged. Perhaps it flew out of his hand and landed under a seat where it was protected from the crushing of the lorry.

As she thought this, Caitlyn got up and went upstairs to the spare room. Almost mechanically she opened the box of

Patrick's electronics and saw his phone lying there, chipped and scratched with a long hairline crack across the screen, but otherwise intact.

Why didn't I think of looking here before?

She tried to switch it on but, just as the tablet had been, it was completely out of power after months of disuse, so she took it downstairs, searched about for her own charger and plugged it in. A few minutes later, it was ready to access. She found the paper with Patrick's codes and passwords and tapped in the pin. The screen popped into life in a mini version of Patrick's tablet, and she wondered why he needed so many of the same thing.

Caitlyn held the phone lightly in her hand, feeling its roughened surface. It had been the last thing Patrick had touched when he was alive. She went to the telephone icon at the bottom of the screen and tapped it. Up came his contacts list. There would be no surprises there. She tapped on the 'recent calls' icon at the base of that screen. There it was – the list of his very last calls. The final one was, of course, to her. One and a half minutes. Was that all it had been? It had seemed so much longer. She would have said five minutes at least. And at what point did the lorry driver take out his phone and start texting? Twenty seconds before the impact? Thirty? At some point while they were talking, Patrick's death had been set in motion, and they'd not realised that every moment took them closer to the final severance, when death would part them forever.

Now his life was here, on this phone, on the tablet, frozen

forever, kept in a permanent limbo. Present and yet not present.

Then she saw that the call before hers was a long one. Twenty minutes. It had started almost exactly twenty-one minutes before Patrick had called her. It was to someone she had never heard of.

Allegra.

She stared at it, her heart thudding. *Who is Allegra?*

Patrick had made his last call to her, his wife, but it was to warn her that Sara had something to tell her. So who was Allegra? The name echoed through her mind, reminding her that she had heard the word recently, but not as a person. It was . . . she grasped at the thought, screwing up her face with the effort of concentration, and then it came to her. *On Patrick's bank statements. A lot of money went to Allegra Communications.* A flood of ideas came into her mind as things began to link together. This must be the key she had been looking for, the one that would unlock Patrick's hidden life.

Allegra.

If she was right, then Allegra was Sara, and in the course of her conversation with Patrick, she had said something that meant Patrick felt it was time to tell Caitlyn the truth. It was something important, something that might threaten . . . what? Caitlyn herself? Her life with Patrick?

She wanted to tell me they were at it and he wanted to get in first, for all the good that would have done.

There was still the sliver of doubt, though. The call was evidence but it wasn't conclusive. She got up and walked around the room thinking, the phone still in her hand. Then, on a whim, she went to the contacts in Patrick's phone. She looked up Allegra and there it was, almost the first name in his contacts list. Then she looked up Sara, and she was listed under her full name. The two telephone numbers were different as well.

But Patrick had called her specifically to warn her about Sara. Not some other person. Sara. Unless Allegra was a friend or . . . someone else entirely?

She gasped at the sudden idea that Allegra was someone Patrick was having an affair with, and Sara had found out and was going to tell her, Caitlyn, unless Patrick did.

But that makes no sense. Because it's Sara who had the flowers and the hotel. And it's Sara who keeps insinuating that she and Patrick were more than friends. It's not beyond the bounds of possibility that Sara has two phones, after all.

She thought suddenly of Nicholas's suggestion that Patrick might have been hiding sexual content on his devices. Immediately, she went to tap on the phone's photo storage icon, her fingertips trembling as she did. There could be photos here that weren't on the tablet. As she watched, the albums came to life in their little stack. At the bottom there it was: an album entitled *Allegra*.

'Oh God,' Caitlyn said out loud. Her heart began racing and her breath was suddenly short. She tapped on it, expecting an array of photographs inside – perhaps obscene, perhaps romantic. Romantic would be infinitely worse, she felt. But there were only two, and one was of a person. She tapped rapidly to select and it exploded into life. It was a photograph of a woman's naked back cinched in at the waist by a tightly drawn corset. Pink stockings encased her legs as far as they could be seen, attached to the corset by silky straps.

It was not possible to see much of the woman's head. But trailing down the naked back was a long russet-red curl.

Caitlyn felt sick. So at last she'd found the proof. It was Sara. It had to be. Who else had long red hair like this, the kind that fell in auburn corkscrews? Had Patrick taken this shot? She looked more closely and realised that it was in fact a selfie, taken in a mirror, the phone held up in one of the woman's hands like a small dead slab.

It had been sent to him.

Her head whirled with an unpleasant giddiness. She had wanted to know the truth and here it was. Sara had sent a near-naked picture of herself to Patrick, and he had filed it away to keep under her pseudonym. It was pretty conclusive.

'No, *no* . . .' she muttered, and then, hearing the pain in her own voice, she realised how much she had been hoping that, after all her suspicions, she'd been wrong and Patrick had not betrayed her with Sara.

Numb with hurt, Caitlyn went back to the album screen and selected the other photograph. It came up as a black screen with a message on it written in red capital letters.

Look for the snake in the grass.

Caitlyn drew in a sharp breath. It was as though she had just heard Patrick's voice in her head. The snake in the grass? Was this a message for her?

This is how I used to feel during the treasure hunts – never quite sure what was a clue and what wasn't. But why would he want me to know about his affair?

Patrick loved his games. But surely he would not be so cruel as to turn an affair into the same sort of game as his treasure hunt.

On impulse she went back to his email and looked at the folders. She had not paid much attention to them before; they had the names of his clients and had seemed to be full of work correspondence. She had ignored the one named Allegra Communications, but now it jumped out at her, setting off another flood of adrenaline as she opened it. There was only one email there, but it contained three threads. The first was sent from Patrick to Allegra. It said, **You know what to do**.

After it came a message from Allegra, without text, containing only the photograph Caitlyn had seen in the album. In response to the photo was another message sent from Patrick. This one said, **Well done**.

'What the hell is going on?' she shouted out loud. 'What game are you both playing?'

Caitlyn stood, shaking, looking at the picture and the messages as though they would begin to reveal more, and give her the answers she wanted.

There is one way to find out.

She went back to Patrick's contacts list. All the innocent names and numbers, accumulated over the years, and hidden in amongst them, one poisonous name.

Allegra.

Her finger hovered over the number. Her mouth went dry

and her breath shortened. Then she pressed down and the phone began to make contact.

She heard the ringing tone. It went on and on, neither picked up nor sent to the answer service.

She was just about to give up when the ringing tone stopped abruptly, and a voice on the other end, slurring with drink, said tearfully, 'Oh my God, Patrick, is that you? Please say it's you. Oh Patrick.' It began to sob. 'I miss you!'

'You know it's not Patrick!' Caitlyn yelled. 'You know who it is.'

'I just want him back so badly,' Sara moaned. 'I loved him more than you ever could.'

Caitlyn hung up and threw the phone across the room.

Chapter Thirty-Four

The atmosphere that night during dinner was the oddest it had ever been. When Gerry and Tommy carried the plates out to the scullery, Gerry hissed, 'It's like there's going to be a murder committed! And now I think about it, being snowed in like this creates exactly the kind of conditions for an Agatha Christie!'

'It is very strange,' Tommy agreed, looking around to make sure that Ada and Thornton, eating their own supper at the kitchen table, hadn't heard them. 'Something seems to be building up.'

'And why is Roger drinking for England?' Gerry said, as they put down the stacks by the sink. 'That's the third bottle he's opened, and I've had barely any, and nor has Mother.'

'I'm sure I don't know. Let's hope it's a sign he's feeling more cheerful.'

But there was a reckless air to the way Roger was knocking back glass after glass. Fred kept up valiantly and Barbara let her glass be filled. Gerry was watching them all with a kind of horrified relish, while Mrs Whitfield did not appear to notice a thing. Tommy drank another and found it only made her feel depressed. Why were things going so wrong? What had happened – in a house where it felt as though nothing had happened for days – to change everything?

She was about to excuse herself and go up to bed when Roger put out the cigarette he'd been smoking and took up a teaspoon to bang against his wine glass.

'Attention, please!' he called out, his voice slurring very slightly. 'I have an important announcement.'

Everyone turned to him to listen, eyes wide with expectation, except for Barbara, who inclined her head and gazed modestly at the tablecloth.

Roger coughed and said, 'I'm sure you'll all be very happy and excited . . . as am I . . . when you hear that Barbara has done me the very great honour of agreeing to become my wife.'

Tommy gasped and Gerry gave a half-strangled exclamation. Mrs Whitfield smiled and said, 'What wonderful news. How marvellous. Congratulations, Roger, my dear. Barbara, come and kiss me.'

Fred raised an eyebrow and said, 'Congratulations. You've kept that deadly secret. I'm happy for you both.'

Roger nodded slowly, smiling, his eyes half closed, as though he were not quite with them. Then he said, 'Yes, everyone is very happy.'

'Congratulations, Roger,' Tommy said in a voice that, despite her best efforts, came out tight and strained. 'What marvellous news.' For a moment she wished she could leap to her feet and shout, *Why are you doing this, you fool? You know you'll be miserable – it isn't possible for you to be happy with her, not ever, no matter how hard you try!* But that couldn't be done. It wouldn't be right. She must pretend all was well, when it wasn't.

'Congratulations, Roger,' Gerry echoed, her tone astonished. She turned to Barbara. 'And every happiness for your future.'

'Thank you, Gerry,' Barbara said in a voice of honeyed graciousness. Even while they were looking at her, she seemed to grow in stature as though assuming the mantle of chatelaine in just a few moments.

Roger, though, was staring at Tommy. 'You don't seem very happy for me, Tommy,' he said. 'Is there something wrong?'

She opened her mouth to say, *Of course not.* But as she spoke, she found she was saying something different. 'I think it's a mistake, Roger. I don't believe it's what you really want.'

'Oh, don't you?' Roger said in a dark voice. He reached for his glass and gulped down another mouthful. 'I think we can all guess why, Tommy. You don't want to be usurped. You've been trying to rob me of my rights for years, using the war to take away what's mine. You thought you could steal the house and everything in it away from me.'

'That's nonsense!' protested Tommy. 'I didn't want the burden of running it. I did it because I had to! And I've no intention of taking the house away from you. You never showed the faintest desire to have anything to do with it. You've always said you'll be back to London like a shot as soon as you're well enough.'

'That's what you wanted me to say,' Roger retorted. 'You've been planting the idea in my head, so that I'd go away and leave you with a clear run at taking over.'

'That's nonsense—'

'No!' spat Roger, his face reddening. 'I was blind to it for ages, and then I saw it. You want to take everything from me. The house, the money . . . even my best friend.' He looked over at Fred, his eyes suddenly tormented. 'You've taken Fred from me too. My only friend, my best friend. As soon as he arrived you had to get your claws into him, didn't you? Something else to sequester. Fine! You have him! The two of you have been cooking up your little schemes between you!'

'Now, old man, what are you saying?' Fred said in a calm voice. 'You're throwing some very wild accusations around here. We don't have any schemes, as you put it.'

'I'm so sorry,' Barbara said suddenly, her high, light voice cutting clearly through the air. 'I'm so sorry, but you do have schemes. You and Tommy are in cahoots. I saw you today plotting. You were kissing her upstairs. I saw it.'

Mrs Whitfield gasped and turned shocked eyes on her daughter. 'Thomasina!'

Tommy flushed red as Roger drank another gulp from his glass. 'Well . . .'

'Don't deny it!' yelled Roger, suddenly furious, slamming down his wine glass. 'You're rumbled, can't you see?'

'A kiss is not a crime,' Tommy said with as much defiance as she could muster.

'Ha! It is when you're planning to steal someone else's inheritance!'

'How ridiculous, of course I'm not.'

'Barbara says differently.'

'What does Barbara say?' demanded Tommy, anger

growing alongside her embarrassment. 'And why would you believe her anyway?'

Roger said, 'If it weren't for Barbara, we wouldn't know what you're up to. She's the one who's on our side.'

'Besides,' Barbara said, 'I'm not the only one who knows your involvement with Fred. Gerry knows it too, don't you, Gerry?'

Now Gerry turned pink and stared at the tablecloth. 'Well,' she muttered. 'Perhaps. Perhaps I saw you kissing Fred.' She looked accusingly at Barbara. 'But I wasn't spying. When I realised what was happening, I went away.'

Fred took out a cigarette and lit it, the only sign he was at all disconcerted by the situation. 'Look, Roger, a bit of romance isn't such a bad thing. A kiss here and there. It's nothing. But accusing Tommy of stealing your inheritance is a bit rich. As far as I can see, she's saved it.'

'Hardly,' Barbara returned, cool confidence emanating from her. 'You two have detailed plans of theft.'

'What?' demanded Tommy, outraged. 'How dare you? Your room was stuffed full of our things, and you're decked in my mother's jewellery!'

'That's beneath you, Tommy,' Barbara said with dignity.

'Barbara has my permission to wear anything she chooses,' added Mrs Whitfield. 'But I don't understand what Tommy is planning to steal.'

'The Gainsborough,' Barbara said. She looked directly at Tommy. 'I think you convinced Fred to make a copy for you. You were planning to take the original and sell it so you could keep the proceeds, no doubt to replace Fred's bombed-out flat with a very nice house in London. Then you could leave the house to Roger without its greatest asset, which would be yours.'

Tommy gaped at her, and Fred turned pale.

Mrs Whitfield rose to her feet, her expression shocked. 'Is this true?'

Roger turned to Fred. 'You've been low, Fred. You know you have. To come here as my friend and then fall in with Tommy's scheme . . .'

'Look here, it's not like that—' Fred began angrily, but Mrs Whitfield, her eyes flashing with anger, talked over the top of him and forced him into silence.

'I know the truth when I hear it,' she declared, icy and furious. 'Thomasina, I'm ashamed of you. I didn't believe Barbara at first, but your reaction to the news of Roger's engagement has told me everything I need to know. Can you promise me that you never intended to replace the painting as Barbara says?'

Tommy opened her mouth but couldn't say anything. Her sense of honesty meant that she couldn't vow it had never crossed her mind. The hesitation was enough.

'How could you?' asked her mother in a low voice. 'How could you betray us?'

'Wait, this is terribly unfair, let me explain!' protested Tommy.

'The evidence is on the easel in the library,' returned Barbara lightly.

Mrs Whitfield looked over at Fred. 'Mr Burton Brown, I'm afraid I must insist that you leave at once.'

Tommy jumped to her feet in her passion. 'It's nonsense. Copying the picture was only ever for fun! It's not even finished. You can't send Fred away, while he's still recovering and the weather is so awful.' She looked over at her mother. 'If he goes, then I go!'

'Very well,' said her mother, sitting slowly down. 'Perhaps that would be for the best.'

Tommy gasped, wounded.

'You may leave the children here until you make other arrangements,' Mrs Whitfield said.

Tommy paled and she whispered, 'You'd really do that, Mother? Make the three of us go? And what about Molly?'

Barbara stared coldly. 'What about her? She stays here with me, of course.'

Fred stood up as well, stubbing out his cigarette. 'Mrs Whitfield, of course I will leave if you wish it, and I'm distressed that you think I would ever abuse your hospitality. But Tommy's done nothing wrong!'

'She has let me down,' said Mrs Whitfield. 'And now she is a force for division in this house.'

'That's not true, Mother. I did my best,' Tommy said in a shaking voice. 'I always did my best and it was never good enough. I don't know why you prefer Barbara over me.'

'Because,' Mrs Whitfield said in a bitter voice, 'at least she is respectable.'

There was a moment of horrified silence and then Gerry burst into tears.

Tommy turned and ran out of the room.

Chapter Thirty-Five

'Are you all right?' Nicholas said when Caitlyn answered the door the next morning. 'You look like you've had a terrible night.'

'I'm fine,' she said mechanically but she knew she looked awful. The tears had come at last, a great storm that had possessed her and shook her to the depth. *I didn't want to believe it. I didn't believe it until I heard her voice. Who were you, Patrick? Did I ever really know you?*

When she woke, zombified, in the first light of dawn, the first thought that floated into her mind was, *I hope I fucking terrified her, calling her from Patrick's phone. She was drunk. For a minute I bet she actually thought he might be calling from the spirit world. Or else she's so spiteful, she wanted to take the opportunity to rub in her supposed love for him.*

Caitlyn looked down now at the girl standing next to Nicholas. She was fair, with a broad open face with freckles and large, wide-spaced brown eyes under straight fine brows. Caitlyn smiled at her. 'Well now, you must be Coco.'

Coco smiled, revealing a double set of train-track braces, and said, 'Hi!'

'Come in and meet Max. I'm just packing up a picnic and we'll be on our way.' Caitlyn ushered Coco in and Nicholas followed, looking concerned.

'Seriously, Caitlyn. What's wrong?'

She turned to him with a sad smile. 'I have my proof.'

'You do?' He looked around. 'What is it?'

'A nearly nude photo on his phone. And I called the number of the last person he spoke to before me, the same person who sent the photo. And guess who answered.'

'Oh my God.' Nicholas put out his arms and pulled her into a hug. 'That's terrible. I'm so sorry.'

'I think she was drunk. She was certainly crying. She couldn't wait to tell me that she loved Patrick more than I had.'

'Nice.' Nicholas stepped back. 'Are you really okay to go out today?'

'Yes, I'm fine. Well ... not fine. I feel like my heart is breaking again, in a different way.'

'We don't have to go if you don't want to.'

'No, I do want to. I think it will help me.'

When the picnic basket was packed, they went outside to where the MG was waiting and Nicholas strapped it onto the back. The soft cool bags were stowed at the children's feet and they sat on the picnic rugs.

'Come on, then,' Nicholas said, getting behind the wheel. 'Ready? Let's go.'

Caitlyn was just about to climb in when there was a

movement from a car across the road, a little way up. The next moment Sara was stalking towards them, a cream hat low over her eyes and a pair of sunglasses hiding their expression. She looked elegant as ever in white trousers and a floating pale green cotton top.

As she got closer, she called out, 'Well, this looks nice. Where are you going? Aren't you going to invite me along?'

Nicholas groaned and muttered, 'Oh God, she must have followed me. Sorry. I forgot she might be on the lookout.'

'She might not have,' Caitlyn replied quietly. 'She might have been there already.' As Sara came up next to the car, Caitlyn looked her straight in the eye. 'Not today, I'm afraid. There's only room for us.'

'Very cosy. But I don't think that's very friendly.' Sara's voice hardened. 'It's not very friendly at all.'

'You know all about not being friendly, Sara.'

Sara stared at her and a smile curled over her mouth. 'So you've finally worked it all out, have you?'

'How could you?' asked Caitlyn, her voice raw with hurt and fury. Then she remembered Max, sitting there listening. 'Actually, I don't want to know.'

'I was doing you a favour,' Sara said coolly. 'Otherwise you might have not kept him as long as you did. Now you've guessed, you may as well know the whole truth.'

Nicholas made the engine roar into life to drown out anything else Sara might say, and Caitlyn slid quickly into her seat, shutting the door with a slam. 'I'm finished with all of it now, thanks. Have a nice day. Bye.'

'You can't get away from it that easily!' Sara snapped. 'You can't run away from it, I won't let you!'

'Try and stop me.'

Reading his cue, Nicholas pulled out into the road and they set off down the street. Caitlyn watched in the rear-view mirror as Sara headed back to her car. 'Nicely done,' he said to Caitlyn. 'I think she got the message.'

But a moment later, Sara's car pulled out into the road after them. Nicholas had to stop at the end of the street, and by the time a space had cleared to pull out onto the main road, she was immediately behind them.

'Oh God,' Nicholas muttered, glancing up into the mirror to look back at the car on their tail. 'She's following us.'

'She has to come this way,' Caitlyn said. 'She'll probably turn off.'

Sara stayed with them all the way to the ring road, followed them tightly round the roundabout and out onto the A34.

Caitlyn watched her with growing unease. 'You're right. She's definitely following us. Can we lose her without doing anything stupid?'

'Even being stupid, we'd have a job. Her car is a bit more powerful than this old thing, which is all bluster and no trousers, I'm afraid. And it's more or less a straight dual carriageway all the way from here to the house. We just have to hope for some luck.'

'We mustn't lead her to Kings Harcourt. If we don't lose her soon, we'll have to turn around.' Caitlyn was filled with a nasty mix of anger and anxiety. Had she pushed Sara too far? *I can see now that that's why I always played it safe with her.*

I never wanted to find out how far she would go. I didn't want to see her nasty side.

A normal person would have been ashamed at being caught out having an affair with the husband of her oldest friend. Perhaps she would have retired, humbled. But no. Not Sara. *She was doing me a favour, apparently!* She wanted a confrontation and she would have it, no matter what.

That's what my power is. I can refuse to take part. I won't give her what she wants.

'Okay,' Nicholas said, his voice low and serious, 'if we don't lose her soon, we turn around.'

The children, unable to hear the conversation in the front seat with the wind whipping around them, were oblivious to the reason why Nicholas suddenly pulled out into the outside lane and accelerated hard. He had chosen a moment that put him just ahead of a stream of traffic that made it impossible for Sara to pull out after them. He kept his foot down as they zoomed along at the MG's top speed, the faster cars behind nudging a little at their rear and flashing them to move over.

'Just a bit longer,' Nicholas said, his hands gripping the wheel, 'just to be sure . . .'

Then, suddenly, he moved over to the adjacent lane, flicked on his indicator again and took an exit that Caitlyn had hardly seen coming.

'Bit of a detour.' He grinned at Caitlyn as he braked and the engine's roar subsided. 'But I think it's worth it. We've lost her.'

*

With Sara now consigned to follow the A34 not knowing they had exited, Caitlyn's mood lifted and she felt a small swell of triumph. She and Nicholas were joined together in a bond of victory.

The drive was soothing. The bitter feelings Sara's appearance had stirred up began to settle, and the beauty of the countryside started to work its magic. As they came into the little village just before Kings Harcourt, she was overwhelmed by its picturesqueness.

Really, it's absurdly beautiful.

The village houses and shops had been gently rubbed by the centuries to a dull, golden gleam, and stone walls were bedecked with climbing roses and clematis. There was still a village shop, she noticed, and an artisan tea room and bakery with windows full of rows of patisserie in delectable colours of passionfruit and raspberry.

Once through the village, they turned right at the lane with its old fingerpost pointing down to Kings Harcourt. In a moment the house was in view, approached almost side on, its windows facing out over the fields towards the village and the spire of the church.

If this were mine, I would never leave it. As they approached she thought wistfully of Patrick – the one she had known before all these sordid revelations. *He would have loved this place. Perhaps we both could have been happy in a house like this, away from the city and all its pressures and people and the way it made us feel.* She wished that they had had the chance to try out a different life, where Patrick would have been home more, and Max would have lived with them all the time and perhaps they'd have had more children to fill a house and make a garden ring with shouts and laughter.

Far away from Sara and her manic world, all her pretence and manicured fiction.

Nicholas turned the car in between the gateposts and pulled to a halt behind the main house. At the back, it was more ramshackle than the gorgeous front implied. An old pigsty seemed to be attached to it, along with various outhouses and sheds. Behind the house, the woods appeared very close. The trees were in full leaf now, bursting with a lime-green haze, and the grasses and hedgerows had sprouted into shaggy life. There was the buzz of insects and bright birdsong and everything seemed full of vigour.

'This is wonderful,' Caitlyn said, as they marched out carrying the picnic basket, over the velvet grass of the tended lawns and out towards the meadow. They walked away from the woods with their pheasant pens, and out over wild grass sprinkled with tiny blue and yellow flowers and alive with bees hovering between them.

Max and Coco seemed to be getting on famously and they engaged in a busy game of frisbee while Nicholas and Caitlyn laid out the picnic. It was a feast of salads, cheeses, cured meats and fresh bread, followed by strawberries and tiny honey meringues, with dollops of thick cream on top. The children drank ginger beer while Nicholas popped open a bottle of cold champagne.

'I've been saving it for a special occasion,' he said, 'and this seemed appropriate.'

The children got up to play again and the grown-ups

watched from their rug, Caitlyn enjoying the feeling of the sun on her face and arms. She felt as if she were being slowly but thoroughly defrosted.

Nicholas observed the children, his champagne glass balanced on one knee and the sunshine glittering on his dark glasses. 'Max seems like a great kid,' he said. 'He looks like you.'

'Does he?' Caitlyn was surprised. 'People always say he looks like Patrick.'

'Well, I suppose as I didn't meet Patrick, it's you I see most of all.'

She felt suddenly deeply grateful that he hadn't met Patrick and never would. That part of her life and this – whatever it was – were separate. The knowledge that she had finally made the break with Sara after all this time was a relief but she felt too that she had been kicked back to the first rawness of Patrick's death because she was, in a way, losing him all over again.

She watched the children running about for a moment, then said, 'I think Coco is amazing. So confident and articulate. I'm sure I wasn't like that at twelve.'

Nicholas smiled proudly. 'Yes, she's wonderful. It's awful living so far away from her, but having her in my life at all is the greatest thing there is. I'm working on her mother to send her over here for school in a few years. Coco could come to Oxford, she's plenty smart enough, and her mother definitely would like that. So the idea is that she'll come here for her sixth form to prepare for university entrance. That's only a few years away now.'

Caitlyn took a sip of the cold champagne which she was surprised to find she enjoyed very much. 'You obviously adore her.'

Nicholas smiled at her, his eyes invisible behind the dark lenses of his sunglasses. 'Maybe I'm prone to adoring,' he said in a low voice.

A prickle went over her skin, lifting the hairs on her arms. She guessed he meant for her to understand something. Somewhere at the back of her mind, she'd been wondering if he thought there might be something between them. Not now – it was far too soon for that – but one day. 'That's nice,' she said quietly. Then added, 'You're a good friend. Thank you.'

Nicholas put down his glass, and leapt up, suddenly buoyant. 'Come on, let's play frisbee!' he shouted, and grabbed her arm to help her up, so they could run and join the children in the sun-warmed, scented meadow.

After lunch, they packed up and made their way back to the house to say hello to Geraldine. She was awake and perky in her sitting room, and talked a while with the children who were both very good at sitting quietly and conversing politely with a lady in her nineties.

Geraldine sent Coco and Max to find Renee in the kitchen, where some biscuits had been freshly baked, and then turned to Nicholas and Caitlyn. 'Well, my dears, how very nice to see you both together again. And to see your children here too. It makes me very happy.'

'Aunt, it's a bit upsetting how eager you are to get me settled down.' Nicholas laughed.

'Is it any surprise?' retorted his aunt. 'You're getting old! You need a wife and a proper home instead of being an eternal student.'

Nicholas turned a sideways gaze to Caitlyn. 'Aunt Geraldine doesn't realise that I'm not a student. I *teach* students, remember?'

His aunt looked at him fondly. 'Because you're a very clever boy. And I'm sure Caitlyn is a clever girl too.' Geraldine looked at Caitlyn. 'And I understand you're moving in next week. What an excellent time of year to arrive. The house is quite at its best in the summer.'

'We're looking forward to it,' Caitlyn said sincerely. She felt safe here. Protected. Hidden. 'I'm going to show Max around a bit now, so he knows the place.'

'Good idea,' said Geraldine. 'Nicholas can stay here and keep me company.'

Caitlyn went off to find Max and Coco in the kitchen.

They drove back to Oxford more slowly than they'd come, the fresh evening air ruffling their hair as they went. In Caitlyn's quiet street there was no sign of Sara's car and the atmosphere was warm and quiet, a holiday evening.

'Come in for a bit,' suggested Caitlyn. She rustled up pasta for Max and Coco and they ate it in front of a movie, while she and Nicholas talked quietly in the kitchen. Now that they were away from Kings Harcourt and its seductive atmosphere, Sara and her unpredictability became an issue again.

'Do you think she'll still be following you?' Caitlyn said, loading the dishwasher as they talked.

'Who knows? Maybe she'll give up now. She must guess where my loyalties lie. She can't try the same trick twice.' Nicholas gathered up the pots and put them in the sink full of soapy water. 'Or maybe she'll just back off altogether.'

'I think it might be too much to hope for.'

Nicholas plunged his hands into the kitchen sink to scrub the pots. 'Whatever happens, I'm in it with you, okay? You're not alone.'

She was filled with a sudden affection for him. 'Thank you, Nick.' She smiled at him. 'Who would have thought we'd end up here, like this? Doing the washing-up together while we talk about Sara.'

'It is strange,' he conceded. 'But life has a way of bringing you full circle. That's what I've found anyway.' He looked down at the pot in his hands, concentrating on it hard, and then he looked up. His expression was hard to read. 'So you decided to look in Patrick's email again, did you? That's how you found the picture?'

'Yes. And that reminds me. Look.' She went and got Patrick's phone and brought up the second picture. 'It says "Look for the snake in the grass". What do you think it means?'

Nicholas frowned. 'It sounds like he means Sara – the snake in the grass.'

'Yes, but it's right next to a picture of her. I mean, I found her. I don't need to keep on looking.'

'I suppose not.'

'And it's a weird way to describe her, if they were having an affair. He'd be just as bad – even worse, really.'

Nicholas looked puzzled. 'I don't know then. Does it sound like him?'

'Yes, it does. He liked leaving me clues.' She sighed. 'But I'm not sure if I even know Patrick any more, not now I've found out what he was really up to.'

'So he wasn't the unfaithful type?'

'Having an affair would have been really out of character. With Sara – well, I would have said it was impossible. But all this proof . . .'

Nicholas put another clean pan on the tray to drain. 'It changes how you feel about him.'

'It has to,' Caitlyn said in a small voice. 'I hate it, but there's no way round it. Patrick isn't who I thought he was after all. And that's the worst thing, the most heartbreaking thing about it.' Grief, bitter and painful, was suddenly hard in her chest. 'I don't know who I'm mourning, or what my marriage meant.'

Nicholas came over and hugged her, his hands hot and still soapy from the water. His nearness and warmth were deeply comforting. 'I'm so sorry. You've been through a horrible, dreadful time. This must make it worse.'

She nodded, pressing her face into the solidity of his shoulder. The hug was everything she needed. 'It does.'

'Don't doubt him too much, Caitlyn. Patrick sounds like a tricky customer to me. I'm sure someone like him would always be two steps ahead. Let's see what happens, and keep looking for that snake in the grass.'

Chapter Thirty-Six

Tommy ran, hardly knowing where to go. The children were asleep, she couldn't disturb them. She stood on the landing, tears falling down her face, unable to decide where she might be able to hide away.

'Tommy.' Fred came swiftly up the stairs. 'I'm so sorry.' He took her in his arms and hugged her. 'What a horrible thing to hear. You should never have to endure something like that. It was repellent to witness.'

'My mother can't bear me. She thinks I'm the lowest of the low.' Tommy sniffed, determined not to sob on his chest, but the temptation to pour out all the hurt she had suffered over the years was strong.

'But why? Why on earth? When you're so wonderful, so strong and beautiful?'

'She doesn't think that and never has.' There was a noise in the hall downstairs and Tommy froze, then said in a low voice, 'I feel as though we're surrounded by spies.'

'Come on.' He pulled her by the hand. 'Let's go to my room. We can be quiet there.' In his room, he drew the curtains around his bed. 'Now we can be doubly sure we won't be overheard.'

'If they know we're in this room together, they'll only think the worst.'

'Let them. They can't think worse than they do.'

She managed a weak smile. 'All right.'

They climbed onto the high mattress behind the curtains. Fred lay back against the pillows and beckoned Tommy to him. She lay down next to him in the crook of his arm, comforted by his nearness. 'What do you think about all this terrible mess?' she asked him.

'I believe that the last thing Roger wants to do is marry Barbara. And he'll consign himself to a lifetime of misery if he does. He's angry and she's poured poison into his ears. A regular little Borgia. He was ripe to listen as well, and that's my fault.'

'How?'

'I've not given him my full attention. He was jealous.'

'What on earth was he jealous of?'

'Of you, of course. Because he could see that I'd fallen in love with you.' He looked at her earnestly. 'You do know that, don't you?'

'Yes, I do.' She smiled weakly but happily. 'I know because I feel the same.'

Fred shook his head. 'Then why have we suffered so much over it all?'

'To spare ourselves – and others – pain. You knew Roger hated the idea of us being together.'

'Yes. But I've always been honest with him. He knows I

don't feel that way about men, and there's no chance that will change. I've told him that if he wants that from me, then I must never see him again. So he hasn't asked. Knowing he can't have that relationship with me, and seeing me want you, must have been a potent mix. That's Barbara's cleverness. She's seen all our weaknesses and played on them beautifully to get what she wants.'

Tommy shook her head. 'But how can she want to marry a man who can't love her?'

'You know why. Security. It's a cold and hard world out there.'

'Yes.' Tommy sighed a trembling breath. 'And now we both have to leave.'

'That's nonsense. I'll go, of course, and I'll write to your mother and Roger and explain the truth. We never intended to go through with a swap.'

'Perhaps I might have considered it,' Tommy said. 'But I don't think in the end I could have.'

'Well, I'll do my best to explain. But you must stay here. You shouldn't surrender the field to Barbara just like that. And where would you go?'

'I have friends in London I can stay with. I'd have to leave the children, though, until I found a place to live. I think it would only be a week or so. I don't want to leave them with Barbara longer than I have to, although I know Gerry will take care of them. It's poor Molly I feel for. The cat's a better mother than Barbara is.'

Fred turned to look at her, his expression serious. 'Tommy, you mustn't go. I mean it.'

'But I want to. I can't stay here, while my mother thinks of me the way she does.'

'I can't imagine why she threw such a ghastly insult at you,' Fred said, his voice tense with anger at the memory. 'No mother should say such a thing.'

'She's very old fashioned. Quite a puritan. She can't stand talk of love or relationships, or face up to any truths about people. Everything has to be proper. Underneath it all, she's a seething mass of sex obsession, I expect.' Tommy laughed wryly. 'But you see . . .' She shifted a little awkwardly. She was wary of telling the facts of her life, in case she provoked the same reaction in Fred that she had in her mother. She was afraid that love would disappear and never come back. *But I trust him. And if I can't tell him, there's no hope for us.*

Fred was quiet, waiting for her to speak.

'I'm sorry, Fred. This is very hard for me. I've kept it to myself for so long. Only my mother knew even a hint of it.'

'You don't have to say anything.'

'No.' She felt his arm tighten around her and took comfort from it. 'I want to. I need to. It's been eating me up for years. I thought I'd been brave and coped with it, and made it all go away, but it isn't true. I'm falling in love with you even though I tried my hardest not to. But we haven't got a hope if you don't know the truth from the start. If I don't tell you now, it's doomed.' She laughed shakily. 'It's just that I'm afraid of saying it.'

'Don't be,' he said. 'And take your time.'

She lay quietly next to him, gathering her courage, wanting to say it right. At last, in a low voice, she began.

'Alec and I didn't fall in love exactly. We got engaged very quickly because . . . well, we had to get married.' She felt a blush staining her cheeks. 'I explained to my mother at the time that I didn't love him but that I was having a baby. I don't know what I hoped exactly – perhaps that she would tell me that I didn't have to marry him. I knew there were other ways. I could have gone away for a year to study art or something, and come back when it was all over. I wouldn't have had Antonia, though, and that's too awful a thought to contemplate now, so I'm glad I didn't. But at the time, I didn't feel that way. I didn't know if I wanted the baby. But my mother – she was shocked, so horrified. She was . . . *disgusted*. And she told me so.' Tommy stopped, remembering that terrible interview. 'She said that everyone else would be too, if they ever found out. She was never the warmest of mothers, but after that she treated me like a . . . something untouchable. Cheap and sordid. I could feel her scorn and contempt every time she looked at me. It was horrible. So Alec and I were engaged and then married – and I thought after that everything would be all right again, especially when Antonia arrived. She was so beautiful. But it seemed that nothing could wipe away my sin.' Tommy stopped again and bit her lip. She shot a quick glance at Fred, who was gazing at her earnestly. 'All right, so now I expect you despise me, don't you? You probably think I'm the lowest sort of woman.'

'I don't think that at all.'

'Well.' She looked away, remembering. The night of Lady Rosse's ball and Alec, the handsome man who, seeing her separated from her party, had introduced himself – a friend of

Isabelle, Lady Rosse's daughter – and offered her a lift home. She'd accepted, and at first it had been rather romantic. When he'd suggested parking his car by Hyde Park so that they could take a moonlit walk to the lake, she'd been enchanted by the suggestion. Giddy on several glasses of champagne, she'd floated in her chiffon dress, a rabbit fur cape keeping her shoulders warm, the reassuring male strength beside her. He said little but laughed at her chatter. And then . . . it had turned very ugly in the shadows beneath the trees. She had gone so suddenly from gaiety and excitement to cold fear and sickening confusion, as Alec had taken her hand in an iron grip, and then grabbed her neck, pulling her to him, ignoring her shocked protests. Each second had stretched out into an endless moment of pain and fear, and the scene had stayed with her ever since, reverberating through the years, endlessly replaying.

Tommy whispered in a small, choked voice, 'I didn't want to . . . have a baby. He made me do it. I didn't even know him then but I thought I was safe with him because he'd been at the ball. It was a dreadful mistake, the worst I ever made. I wasn't safe after all, not a bit.' She stopped, unable to go on for a moment, chilled by the memory of that terrible night and what it had started. 'I can't believe I'm telling you this. I never told anyone before. I didn't even really explain to Mother, though I think she guessed.'

'Did he hurt you?' Fred's voice was low and gentle.

'Yes, horribly. Because it wasn't what I wanted at all.'

Tommy had another flash of recollection: she was pushing at the stiff dinner jacket, shirt buttons pressing hard on her chest, rough grass under her thighs as the stranger hoicked up the light-as-air chiffon; her own pleas and cries and the hurricane of his heavy breathing in her ear.

She gasped, tears stinging her eyes, and shuddered. Fred tightened his arm around her.

'He said that I'd led him on. But I hadn't. At least, I hadn't meant to. He took me home afterwards; I could hardly speak, all I could think about was the shock and pain and how I must have deserved it somehow. I hoped it would all go away and I could forget about it. But then I found out that . . . Antonia was coming. I didn't know what to do, I thought there was only one way. So I got his address from Isabelle and I wrote to him, and we met for tea.'

'You were very brave.'

'It was stupid. I was sick with fear seeing him again, shaking with it. But he was so normal, as though nothing unusual had happened, meeting me in the tea room so beautifully turned out, so handsome and polite. He acted as though we'd been in love and that's why the baby was coming. It made me think that somehow I'd misunderstood and that perhaps I had wanted him to do it – not wanted, but done as he said, led him on. He said he was happy about the baby and proposed marriage at once. I thought that I didn't have a choice, I had to say yes. I didn't have a clue what I was letting myself in for. I thought I'd get used to it, perhaps even grow to love him. But I never could. I could never forget.'

'You poor thing. Poor girl.'

Tommy was engulfed suddenly by a sadness she rarely let herself feel: a deep sorrow for that eighteen-year-old girl, who had only done what she thought she had to, signing away her life to the man who had destroyed it. 'My mother was desperately ashamed. Everyone kindly kept quiet about the fact Antonia was so early and so bouncingly healthy but I'm sure it didn't go unnoticed. Then Harry came along too the year before war broke out.' Tommy paused, struggling to find the words. 'We seemed happy enough, I suppose. But no one knows what goes on behind closed doors.'

It had turned out that Alec liked his wife's resistance. There was nothing he enjoyed more than taking her against her will. Tommy had soon learned that it was easier, gentler, shorter if she acquiesced. To bear her life and the deep hatred she had for her husband, she closed down all her emotions except the love she felt for her children. She could love them in torrents, but for Alec she had nothing but the coldest scorn and loathing. He felt it and it made him worse towards her, as though he could force love and respect into her with cruelty. She had shut up her heart and resolved to survive alone even if she spent her whole life with him. She would endure it for the sake of the children, the precious gifts Alec had given her.

'If he weren't already dead, I'd kill him myself,' Fred said, his voice now hard, his eyes set steely.

A warmth rushed through her: he understood. She'd been afraid that he would be repelled by her if he knew the truth. But without hesitation, he was on her side.

Fred said, 'I thought you must have loved him very much. I thought that was why you kept running away from me. I was blind and yet, I should have guessed. There were no photographs of him, you see. Nothing on display. And when we talked about Venetia and her heartbroken husband, you said that there were other reasons not to be able to look at a picture. I had the sense then that you were telling me something that I couldn't hear.'

'I had no idea I was.' Tommy rubbed her cheek along the wool of his jumper, taking comfort from the warmth below it. 'The day Alec left for the war, I began to live again. And when he died, I couldn't tell anyone that I was glad, that I got down on my knees and gave thanks that he would never come back and make me suffer again.'

Tommy remembered the day of the telegram, walking out of the kitchen away from her family. They hadn't seen her turn her face to the sky and close her eyes, like a prisoner taken from a dungeon and shown sunlight again. She was unshackled. Free. She was reborn.

She went on: 'I sound like a monster, I know. Of course, I was sorry too, for the children, to have lost their father. He was very good with them in a way he was never able to be with me. But then I thought, well, now they need never learn the truth. He'll always be that wonderful, half remembered father, a hero who was killed in the war. We look at his photograph and I create a new Alec for them, one they can love and be proud of. The pictures can never talk back and reveal the truth.'

Fred stroked her hair lightly. 'No wonder you felt you'd had a lucky escape. Any sane person would have felt the same.'

She looked up at him. 'You don't think I'm wicked?'

'Of course not. It makes perfect sense. And you quite sensibly decided never to let anyone close to you again, in case they hurt you the way Alec did.'

'Yes!' She was drenched in sweet relief that he understood completely. 'That's right. I couldn't risk it again.'

'But . . .' He rested his warm palm on her hair and looked at her seriously. 'My darling Tommy, will you risk it now? I give you my word that I'll never hurt you. I'm not like Alec, not a scrap.'

'I know that. I knew it at once. But I made a promise to myself that I wouldn't let any man close to me again.'

'Can you break that promise?' he asked with hope in his voice.

'I think so.'

He took her face in his hands, his expression intense as he stared into her eyes. 'Tommy, I hope you'll let me love you. Let me show you that it doesn't have to be like that.'

'Yes, please.' She felt his arms, warm and solid around her, and a new, unknown warmth inside herself. Her heart was beating hard, and she was aware of her skin, her nerve endings, her whole physical self. *I thought I was dead. But I'm alive after all.* 'I want you to.'

Chapter Thirty-Seven

Oxford was full of the sound of bells when Caitlyn woke. It was Sunday morning, the sun was obscured by scudding clouds that quickly turned grey and the air had a chill in it. Jen arrived at the front door, wearing her blue boiler suit and a bright red headscarf.

'Morning!' she said. 'I've come for Max.'

'Have you?' Caitlyn said, surprised.

'Didn't he tell you? He did so well last time, he wanted to come again. We're going to make coil vases.'

'Oh. Great, I'm sure he'll love it. I'll call him.'

While they were waiting for Max to come down from his room, Jen said, 'You've got a fan or something.'

'Have I?'

'Yes. Some woman was sitting outside your house last night. In her car. She was there for ages, watching your front door.'

'Really?' Caitlyn looked impulsively over to the front window where it was possible to see all the way through the ground floor to the kitchen. 'How long was she there?'

'She wasn't there when I went up to bed. But I saw her again this morning. Bit weird.'

'Yes,' Caitlyn said faintly.

'Do you know anyone who might do that?'

'I . . . perhaps. I'll keep an eye out for her.'

'I should. Max! Get a move on, matey!'

When Max had gone, Caitlyn went straight to the window and looked out, feeling suddenly chilled. There was no sign of Sara or her car. Could Jen have imagined it? That didn't seem very likely. But neither did the fact that Sara might have sat outside her house for hours on end. Why would she? What did she hope to see?

Her phone chirped and she went to check it. A text had arrived. It was from Sara.

I'm watching you. And I know exactly what you're doing.

A rush of adrenaline sent the tips of Caitlyn's fingers prickling as she fired back a text.

Leave me alone.

Another arrived a moment later.

How dare you betray Patrick like this?

Caitlyn gasped with the effrontery of Sara accusing her of betrayal. *She obviously thinks Nicholas and I are involved.* She switched off her telephone and put it under a sofa cushion so she couldn't see it, then took some deep breaths to calm herself down. *I have to behave naturally. She can't do anything to hurt me.*

After breakfast, she went to the window and looked out. There was no one there, and she told herself she was being paranoid. Sara might be a drama queen but she still had a job to do and a life to run; she couldn't start spending her entire time spooking Caitlyn.

Nevertheless, she was glad that Max was at Jen's.

She had relaxed by the time she sat down at her computer to check her emails. There were ten from Sara, all with the subject heading **You Never Loved Patrick.**

Caitlyn started shaking properly. How had Sara turned the tables like this – accusing Caitlyn of a kind of infidelity? *What gives her the right?*

She rang Nicholas and told him in a frightened voice what was going on.

'She's insane,' he said frankly. 'But emails and texts ... they're annoying but you can ignore them. I don't like the fact that she's watching the house.'

'I suppose it was her,' Caitlyn said. 'But I don't think she's there now.' She got up and went over to the window, then gasped. Sara was standing across the street, staring blankly at the house. She darted back out of view, her heart pounding. 'Oh my God, she's there.'

'Okay. That's not good.' Nicholas sounded worried. 'I'll come and tell her to get the hell away from you.'

'What does she want?' Caitlyn said, panicked. 'Why doesn't she leave me alone? She ought to be too ashamed to look me in the face, instead she's attacking me!'

'She can't accept she's in the wrong. I don't think she's ever been able to admit her actions, even to herself. You've always given her reassurance that she's a normal, likeable person. If you desert her, she'll probably collapse. Does she have many other close friends?'

'She's got loads of friends . . .' Caitlyn broke off, trying to think of Sara's really close friends. 'She knows a lot of people, I suppose. But I'm her only real friend.'

Nicholas said firmly, 'I think you should call the police.'

'What good would that do? She's only standing across the road, that's not a crime.'

'Harassment is.'

'Not a few hours' worth. I don't see how it would help.'

'Register it. Just in case.'

Caitlyn sank down against the wall until she was sitting on the floor. 'I can't bear it,' she whispered. 'I only wanted peace for me and Max. I don't deserve this.'

Nicholas said, 'Sweetheart, I'm so sorry. I'm coming to you as soon as my tutorials are over.'

Caitlyn was filled with impotent rage. Every time she looked out of the window, Sara was there, standing across the road by the neighbour's wall, her hands in the pockets of her light summer mac, her sunglasses on and her face expressionless. At one point, Caitlyn saw a neighbour come out of her house, go up and talk to her briefly, obviously asking if she needed any help, but Sara brushed her off with a few words, so the woman shrugged and went back inside.

Caitlyn fought the impulse to open the door and shout at Sara to go away but she knew that interaction would only make things worse. She had already blocked Sara's email address so that no more of the messages would pop up in her inbox but confronting Sara would surely feed her resentment and fury.

'Patrick,' she said out loud. 'How could you have had anything to do with her? Did you really love her? Even if you just enjoyed the sex, was it worth it? You always said she was nuts, and you were right.'

In her head, she heard Patrick's sardonic laugh and the way, coming back from Sara's drunken dinner parties, he would shake his head and say, 'She has no limits. I don't think Mark knows how to keep her in tow. He can't control her.'

He always seemed to feel sorry for any man Sara got involved with. And yet it occurred to her that Sara was one of the few people whose taste Patrick didn't criticise. He admired the way she could transform interiors. He was scornful, on the whole, of interior designers, but he made an exception for Sara. She had a quirkiness that meant she could put clashing colours and patterns together to create a brilliant harmony. Her interiors looked stylish and fresh and yet timeless. She never used anything she'd seen in a magazine. 'Once it's in print, it's over,' she said, although she didn't mind her own work appearing in glossy design magazines. She yearned, really, to be discovered for a television show and to find a new level of fame. But it hadn't happened, even though she'd been tested. Caitlyn suspected that, despite Sara's shimmering photogenic qualities, she would be stiff and affected once the camera was on her, just as she had been so painful to watch when she attempted her flirting.

She wondered what it would have been like if Patrick had married Sara instead of her. Perhaps everything would have been different if it had been Patrick, not Rupert, Sara had chosen that night. But Sara would always have opted for Rupert over Patrick, and even if she hadn't, he would have become just another in her endless line of conquests, eventually to be rejected with that delicate wrinkle of the nose and the cutting judgement that he was, in the end, rather common. Sara would never have come to terms with Patrick's Australian family, the strident, suntanned Aileen and the rest of the salt-of-the-earth tribe. She'd have laughed, openly, at them.

Patrick wouldn't have been able to take that. He was so proud.

Caitlyn could see, suddenly, the constant attraction and repulsion that had existed between Patrick and Sara. They were cut from the same cloth in some ways: both charismatic, attractive, obsessed with appearances and determined to live in the way they deemed the best. Both needed to be the top dog.

It would have been awful, if they'd been fighting each other to be in control.

Whereas all the checks and balances had made her relationship with Patrick work, it would never have been like that with Sara.

And I loved him. I really did.

'Then why?' she said out loud. 'Why, Patrick?'

But there was no reply, and still Sara was outside, watching.

When Nicholas arrived thirty minutes later, roaring up in his MG, Sara had gone. At least, she was nowhere to be seen.

'I really don't like this,' Nicholas said, looking out at the pavement from the sitting room window. 'All we need is for her to go a bit *Fatal Attraction* on you. Do you have any pets?'

'Thankfully, no. Not even a hamster.'

'Still, I think you ought to report it.'

'I will. If it gets worse.'

He went over and hugged her. 'I want to stop this.'

'You can't. She'll love it if you get involved, honestly. I know her.'

The sound of a loud thumping on the front door startled them. Caitlyn was instantly alert, her eyes turning at once to the window. A loud shouting came from the street outside.

'I know what you're doing in there! What would Patrick think? You're betraying him, you whore!'

'Oh my God.' Nicholas turned towards the door, his expression determined. 'I'm going to tell her what I think of her.'

'No!' Caitlyn had gone pale, her heart racing and her palms prickly. 'I won't have a fight on my doorstep. You'll make her much worse. Ignore her.'

The shouts continued – 'You're with Nicholas, I know you are! It's disgusting!' – as Caitlyn went to the window and peeped out. Sara was on the doorstep, still thumping on the door. When she looked over at the window, Caitlyn darted back out of sight.

'I can't stand this,' she said in a shaky voice. 'What if Max hears her? He's only next door. I can't have that. She's got a bloody nerve!'

Nicholas shook his head. 'She's unbelievable!'

Caitlyn ran to the front door and opened it in one swift movement. Sara stood there, quietened by the surprise, her cheeks flushed and her eyes glittering with anger. Before she had time to gather herself, Caitlyn said, 'I will call the police if you carry on shouting and banging on my door. You have thirty seconds to leave or I phone them. Understand? Leave me alone, Sara. Treating me like this does not lessen your guilt. I have nothing to be ashamed of.'

'He loved me!' shouted Sara. 'That's the truth and you can't accept it!'

'Twenty-five seconds,' Caitlyn said coolly, and shut the door. Then she started to shake, her breath coming in stutters as she tried to keep calm.

'You were magnificent,' Nicholas said.

'I can't let Max see this. It's too awful.'

The thumping and shouting stopped and when Nicholas looked, Sara had gone. He went back to Caitlyn and took her hands in his.

'Listen, why don't you move now? Today? Take what you want, and let the movers do the rest later. I don't usually recommend running away, but in this case, it makes sense for you to get away from her.'

'Go to the house today?' The thought was like being wrapped in warmth.

'Of course,' he said simply.

'Yes.' She knew at once that it was what she wanted more than anything.

Chapter Thirty-Eight

In London, the snow was melting a little, though it was still thick on the rooftops and at roadsides. Nelson, looking chilly on the top of his column, was wearing thick white epaulettes and his hat carried a blanket of snow like a layer of cotton wool padding.

Tommy looked out of the window as the bus lumbered slowly around Trafalgar Square. The weather was still freezing cold but the worst of it now seemed to have passed, and the south-east was feeling a moderate recovery. There had been enough trains running to get her to Oxford and from there to London. But it was hardly the place she had known before the war, when it had glittered with lights and the enticements of cafes, bars and nightclubs. Now even the great hotels looked shabby and the city and its people seemed tired and battered by everything they had suffered.

Perhaps if I'd lived through it, I wouldn't notice the contrast as much. As it is, I can hardly bear it.

London had retained its glamour in her mind. Even the worst newsreels of destruction and bombs and fire and death had not quite been able to dent her memories of it. Now it was only too plain what the city had suffered, even through the snow and ice.

It will never be the same again.

The journey down from Kings Harcourt had been long and arduous but nothing like as difficult as staying at home. After the announcement of Roger's engagement, the atmosphere inside the house had grown colder than that outside. The following day, Fred had begged Thornton to get the old truck out and help him clear the snow along the lane. It had taken all day and part of the next, but at last they had met up with the clearers approaching from the village, and the way had been cleared for Fred to leave.

'I can't stay now,' he'd said to Tommy. 'But you should. Fight your corner. Don't let her win.'

But she felt that life at home was now insupportable. She couldn't go on, with Roger's accusatory glances and her mother's scorn. Worst of all was Barbara's air of triumph, and the way she began almost immediately to go about the house making changes. The electricity burned whenever she pleased, and things were rearranged to suit her. Ada was both more humble in Barbara's presence, realising that her future now lay in Barbara's hands rather than Tommy's, and also more enraged.

'Do you know what she said to me, miss?' Ada said in shocked tones. 'She said she trusted that Thornton and me are eating according to the rations. She said she wouldn't like it if we were found to be taking more than we're entitled to from the household. Well, miss! Would you believe it? As if we would.'

'You're entitled to as much as any of us have, Ada,' Tommy replied. 'Don't listen to her.'

But Tommy knew that when the thaw came, plenty of black market produce would be making its way to the table. Barbara would see to that.

Once the road to the village was clear and her little car had been dragged back to the house, probably never to recover, she felt that the crisis was over. The snow was still thick on the ground but the worst blizzards had passed and not come back. The village had begun to receive a little more in the way of supplies. Milk and bread were now available, even if meat was scarcer than ever. A very great amount of livestock had frozen on the hills and in the fields, and no one would know the extent of the losses until spring finally came.

But will it ever come? Tommy wondered, as her taxi made its way along Piccadilly and up into Mayfair. *It's hard to believe that it will ever be summer again.*

She had told the children she would be back soon, and left them in Gerry's care. Thornton had driven her in the truck to the station and from there she had telegrammed ahead to her friend Celia to say that she would be coming. Celia had always urged her to drop in at any time she wanted.

Now, as they made their way to South Audley Street, it occurred to Tommy to wonder if Celia and her flat were still even there. But as they approached it was obvious that there was less bomb damage here and the taxi pulled to a stop outside Celia's. Once inside, Tommy was blissfully warm. The fire seemed to throw out so much heat in comparison to the feeble efforts of the fires at home.

'How marvellous to have you here!' Celia cried, throwing her arms around her and kissing her. 'You've been gone for far too long. We have gin. We will make cocktails. Why, you silly thing, you're crying!'

'I'm sorry, Celia, I'm just thinking of the children. It's so cold at Kings Harcourt.'

'Cold everywhere, darling,' Celia said, moving to the drinks tray. 'But that's where a little flat beats a country pile hollow. Peanuts to heat this place, my love. You should come back to town.'

'Perhaps I will.' Tommy took off her coat. Her prized fur looked a little tatty in Celia's elegant surroundings. 'But the oddest thing. I had Barbara Fallon to stay, and now she's engaged to my brother.'

'Barbara Fallon?' Celia looked blank as she tipped gin into tall glasses and opened her ice bucket. 'I don't think I know her. Is she somebody?'

'No, not really, not the way you mean. I don't think I am either, come to that. We were at school together. And then . . . oh, she got married. Now she's Barbara Hastings.'

Celia added two large measures of Dubonnet to each glass and passed one to Tommy. 'Now that name I do know. Barbara Hastings . . . I can't think why it rings a bell but it does. Here you are – drink this and relax.'

It was very otherworldly to be away from Kings Harcourt after so long. She felt in one way quite lost and in another delighted to be free of all the pressure it had imposed upon her for such a long time. As she sat on Celia's sofa, drinking while she listened to all the silly gossip she had missed, she thought almost recklessly, *If Barbara wants the house and all that goes with it so very badly – so badly she'd marry Roger – then let her have it. She can deal with the leaking roof and the failing heating and the moaning tenants and all the rest. I've got my little income from Father. I can manage if Roger pays for the children's education. I don't think that's too much to ask.*

'Bianca Montgomery is having a party tonight, if you want to go along. I said I might bring you and she was quite excited.' Celia exhaled a plume of smoke from her cigarette. 'Do come if you're not too tired.'

Tommy smiled at her. 'I'd love to,' she said.

After a week at Celia's, Tommy was quite exhausted. She'd forgotten what it was like to run on such late hours, and to spend so much time talking and drinking and going from one place to the next in order to do more talking and drinking. The weather hadn't stopped everything as brutally as it had in the countryside and now, with a break from the snowstorms, the streets were relatively clear, if bordered with nasty black slush. The Thames was still frozen, though, and there were stories of people cycling the length of the Boat Race on its glassy surface; and it was still bitterly cold. But life was resuming some of its normal pace.

Celia certainly lived at a hectic speed and Tommy found that the daily round didn't leave much time for introspection.

There were regular lunch engagements, and appointments to keep Celia well dressed and polished for her never-ending social diary. Tommy had quite forgotten what it was like to have one's hair done by someone else, or to think of putting polish on her nails. She had little to wear by Celia's standards, but Celia generously opened her wardrobe and shared what she had left from the heady days before clothing was only purchasable with points.

'Unless,' Celia said knowingly, 'you have a dear little lady who will kindly run you something up from the rather gorgeous French print that washed up on a beach somewhere.'

It was fun, Tommy couldn't deny, and it felt so louche to spend money in restaurants and on frivolities, when they could be found, instead of eking out bread by candlelight. But she missed the children, even knowing that Gerry was there to look after them, and was wracked by a longing for Fred. They had parted with little more than a clandestine touch of their hands as he climbed into the truck beside Thornton to make the journey to the station. Tommy had been far too aware of Barbara's pale stare and Roger's grim expression to want to show them how much she cared that he was leaving. Mrs Whitfield did not come out to say goodbye.

'I'll write to you,' he murmured, 'when I know where I'm staying.'

But she had left before anything arrived from Fred.

I should start looking for somewhere for me and the children to live. Not here in Mayfair, obviously. I should look somewhere cheaper. Islington perhaps, or Clapham.

She never did go out to find out about a reasonable lease,

though. The more she tried to imagine it, the less she could see their lives here in London. She wanted to be at home, and that was that. London was fun but it was not home.

But Barbara was there, sitting cosily in Tommy's place like a spider in the centre of her web.

A letter came for Tommy, brought to her breakfast plate by Celia's maid Simpson. She recognised Gerry's round hand on the address and opened it to find a letter from her sister, notes and drawings from the children and an envelope addressed to her in a thin, elegant hand with a London postmark.

She read Gerry's letter first.

Dearest Tommy,

You're very well out of this dreadful place. You can't think what a swank Barbara has become since you went away. She's swanning around like Lady Muck, and what's more, she's started wearing more of Mother's jewellery. If I didn't know better, I'd say Mumsie is beginning to regret sending you away and keeping Barbara, and is wishing it was the other way around. Barbara can be very strict and bossy when she feels like it and she's not being as sweet as she used to be by any means. I suppose she thinks it's all settled as far as it can be and she can stop being the ministering angel.

By the way, some steak was served here for dinner the other night. Steak! You can't imagine! Babs looked so pleased with herself but when I tasted it, I said I was certain it was horse. Well, her face, you would have hooted. I wish you could have seen it. I could read all over it that she thought she'd been had by some spiv. I don't know if it was horse, but I hope now it was.

The bad thing is Roger. I've never seen him so low. As soon as you and Fred left, all the fight just went out of him and he collapsed. He was in bed three days at least. Now he's up and about and floating around like a sad ghost of a creature, being nagged all the time by Barbara for her engagement ring. He spends more time with the children than he ever did. He seems to be happier with them. The thing is, Tommy, I'm worried for him. I really am. He seems so very hopeless and is trying to drink the cellar dry all on his own.

The children send best love and some notes from them are enclosed. They are both well.

This letter came for you – I thought you'd like it as soon as possible.

Write soon and tell me your news and when you'll be back.

Love from
Gerry x

Tommy folded the letter carefully and picked up the notes from the children, which she read with pleasure then put neatly to one side as well. She picked up the other envelope, slid her knife under the fold and opened it. She extracted the paper inside and opened that too.

My darling Tommy,

I hope you're well and fighting the good fight. I think about you all the time, and wish I could see you again and hold you in my arms. You are the bravest and best, and I cannot bear being apart from you. I miss you every second and hope you think sometimes of me.

I am staying with my sister Octavia in her place in Aldgate. You've never seen anything like the terrible destruction around here, but plenty still remains. I will set about finding a new place to live and seeing if I can resume my career at the BBC. My wound is almost healed. I haven't forgotten, my darling, that I owe you my life.

The thing that pains me most is that I don't know when I will see you again. Please tell me if you come to London and can spare me an hour. I live to see your sweet face again.

All my love,
Fred

She flushed as she read it, a swoop of pleasure dropping through her body, and then held it tight while she thought of it, and read it again.

'Anything nice?' Celia said, looking up from the morning newspaper.

'Just some news from home. You know – ordinary things. But lovely anyway.' Tommy held the letter to her heart, as though the slender slip of paper could warm and support her.

Chapter Thirty-Nine

As they left the house in Oxford late in the afternoon, Caitlyn looked around anxiously, worried that Sara was watching, but there was no sign of her. She packed everything into the car and set off, still alert for her watching them.

Every mile that stretched between her and Sara lightened the feeling of oppression. Sleeplessness and the constant sense of wariness had strained her nerves and exhausted her. Kings Harcourt lay ahead, a peaceful retreat from all of the recent tumult. Even knowing that Patrick's past was contained in the boxes in the spare room liberated her. Max had been happy to hear that they were going back there, if surprised at the sudden departure, but he didn't complain. It felt strange to leave a place, probably for good, with most of her possessions still in it, but the movers would come and collect them during the week. Nicholas had told her that there were plenty of barns to store things in.

The evening brightened and the sun came out as they neared the house. A good omen, Caitlyn thought.

'The old lady's asleep, dear,' Renee said when Caitlyn

knocked on the side door. 'Down, you rascals,' she scolded the dogs who were yapping and jumping about as usual. 'But we knew you were coming. She said to take you straight over to the main house. You can use our kitchen till all your bits and bobs arrive.'

'Thanks, Renee, that's very kind.'

Renee led them through the sitting room, into the hall and up the stairs to a bedroom papered in faded roses. Along the landing was another smaller room for Max. 'It's a touch dusty,' Renee said, 'but generally clean. The lady who cleans only does the rooms in rotation when they're not used. You can have her in more often if you want.'

'It's perfectly wonderful. When I've made the beds, it'll be very cosy,' Caitlyn assured her.

'I've made a cottage pie for supper, so come to us at seven o'clock.'

'Thank you, you're very kind.' Caitlyn smiled. 'I'll come and get the sheets from you and get started.'

'Max, you can watch the television while your mum gets settled. Come on, young man, this way.' Renee bustled him out and Caitlyn followed her to get the bedding.

The house was calm and as she worked, Caitlyn felt a serenity returning. The evening sunshine fell in warm pools on the floor, and birdsong floated through the open window. *I feel safe here. I feel as though everything will be all right.*

Once the beds were made and the contents of the suitcases put away, Caitlyn wandered about, taking everything in. The kitchen was like a time capsule with an ancient gas stove where a range had probably once been, and a scrubbed pine table. There was a fridge but it was at least forty years old. Everything else looked older than that but she liked the echoes of lives lived and meals cooked, and it seemed to be in working order.

Going back down to the hall, she looked up at the magnificent Gainsborough hanging in shadow. Really, she thought, it should be illuminated so that it could be seen and enjoyed properly. But then again, who would see it? It was very odd to have this valuable painting hanging here, in an empty house.

When she went back to find Max, Geraldine was awake and watching a television quiz with him, which they both were apparently engrossed in.

'I'm delighted you're both here, I shall enjoy having some company,' Geraldine said, as Caitlyn kissed her soft, powder-scented cheek. 'It's so nice to meet someone who likes the television as much as I do.'

'You definitely have an ally in Max,' Caitlyn said with a laugh. Then it came to her that she had laughed a few times lately. *When I thought I never would again.*

'We all need allies,' Geraldine replied. 'Now, I think our supper is nearly ready.'

When Caitlyn woke the next day, she was bewildered by the pattern of roses everywhere and, for a moment, forgot where she was and panicked. Then she remembered that they were safe. Today she'd be driving Max to school from Kings Harcourt. If Sara went back to watch the house, there would be no one there to observe and no way to find out where they had gone. That thought alone made her relax.

Outside it was bright and fresh, the green lawns velvety and smooth with just a hint of new clover bursting out. Fat pigeons were patrolling the lawns for insects and grubs, while sparrows, wrens and blackbirds darted down to pick up a morsel and flutter off with it to a branch or wall. The grass glittered with the remnants of the dawn dew, and the flower beds were riotous with full-blown peony heads, lavender and tiny, tissuey white geraniums on long spindly stalks. All around them, life was bursting out. Caitlyn went to wake up Max with a hope in her heart she had not felt in a long time. The buzzing of nature all around her made her aware of a future beyond this dark tunnel of misery she'd been walking through for what felt like an age. It might not be here yet, but there was something good still to be had from life. It always renewed itself. There was no other way.

'Come on, Maxie, chop chop! Get your uniform on and we'll go to Renee for some breakfast.'

Max groaned but began to haul himself out of bed, and Caitlyn went to run herself a bath.

By the time she got back from dropping off Max and picking up some shopping at the small supermarket in the nearest town, the morning was well advanced.

'Geraldine says would you like to have a cup of tea with her?' Renee asked, as Caitlyn was unloading the car.

'Of course. I'll be right over when this is done.'

She stowed her shopping in the old kitchen, rather charmed by the lack of cupboard space. There were no wall cabinets, just open shelves, and all the food was clearly supposed to go into the cool larder with its marble shelf for butter and cheese. Then she went over to the other half of the house, where Geraldine was up and about, moving with the help of a three-footed walking stick.

'Hello, my dear, how was your first night?'

'Excellent. It's so quiet here!'

'Isn't it? You can forget street lights and traffic and all the rest. The sky is like black velvet here. Now. I'm feeling rather mobile today and I thought you might like to see some of the paintings we've got. Nicholas tells me you worked in the art world.'

'Yes, I did, a long time ago – but I'm no expert.'

'Perhaps not, but you'd probably enjoy having a look, wouldn't you? Yes? Excellent. Come on then, while I've got the energy. I never quite know when I'm going to flag.'

They went almost directly to the Gainsborough, via a couple of pleasant but unremarkable oils of landscapes. The beautiful Venetia gazed out in her mournful way, half obscured by the shadow of the staircase. A picture light bent over the painting, but was not switched on.

'I'm still getting my head around living in a place where there's a Gainsborough hanging in the hall,' Caitlyn said, gazing at it with renewed awe. 'It's a shame more people can't see it.'

'Oh, people do come to see it,' Geraldine said, 'they make appointments to view it. But I feel rather guilty about it.'

'Really? Why?'

'I'm not entirely sure it's the real thing. But I don't want to disappoint people and they seem to like it very much as it is, so I don't say anything at all. If the picture light were switched on, I'm sure it would be revealed in no time. So I leave it off and pretend it's broken. That way it can't do any harm to just leave it hanging there making people happy.'

'She is so gorgeous.'

'She is, but if you know the history, the sadness of her early death almost overwhelms the picture, don't you think? All one can think of looking at her is the brevity of her life. You remember I told you about her.' Geraldine stood in front of it, leaning heavily on her stick. 'Her death must have caused great misery to all those who loved her.'

Caitlyn gazed at the painting. This young woman must have seemed so full of promise, even in an age of precarious existence with all the dangers of sickness and childbirth. It was easy to accept her death now, when it was two hundred and fifty years since she had lived, and all the rest of her generation and the ones that followed were long dead too. But one day, in a flash, she had moved unexpectedly from living to dead, leaving agony and grief behind. Those who mourned were gone and forgotten but her short life had left this mark behind it, a window from now to then.

Geraldine said softly, 'You spoke before of your own grief.'

'Yes. I am mourning too.' She thought of Patrick, now alive only in pictures and memories.

'The pain you feel now will change and lessen, I can promise you that.'

Caitlyn turned to look at the old lady. 'I thought I understood it at the beginning, and that I could cope, but now I know it was just the start of a much longer, more difficult journey than I expected. The pain at first was so awful – waking up every day and realising that it was still the same. He wasn't there and he never would be there. I hated every minute that took us further apart. And yet I also thought that I would get used to a world without him in it, and I longed for that moment to come when I wouldn't mind any more. It's not come yet. I can't see when it will. I fight every day like an Amazonian explorer hacking through the massive forest with a machete. It's such hard work, and it achieves so little, but I have to do it, or sit down and be overcome by it. It was all so paradoxical – I clung on to the memory of him at the same time as trying not to think about him. I hated the way that time and random fate had separated us. And . . . and I'm tormented by the knowledge that he hasn't escaped the void, and neither will I, and neither will Max.' She stopped, choked.

Geraldine nodded her white head slowly. 'I'm closer to it than you are, most likely. I can tell you that it is natural to be afraid. The only comfort I can offer you is that when your time comes, you will make your peace with it. The great tragedy is not death in itself. I can see a time when I will welcome a release from this old body of mine. It's being untimely ripped – taken for no purpose, before a life has been lived, through stupid accident or pointless circumstance or malevolent ignorance. That is where you and your poor husband are left – without peace and understanding.'

'Yes.' Caitlyn's voice came out thicker than she'd expected, freighted with longing and grief. 'And I feel I understand him less now than I did when he was alive.'

'Well . . .' Geraldine leaned on her walking stick, shifting her feet to be more comfortable. 'You mustn't let that fester, my dear. It will destroy something precious in you if you do. Do all you can to reconcile yourself to his death and trust in the past you knew. Even if something comes to light that gives a new facet to the person you loved – and it does happen, my dear – don't let it destroy the truth of your experience of them. We all look for ways to keep our loved ones alive, to maintain our relationship with them – and sometimes not in the best way. Sometimes anger and resentment can be a relationship too, but not a healthy one. Not one that will give you peace.'

Caitlyn nodded. 'Yes . . . I see.'

'Recovering from loss is not the work of a day or even a month, or a year. Grief must be worked through, it cannot be escaped, and it is a persistent creature, always tugging for attention. But ignore it at your peril – it will only appear when you least expect it, or in a guise you do not recognise: dressed up as anger or depression or self-destruction. Take a step every day out of the darkness – don't try and run – and that step will lead you inexorably towards acceptance and a new, different life.'

'You sound as though you know all about it,' Caitlyn said softly.

'I've lost many people. I have learned the ways of grief. But I also know that love lives on when those you love have gone.' Geraldine looked around the flag-stoned hall. 'This place is so familiar to me even though I come across that threshold rarely now. It seems like only yesterday that I was running down the stairs, just a child myself. Only days since my sister was here, gazing at this picture as she so often was. And there were other children here, running around and screaming their heads off. They are all gone now.'

Caitlyn pictured youngsters racing about the large room, which seemed made for chasing. One of them must have been Nicholas's mother. She recalled him saying that he had been a late arrival in his mother's life. She had been too busy trying to ban the bomb and fight for women's rights to get around to motherhood until it was almost too late.

'What happened to Nicholas's uncle? He said something about him dying young.'

Geraldine sighed. 'Harry was a little firebrand. He was killed in a car accident, far too young. Luckily my sister didn't live to see that, it would have broken her heart. I still miss him too. He would have been an old man himself by now – but that wasn't his story. Now, my dear, I want to show you the plasterwork upstairs.'

It was a long, slow process to get Geraldine to the top of the landing. She needed to pause on every step and prepare herself for the next one. At last they reached the top and walked slowly to the plaster frieze on the far wall of the landing. Geraldine examined it for a while, then sighed. 'Oh dear. The truth is that I can hardly see. I used to know them so well, these little figures.' She reached out a finger and traced it over a tiny plaster ringmaster, holding up his whip high above his top hat. 'I loved them. We all did.'

'But they're relatively new, aren't they?' Caitlyn said, bending to look closer in the gloom. She could smell the violet scent of Geraldine's cologne and it was somehow very comforting. 'Not the same age as the rest of the house. Nicholas said they were done during a long and hard winter that his mother often talked about.'

'The winter of '47, just after the war ended and all the men were coming back. That's when this work was started. The children came up with the idea, I think. How they longed to go to a circus. About as much chance of that as going to the moon back then.'

'I don't think I've heard of the winter of '47,' Caitlyn remarked.

'Everyone thinks now of the other great freeze – '62, was it? Something like that. Those of us who remember the other one are dying out. That's the thing with history, my dear. It loses its resonance once the eye witnesses are gone. That's why you'll see terrible things coming back into this world, as those of us who remember the horror of war disappear.' She gave Caitlyn a sideways look. 'Listen to me – like an oracle, just as Nicholas says. The winter of '47 was quite the most horrible thing, worse than the war, or so it seemed to me at the time. We were so beaten already, you see, after six years of privation and effort to win the blessed thing. And what was the reward for victory? Harder lines, more frugality, a freezing winter and all that came with it. It brought the country to its knees – oh, the suffering of it. Cold and more cold, no electricity, no supplies, the wireless silent. We were cut off and left to ourselves for weeks.'

'I suppose the house is quite remote.' Caitlyn found it hard to imagine the kind of conditions Geraldine was describing. Would it be possible to be as stranded today? Surely not. The internet, cable, mobile phones ... *But no electricity. What then? As soon as we ran out of charge for our devices, boom. We'd all be alone. Perhaps even more alone than back then because we're so dependent on our communications.*

Geraldine went on: 'I suppose what made it bearable was that we were used to it. Lack of food, lack of everything. And we knew very well that here we were fortunate – we had supplies. Others were not so lucky.' She turned back to the plaster. 'And this kind of thing kept us all occupied.'

'So who did this?' Caitlyn asked.

Geraldine looked vague suddenly, her blue eyes misty. 'Dear Fred ... Another loss. But he brought our family joy when we most needed it. Shall we look at some of the other paintings up here? I should like a wander around. It's been so long.'

They walked about the upper floor, opening doors and peeking inside. The rooms had an old-fashioned feel with their dark furniture and heavy curtains. Caitlyn thought again how much Patrick would have loved this house, with its patina of age. The pictures in the bedrooms were nothing special: watercolours, prints and the odd oil painting, mostly of landscapes. Caitlyn's vague thoughts of finding an over-looked masterpiece hanging above a fireplace – an early Leonardo or a long-forgotten Picasso – were not realised.

'Thank you for this, my dear,' Geraldine said as they began the slow climb back down the stairs. 'I've enjoyed talking to you very much.'

'So have I. To you, I mean.' Caitlyn went on one side of her, helping her negotiate each new step.

As they reached the bottom, Geraldine said, 'I'm afraid I'm very tired now. Please ask Renee to give you some tea if you'd like some. I must go and lie down.'

'I won't bother her. I must go and get Max.'

'Yes, of course. I'll look forward to seeing him later. Goodbye for now, my dear.' Geraldine kissed her cheek, then shuffled away, her shoulders bent with fatigue. Caitlyn looked at the painting hung opposite the door, nestling in shadow. With its picture light on, it would be illuminated and easy to examine but now it was a beguiling and beautiful portrait rendered out of focus by shade.

Chapter Forty

'I know a little place not far from your friend's flat,' Fred said when she telephoned him at the number on his letter. 'We can meet there. It's a tiny restaurant but it does a very good dinner.'

He had been elated when she rang. The woman who answered had asked her name and then said, 'Oh! *Tommy*. The wonderful Tommy. Delighted to make your acquaintance, even if only by telephone. I'm Octavia Burton Brown, Fred's sister. And he's quite your biggest fan.'

'Is he?' Tommy said, blushing, even over the telephone. 'How . . . nice!'

Fred had been excited to hear from her and even more so when he heard she was in London. 'Can I see you tonight, darling?' he asked. 'Can you get away?'

'Of course. Celia is dining out. I was staying in with a tray on my knees and a book anyway.'

'We can do better than that. Here, have you got a pen?'

Fred was right, it wasn't more than ten minutes away from the flat; a short walk to Curzon Street and then a sharp turn down an alley to an area that might as well have been miles from the smart building that Celia lived in. Lights glowed red in upstairs rooms and women in shabby overcoats and scuffed shoes smoked in small groups on the corners of the twisting streets. Several pubs were open, their clientele spreading out into the street despite the cold and the banks of snow against the walls. From inside the pubs came a fug of smoke and sweat and hot breath and laughter and chatter.

Can this be right? It's very insalubrious.

Nevertheless, she pressed on and found a restaurant set on the corner of a small street across the road from a pub. Its corner frontage shone brightly against the darkness and it seemed that plenty of people were making the most of the hours of electricity as it was quite full. She opened the door and went in. The customers were a mixed bag but she stood out with her smart suit and the fox fur over one shoulder, and she glanced nervously about looking for Fred. He spotted her at once, and stood up to wave her over to his table.

'Hello, Tommy!' He kissed her on the cheek, his eyes glowing with happiness to see her. He pulled a chair out for her so that she could sit down.

'Hello, Fred.' She was suddenly shy, despite having been desperate all afternoon for this moment to arrive. 'This seems an interesting place.'

He laughed. 'I like to think of it as a well-kept secret. I don't know how the chef does it, but he conjures magic out of very scrawny ingredients. He's French of course. Now – here's the menu. It's even barer than usual but everything will be good.'

'It looks lovely,' she said politely, though she didn't much care about the food. 'How are you, Fred?'

'I'm much better. The dressings are off completely now and I'm almost good as new.' He smiled at her, his face illuminated by the evident pleasure he felt in seeing her again. 'You look beautiful. Are you well?'

'Yes, quite well.' She told him some of her recent doings, and then recounted what Gerry had said in her letter. 'Roger isn't at all happy, according to Gerry. In fact, he's horribly miserable.'

'I should think it's only just dawning on him what it will mean to marry Barbara. There'll be no going back.'

Tommy looked at the table. 'I know better than most how awful a mistake like that can be. I want to help him if I can.'

'He has to make his own choices, Tommy, you know that. He's not compelled into marriage, the way you were. He can't blame anyone else for this mess. And he still has time to get out of it.'

'Gerry said Barbara has them all under her thumb. I can't imagine Roger standing up to her.'

Fred put his hand on hers across the table. 'If he wants us, we'll help him. Until he asks, there's nothing we can do.'

They ordered their food and talked of anything but what was happening at home. Fred told her about his sister's life and her friends and the large house they had bought in Spitalfields which would be a community for women who wanted to live independently but with like-minded friends. He made it sound cheerful and free and new.

'I'd like to meet her,' Tommy said. 'She sounds very interesting.'

'She's dying to meet you. I had to hold her back from coming here tonight, she's so curious. And she told me how I could make moulds for my little circus figures – remember how I was trying to work it all out? She has some sort of rubber substance that I can set around my carvings. Then, when it comes off, I have a very flexible mould for the plaster. When I come back to Kings Harcourt, I'll finish the mouldings.'

Tommy was suddenly melancholy. 'Do you think you'll come back?'

'I'm sure I will. And so will you. If you don't want to live in London, take a house in the village. Don't let Barbara push you out if you want to stay there. And if Gerry is right, your mother may well have a change of heart about dear Barbara.'

'Yes.' She felt more cheerful. 'You're right. I'll find a way to stay close by. Then I can be there when they need me.'

The evening was over too soon. At eleven o'clock the last dishes were cleared away and the lights turned off. Over the road, the raucous fun in the pub was reaching its peak. The bell for last orders rang as they went past.

They strolled up Curzon Street and then up to South Audley Street, where Fred took her in his arms by some railings and kissed her deeply. 'Tommy,' he said quietly. 'I want to be with you all the time. We must live together.'

'I want that too. But you're homeless and so am I. I have two children to raise . . .'

413

'I'll raise them with you. I think your children are marvellous and I'd do my best to be a father to them.'

'I believe you – but it's such a lot to ask when you have no job, no home . . .'

'We can start again together. We can make a life.' Fred held her tight and then said, 'I can see the lights of the Dorchester over there. Shall we see if the bar is still open?'

At the entrance to the bar, a waiter tried to turn them away, saying that only residents could now buy a drink there, but then someone squealed Tommy's name and they saw Celia sitting there with a friend.

'Very well, if you're with Lady Celia,' the waiter said, letting them pass.

'They always let me in,' Celia said when Tommy and Fred had joined her. 'I'm here so often I'm practically a resident. I used to come to their shelter in the raids during the war. My dear, the best people were taking cover here! It was quite a party when we weren't shaking with fear. This is Amanda Lillington. We escaped from Jonty's party and came here to blot out the memory. Amanda, this is Tommy Eliott, and . . . ?' Celia raised her eyebrows.

'Fred Burton Brown,' Tommy said.

'How do you do,' Fred said politely. 'I'll go and find the waiter, he seems to have disappeared.'

Celia wanted all the gossip about their night. 'You were in Shepherd's Market? How brave! It's rather colourful, by all accounts. But you were always plucky, Tommy, I'll give you that. Oh!' Celia put her hand on her friend's arm. 'But

414

Amanda, you know Barbara Hastings, don't you? You were the one who told me you knew her – that's right, it's coming back to me.'

'Yes, I know Barbara Hastings. Not well, but I certainly know her.' Amanda took a sip from her cocktail. 'I was out in India for a while, that's how our paths crossed.'

'Tommy knows her too,' Celia said confidentially. 'Very well, as it happens.'

'Not that well. We were at school together.'

Amanda laughed. 'I bet you have some stories then, if she was anything like that at school!'

'What do you mean?' Tommy asked, wondering where Fred had got to. She tried to spot him through the gloom.

'In India, she was quite the most scandalous English-woman there. She had several affairs but the most brazen was with an officer in the army. A major-general. It was talked about everywhere. She seemed to take great pleasure in humiliating the man's poor wife, and her own husband. She didn't make any effort to hide what was going on. If anything, she flaunted it. I think she thought something would come of it – but of course it didn't. And then the war came. She might be unknown here, but those of us who saw her in action know better. She's an adventuress, always on the prowl for rich men to buy her luxuries. We all felt sorry for her poor husband. I don't know how he tolerated it.'

'Oh dear,' Tommy said, feeling depressed though not surprised. 'That is a shame because she's marrying my brother.'

Fred appeared and said, 'The waiter's bringing a jug of

Singapore Sling. I thought that sounded all right.' He sat down at the table.

Amanda didn't appear to hear him. 'Marrying your brother?' she said to Tommy, disbelievingly. 'I don't think so.'

'Yes, she is. They got engaged last week. I should think it will be in *The Times* before too long.'

'No, she can't be,' Amanda said decisively. 'Because I saw Duncan Hastings just the day before yesterday lunching in Glover's in Piccadilly. I'm sure it was him. So unless they're divorced, how can his wife be engaged to marry someone else?'

'We have to tell Roger at once!' Tommy said urgently, as she and Fred stood on the doorstep of Celia's flat. Celia had tactfully withdrawn inside to leave them alone to say their goodbyes. 'I'll ring home tomorrow and explain that Barbara is a fraud!'

'Wait,' Fred said, 'we don't know for sure that Celia's friend really did see Duncan Hastings. She might have been mistaken.'

'But she knew him in India!'

'Yes, but why would Barbara allow Roger to propose to her if she has a husband living? She's not stupid enough to think she wouldn't be found out at some point. She must already be divorced.'

Tommy frowned. 'Yes, I suppose you're right. But why pretend to be widowed? Why say her husband was dead, if he might turn up at any moment?'

'Perhaps she thinks it sounds more respectable. But it's a

rum case. I think we need to do some investigating. Leave it with me and I'll see what I can find out from my army friends. I'm sure someone will have heard of Duncan Hastings and be able to help me track him down. Meanwhile, don't alert Barbara to this. If she's guilty, it'll give her more time to cover her tracks. And if she's innocent and we accuse her unjustly, it will make us look much worse than she does.'

'Yes, I see all that. I just want to save Roger any more pain.'

'I know. A day or two more won't make any difference.' He kissed her tenderly and she hugged him tightly. 'I'll telephone you as soon as I have some news. Sleep tight, my darling.'

'Goodnight, Fred. Sweet dreams.'

In the morning, Celia said, 'What a turn-up, Amanda knowing your friend! She sounds quite a piece of work.'

'Yes. She is,' Tommy said. 'The worst thing is that I thought I was helping her by taking her in, and she had no compunction about turning me out of my own home.'

'She's a cuckoo in the nest, chucking out anything that might threaten her security,' Celia remarked. 'I know the type. The war seemed to bring out the best in some of us, and the worst in others. Most I know found their best selves. But I saw some shoddy behaviour and I'm sure you did too.'

Tommy nodded. 'Yes.'

'Well, good luck, darling. I hope you get rid of the viper in the bosom.'

Chapter Forty-One

'How are you settling in?' Nicholas asked down the line.

'Very well, even if my phone signal is a bit patchy.'

'I don't think Aunt G has got round to installing a broadband connection yet, I'm afraid,' he said with a laugh. 'Any news from Sara?'

Caitlyn stood at the window on the upper-storey landing, looking out over the fields that stretched towards the village. They glowed with a luminous, almost acid green under the clear blue sky. 'No. I was expecting something, but there's been nothing. The movers are doing their thing today and I'm going back to the house to take a look. My neighbour Jen said she hadn't seen anyone loitering about when I called, so Sara must have given up.'

'She probably knows you've moved, and you're serious about breaking off contact. She'll have to just accept it. Coco and I are off visiting relations today and tomorrow but shall I come over with her when we're back?'

'Yes, that's a good idea. I've got Max's end-of-term

prize-giving this week. Then he'll be on holiday and needing some amusement.'

'Perfect. We'll look forward to it.'

Caitlyn drove back to Oxford, anxiety rolling in the pit of her stomach. She hadn't wanted to tell Nicholas but she had woken in the night with the sudden realisation that she'd left Patrick's tablet in the Oxford house when she'd meant to bring it with her. All his other things were there too, but boxed up and sealed, whereas she had hidden the tablet when Sara was hanging around outside, tucking it under the sofa cushion. Not a great hiding place but it was all that occurred to her on the spur of the moment. Now she was worried that the movers would damage it not knowing it was there.

When she arrived back at the terraced cottage, the van was parked outside and the movers were filling it up with large boxes from upstairs.

Caitlyn greeted the movers and went straight to the sofa. The tablet was still there, underneath the cushion and, as far as she could tell, unharmed. Relieved, she tucked it into her bag and went to make them all mugs of tea while there were still cups in the kitchen.

Jen put her head around the kitchen door while Caitlyn was brewing up the tea. 'Hello! You left in a hurry!'

'Sorry, Jen, we've had a bit of trouble that meant I needed to head off before I expected to.' Caitlyn tossed the teabags into a plastic rubbish sack. 'I meant to say a proper goodbye.'

'Anything to do with that woman hanging about here?'

'Well . . . yes. A bit. She's a little over-attentive.'

'You could say that.' Jen came in. 'Can I help?'

'You could carry some mugs for me if you like.'

They took the tea out to the movers and then stood on the street, watching them as they expertly emptied the house of Caitlyn's possessions.

Jen said, 'So you're on the run from a stalker?'

'That's putting it a bit strongly,' Caitlyn answered with a laugh. 'But . . . well, I was glad to have the opportunity to get away. Have you seen her since then?'

Jen shook her head. 'No. Not a sign.'

'I was worried she could turn up and just ask the movers where they were taking all the stuff. So I've asked the head mover to keep it private just in case.'

'Good idea. I'm sorry you're going through all of this on top of your husband's passing. I'm sending out as much good energy as I can.'

'Thanks, Jen.' Caitlyn smiled. 'It's much appreciated.'

One of the movers came up to her and said, 'What do you want us to do about the situation in the spare room?'

'Er . . . sorry?'

Jen said, 'I'll leave you to it, love, but come and say goodbye before you go.'

'The spare room,' said the mover. 'You want us to box it all up, or what?'

'It's all boxed up already.'

'No it's not, love. Come and see.'

In the spare room, Caitlyn looked around in horror. Patrick's boxes had been opened, some ripped apart, and his things were scattered everywhere in a storm of papers, files, books and photographs.

'Oh my God,' she said weakly. 'She's been here.'

'Sorry?' asked the mover.

'Nothing. I . . . I'll pack it up myself. Do you have some spare boxes?'

She set to work piling the stuff back into the boxes that were still useable, trying to see if anything was missing. It sickened her to think that Sara had somehow got into the house and helped herself to Patrick's life. All his private possessions seemed soiled by her touch.

I mustn't think like that. It will make her more aware of how much of him she didn't know, and never could. Talking to Geraldine helped me. It's made me see that I can put a fence around my memories of Patrick and our life and keep them for myself, no matter how hard Sara tries to change or destroy them.

That was always Sara's game. Perception. She was always persuading Caitlyn to change her version of events to Sara's own – whether it had been about Nicholas, or any of her early relationships, or even about situations they had both been in.

And I let her do it. I let her change my viewpoint. And she's still trying to do it.

She picked up the mass of cables and chargers that sat on top of Patrick's old laptop. Sara had evidently not considered it interesting enough to investigate. *But where is his phone?*

She stared about for it, but it was nowhere to be seen, then she began to scrabble through the remaining stuff on the floor, sure it must be here. She had put it back in the box with the other electronics but now there was no doubt about it. It was gone.

Caitlyn sat back on the floor, tears pricking her eyes. The last thing that Patrick touched, Sara had taken it.

'Just leave us alone!' she cried out. 'Patrick's dead and you can't have him now . . . and neither can I.' Then she put her face in her hands and cried.

Caitlyn went in to say goodbye to Jen before driving off to pick up Max from school on the way back to Kings Harcourt.

'Are you okay? You've been crying,' Jen said, hugging her.

'Yes, I'm okay. But that woman was in the house. She's taken something of Patrick's.'

'Oh.' Jen's eyes went round. 'Ah, I see. Was she – excuse me for saying it – a lover of his?'

'I don't know. I think so. Yes. She was.'

'She's in a struggle with you, is she?'

Caitlyn nodded.

'I'm sorry to hear that.' Jen took her hand. 'Listen, love. He was your husband, not hers. Don't forget it. What did she take?'

'His phone.'

Jen squeezed her hand. 'I know that must hurt. But you've got what really matters from his life – you've got your son, right?'

Caitlyn nodded. 'Yes. I've got him.'

'There you are. Let her have the phone, it's a dead thing. Concentrate on what's alive – you and Max.'

'Thanks, Jen.' Caitlyn managed a small smile. 'I'll try. Goodbye – and thanks.'

Despite Jen's words, Caitlyn felt horribly depressed on the drive back. Even Max, happy and full of stories of his afternoon cricket match, couldn't lift her spirits out of the doldrums. She had begun to feel more hopeful now that they had moved to Kings Harcourt. Geraldine's words had resonated with her, and the combination of the beautiful, vibrant countryside and the solid, graceful permanency of the house had given her the sense of a new start, or at least, the possibility of one.

Now Sara had tainted it all again, rifling through Patrick's life, taking his things. It brought back the rancid bitterness of jealousy and betrayal, and that dragged her spirit down into darkness again.

Back at the house, she and Max ate on the terrace, and Max talked excitedly about the prize-giving the following day.

'I don't think I'll get a prize because I wasn't top in the end-of-year exams, but I might get something for cricket, 'cos I got two wickets this afternoon and Mr Reynolds said I'd contributed a lot to the team this term.'

'That's wonderful, darling, I'm so glad you enjoyed it.' She smiled at him, happy to see how his attitude to school had been transformed. Then she thought of how Patrick would have loved it, and the same dark bleakness engulfed her again.

Later, lying wakeful in bed, she got up and collected Patrick's tablet from her bag, and plugged it in. She switched it on and began to swipe through the screens, thinking of Patrick as she did. She tapped on the folder marked 'Games' and up came his backgammon app, and the game of snake. The old-style-computer snake was made of little squares and was curled clunkily on a plain green background, rearing up towards a square apple so that he formed a kind of 'S' shape. Caitlyn stared at it. S was now, appropriately, a letter that seemed full of poison, a venomous and destructive letter.

As she stared at it, she heard Patrick's voice in her mind. It said: 'Look for the snake in the grass.'

The words on the other photograph in his Allegra folder. And here she was, looking at a snake on a green field, making an S shape.

She gasped.

It burst into her mind in an instant. She thought of Patrick and the way he liked to control everything. She remembered the odd message in the addendum to his will, the one that granted her access to his online life. He said she would know what to do with whatever it contained. *It was such a strange thing to say – that if I needed them, I would know what to do.*

Patrick had laid a trail for her to follow; she could almost hear him scolding her, telling her to open her eyes and see the clues that were in front of her.

Would he actually leave a picture of Sara on his phone? He was never careless like that.

She heard his sardonic tones. 'Poor Mark can't control her. He doesn't know how.'

But Patrick knew how. He always did.

With a shaking finger, she clicked on the snake game, and

it opened. She began to play it, and immediately crashed the snake into the border and the game was over with a score of zero. She started again, clumsily manoeuvring the snake with the arrow keys on the screen, but she couldn't get the hang of it and crashed the snake at once again.

'Oh bother, this is impossible.' She felt stupid playing a game like this, but each time she thought of giving up, she decided to have one more go, and gradually got more used to moving the snake around. Before long, she had scored some points but as the snake grew not just longer but faster, it was tricky to keep on top of the game. Then, completely absorbed in moving the snake around and eating the apples, which disappeared with a satisfying electronic beep, she was thrilled when she had eaten enough apples for a gate to appear at the top of the screen, and she sent the snake off through it, on to the next round.

As soon as the snake's tail disappeared, there was a tiny click and a movement in the small round camera eye built into the tablet's frame.

Did I just have my picture taken? she thought, surprised.

Then the screen abruptly changed. The snake game vanished, and she was looking at a new screen and gazing back at her, smiling, was Patrick.

'Ah, Caitlyn,' he said breezily. 'Hello! I was wondering when you'd get here.'

Chapter Forty-Two

It was hard for Tommy to concentrate on anything other than what they had learned about Barbara, but she knew that, as Fred had advised, patience was their best course. Fred promised that he was making enquiries as quickly as he could.

'I'm meeting a friend in the Army and Navy Club this afternoon. I hope he'll be able to help me.'

They met in the Ritz bar afterwards, and he told her that his friend had been very helpful. 'A pal of his knows Duncan Hastings. He was a prisoner of war – and presumed dead for a spell. But then he was reported alive, and was sent home in the autumn of last year.'

Tommy said excitedly, 'Perhaps he was in touch with her then. And that's why she went to ground, moving from friend's house to friend's house. Duncan Hastings might not know Veronica. He certainly didn't know me. How would he track her down, if she doesn't want to be found?'

'We could be charitable and assume that she doesn't know he's alive,' Fred said. 'It's risky to get engaged to a man with a husband still living. But we'll find out what we want to know tomorrow. I'm meeting him at the Reform for tea.'

'Let me come,' she begged.

'I suppose it can't hurt,' Fred said thoughtfully. 'All right. Meet me outside at a quarter to four and we can be ready for him.'

Tommy had barely slept when she arrived at the Reform Club in Pall Mall the next day. Fred was waiting outside for her, smoking under a street lamp, and greeted her with a kiss as she came up.

'Hello, darling. Well, here we are. In a few minutes we ought to know everything we need to about Barbara Hastings.'

He took her inside and the porter directed them up the staircase to the upper landing that ran around the great inner courtyard. Tea tables were positioned all around the square so that those sitting at them could look over and get a view of the splendid mosaics of the ground floor.

A waiter came to take their order for tea, and then they waited. Tommy took a cigarette from Fred and smoked nervously, looking up every time anyone appeared on the landing.

'What time is he due?' she asked fretfully.

'Any moment now,' Fred said. 'Don't worry. He'll be here.'

A few minutes later, Tommy saw a man emerge from the mouth of the staircase at the far side of the landing. He was tall and disconcertingly thin, with the shadow of a tan on his skin despite the lack of sunshine outside, and dressed in a shabby demob suit and a thin overcoat. He spotted them at once, and made his way over, ignoring the few single men with their newspapers and air of concentration.

'How do you do,' he said as he reached them. 'Duncan Hastings.' He held out his hand to Fred, who stood up and took it.

'Fred Burton Brown. And this is Mrs Eliott.'

'How do you do.' Hastings nodded politely and then took off his hat and sat down at the chair indicated by Fred. 'How can I help you?'

'Did Bowles tell you anything about why I wanted to see you?' Fred asked. He looked grave and businesslike as he took out a packet of cigarettes. 'Smoke?'

'Thank you.' Hastings took one and let Fred offer him a light. He said, 'My doctor wouldn't be happy about this. He says my lungs are shot. I told him it was all that kept me going during the years in my holiday camp, and if that meant I lost a year or two, it was damn well worth it, considering I didn't expect to get out at all.' He glanced at Tommy. 'Excuse my language, Mrs Eliott.'

'That's perfectly all right,' Tommy said. She reached for a cigarette as well, hoping that her hands weren't shaking too obviously. Fred leaned over to light it. 'You must have had a bad time of it.'

'Pretty much.' Hastings took a long drag of his cigarette and said, 'Ah, here comes your tea.'

The waiter set out the tea things and brought a cup for Hastings. He passed the bill silently to Fred, who shut a note into the red leather folder and gave it back to him with a nod.

When the waiter had left, Fred turned his attention to Hastings.

'We want to ask you about your wife.'

Hastings looked surprised for a moment and then collected his cool demeanour. 'I see. Know where she is, do you?'

'Perhaps. More to the point, do you know where she is?'

'Haven't a clue,' Hastings said. 'She's being very clever about keeping herself and my daughter hidden. I'm getting information through a solicitor, that's all. But I don't know where to find her.'

Tommy felt a rush of elation. So Barbara did know that her husband was alive. 'I take it your marriage is not a success, Mr Hastings? If you'll forgive the personal question.'

'Of course.' Hastings looked at her with a small smile. 'I have the impression you know Barbara. In that case you'll be aware that she's a cool customer with a strong instinct for self-preservation. She's damned attractive too, and can make a man feel he's just about the best there is. That's what she did for me, and I fell for it. But in the end, it was all just a big pretence. She made a fool out of me more than once, and I took it, not just for her but for the child.' He gave Tommy a sudden swift, almost pleading look. 'Have you seen Molly? Do you know if she's all right?'

'She's perfectly fine,' Tommy said softly, feeling sorry for him. 'She's a sweet little thing, with lovely manners. We all like her a great deal.'

'I'd love to see her,' Hastings said wistfully. 'But I never worried too much – I knew Barbara would look after her. She's good that way.'

'What contact have you had with your wife, Mr Hastings?' asked Fred.

'Not much. I tried to find her but with no success. I put the word out among our old pals that I was looking for her. Old Lazarus, you know, back from the dead. I hoped she might be pleased but I was rudely awoken from that little dream quickly. The word must have got back. I told people that any correspondence should go to me at my old club – not a grand place like this, a little place north of Bloomsbury, more of a boarding house really. That's where the letters started to come. She wanted a divorce. But we would have to do it secretly. She would move to a town in the north where no one knew her, establish residency and divorce me there, so long as I'd provide evidence of infidelity. I said, that's all very well, but asked her why, and sent the reply back to the lawyer she appointed.'

'And what did she say?' asked Fred. He sipped his tea and watched Hastings intently over the top of his teacup.

'Answer came there none,' replied Hastings with a laugh. 'Not right away at least. Then I got a very short, sharp reply. "How much?" or words to that effect. I wondered how Barbara had come into enough money to pay me off. She never had much before beyond what I gave her.'

'When was this?'

'Oh, last year. Not long before Christmas. She was evidently in a hurry to be rid of me, for whatever reason. She probably had her eye on some poor sap.'

Tommy frowned. *Perhaps . . . perhaps that's why Veronica wanted her gone so badly. It's possible Barbara was eyeing up her husband and considering making a move.* She looked over at Fred, but there was no way to convey all this, and anyway, he was looking at Hastings.

Fred said, 'Did you decide to give her a divorce?'

'I wasn't going to roll over,' Hastings replied, and took a long pull on his cigarette. 'I know Barbara and I wasn't going to let her win just like that. I knew we'd both enjoy a final tussle a little too much. And she had my girl. I had my conditions. Access to the girl. And five hundred pounds.'

Tommy gasped. 'Five hundred! I don't know how Barbara would get that kind of money.'

'She can get money if she needs it, all right. She'd do anything for cash. She was free enough with her favours in India if she could get some return on it.'

Tommy blushed deep red at the implication. Had Barbara really stooped so low? If she had, there was no knowing what else she might do. 'If that's what you think,' she said in a tremulous voice, 'how can you leave your daughter with her?'

'I'd like nothing better than to have Molly to myself. However, I know Barbara can be a lot less than a paragon but I do know she'd never expose Molly to anything unsavoury. She has a strong sense of decorum, believe it or not.'

'Yes,' Tommy said thoughtfully. 'I know what you mean. But still, Mr Hastings—'

'Listen, you two,' Hastings said, suddenly brusque. 'Is this some kind of church meeting or what? What's your offer?'

'What do you mean?' Fred said quietly, flicking a quick glance at Tommy.

'I presume you've been sent by Barbara to move this

divorce along. So you've come to offer me money. I know five hundred pounds is steep but it's what I need to set myself up and I believe Barbara could be good for it, and I deserve it if I'm to lose my girl.' He held up a warning hand. 'Though I'll have some visiting rights, you can be sure of that, or I'll drag her through the London courts, sue her on the grounds of *her* infidelity and be sure to scupper her chances of ever marrying a decent man again.'

Tommy and Fred looked at one another and burst out laughing.

'What is it?' asked Hastings crossly. 'What's so funny?'

'Nothing,' Tommy said, giggling. 'It's not funny. It's just . . .'

'We would like nothing better than for you to decide to divorce your wife in a blaze of publicity, that's all,' Fred said. 'But I have a feeling you won't do that if you think it would serve our purpose. So let's come to a compromise. A letter from you, confirming that you are legally married to Barbara Hastings, and your whereabouts, should we need to contact you. After that, you're free to work out the end of your marriage in any way you choose. So . . .' Fred took another sip of his tea then put the china cup carefully back in the saucer. 'I suppose the only question to resolve now is your price.'

When Hastings had left, having signed a letter quickly written out by Fred in the nearby library and pocketed a cheque for fifty pounds, Fred and Tommy faced each other over the tea table. Fred leaned across and took her hand.

'Darling, we've got her,' he said exultantly. 'She's known all along her husband is alive. She's guilty of attempted bigamy, and we've got her on the ropes. Roger is going to be free, just as soon as we can get down to Kings Harcourt and confront her. I have some appointments tomorrow. Shall we leave on Friday?'

'Yes, Friday.' Tommy clutched his hand. 'My God . . . we've done it. I can hardly believe it. They'll have to believe us now. And you know what this means, don't you, Fred? I can go home.'

When she got back to Celia's flat that evening, still hopping inside with excitement from the plans that she and Fred had been making, she found a telegram addressed to her on the hall table. She opened it quickly and read the brief message on the piece of paper inside.

COME HOME AT ONCE STOP ROGER MISSING STOP

Chapter Forty-Three

'Patrick!' Caitlyn was dizzy, astounded. Here was Patrick, talking to her. Alive. Her head whirled and she thought she might faint. 'Patrick!'

But Patrick went on talking as if she hadn't spoken and she realised she was watching a recording. She spooled it back to the beginning, her finger trembling so much she could hardly make the arrow move, so she could watch it again. The image of Patrick was frozen now. She could see he was sitting in his study in their old house, around him all the familiar objects of a life now utterly vanished. He was history now, and so was that moment and those things; all scattered and gone.

She pressed play and the still image came to life.

'Ah, Caitlyn. Hello! I was wondering when you'd get here. Pretty good, isn't it? You're looking around in my tablet, aren't you? And, at last, you've stumbled on my little games folder. So I think you found the clue that directed you to play this game of snake and you managed to get past the first round. Well done. Once you did that, my tablet took your picture and recognised your face, and set in motion this little recording for you. Only you could possibly see it.' Patrick smiled at her across the gulf of time and space. 'Now. If you're looking in my tablet, then you must have the code which I left with the lawyers to be given to you in the event of my death. I know you, Caitlyn. You're only looking around because you suspect me of something heinous. Hmmm . . . let me guess.' He made a face and stroked his chin in a theatrical way.

He's enjoying this. He always did like his games. It was the oddest sensation to see him alive like this again. Wonderful in some ways, but also horrifying. All the old feelings of being controlled came back along with the happiness of seeing him. *And he still knows how to pull my strings.*

'Here's my guess,' Patrick went on. 'You think I'm having an affair with Sara. Maybe that's what she told you. Did she tell you that?' Patrick suddenly leaned in, closer to the camera and she could see the way his shirt crumpled open a little and the skin below. She remembered that shirt. *Where is it now?* As she glimpsed his chest, she remembered the weight of his body and the scent of him. She missed him deeply and ravenously in that tiny moment. Then she was listening again.

'My darling, do you really think I would have an affair with Sara? I don't think so. But my relationship with her is . . . complicated. She is a complicated person. She wants what she can't have and she hates what she loves and loves what she hates. Right from the start, she thought I would be hers if she just twitched upon the thread. She thought that, like all the rest, I would come running when she snapped her fingers. Of course, there are plenty who don't want her. You'd be surprised. But she filters most of those people out of her

435

consciousness very effectively. Over me, she expected to triumph for some reason. She seemed to find my imperviousness a challenge, or an elaborate pretence on my part that I was begging her to take apart. You, my darling, were allowed to have me until she wanted me, a kind of human duvet, keeping me warm until needed. I knew that she would try her luck with me one day; she sent me that message all the time with her fluttering eyelids and heavy-handed flirting. Any excuse and she'd be touching me, stroking me, pouting at me – even when she was with Rupert. On the day she married him, she took me to one side and said, "Don't worry, Patrick, you'll get your chance one day."' Patrick laughed mirthlessly. 'She really is incredible. Her self-confidence is mesmerising.'

Caitlyn felt a stab of pain and a plunging feeling in her stomach. So that's how it was. She'd always known it somehow.

'There, there,' Patrick said. 'I can see your sad little eyes right now. My God, how she's made you suffer over the years. Why do you let her, Caitlyn? I never could understand it. I'd watch her toy with you and use you, and work out her little ways of undermining you. I think she sometimes didn't even know she was doing it but there was nothing you did or said that she didn't notice and work on. I could see why she did it. It was warped but it made a kind of sense. She didn't want you to be happy because she didn't see why you should be. You weren't as beautiful or talented – I'm sorry to say that, because it's not what I think, it's what she thinks – so why did you keep winning at life? Why did you get the scholarship? Why did you fall in love – really in love – with me and have a happy marriage?' Patrick smiled at her conspiratorially. 'We know we have our problems and I know I'm not easy to live with, but we love each other, don't we? We have Max. We have our home. We're happy, despite my being a prize shit from time to time. I'm a control freak, I know that. But that's because I want to make life good for all of us.' His expression was warm and he looked wistful for a moment.

She nodded without thinking that he couldn't see her and said, 'Yes, you're right.' Tears came to her eyes and her nose tingled. 'You're right. We were happy.'

Patrick was going on, heedless. 'So that was Sara's thing. Why were you happy and not her? She was the girl with the mostest. With the beauty and the style and the class. How come you kept being the real winner at life? So she thought she would wait for her moment and then destroy your marriage when she felt like it, or when she needed a boost. I knew that was her plan. I knew it from the very first day. And so . . .'

'What happened, Patrick? What? Did you do it? Please don't say you did!' Tears slipped out of her eyes and rolled down her cheeks but she barely noticed.

'One day when her marriage to Mark was failing, she obviously decided that now was the time. I suppose that while she'd ruined two relationships, I'd been on the up. We'd bought our lovely house, my career was going well, we had money, we had Max. I think she thought she would like a little piece of that for herself. So she invited me out for lunch and told me what she wanted: an affair. You should have seen it. I often wish I'd told you about it so we could have laughed about her together: her incredible ego that made her certain I'd betray you at the first opportunity.'

Patrick gazed out at her across the gulf of time.

'My darling,' he said in a soft voice, 'I didn't say yes, and I didn't say no. It gave me great pleasure to make her life hell. She didn't know it. She thought she was winning and that's what I let her think. Because as long as she thought that she was beating you, she was happy and that took the heat off you. She was kinder and nicer to you, she stopped being quite such a grade A bitch. And I knew she was going to be in our lives.' He nodded and said wryly, 'Let's face it. We were both fascinated by her. She is compelling.'

But what did you do?

'So,' he said, as if in answer, 'I didn't have an affair with Sara, but I did something else. You may not like it – in fact, I'm sure you won't – but try to understand. I told her that she had to learn to obey me. I wanted to become her controller. I held out the vague idea that at some point, I'd give her what she wanted – and that made her want to win me even more. She liked that idea that I was her master: it tickled her sense of naughtiness, her rather basic sense of drama. But most of all she liked our secret conspiracy, of which you were completely unaware. So she played my game. I gave her orders to carry out: some simple, some more complicated and difficult, some that would titillate her. I liked the fact that she would obey me when she obeyed no one else. She went where I told her, did what I demanded. I set her tasks, treasure hunts and challenges. You know the kind of thing, darling. Like our games, but with the joy taken out.'

Caitlyn couldn't take her eyes off him, her breath coming in short bursts. She could see it all in her mind as he spoke.

'But she's always trying to spin it into a sexual situation. She can't resist sending me pictures of herself – ones she thinks are erotic but aren't. You know Sara's clumsiness in the area of seduction – she flirts like someone from another planet who's been told how to do it but doesn't understand the first thing about how it works. She's tasteful and sophisticated but incredibly simple, almost burlesque, when it comes to sex. She boasts to me of the parties she goes to – I doubt she's told you, but she belongs to one of those clubs that have civilised little orgies in hotels and houses all over Europe. All the elaborate underwear and masks and feathery bits and bobs, and the emotionless encounters with supposedly sexy strangers are right up her alley. She loves to tell me how she sleeps with men and women, or hangs from the ceiling in latex slings and whatever else.' Patrick laughed. 'She never realises how funny I find it. She thinks it's fashionable and edgy, and that I must be crazed with lust at the idea of a load of people writhing on velvet cushions in bondage gear while getting out the whipped cream and the nipple clamps.' He laughed again, shaking his head. 'She really doesn't mind abasing herself if she thinks it will get her what she wants. She's sent me the most ridiculous film and pictures of herself. I have it all. You'll find them in a secret stash on here, just in case you ever need them. You'll have to win a few rounds of snake in order to get more clues but hey, that's what will make it fun.' Patrick winked at her. 'You know how I like my games.'

He looked serious suddenly. Clasping his hands together as

if in supplication, he leaned towards the camera again and now she saw his lips and teeth and eyes in amazing clarity, and the way his face moved and the breath going in and out of him. He was alive, utterly and completely alive.

'But Caitlyn, I never slept with her. And I never would. I've done it for you. To protect you and to prove to you that she really is not worth agonising over. She'd sleep with me in an instant, and she's almost made herself believe that we have a sexual relationship. She's probably told you that. But we haven't. Never. I've never loved her or anything like that. Good God, I don't think I even like her all that much.' He was thoughtful for a moment. 'I suppose . . . if I'm honest . . . that part of me enjoys these games with her. Maybe I do get a kind of kick out of the way she's pursuing me while pretending to be my creature. I'm amused by all the hopeless, soulless stuff she thinks is sexy, and the elaborate pretence that I might, one day, give her what she wants. What's the point in lying now? You know me too well anyway. But that's not love. If she says differently, you can show her this. You've got all the proof you need to destroy her if you want to. It's up to you.' Patrick leaned back in his chair again and sighed. 'I guess if you're watching this, then I'm dead. I was flying back from Geneva the other day and it occurred to me that if I died in a plane crash, Sara would have all the tools necessary to make it look as though we were engaged in an affair. I pay for all her little adventures and the things she needs for them, and she could easily twist that if I'm not there to deny it. I know that she would want to destroy our happiness retrospectively if she could. So I decided then that I would record this message for

440

you, just in case. But actually, it's a good idea, isn't it? We should all record our just-in-case farewell, and renew it every year. I know you, Caitlyn, and I knew it wouldn't occur to you to look through my private things unless you had a very good reason. And Sara would be it. So I've laid some clues for you if you happen to come looking. That way you can live in happy ignorance if Sara behaves completely out of character and chooses to let the past go, but the truth is right here if you ever need it.'

'I can't believe it,' Caitlyn murmured, sniffing. He had always had that ability to look ahead, and a perception so acute that sometimes it seemed like second sight. He had considered his own death and what might happen, and countered it with this message, just in case.

Patrick blinked his handsome grey-green eyes and smiled at her. 'So, darling, I'm dead. I wish it weren't so. I'll miss you and Max, and I hate the idea that I'm not going to grow old with you, and see how our boy turns out. But I know you'll look after him and love him and do your best by him. You're a great mother, Caitlyn. I never tell you often enough. You are a wonderful wife as well. I love you. Please forgive all my shit behaviour and my inability to give in. I hope it wasn't too bad. And now I'm dead. I've gone ahead into that great unknown.' He smiled at her. 'I'll tell you what it's like if I can reach you but my guess is that I won't be able to. And of course I'm really pissed off that I don't know the end of my own story. I just hope it wasn't too awful. I hope it was fast. Was it fast? Did I suffer?' He shrugged. 'Well, it's academic now. It's in the past, right?'

441

'Oh Patrick.' She was crying hard now, her finger lightly touching his face. 'You didn't suffer. It was fast. I'm so sorry. I wish you were here.'

'But here's the thing,' Patrick went on, oblivious to her and to his own future. 'I want you to go on and not look back. Sell everything and start your life anew. Do what you think is right for Max, even if it's taking him out of Spring Hall.' He made a silly stern face and said in a growly voice, 'Don't take him out of Spring Hall!' then laughed. 'I'm kidding. Do what's best. Follow your heart. Fall in love again. Be happy, with my blessing.'

'I will,' she said, tears falling faster. 'Thank you.'

'But I have one last thing for you to do. Okay? It's very important so listen carefully.' Patrick leaned forward to the camera again. 'Get Sara out of your life! I mean it. You're better than all that. You'll only really flourish when she's gone. Right? That's it. Goodbye, my darling. Tell Max I love him to the end of time. And I love you too.' He leaned forward and switched off the recording. The screen went blank.

Goodbye, Patrick. Goodbye, goodbye.

Chapter Forty-Four

It was strange for Tommy to return to the world of snow and ice after the sojourn in London, where the weather had been tamed and pushed back. Once outside the city centre, there was the familiar view of acres of white roofs and chimneys and roads thick with drifts. A short while later, as they headed out into the countryside, there was a sea of white almost as far as they could see.

Tommy couldn't think of anything but getting home as quickly as possible. Fred had cancelled his appointments so that he could meet her at Paddington and catch the train back to Kings Harcourt and now the two of them sat, agitated and unhappy, urging the engine on as they sped ever closer.

'We should have rung immediately to tell them about Barbara,' Tommy said under her breath to hide their conversation from the others in the carriage.

'How could we?' Fred replied. 'The lines are down.'

'We should have told them about Barbara in the wire I sent, instead of waiting.'

'Perhaps. But we thought there was time. We had no idea.'

Tommy clenched her fist inside her glove and hit down into her lap. 'We should have guessed. Oh God, where can he have gone?'

Fred looked grim. He stared out of the window at the snowy fields beyond the train and she knew he was thinking the same as she was. In this weather, where could he have gone? He couldn't drive far, or get to the station without help. And as for walking somewhere . . .

Surely he wouldn't have done that. Oh Roger.

She had sent a telegram to Gerry to let her know that she was returning and that they would need Thornton to collect them. He was waiting at the station in the rusty old truck, his eyes anxious.

'It's good to see you, Miss Tommy,' he said as she and Fred climbed in. 'It hasn't been the same since you left.'

'Is there any news, Thornton?'

He shook his head. 'Miss Gerry went to report to the constable yesterday afternoon, and they sent out a search party this morning but there's no sign of him yet. And there's snow due to come tonight.'

'Oh no. Let's get home, Thornton, please.'

They made the journey back in near silence, the grinding of the engine too much for them to talk over. Tommy found herself shivering hard inside her fur coat. She had forgotten the bone-gnawing cold. It was only when they turned into the lane and saw the house, so familiar and beloved, at the end of it that Tommy felt a lump in her throat. Fred must have sensed her reaction, for he quietly took her hand and squeezed it. She smiled at him gratefully.

It was already growing dark as they approached the house and Tommy could see people with sticks and lanterns standing by the gates. One of them was the constable in a huge black great coat, his constable's hat buckled firmly under his chin. As soon as Thornton had stopped, she jumped down and ran over.

'Constable, is there any news? Any sign of my brother?'

'No, Mrs Eliott, I'm afraid not.' The policeman gestured at the crowd of volunteers. 'I'm calling them off for the night. It's getting dark and more snow is forecast. We can't stay out.'

'No. Of course not,' Tommy said miserably. 'I quite understand. Would everyone like cocoa or something before they go?'

'No, thank you, ma'am, we appreciate the thought, but it's as well to get home while there's some light left. We'll be back tomorrow, depending on the weather.'

Tommy felt awful as she watched them begin to trek off. Just then a dark shape came flying out towards her from the house and the next moment, Gerry was hugging her tightly.

'Oh Tommy, you're back! I'm so happy to see you.' Gerry started weeping the moment she was close to her sister. 'We're all in a terrible state, Mother too. You must come in!' She noticed Fred. 'Oh Mr BB, you're back too. I'm so pleased. Come on.'

They followed her in and found the family in the sitting room, the children playing a muted game of draughts while Mrs Whitfield sat on the sofa, not sewing now but staring into the flames. The children jumped up, shouting with pleasure, as Tommy walked in, and came running over for hello hugs, except Molly who hung back. Mrs Whitfield watched, despair all over her face. When Tommy caught her eye and said, 'Hello, Mother,' she put out a trembling hand.

'Oh Tommy,' she said in a choked voice. 'You're back. Then they haven't found him?'

'Mother, no. I'm so sorry.' Tommy went over to her mother and hugged her, and her mother seemed to fall into her arms, suddenly small and frail and very old.

'You shouldn't be sorry,' her mother said quietly. 'I sent you away. This wouldn't have happened if you and Fred had been here.'

'We can't possibly know that,' Tommy said quickly. 'Let's not blame anyone at all.' She looked around. 'Where's Barbara?'

'She's gone to her room,' Gerry said, her eyes wide and almost frightened. 'She hasn't come down today. She's not in a good way at all.'

Tommy and Fred exchanged looks. 'I'll go and see her,' Tommy said.

'Call me if you need me,' murmured Fred as she went by. 'I'll be near and waiting.'

She nodded and walked slowly to the hall and then up the stairs. Below her, the sad eyes of Venetia and her paper-white skin gleamed in the twilight.

Tommy knocked at the door of the rose bedroom. 'Barbara?'

There was silence, perhaps the slightest shiver of movement from inside.

'Barbara, it's me, Tommy. I'd like to talk to you.'

446

There was no reply.

'I'm going to come in now.' Tommy turned the door handle and pushed the door ajar. It opened easily to reveal the gloomy room beyond. Despite her love of electricity, Barbara had not put any lights on.

Tommy went in, blinking as her eyes adjusted to the murkiness. Then she saw Barbara lying fully clothed on her bed, staring up at the ceiling.

'So you're back,' she said flatly.

'That's right. We're worried about Roger. Do you know what's happened to him?'

'Of course not,' Barbara replied.

'Did he say anything before he left?'

Barbara turned her head to fix her with cold blue eyes. 'No. He told me he was the happiest man in the world.'

Tommy gazed back at her. 'I think we both know that isn't true. I've got some interesting news for you. I'm sure you'll be pleased to know that your husband Duncan wasn't killed in Burma after all. He's alive and well and living in London, and very keen to see you.'

Barbara stiffened at the mention of her husband's name, an expression of shock flitting over her face, then quickly recovered herself. 'It's true I said I was widowed, but in fact we are divorced,' she said coldly. 'I've said nothing about it as I truly believed he was intending to live abroad in future and I thought it would spare Molly.'

'How thoughtful.' Tommy's voice was just as cold but there was an anger in its depths. 'You can stop lying now, Barbara. We know the truth. You're not divorced and not likely to be for months. You got engaged to Roger knowing you had a husband living, and we have your husband's signed affidavit to that effect.'

Barbara drew in a sharp breath, but retained her composure.

She's a cool customer, all right.

'And how much,' Barbara asked, 'did you pay for that bit of fiction? You can't believe a word that man says; he's a crook and a con artist. I'll sue him for defamation.'

'I would really like to see that, Barbara, because I think you've overplayed your hand. You got a little bit cocky. You thought you were so clever that you could divorce your husband without ever being found out, and get engaged to someone else at the same time. No doubt you'd have found some reason to go on an extended trip to establish your residence somewhere and get your case through the courts in secret. But while you were busy sorting out that business – and you might have got away with it, too, as Duncan was quite willing to give you your divorce for a price – you forgot about Roger. That poor, deluded man who thought he must be doing the right thing marrying you – because that's what you told him. You thought he was in the bag, didn't you? You stopped trying to make him happy.'

'Your mother was also keen on the whole idea,' Barbara said, apparently untouched by Tommy's words. 'She fought my battles for me if you must know. Roger knew full well that she wanted him to propose to me. So he did. If he wasn't the marrying kind, that's hardly my fault.'

'Her role in it all is something that will haunt Mother, I have no doubt.' Tommy went over to the armchair by the window and sat down, not taking her eyes off Barbara. 'And it might have been all right if you hadn't decided to bully Roger. It wasn't enough to make a man marry you when he didn't love you, or even want to be married at all. You had to humiliate him too, make him your lap dog, show off the fact that you were now in charge. My guess is that it didn't take Roger long to realise what a mistake he had made, and he was too fragile to cope with that knowledge. He was cast into despair. He couldn't bear the misery that a future with you would entail. Gerry knew it – she saw it.' Tommy got up and walked slowly towards Barbara. 'You could have had everything you wanted. Now he's run away and you'll get nothing because we have all the information we need to stop you.'

Barbara sat bolt upright on the bed and sneered at Tommy. 'You make me sick,' she hissed. 'Your self-righteous priggery is unbearable! How is it my fault? Did I make him disappear? I could have brought some style to this dump. I could have made life exciting. Instead he turned out to be just another coward, like all the rest. I have no sympathy for him. I don't know where he's gone, and I don't care.'

'You never understood him for a moment, did you?' Tommy said angrily. 'He isn't like you, he isn't tough and selfish and hedonistic and pragmatic. He's a romantic with his head in the clouds, who believes in ideals whether or not they could ever exist in the real world. If he hadn't been heir to this place, you would never have looked at him twice.'

'Maybe. But I won't be lectured by someone born to all of this, who has never had to worry about the bread in her children's mouths. You don't know what it's like to struggle, as I have! It's easy to be moral when you're not put to the test. If you had to, you'd do exactly what I have.'

Tommy straightened her shoulders. 'Perhaps that's so. But I'm pretty sure that whatever happened to me, I would try to do my best to live honourably, even if it wasn't always possible. You, Barbara . . . you don't even try.'

Barbara patted her hair, smoothing escaping hairs back down. 'I expect you're glad you got that off your chest.' She got up off the bed and slipped on her shoes. 'I'm prepared to go away as I assume that's what you want. I'll leave a very sweet letter for Roger explaining why I'm releasing him from our engagement. I can be packed and Molly and I can go today.'

'Very well,' Tommy said. Inside, she felt disgust for this woman, who clearly didn't give a fig what might have happened to Roger and appeared to have no remorse for her part in it all. Still, she was surprised that Barbara was prepared to give in so easily. 'I think it's best if you go as soon as possible in the morning.'

'I agree.'

'Where will you go?'

Barbara shrugged. 'I don't know. London. Eastbourne. Somewhere.'

Tommy felt a pang of pity for poor Molly, dragged away to . . . where? What kind of a future? *And I promised I'd look after her.*

Barbara turned to Tommy. 'I'll go, don't you worry. But . . .'

The defiance was clear on her face despite the darkness in the room. 'I have my price.'

'Your price?' *I might have guessed she wouldn't go without some kind of pay-off.* 'And what is it?'

'The Gainsborough.' Barbara lifted one slender eyebrow and her mouth twitched with tension. 'I want the Gains-borough.'

Tommy laughed in disbelief. 'What? You seem to have forgotten that you're guilty of attempted bigamy. I don't know why you think we should pay you a penny.'

'You have no proof of my engagement. No notice in the paper, no party, no ring.' Barbara shrugged. 'But I can make things very sticky for you if you don't give me what I want. I can spread rumours. And I have proof of lawbreaking here – electricity turned on, black market goods bought, stolen army medicines used. If you give me the Gainsborough, I'll give back your mother's brooch.'

'That brooch is worth a lot of money,' Tommy said. 'Why give it back when you could take it and go?'

'Because the Gainsborough is special. It's all that raises this place from being a glorified farmhouse. I want it.'

Tommy stared at her for a long minute, realising that Barbara, for all her pragmatism, could not resist this attempt to hurt Tommy where she thought it would cause most pain. The brooch would be forgotten, but the loss of the Gains-borough would be an open wound forever. *But what does it really matter? They're just things. Roger's gone and I'm sure he's not coming back. That's our real loss.*

Venetia's beautiful portrait was expensive, a treasure, a

masterpiece; but it had been too much for her grieving husband to look at, no matter what it was worth.

We have to choose what is most valuable to us.

When Tommy spoke, her voice was low and serious. 'All right. Here's my suggestion. It's a gamble if you like. Tomorrow morning, before you go, you can look at the two paintings. You will have two minutes. You can choose one. Whichever one you choose will be taken out of its frame and rolled up for you to take away with you. You'll have either the genuine or the fake, but you won't know which until an expert looks at it for you.'

Barbara looked surprised as if she'd expected Tommy not to give in so easily but to offer more money, more jewellery. She eyed her suspiciously. 'You'd do that? You'd risk losing the Gainsborough? Surely you must know I'll identify the real thing and take it with me.'

'Perhaps,' Tommy said. 'Perhaps not. But whichever you choose, you leave Mother's jewellery behind.'

There was a pause while Barbara considered. Then she said coolly, 'I'll take the earrings but you can have the rest back.'

'Very well, you can have the earrings. On one condition. You leave Molly here too.'

Barbara looked astonished. 'You want Molly to stay here?' She half laughed. 'Why on earth . . . ? Let me be clear. So I can take the earrings and Molly, or I can take the painting and the earrings, and leave Molly here? Indefinitely?'

'Until you can prove that you can provide a decent, stable home for her.'

Barbara's eyebrows lifted slightly. 'I see.'

'Whichever painting you choose, you leave Molly behind. That's the only deal I'll make with you. Take it or leave it.'

Barbara hesitated, then smiled. 'All right,' she said. 'I'll take it. The Gainsborough and the earrings.'

'I'll see you tomorrow morning at nine o'clock.' Tommy turned to make her way out, then looked back to Barbara. 'Oh, and I'm sure you'll understand if we lock your door tonight – from the outside.'

'There's no need. I'm a woman of my word.'

'That's not what I've heard. Very well. Goodnight.' Tommy went out, taking the key with her as she went. As she turned it in the lock behind her, Fred came up.

'Is it all fine? What happened?'

'Oh Fred.' Tommy threw her arms around him. 'I hope you painted that picture well. I hope you've never done anything better.'

The next morning, she and Fred went upstairs and let Barbara out of her room. She was dressed for a journey, well wrapped up in her coat and hat, her handbag over her arm. She looked at them with hard set eyes.

'You haven't decided to go back on our agreement, have you?'

Tommy shook her head. 'No. But there's another condition. The pictures will hang side by side, and you must choose from six feet away.'

Barbara laughed. 'I don't think that will be a problem. I'm not an expert but I think I can just about manage to tell the difference between a Gainsborough and a copy by Mr Burton Brown.'

They went down to the hall. The paintings were already there, set up by Fred. The second frame, very like the one that belonged to the original, had been taken from a painting in the attic and used for the copy.

'But don't let the frames fool you,' Fred said pleasantly. 'I may well have moved them around.'

'You can do what you like, Fred,' Barbara said acidly. 'But you can't make yourself into Gainsborough.'

'Here's the mark on the floor,' said Tommy, pointing to a chalk line on the flags. 'It's six feet away. You have two minutes.'

'Thank you.' Barbara took her place and regarded both paintings coolly. 'Hmm,' she said. 'I admit you've done a good job. And the gloom makes it much harder to tell the difference. Hmm.'

Tommy watched her anxiously as she assessed the paintings. Inside her pockets, her fists were tightly clenched, her nails digging into her palms. At last she could bear it no longer.

'Time's up,' Fred said, looking at his watch.

'Well?' Tommy demanded. 'Which one do you want?'

Barbara pointed at the picture on the left. 'That one. That's my choice. I'm taking that one with me.'

Tommy turned agonised eyes on Fred, who looked back, disappointment all over his face. Unseen by Barbara, he gave the smallest shake of his head and mouthed a word.

Sorry.

Tommy smiled back at him. 'No,' she said in a low voice. 'You don't understand. We've won.'

Chapter Forty-Five

After watching Patrick's message, Caitlyn slept deeply and well, and woke feeling happy for the first time in months. She lay there staring up at the ceiling with a feeling of intense closeness to him, revelling in the sensation that he was alive to her. It would be the last time, she knew that. When she got up and started the day, he would be gone again, vanished back into the mysterious place where death had taken him. But she had been given him back, just for a short while, and she knew now he'd loved her and not betrayed her. Patrick's solution to the Sara problem had been typical of him: a convoluted game, full of control and manipulation, for his own amusement.

He said he was protecting me from Sara, but perhaps he was also protecting me from him. He could channel his darkest needs to control onto her. She could absorb them – she was certainly tough and ruthless enough. Perhaps, in a strange way, that saved our marriage. Caitlyn laughed wryly to herself. *Maybe Sara was right – she did do me a favour. Just not in the way she thought.*

She saw that the three of them had been in a triangular relationship right from the start; she and Patrick had been brought together by Sara and even held together by her, each one yearning after something the others had.

But with Patrick gone, it's all wrong. It's destabilised. It can only go to bad without him. That's why he told me to get Sara out of my life.

That thought made her feel stronger, more able to face Sara down than she ever had before.

In the morning, after breakfast, she telephoned Nicholas and told him some of what she had discovered.

'A message from beyond the grave,' Nicholas said soberly. 'My God. What a thing to plan. As if he knew he was going to die.'

'Patrick was good at planning. He didn't leave much to chance. He made sure we renewed our wills every year, just in case. I should have remembered that. Perhaps he even recorded new messages to me all the time.'

'Are you going to look for all the things he's hidden on his tablet? The films of Sara? The pictures?'

Caitlyn paused. 'No. I don't think so. I don't want to see that stuff.'

'So you won't play his last game?'

'I suppose not. My final defiance. But I know it's there, and I suspect that's what he really wanted. He wanted me to know that he had, in his own way, taken Sara on and beaten her and that he did it for me. I really believe he was protecting me, in all sorts of ways.'

456

'A curious kind of gift.'

'Yes.' She laughed. 'Not standard husbandly behaviour, by any means. But that's Patrick. And who knows what would have happened or how long it would have lasted if he hadn't been killed? If he'd died a year or two down the line, I might have got quite a different message.'

'Will you tell Sara what you know?'

'I don't think so. I hope she's vanished. Maybe now she's got Patrick's phone, she'll be happy.'

'What? How did she get his phone?'

Caitlyn told him about the mess in the Oxford house. 'She'd broken in somehow and gone through everything, found the phone and taken it.'

'That's a step too far. I don't like it at all,' Nicholas said sombrely. 'Listen, I was planning to bring Coco to visit Geraldine today anyway, but we'll stay over for a couple of days while you and I work out what to do.'

'I won't be around till after Max's prize-giving.'

'That's okay, we'll come in the afternoon. Then we can decide what to do about it.'

'Don't bother getting here till after two. Geraldine told me this morning that she's had a request to see the Gainsborough so there'll be a party going through the house around then. Come after and you'll miss them.'

'Good point. I won't hurry.'

'I had a nice chat with your aunt about the painting. She seems pretty convinced it isn't the real deal. But you think it's genuine, don't you?'

'That's right,' Nicholas replied. 'My mother told me that

her mother – my grandmother – had been quite clear. There was a copy floating around but the real Gainsborough is in Kings Harcourt. So Aunt Geraldine must be mistaken. She's probably getting confused in her old age. I guess it had to happen. I'll see you later, okay?'

'Yes. I'm looking forward to it.'

At lunchtime, Caitlyn put on a floaty summer dress in honour of the Spring Hall prize-giving and drove to the school. A large white marquee had been set up in the grounds and she took her place on a sticky plastic chair at the end of a row. The boys had been seated on benches at the side of the tent and she made out Max sitting with his friends and gave him a wave.

It was benign tedium but not without its moments of sweetness and laughter. A speech was given by a local athletics hero. The chairman of the governors droned on at great length, then there were some choral performances. Then, at last, the headmaster's address and the prizes. To Caitlyn's delight, Max won the prize for most improved cricket player in his year and she applauded enthusiastically when he went up to get his certificate and book.

Afterwards the boys were taken back to their form rooms to prepare for leaving, and the parents and guardians were offered sandwiches and coffee at the back of the marquee. She wandered about, chatting to the parents of Max's friends and to his sports teacher, then spotted Mr Reynolds, so she headed over to talk to him.

'Hello!' she greeted him as she neared him. 'I was so pleased to see Max win the prize for cricket! Who would have thought it?'

'Yes, we're all very proud of him.' Mr Reynolds gave her a puzzled look. 'What are you doing here, Mrs Balfour?'

'I've been watching the prize-giving, of course. Why?'

'Well . . . because your friend said you weren't able to make it. That's why she was here. And she's just taken Max off.'

Caitlyn went cold all over, her smile dropping away. 'What?'

'Your friend . . .' Mr Reynolds went white. 'I wouldn't usually release a boy without permission but she was here when you came to tell Max about his dad so—'

'Oh my God.' Her heart started pounding hard in her chest and a rushing noise filled her head. 'She's taken Max? When?'

'She went off with him just a few minutes ago. In her car. She said she was taking him home.'

'But she doesn't know where we live!' Caitlyn turned and ran for the door of the marquee, pushing past other parents without a second thought as she raced to the car. As she went, she heard her phone beep and she pulled it out of her handbag. She felt shocked for an instant when she saw it was a text that came from Patrick's phone.

You are betraying me. But I don't care. I love Sara not you.

Caitlyn almost laughed. *She's an immature child playing stupid games. Really, Sara, Patrick was right. You're clumsy and unsophisticated.*

Panic was making her slow and fumbling but when she reached the car, she stopped long enough to type a reply:

Where's Max? Tell me right now.

She got in the car, panting, and started the engine. Where would Sara take him? *Stay calm. Sara won't harm him. She's using him to get to me. I just have to think clearly, that's all. Would she take him to the Oxford house?*

That seemed most likely and she was just about to pull out of the car park when another text beeped in.

Are you enjoying your stay in Nicholas's beautiful home?

A nasty chill fluttered up her back. So Sara knew where they were living. Of course. It was stupid to think she wouldn't have tried to find them, and it wouldn't have been difficult. She could have followed them, or bribed one of the movers or something. She might even have asked the school office. Another message popped up.

I think it's very nice. I might move in here myself.

The words danced in front of her eyes. *Here?*

She's gone to Kings Harcourt. She's taken Max and gone to the house.

Caitlyn roared the car through the school gates and out onto the road, heading back to Kings Harcourt.

Sara's car was parked in front of the house on the grassy verge and the sight of it was both terrifying and a relief.

Caitlyn parked on the verge behind Sara's car, and ran around the back of the house to her kitchen door, inside and up the back stairs to Max's bedroom. She flung open the door, panting his name, but the bedroom was empty. 'Oh God, Sara, what have you done with him?' she cried breathlessly. She had expected to find her sitting with Max, playing cards or something, waiting for her to get back, reeling her in with the bait of seeing her son safe and well, so she could get the confrontation with Caitlyn she'd been denied.

Caitlyn hurried out onto the landing. Sara had to be somewhere nearby. Her car was outside. Just then Caitlyn's phone throbbed again with another message. It was so horrible to see Patrick's name flashing up, even though she knew it was Sara.

You're going to be sorry.

She felt clammy with sudden panic and fear pulsed through her. A voice floated up from the hall below. It was Renee explaining the history of the Gainsborough to the visitors. 'And so, once she died, he couldn't bear to see it. He was broken-hearted. He put the picture away so he never had to look at it again. Of course, it's now worth a fortune. Strange to think of it up there in the attic when it's so valuable.'

'That's an amazing story,' said a melodious voice from below. 'Thanks so much. And can I take a closer look?'

Caitlyn gasped and her knees went weak. She grabbed at the banister to hold herself up. She knew that voice so well. She'd heard it thousands of times in many different moods. But she had a feeling she hadn't seen this mood before. *What's she doing here? Where's Max?*

'You're very welcome, Allegra,' Renee said. 'Shall I leave you here to have a look at it? You're welcome to come back and find me when you're finished.'

'Thank you. I'll do that.'

Renee's footsteps faded as she left the hall. Caitlyn froze. *What is Sara going to do now?*

She heard soft footsteps across the flagstones and then the

sound of a foot on the staircase. Sara was coming upstairs.

No. She's not going to invade my home again.

She was filled with a mixture of anger and determination to stop Sara in her tracks, and without stopping to think she stepped out to the top of the staircase and put out her hand.

'Stop!' she yelled.

Sara halted and looked up, taken by surprise. Then a slow smile spread over her face. 'So there you are. I didn't realise you'd get here so fast.'

'Where's Max?' Caitlyn demanded, her eyes flashing with fury. 'Tell me where he is right now.'

'What are you afraid of?'

'I'm not afraid of anything, but I demand that you tell me where Max is. And you stay right where you are, you're not coming any further.'

'You've certainly made yourself at home if you can give an order like that,' Sara said in a sickly sweet voice. 'I don't think this is your house, is it? It's Nicholas's. Or does that count as the same thing nowadays?'

Caitlyn began to walk down the stairs towards her old friend. *Did I ever even know her? Did I ever even like her? Why on earth did I waste so much time and energy on her?*

She remembered Patrick saying, 'We were both fascinated by her.'

Maybe I was. But that's over. Now she bores me, with her endless drama, her desperate selfishness and the unending dissatisfaction with everything. She's eaten up with envy. I don't need that in my life.

Strength began to flood through her, and the fear vanished.

She thought of Patrick and that thought made her powerful. He had told her the truth, she knew that. He'd asked her, as his last request, to get Sara out of her life. And that was just what she was going to do.

'I've had enough of these games, Sara,' she said in a voice of steel, getting closer to her. 'I don't know how you tracked us down, but you've gone too far this time. You can't involve Max in your sick little games. Patrick was a grown-up and he could take care of himself. How dare you bring a child into this?'

'I'm not going to hurt Max, for God's sake,' hissed Sara. 'But you can't get away with ignoring me any longer. You won't know where he is until I have my say!'

'This has to end,' said Caitlyn, setting her shoulders. 'I want you gone, Sara. Our friendship is over, and you know why. Now tell me where Max is, and leave.'

'I'm doing this for Patrick!' cried Sara as Caitlyn came near her. 'I still remember him even if you don't! You're pissing all over his memory, jumping into bed with Nick. Well, guess what, Nick was with me last night!'

'Don't even try it,' Caitlyn said in a bored voice. She walked past Sara and down into the hall. 'I'm immune to your lies now. Of course you weren't with Nicholas. He can't stand you and never has. I know all about how you kept us apart, and I expect you guessed I did. You never have liked me knowing the truth about how empty and jealous you are.'

'Have him, you're welcome to him, he's a jumped-up no one,' declared Sara, turning to watch Caitlyn, her nose in the air.

'Yes, that's right. A no one, with this beautiful house and grounds and a priceless picture. I bet you're kicking yourself that you missed that one, aren't you? Because if you'd known about this place, you'd have really thrown yourself at him, wouldn't you? You're a grasping, silly snob. A greedy, selfish woman who thinks only of herself and always has.'

Sara laughed. 'Oh, now we see it. The worm has turned! The little drab, plain nothing who owed everything to me has decided she's better than me after all, because she's shagging a man with a big house! You never would have met Patrick if it hadn't been for me. He was too good for you!'

'No. He was too good for you.'

Tears filled Sara's eyes. 'You must know by now. You called me from Patrick's phone on the handset he gave me for his private use. You must have guessed that we were lovers. He'd been with me that weekend, when he died. I was at the same hotel in Switzerland so we could be together. I'd been with him loads of times. I told him to buy that perfume for you, the one I always wear. See? How would I know that otherwise?' She adopted a tragic look. 'I was never going to tell you this, but you've forced me to! I was going to take it to the grave, to protect you!'

'Bullshit,' Caitlyn said smoothly. 'You could hardly wait to start dropping clues about you and Patrick. You intended to make sure that I worked out that you and he were having an affair.'

Sara looked mutinous and then her expression cleared. 'Yes! All right, I did. You had to know the truth in the end. I couldn't let you live in ignorance any longer. He wanted to be with me. I'd told him that we had to tell you, and that I would if he refused. He was on his way home that night to say he wanted a divorce so that he and I could be together.'

For a moment Caitlyn wavered. It was true that Patrick had been trying to tell her something about Sara. Something important. He knew that Sara was going to do something, or had said she would. Was she right – they'd been together and she'd demanded he end his marriage, and he'd agreed?

Then she recalled his face on the screen, heard his words and felt the comfort of his love around her. Sara might have been with him that weekend, Caitlyn would probably never know for sure, but she was certain that he had probably decided that if Sara was serious about revealing everything, then he would do it first.

But her guess was that Sara hadn't intended to tell her at all. It had been another move in her endless game with Patrick. Sara didn't want the game to be over – there would be no fun in that. Perhaps Patrick had tired of her at last. Perhaps he'd got jaded with pulling her strings, manipulating her and making her obey him. And then, before he could get home and explain, or change the message he'd recorded to her, he'd been killed.

No wonder Sara had asked 'Is it Patrick?' when Caitlyn had called her on the night of his death, before she knew anything of the accident.

Caitlyn faced Sara full on and put her hands on her hips. 'Sara, you tell so many lies, you've forgotten what the truth is. You probably believe half of the fantasies you concoct. I know that you and Patrick were not lovers. He's told me everything about you and him, and I know that he was your partner in a sorry little game of dare. He strung you along, just as you strung along so many others. He used you, just as you've used dozens of men. And he made you into his puppet, just like you tried to make me into your creature. How did it feel? I bet you couldn't understand why he never actually succumbed to your charms. It must have been tormenting.'

'Shut up!' shouted Sara, her eyes flashing with fury. 'I don't want to hear this. It's all lies. How dare you talk me to like this?'

'You're right about one thing – the worm has turned. I won't be walked all over by you again. I'm not proud of some of my own behaviour. You're right that I liked your glamorous life and the doors you opened. But when I saw how cheap you made yourself – sold for a glass of champagne and a free dinner to whoever would pay – I realised that was not a life I wanted.'

'How very noble,' sneered Sara. She took a step towards her. 'I might have known you'd turn saintly in your old age. You're fine now, aren't you? You've got all of Patrick's money and now you've got your claws into Nicholas as well. The truth is you don't deserve any of it. You weren't good enough for Patrick. You aren't good enough for a house like this. You ought to be taken down a peg or two.'

'You've devoted most of your adult life to doing just that,' replied Caitlyn. 'But you're going to have to accept that it hasn't worked. I've won.' She smiled. 'And I have the proof. I have all the films and pictures you sent to Patrick, and I know the truth. He didn't love you at all. You were his pawn. He knew the truth about you and the reality is, he didn't even like you.'

Sara screamed a long piercing scream, her hands in her hair, tearing at it, pulling it. 'No, no no!' she shrieked. 'He loved me. I won't have it any other way!'

'I have it on tape!' countered Caitlyn, talking loudly over her screams, 'and I'll play it to anyone you tell that Patrick was your lover. Now, tell me where Max is.'

Sara's eyes were wide, her mouth twisted with rage. 'You didn't deserve Patrick, and you don't deserve Max. You never were good enough for them.'

'Tell me!'

Sara snarled and darted towards the fire irons that stood at the side of the great fireplace. A second later she was holding a poker in her hand, its long cold iron shaft pointed directly at Caitlyn. 'You've always thought you were so much better than me. So saintly and sweet, practically untouched by human hand. Did you think I didn't notice that you were standing in judgement of me all the time? Of course I did! But you never had half as much fun as I did. You don't have it in you.'

'Put the poker down, Sara,' Caitlyn said, trying to sound calm, though she was churning inside. What was Sara really capable of? 'Come on, we don't need to settle our differences like this. We can just talk about it.'

Sara didn't seem to hear her. 'You don't know what it is to live, not really. Patrick did. I do. That's why he loved me.'

'Believe that if you want to. But please, Sara . . .' Caitlyn couldn't take her eyes off the slender iron rod that Sara had in her hand, still held out menacingly in front of her. 'Please, put the poker down now.'

Sara frowned, her grey eyes cold. 'He did love me.'

'All right . . .'

'No, he did.'

'I'm agreeing with you.'

'You don't mean it!' she howled.

Caitlyn's nerve, strained to breaking point, snapped. 'Of course I don't! I know exactly what he really thought about you. He knew you for what you are – a phoney and a fake.'

Sara's face contorted. 'No, *you're the fake! You're the fucking fake!*'

Caitlyn gasped as she saw the rage blossom in Sara's face. Decades of bitterness and jealousy had worked their way to the surface and were ready to explode. She was on the brink of losing control.

She's a drama queen. She wants the ultimate last act. She wants to be the winner in our little psychodrama.

Caitlyn took a step away, her hands out in a placatory gesture. 'Calm down, Sara . . . please.'

Sara took another step towards her, still glassy-eyed. 'Patrick loved me. If he told you he didn't, it was a lie. He loved me. Say it.'

Caitlyn stood still, wondering if she should run. But somehow she felt that if she tried, it would spur Sara on. She tried her best to relax, despite her pounding heart and the adrenaline coursing through her. 'Okay, Sara, you're right. Patrick loved you best. It's so hard for me to accept that you were the one he wanted.'

Sara narrowed her eyes. 'You're lying.'

'No. The message he left me – it said . . . well, it told the truth about how he felt. You can see it if you want to.'

Sara's eyes immediately filled with tears and her expression changed to one of pleading. 'Really? Did he say it? Oh God, I miss him so much.'

'I know. So do I. But' – Caitlyn licked her dry lips – 'it was you he preferred.'

'Did he really?' Sara asked, her voice high and girlish. She looked at Caitlyn but didn't seem to see her. She was seeing Patrick. Her expression was almost beatific, as if she were having a vision of heaven. 'He wanted me?'

'Yes. Give me the poker, Sara. You've won.'

Caitlyn held her breath as Sara took another step towards her, the poker shaking slightly in the air, and put out her hand for it. 'Good girl, Sara. You're the winner.'

'The winner.' Sara sounded happy. She began to proffer the poker to Caitlyn, who stretched out to take it. Her fingers were just about to close on the handle when there was a loud noise and Nicholas burst in from the door into the hall.

'For Christ's sake, Sara, what the hell are you doing? Leave her alone!'

Sara started as though woken from a trance, and seeing Nicholas, her expression transformed. 'You!' she spat. 'I know all about you and your horrible lies.'

Caitlyn watched her in horror. There was no end to Sara's need to be loved. She was a great, empty pit of a person, desperate to be filled up by other people's admiration. It was pathological, there was no doubt about that. Caitlyn had never known how deep it went until now.

Nicholas had stopped and was staring at her. 'You're crazy. I really think you believe that shit.'

'You wanted me!' Sara screamed.

'I bloody didn't! I couldn't get away from you fast enough.'

Sara bared her teeth at him in a kind of grimace.

Oh God. Nicholas, you don't understand ... that's her weakness. The thing that drives her wild.

Nicholas gave Sara a look of scorn. 'Put the poker down and get out of here. I've got Max safely in the car with Coco and if you ever come near any of us again, I'm going to the police.' The contempt in his voice was withering. 'You're pathetic. And you know it.'

Sara started to scream in a strange, high-pitched thin wail. Then she turned, ran at the painting on the wall. Venetia hung there, sad and still as ever, gazing out over the centuries. She stood, always young and beautiful, in the shade of the tree. Her soft hair rose in powdery perfection, her curl resting on her collarbone. She would never move or change. She would always be taking a half-step forward towards her death. Caitlyn watched, stunned, as Sara lifted the poker and stabbed it hard into the centre of Venetia's gentle face. It punctured her between the eyes, the dark shaft entering her white skin. Sara tore the poker downwards with all her might, shredding the canvas all the way to the bottom so that Venetia was gone. Now it was just a painted canvas that hung in two loose pieces, flapping inwards, the image lost. Sara drew out the poker and turned to look at Caitlyn in a kind of wild triumph, then began to weep, just at Nicholas dashed forward, grabbed her hard and restrained her in a strong embrace.

The poker fell out of her hand and skittered away.

'Caitlyn,' Nicholas said as he held the sobbing Sara still, 'I think you'd better call the police.'

By the time the police took Sara away, the fight had gone out of her. She was sobbing quietly, letting Nicholas keep her sitting in a chair in the middle of the hall. Caitlyn left, feeling that her presence was not right at that particular moment. Besides, it was too weird to see her sitting there, muttering about Patrick.

'I was his best girl,' she said in her high voice. 'It was me he wanted. Caitlyn said so.'

Caitlyn, saddened by the spectacle even through her relief, went outside to find Max. He and Coco had climbed out of the car and were eating ice creams on the grass. Caitlyn rushed over to him and hugged him.

'Maxie, are you okay?'

He nodded, and said, 'Yeah, but it was kind of weird. Sara said you wanted me to go with her, and then she took me to the village shop and left me there with ten pounds to spend on whatever I wanted. She said she'd pick me up later. So I bought some sweets and sat outside until Nicholas came by and stopped in his car. I told him about Sara, and he bought me and Coco these ice creams.' Max took another lick thoughtfully and said, 'Did you want me to go with Sara?'

'It was perfectly fine that you did. But she's not very well. I don't think we'll see her for a while now. And one of the paintings has been damaged so the police are coming, but there's no need to be frightened. You and Coco go and play in the garden till we come and find you, okay?'

'Sure,' Coco said cheerfully. 'Come on, I want to go and see those cages in the woods.'

The children walked off together.

Caitlyn stayed away and didn't witness the arrest, but from the window she saw Sara being walked to the waiting police car between two officers and driven away. When she went downstairs, Nicholas was waiting for her, pale but calm. He put an arm around Caitlyn.

'Are you all right? There's a police officer waiting to take a statement.'

'Yes, I'm fine. It's just so shocking. She took Max – it was horrible.'

'I saw him sitting outside the village shop and guessed something like that had happened.' He shook his head. 'Do you really think she was going to whack you with that poker?'

'I don't know – I don't think so. She just wanted the drama of it. She didn't want it all to end and she couldn't just walk away, she's not secure enough in herself for that.' Caitlyn looked sombre. 'You were right, I should have listened. She needed me, and once I didn't need her any longer, she collapsed. And . . . oh Nicholas. Look at the Gainsborough!' She turned agonised eyes to the flapping canvas. 'She's ruined it.'

'It's looked better,' Nicholas said and smiled ruefully. 'But we'll see what restoration can do.'

'I don't think there's any need for that.' From the connecting door, Aunt Geraldine came walking forward slowly and carefully, supported by her stick.

'What do you mean?' Nicholas asked. 'We'll have to get it mended, Aunt.'

'There's absolutely no point. That painting is a fake.'

'But Aunt . . .' Nicholas looked perplexed. 'My mother told me that the Gainsborough in the house was the real thing. She said that ages ago someone took the real Gainsborough – but it came back. Her mother told her specifically that the Gainsborough was hers.'

'Yes, that's true. But she should have said that *a* Gainsborough in the house was real. And it's not that one. That one was painted by your grandfather, Fred Burton Brown.'

'Really?' Nicholas appeared even more confused. 'Then . . . there's another Gainsborough?'

'Yes,' Geraldine said. 'It's hanging in my room. I thought it would be safer there. Thieves, you know. Vandals. Perfect strangers want to come into the house and look at the painting. I thought it was best to put out the fake, in case of accidents. A rather prescient thought, as it turned out. Today's visitor obviously didn't like Gainsborough very much. She quite took against the painting.' A smile flickered on the old lady's lips.

'Then my mother was right.'

'She was. But your mother didn't mean my sister, Thomasina Burton Brown. She meant her *real* mother. Barbara Hastings.

Or Barbara Evans. Or Barbara de Chalincourt, or whoever her last husband was.'

'Your mother was adopted?' Caitlyn turned to Nicholas. 'Did you know that?'

Nicholas looked baffled. 'Well, yes, I did. But when she said her mother had told her that the Gainsborough was real, I assumed she meant Granny Tommy. She always called Tommy her mother. I didn't know she was in touch with her biological mother.'

Geraldine said, 'She wasn't really. Barbara left the poor girl here and never came back. She rarely wrote. Her father visited once or twice but died in a brawl in Soho in the fifties and that was that. Dear little Molly grew up here and became another daughter to Tommy. She was a great comfort to us all. We loved her. Barbara left her the Gainsborough in her will. And it's because of Molly that you will get this place from me when I die, young Nicholas. And a real Gainsborough. So there you are. You can mend that one if you like, but I should think the glue will be worth more than the painting.' Aunt Geraldine turned to head back to her sitting room. 'I've called those children to watch the game show with me. I do like a quiz when I've got some company.'

When they were alone, Caitlyn hugged Nicholas hard.

'That,' he said in a heartfelt voice, 'was bloody terrifying.'

She nodded against his chest. 'I'm just glad the painting was a fake.'

'Sod the bloody painting, I'm glad you're alive.'

'I don't think I was really in danger. But . . . me too.'

They hugged for a while and then went through to the old kitchen and out the back door into the late afternoon sunshine. 'I'll need to give my statement, I suppose,' Caitlyn said.

'The officer is currently being plied with tea and biscuits by Renee. We've probably got a few minutes.' Nicholas took her hand and they walked into the garden.

'What do you think will happen to Sara?'

'It depends what you decide. If you think she was going to thwack you with the poker, it could be pretty bad. Attempted murder, at worst. Criminal damage at best. I'm afraid it might go on for a while.'

'That's all right. She's out of our lives because she can't hurt me any more.'

'You were brave back there, facing her down.'

Caitlyn smiled at him. 'I finally found my best self. Thanks to Patrick, oddly.'

'How do you feel about him now?'

They walked to a stone bench near a border of pale pink rose bushes and sat down. Caitlyn caught their sweet, rich scent on the air and felt the warmth of the sun-heated stone against her back. 'I loved him, and I miss him. I'm grieving and I will be for a while. But our relationship was a complicated one. He called his activities "games" but they were darker than that. He lied to me – perhaps to protect me, but still . . . he lied. He did have a relationship with Sara even if it wasn't straightforward infidelity. I need to come to terms with all of that. It helps to remind myself that our marriage wasn't perfect, and that Patrick knew that too, but it was still possible to love him and treasure what was good.' She turned to

Nicholas. 'I feel some closure now, though. I can move on and look to a future without him.'

He took her hand in his, his brown eyes gentle yet intense. 'That's good, Caitlyn.'

For a moment, she wondered if he would kiss her. She remembered with a sudden vivid sensation that kiss twenty years ago in another garden – the musky, honeyed sweetness of his mouth, his soft skin, the excitement of his embrace.

All that potential. And here we are, together again. Perhaps . . .

Patrick had said, *Be happy . . . follow your heart . . . fall in love again.*

After a while, Nicholas spoke. 'How would you feel if Coco and I came here for the rest of her holidays? Do you think Max would like it?'

'I'm sure he'd love it.'

'Would you?'

She smiled at him. 'Yes. I would.'

He said softly, 'I'd like to spend more time here. I need to think about the future of this house and what I could make of it. And I want to hang out with Geraldine a bit more. What do you think?'

'I think it sounds amazing. I'd love you to. As long as we're together.' She held his hand tightly. Everything felt right. 'I should warn you, I do have a parcel of nephews and nieces who are going to love this place. A lairy brother-in-law and a very nice sister. And a lot of cousins.'

Nicholas laughed. 'The more, the merrier. This house was made for people.'

Caitlyn gazed into his brown eyes, her expression suddenly solemn. 'And if you're thinking of doing this place up . . . well, I know a great interior designer with some time on her hands.'

There was a pause and then he threw back his head and laughed. Caitlyn joined in, and they went together back into the house.

Epilogue

The thaw, when it finally came, was almost as dramatic as the great freeze. Torrents of water flooded the countryside. Kings Harcourt stood alone in a vast lake, cut off again from the world. Now it was not skis they needed, but a boat.

It passed, as all the crises did, and the world went back to normal, more obsessed with Princess Elizabeth's forthcoming wedding than with the trauma of the winter and the torrential spring. The fields, empty for a while, gradually refilled with livestock and life moved ever closer to normal.

I suppose it is normal, the way we are now.

Tommy stood at the window, looking out and watching the three children playing in the garden. The sun was bright now and the girls were in light dresses. Harry was in shorts and ankle socks. Summer was coming, and it promised to be a hot one. Near them in a chair sat Mrs Whitfield, watching them play, a cup of tea on the small table beside her. She looked older than she had during the winter, but she seemed calmer and more relaxed. Despite the loss of her son, she was happier somehow.

Tommy knew that her mother had been much altered by her experience with Barbara Hastings. After the woman had left, the Gainsborough tucked under her arm and a smile of triumph on her lips, Mrs Whitfield had turned a white, shocked face to Tommy.

She's going to tell me that it's my fault we've lost the painting, Tommy thought, and waited for the tongue-lashing.

But her mother said in a trembling voice, 'She didn't even say goodbye to Molly.'

It wasn't until some weeks later, though, when Molly already seemed a part of the family and the snow had begun to melt, that Mrs Whitfield had been able to say anything more to Tommy. She had found her daughter in the drawing room one evening and said stiffly that she had something to tell her.

'Yes?' Tommy said, mystified, as they sat down side by side on the sofa.

Her mother took her hand. 'Tommy, I owe you an apology. For many things. But I'm sorry in particular for the way I treated you before your marriage. I should have been kinder to you. Your situation was awful and you did the brave thing of marrying a man who was cruel to you in order to give your child a family. I respected that. But I never said it. I punished you for it instead.' Mrs Whitfield paused, and looked downwards for a moment. Then she met Tommy's gaze again. 'It was only when that woman came here and did what she did . . . well, I realised your excellent qualities. I know Roger isn't coming back. I wish he'd been strong like you, but he wasn't. And I also know you will take on the burden of this house and shoulder it successfully, as you have everything else. You saw us through the war and through the winter. I'm very proud of you.'

Tommy felt choked for a moment. 'Thank you, Mother. That means so much. You can't think how much.' She paused, then said, 'I thought you were going to tell me off for giving Barbara the chance to take the Gainsborough. I knew it was a risk but I also wanted her off our backs once and for all.'

Her mother sniffed. 'I'm sure she's regretted it since. She'd have been better off with my diamond brooch. She will never be able to sell the painting, it's quite famous. Perhaps she might have found a buyer on the black market ... but as there's a question mark over its authenticity, she might find that difficult too.'

'Really?' Tommy blinked at her. 'I had no idea. It might not be genuine?'

'I don't think it is, if I'm honest, although I've never said anything. What difference does it make? If you like it, you like it, no matter who painted it. And we still have Fred's copy. It's just as good, in my opinion.'

Tommy laughed. 'Mother, you do surprise me. I would have thought you cared enormously. After all, the money could make a significant difference to us.'

'Oh, we would never sell it,' said her mother. 'In a way, I'm glad it's not there any more, making us all anxious thinking about the money we could have if we sold it. Now we can get on with things.'

Tommy hugged her. 'I'm so glad you said it. I must remember to tell Gerry that Barbara might have a fake, it will cheer her up no end. Oh, and there's something else. Fred's asked me to marry him, and I said yes.'

'Good. That's very good,' said her mother. 'Yes. Now, I can tell with you and Fred . . . that's the real thing.'

That had been the beginning of a phase of unaccustomed warmth in their relationship, and it had transformed the atmosphere in the house.

But I never did tell Gerry about the painting. I must remember to.

Tommy thought of Barbara often when she passed the copy of Venetia, wondering what on earth she was doing with the original. Perhaps it was rolled up under a bed in a cheap lodging house, or hanging in pride of place in some new home. Wherever it was, Venetia was still here, gazing out from the shadows with her sad eyes.

Just a different version. But it still seems to have her essence in it.

'I rather like Fred's effort,' Gerry said one day when she came into the hall to find Tommy standing in front of the portrait. 'I don't think I could tell the difference now myself.' She looked over at her sister. 'But I always wondered why you thought Barbara wouldn't be able to guess the real one.'

Tommy smiled at her. 'I guessed she would probably get it right. But it was the only way I could think of to make her leave Molly behind. She wasn't thoroughly bad, she loved Molly in her own way. But in the end, she had a price.'

Gerry stared at her in astonishment. 'That was the deal? Molly or the painting?'

Tommy nodded.

Gerry whistled. 'Well then. I think we got the better half of the bargain.'

'So do I.'

At that moment there was a clatter of shoes on the stairs and the three children came hurrying down, dressed in their best clothes. They stopped short at the sight of Tommy and stared.

'Oh Mummy, you look beautiful,' breathed Antonia.

'Like a princess,' Molly said shyly.

'Very nice,' agreed Harry, who had neatly combed hair and a freshly washed face. 'You too, Aunt Gerry.'

'I'm glad you like my get-up,' Gerry said. She was wearing a cornflower blue dress and a silver organza wrap. She held up her hands. 'I've even got gloves on! Now off you go and get into the car, children. Shoo!'

They ran out through the hall, leaving the sisters together.

Gerry said, 'They're right, you know, you look wonderful.'

Tommy glanced down at her pale pink suit. 'Thank you. It's not really like a princess's wedding dress, but I think it's right for me.'

'Oh Tommy, I wish Roger were here. I do miss him, the idiot.' Gerry sighed. 'I wish we knew where he is.'

'Sometimes I think he's quite near to us,' Tommy replied. 'And other times, I imagine him travelling the world far away from here, free at last to live the way he wanted.'

'In Russia, then,' Gerry said with a laugh. 'He seemed to think that was the earthly paradise he was seeking. We'll toast him today at any rate. Now, I'll go and make sure the children are in the car. Then it's time to go.'

'Just a moment more,' Tommy said.

'All right, darling. We'll be waiting.' Gerry went out to the car.

She was still gazing at the portrait when Fred came in, smart in his double-breasted suit. 'Tommy, darling, it's time to go. We don't want to miss our appointment at the town hall.' He looked at her searchingly. 'Are you all right?'

'Yes.' She smiled, full of love and tenderness for him. 'I was just thinking of everything that brought us together.'

'You're not afraid, are you? Of marrying me? You're happy that you broke that promise to yourself?'

Tommy laughed, her eyes shining with sudden tears. 'Of course I'm not afraid. I feel brave enough to face anything now we're together. I'm only wondering how I managed to be so lucky as to be given you and Molly to make my family complete.' She looked over at the portrait of Venetia. 'But she reminds me how brief it can all be.'

'Don't think about that.' Fred took her hand and smiled. 'The worst is behind us now. We have so much to look forward to.'

'Yes, we do.' She squeezed his hand and felt a thrill of anticipation. She had come out of the cold and dark at last and into the light and warmth of a life with Fred.

'Now,' he said, 'I think we have a wedding to go to. Come on. Take my arm.'

They walked out arm in arm into the morning sunshine.

Acknowledgements

Thanks to everyone at Pan Macmillan, in particular the marvellous Wayne Brookes, my editor, who is hugely cherished for his brilliance, good humour and the enormous care he takes of his authors; and to Alex Saunders, for endless patience and thoughtfulness. I'd like to thank Katie James and everyone in the publicity department, and Amy Lines and the fabulous marketing department. Thank you, of course, to the sales force for their amazing championing of their books. And endless gratitude to the talented art department for the brilliant covers. Macmillan is a very special place.

Huge thanks to Lorraine Green for her usual excellent and thoughtful copy edit, and all her patience and encouragement.

Thank you to my wonderful agent Lizzy Kremer, Harriet Moore, and all at David Higham Associates.

Thank you to all those who support the books and work behind the scenes to ensure their success, and to all the readers and book-buyers who keep writers writing.

A special mention of my friend Alice, whose beautiful house partly inspired the one in this book. You can see it at www.midelneymanor.co.uk or on Instagram at midelney_ manor. It's a beautiful and magical place.

I'm lucky enough to have a circle of kind, thoughtful and supportive friends (not at all like Sara!), and I thank them for their love and friendship over the years.

Thanks to those who contact me via Twitter and Facebook to send their support – it's wonderful to hear when someone has read and enjoyed a book.

And of course, thank you to my family for all their love and encouragement, in particular to James, Barney and Tabby.

Lulu Taylor
Dorset 2017

THE SNOW ANGEL

A forbidden passion. A lifetime of consequences.

Cressida Felbridge is living the high life as a debutante in 1960s London society when she is courted by a friend of her brother's and set to marry. Wishing only the best for his daughter, her father decrees that she must have her portrait painted to mark the occasion. But as soon as she meets the painter Ralph Few, Cressie knows her life will never be the same again. Soon, she is deeply in love with Ralph, but there is one problem: Ralph is still married to Catherine. As Cressie is drawn into a strange, triangular relationship, Catherine's behaviour becomes increasingly erratic and Ralph and Cressie escape to Cressie's family home in Cumbria. But Catherine will not give up Ralph that easily . . .

In the present day, Emily Conway has everything she could wish for: a huge house in west London, two beautiful children and a successful husband, Will. But as Emily and Will drive to a party, Will reveals that he has been betrayed by his business partner. Steering the car off the road at high speed, he ends their perfect life abruptly. When she wakes from her injuries, Emily is told of a mysterious legacy: a house in Cumbria on the edge of an estate, left to her by a woman she has never met. Could this house provide the chance to start anew, or does it hold secrets that she must uncover before she can be at peace?

Praise for Lulu Taylor

'Utterly compelling. A really excellent winter's story'
LUCY DIAMOND

THE WINTER CHILDREN

Behind a selfless act of kindness lie dark intentions

Olivia and Dan Felbeck's dreams of a family are finally fulfilled on the birth of their twins. The longed-for babies mark a new and happy stage in their lives.

Soon after, Dan's oldest friend, Francesca, offers them the chance to live at Renniston Hall, an Elizabethan house she is renovating. They can stay rent-free in a small part of the unmodernised house, which was once a girls' boarding school.

The couple accept, and just as they are enjoying the family life that they have craved for so long, Francesca arrives at the Hall and doesn't seem to want to leave. What exactly happened between Dan and Francesca years ago at Cambridge? As Olivia wonders how well she knows her husband, she starts to suspect that her perfect life could be built on a lie.

Meanwhile, Renniston Hall holds dark mysteries of its own, and slowly the old house starts to surrender its long-held secrets . . .

Praise for Lulu Taylor

'I raced through this gripping tale about secrets and lies and long-buried emotions bubbling explosively to the surface'

DAILY MAIL

THE SNOW ROSE

I know they think I shouldn't keep her . . . That's why I've escaped them while I can, while I still have the opportunity . . .

Kate is on the run with her daughter Heather, her identity hidden and their destination unknown to the family they've left behind. She's found a place where they can live in solitude, a grand old house full of empty rooms and dark secrets. But they're not alone, for there are the strange old ladies in the cottage next door: Matty and her sister Sissy. They know what happened here long ago, and are curious about Kate. How long can she hide Heather's presence from them?

When an eccentric band of newcomers arrive, led by the charismatic Archer, Kate realises that the past she's so desperate to escape is about to catch up with her. And inside the house, history is beginning to repeat itself . . .

Praise for Lulu Taylor

'Pure indulgence and perfect reading
for a dull January evening'
SUN